Other Titles by TW Brown

The DEAD Series:

DEAD: The Ugly Beginning
DEAD: Revelations
DEAD: Fortunes & Failures
DEAD: Winter
DEAD: Siege & Survival
DEAD: Confrontation
DEAD: Reborn
DEAD: Darkness Before Dawn
DEAD: Spring
DEAD: Reclamation
DEAD: Blood & Betrayal
DEAD: End

Zomblog

Zomblog
Zomblog II
Zomblog: The Final Entry
Zomblog: Snoe
Zomblog: Snoe's War
Zomblog: Snoe's Journey

That Ghoul Ava

That Ghoul Ava: Her First Adventures
That Ghoul Ava & The Queen of the Zombies
That Ghoul Ava Kicks Some Faerie A**
That Ghoul Ava On a Roll
That Ghoul Ava Sacks a Quarterback

Dead:
Alone

(Book 2 of the New DEAD series)

TW Brown

Estacada, Oregon, USA

DEAD: Alone
Book 2 of the New *DEAD* series
©2017 May December Publications LLC

Printed in the U.S.A.

978-1-940734-58-3

Things you should know before reading...

Starting a new series can be difficult. Starting a new series set in the world another series has already established can be even trickier. Fans of the original are going to hold them up side-by-side and look for something wrong or perhaps repetitious. Therefore, there is a balance that I must find to bring in new fans, bring back old ones, and maybe even convert a few people who walked away from the other series for whatever reason.

With this reboot of the **DEAD** series, I have decided to give the story of one person and his group. Many of the zombie series out in the market give you a clear-cut hero that is good and wears a very white hat. Or...they go the exact opposite and you get to follow in the shoes of evil. I believe that humans have a much broader spectrum that they exist in. We live in varying shades of gray. Nobody is absolutely good, nor are they usually completely evil. But this is not a debate about such things, I am speaking in generalities before you start flooding me with emails about Manson, Hitler, Jesus or Mother Teresa.

Evan Berry is the guy next door. He is you, me, and all the regular folks. He has certain things that he excels at, and others...not so much. He makes mistakes that he, and sometimes others, pay for—sometimes with their lives. He is not Steve, nor is he Kevin, and I know that some people might not be sure how to feel about him. All I can say to that is perhaps go into this with new eyes. Yes, it is has the **DEAD** logo, and there might even be a bit of crossover. You've already had appearances by Steve, Thalia, Teresa, Barry and Randi. Could there be more? Anything is possible.

So, what lies ahead? For one, I want to really bring the zombie children into the forefront. Yes, they are different. But how much so remains to be seen. And then there are some other aspects that I also want to explore. I don't want to be rushed. Evan's story allows me to do that.

A few more things before you venture forth. Sometimes, writers push the envelope of reality. One of the things I will say is that this book covers a span of about ten days. As you read, ask yourself, if you were in Evan's shoes, how hard would you push your body? We see athletes play with injuries that we take a week of from work for. Is Evan on par physically with a pro athlete? No. But he has few options and must ignore things that we might tend to look at from eyes that are not facing life or death. But, the bottom line is this…my book is just a story. You are already suspending belief to accept zombies. Open it just a fraction more.

The last thing I will say before I get to the thank you portion of this little introduction is to say that I look forward to where this story will take us together. Here is where I do that little bit of begging. Your reviews are priceless. Good or bad, your reviews are the commercial for others to see and perhaps join you on this journey. You might think, "Well, I'm sure there will be plenty of *other* people who review this book." Yet, of the almost one thousand copies of the previous book in this series that was purchased, to date, it has thirty reviews. I suck at math, but even I know that is a pretty low percentage. Believe it or not, Amazon increases visibility of a book or product if it surpasses a certain number of reviews with a decent average rating. And no, this is not a plea for just a glut of 5-star reviews. It's okay if my book doesn't hit all your buttons. Be honest. I read them all, and sometimes a well-crafted critical review can be helpful. And sometimes, those glowing reviews arrive on the day when I need a boost. You are the ones who write my job performance review. The difference between the one you write me and the one you might get from work is that mine are public, for the entire world to read.

And now…the thanks. I will make these quick because I know that, unless your name appears here, these are just random names that mean little to nothing: First and most important, I must thank my wife Denise for all the support, I could not do this without her; Debra, Sophie, Todd & Amy, Cassie, Malik,

Andrea, Caron, Hope, Justin, Kathy, Abby and Terri, each of you has my deepest thanks; to Evan for lending me a name for the new main character for this series; to another really cool guy, Don Evans, trust me, the REAL Don Evans is nothing like the man you will meet in these pages; while I'm at it, I want to thank many of the local Portland, Oregon Tribute Band performers who have pulled me aside at a show and asked if I might need another name for a future volume. Before this series ends, I might end up exhausting every band roster under the J-Fell banner. So, I guess I should also thank Jason Fellman. Hmm…that might be a name you will see in the next book. Stay tuned.

Hello.
TW Brown
January 2017

Andrea, Caron, Hope, Justin, Kathy, Abby and Terri, each of you has my deepest thanks; to Evan for lending me a name for the new main character for this series; to another really cool guy, Don Evans, trust me, the REAL Don Evans is nothing like the man you will meet in these pages; while I'm at it, I want to thank many of the local Portland, Oregon Tribute Band performers who have pulled me aside at a show and asked if I might need another name for a future volume. Before this series ends, I might end up exhausting every band roster under the J-Fell banner. So, I guess I should also thank Jason Fellman. Hmm…that might be a name you will see in the next book. Stay tuned.

Hello.
TW Brown
January 2017

To Don Evans
You Said You Wanted to be Bad

Wish Granted

Contents

1	Slipping Away	1
2	The World is a Graveyard	19
3	Who Can I Trust?	37
4	Sunday Driver	55
5	Stranger Danger	73
6	Monsters	89
7	One of Us	107
8	The Guilt of an Executioner	125
9	A Ray of Hope	143
10	Proof	161
11	Survivor	181
12	Delaying the Inevitable	197
13	Stepping Off the Ledge	215
14	Overload	231
15	New Friends and Enemies	241
16	Small World	263

ZOMBIE
The Little Girl in the Garage 275

1

Slipping Away

I stuffed the socks into my knapsack and then checked my inventory. I would not take more than I thought was absolutely necessary to keep myself from being eaten alive. I only had the one Glock and three spare magazines. If I was going to die in the next few days, it would be on my terms. I had a few sturdy blades and my trusty hand axe as well.

Slipping out of my room, I was once again struck by the absolute silence that falls over a dead world. Heading downstairs, I stopped and grabbed a jug of water. I would probably find some, but I wanted a little insurance. I still wasn't even sure that I had what it took to shove the end of my Glock into my mouth and pull the trigger. Did I want to become a zombie? Hell no. But I was still not very excited about killing myself. Would one less zombie make a difference in the bigger scheme of things? No. If they were driven by some sort of base inner drive, I did not want to be like Stephen "Fly Boy" Andrews at the end of *Dawn of the Dead* and bring a horde of zombies to the gates of the people who had been my fellow survivors. I just did not like the idea of an undead version of myself roaming the streets.

I pinned my note on my door explaining about how I'd discovered the scratch on the inside of my arm and how I would not make them watch over me as I turned. I made sure to include a small plea that my Newfoundland, Chewie, be taken care of and not tossed out or simply killed. There was some sort of bond between her and that autistic boy, Michael. Perhaps that would be reason enough to continue to care for her in my absence.

I didn't think Carl would do anything to my dog or the children despite his earlier statements of how they were useless drains on our resources. He has a softer heart than he would admit. Also, I did not believe that Betty would allow it. I didn't care much for the woman and her people skills were severely lacking…when it came to adults. She was actually very good with the kids, and I had no doubts that she was aware of the bond that was developing between Chewie and Michael.

The only one in the original group that I did not have a real read on was Selina. The girl was almost twelve, but she seemed much more observant than I was at her age. She also seemed to be a good shot based on the one time I'd witnessed her in action. She'd shot a zombie that was coming for me from about a block away. That was how we'd first met.

I made my way down the stairs and paused when I reached the front door. Once I walked through it, I was pretty much committing myself to the fate that this scratch held for me. By morning, my note would be found and I would be long gone.

I was terrified. I did not want to be alone but I could not stay knowing that I would become one of those things. According to the reports I'd heard, turning happened within the first seventy-two hours. I was just glad that I hadn't turned in my sleep. Michael had slipped in with Chewie at some point and fallen asleep on my bedroom floor.

While I am pretty certain that, as a zombie, I would not feel remorse, I was bothered deep down about the fact that I *could've* turned, gotten up, and attacked that boy. Even worse…I could've attacked my Chewie.

Opening the door, I stepped outside and pulled it shut behind me. The night air was verging on cold as spring had just started when all this madness began. I zipped up my jacket and headed for the brick wall that surrounded this place.

Up until this very moment, I had not decided where I would

go, but now I knew where I would start this last adventure. Across the way was a gated community. We'd sealed it up from the outside, and now all we needed to do was kill the zombies inside and we could use the place for supplies.

My last act on this earth would be to take down as many of the walking dead as I possibly could. That would make it easier on Carl. I was pretty sure that he would have to make these trips alone now that I would be gone. The kids sure as hell wouldn't be able to help, and Betty would not leave them all alone while she and Carl left the relative safety of our...*their*...little compound. As for that new girl, Amanda, she was a mystery to me. I had no idea how she might fit in with things or if she would even stay. I could not count on her in any of my assessments of how things might unfold in my absence.

I climbed up on the wall and looked around. From this vantage point, I looked down onto Johnson Creek Boulevard. That main road wound its way up this little hill. On the other side and up a grassy slope was the gated community where I would go to die.

The clouds above made it darker than normal which meant I could barely see my hand in front of my face. I pulled out the small battery-operated lantern from my bag and switched it on. I didn't like the fact that I would be a visible target for miles around, but I liked the idea of walking into or stepping on a zombie unawares even less.

I was just swinging my other leg over when a small voice froze me in my place. "Are you going out to do more murder?"

Michael Killian. At nine years old, he was the youngest survivor in our group. He was also autistic. I can't say that I know much about such things, but what I have noticed is that he almost never makes eye contact with any of us. He seems much more comfortable talking to my female Newfoundland. Speaking of my beloved dog, she was standing right beside the boy on the pathway that I'd followed to the wall. Her tail swished when she and I made eye contact.

"Umm..." I honestly didn't know what to say to the boy.

"Chewie needs more of her special treats."

3

I was about to ask what treats those might be when the boy pulled out a package of beef jerky. I wasn't sure where he'd found it, but the boy pulled a piece out of the plastic pouch and held up one finger on his left hand. She sat down on her haunches obediently.

"That's new," I breathed.

"There is more of it at the dinner place." With that, Michael turned and started back for the house.

Chewie stayed put for a moment, her head tilted and her tail wagging. I could see her dark eyes glitter and reflect the light from my lantern.

"Take good care of them, girl," I whispered.

As if she understood me, she gave me a huff and then turned around and plodded after the boy. I watched her vanish into the blackness of the night and felt my eyes begin to sting with tears that desperately wanted to come. I forced them back and swallowed the grief that made my heart ache and my stomach twist into a knot.

Turning back to the task at hand, I dropped to the ground and started down the hill. I would need to stay alert. If I was forced into hand-to-hand combat with a zombie, I would do it because there was no other choice. But with my busted arm wrapped in Ace bandages, I doubted my efficiency.

Betty had said that my healing could take as long as ten weeks or as short as four or five. I would not live that long no matter where I fell in the healing spectrum, so I guess it didn't matter if I ruined my arm to the point of not being able to use it any more.

By the time I reached the road, I knew that I would not make it up the other side without having to take down at least one zombie. It was probably due to the darkness reducing my vision, but I now found myself sort of trapped between a group of three to my right and two to the left. They were coming down at me from the direction of the gated community.

Sure, I could change my mind and just head someplace else; but no, my mind was made up. Besides, the worst that could happen to me would be to get bitten. Since I was already scratched up, that would only suck in that it would really hurt. It wasn't like I could be infected twice. And if it looked like I was about to go down, then I would shove the Glock in my mouth and pull the trigger.

I doubted my ability to do it unless it was the final option. I just hoped that I would be able to eventually do it once I reached the point where I was really sick. I remembered Morey and how he became listless and unresponsive. I told myself that he wasn't quite aware of what was happening to him, and that I knew my eventual fate if I did not go through with it.

I closed on the zombies to my left, effectively putting distance between me and the ones on my right. This would be tricky and I pulled up just about ten feet from the closest of the two. As it stumbled towards me, arms out and hands grasping at the air, I tried to time my move. Just as he was taking another unsteady step towards me, I lunged forward, gripped the thing by the wrist and jerked it towards and then past me. I heaved with all I could and the zombie stumbled and then fell. The second one I simply shoved away and then I broke into a jog for the wall at the top of the hill.

I climbed up and over where I'd entered the place just yesterday when I'd sort of saved Carl. Already, the moans of the undead drifted on the night air. Just as I slid to the ground, I felt the first drops of rain on my face. Since I had no idea what the insides of these houses might have in store for me, and one was pretty much like any other, I took the one right across from me.

Crossing the street, my lantern's dull glow gave me a good ten or so feet of illumination. The shadows all around had me jumping every few steps as the wind made things shift and move. The rain and breeze did nothing to eliminate the stench of the undead, so even though I couldn't see them, I knew they were near.

When the first one came into view, I stopped in my tracks. She couldn't be any older than sixteen. Her death had been violent and gruesome. Not that anybody being eaten alive doesn't suffer such a fate, but this had me wincing in sympathetic pain. I suddenly wished for my lamp to go out. Looking at this girl hurt my soul.

From what I could see, one of the undead had latched onto her face just to the side of her right eye. The flesh was peeled away, enlarging the eye socket to gross proportions. The eyeball was only still in place due to the optic nerve and actually jiggled in an unsettling manner with each labored step. Her belly was torn open wide and a wad of unspooling intestines were bunched up at that hole, just waiting to be knocked loose and spill to the ground. Her nose was nothing more than a gaping wound that appeared pitch black. Her left hand was missing all its fingers and the right hand only had the thumb and index. All of these terrible details were surprisingly visible. Perhaps it was because my eyes could not tear themselves away and allow me to detach myself from any feeling as I prepared to kill this pitiful creature.

I desperately wanted to end this zombie girl. I could not explain why, at first, as I allowed her to approach close enough so that I could sweep her legs out from under her. She landed hard and that proved to be enough to dislodge the wad of entrails that were clogging the rip in her belly. I heard the wet squelch as I stepped in to finish her off with a blow to the head with my axe. Maybe it was the dangling eyeball, or maybe it was my awkwardness with using my left hand, but the blow came in off-center and buried the head of my hand axe in her face right around the center of that empty eye socket. The results were still the same as I ended her pitiful existence for good.

I had to plant a foot on her chest to wrench the axe free. I did this just in time to come up and shoulder a second zombie aside. This one had a mangled arm that did not look right for some reason. It took me a few seconds to realize that this person almost had his arm wrenched off. It had been severely dislocated and turned almost completely backwards.

I ended this one with a surprisingly clean blow considering the circumstances. The downside was that I ended up losing my grip on the trusty hand axe. The sounds of approaching moans caused me to scurry away frantically, leaving my favorite weapon jutting from the forehead of my last kill as I ran for the front door of my target home.

6

Slipping Away

I tried the knob and breathed a sigh of relief when it opened. Slipping inside, I sniffed the air. Other than what I identified as rotting food or garbage, the air was relatively fresh. I ventured down the hallway of what had been a rather stylish residence just a short time ago, pausing to glance at a large family portrait that hung on one wall of the hallway.

The family that smiled back at me seemed strangely familiar. It took me a moment to recognize the man in the photo as one of the members of the professional basketball team in Portland. His smile was what had thrown me. He was known for being a bit ferocious on the court and had a very recognizable sneer that had become a bit of a trademark. His huge hands rested on his wife's shoulders and she was looking over the head of a young girl with long, wavy black hair.

I moved into the living room and plopped down on a very expensive-looking couch. I almost felt guilty. The snow-white couch would forever bear a dark smear from my blood splattered clothing.

I only intended to simply catch my breath. I started awake when a beam of sunlight stabbed through my eyelids. It was well past sunrise.

Getting to my feet, I made a full tour of the house. The first thing I did was locate the ibuprofen. My head was pounding.

"That must be the first sign," I muttered to myself as I popped six tablets into my mouth and swallowed them down with some tepid water. The next thing I did was rifle through the cupboards.

Eventually, I was seated at the expansive oak dining room table with a box of dry cereal and a bottle of Gatorade. I could look out the floor-to-ceiling windows of the dining room and see the street with a handful of walking dead staggering past. As I munched, I made up the conversations I imagined would take place. Sort of doing my own riff of the opening fish tank scene of *Monty Python's Meaning of Life*.

"Hey, somebody left an axe in Herbert's face."

"Seems like a waste of a perfectly good axe."

"Morning Missus Bennington, you're looking particularly pale and ghoulish today."

"Have you lost weight, Mister Jones?"

"Thank you for noticing, had my insides pulled out a few days ago. Already up and about…almost as good as new."

"Amazing what they can do these days."

I wondered briefly if madness was another symptom that I was slowly becoming one of the undead. I had a mouthful of Crunch Berries in my mouth when a realization hit me like a ton of bricks.

Jumping to my feet, I sprinted to the bathroom where I'd located the ibuprofen. Holding up my lantern, I switched it on. I squinted from the initial glare, then leaned forward and stared at my reflection.

"Why aren't the tracers showing up yet?" I asked the empty bathroom.

I don't know how long I stood there staring. Eventually, I headed back into the living room and then upstairs. I went from bedroom to bedroom, not entirely sure of what I was looking for. Certainly none of the clothes would fit. If I remembered correctly, this guy was listed as being almost seven feet tall.

After not finding much that I needed, at least at the moment, I returned downstairs. That entire venture had used up maybe twenty minutes. Time seemed to have stopped.

"I might kill myself to escape the boredom of waiting," I groused as I opened a cupboard under the island in the kitchen.

I pulled out all sorts of instruction booklets for the assorted appliances and smoke detectors as well as a few phone books that were from almost five years back. A pamphlet stuffed in the rear of the cabinet caught my attention and I pulled it out.

A map of the local area.

I don't know why, but this made me laugh. I'd searched for one earlier in order to try and locate a local vet. Chewie's tail injury had been a point of concern those first days. Betty had helped get her all cleaned up and on the mend.

"What the hell," I muttered and spread the map out on the kitchen table.

I traced the route with a pencil, making notes on a piece of paper as to where I needed to turn. If I drove the majority of the way over, I could abandon the car someplace close by. Then, after I made the last bit of the journey on foot and gathered a good bit of supplies and much needed dog food, I could load the car up again and drive it back. I could park it at the foot of the driveway up to the compound where Carl and the others were staying. Maybe I would even see about getting some gear for the humans.

Next, I went out to the garage. I couldn't help but let a low whistle of appreciation escape. I don't know what sort of vehicle was used by this family when they evacuated, but I was more than a little impressed with the luxury Mercedes-Benz GL parked inside. Now all I needed to do was find the keys.

That quest proved to be harder than I'd expected. I emptied drawers, searched through every room and then my eyes fell on them. Wadded up in a corner of the master bedroom were a pair of pants. The size told me they were his. The nasty black stain on one leg told me somebody had met with an accident. Sure enough, in the front right pocket was a key ring.

I stuffed them in my own pocket and then went about the process of tossing a few things in the passenger side of the luxury SUV. All that remained was to physically climb behind the wheel and make my way out of this place.

That is when it dawned on me that there were a few problems with this plan. For one, Carl and I had gone around and pulled all the gates shut to this community. We'd even managed to block it with some cars from the outside that he'd rather smartly disabled. We'd wanted to at least make any passing scavengers work for what they would take. It wasn't that we had any right or claim to this area, but it was one of the closest communities, and so we'd sorta called dibs even if nobody else knew.

It had been quite a job for the two of us. I wasn't sure how well I would fare trying to pull it off by myself.

"There went a day wasted," I snapped as I returned to the living room and collapsed into the couch with a feeling of utter defeat welling up inside me.

I'd just wanted to do one last thing for my Chewie. Yes, I'd planned on going through this neighborhood and trying to take down as many of the zombies as I could so that it would be an easier run for Carl, but I'd really had my heart locked on doing one last thing for my dog.

I was being an idiot. I was not thinking things through. I had walked out with no real plan. I was just lunging after any random idea that drifted through my brain.

I'd always considered myself to be at least marginally smart. So why was I acting like a complete moron? It had been so easy from the comfort of my couch to watch a movie and point out all the stupid things the characters did. So far, I was doing much worse. I'd willingly walked into a hospital and then fallen asleep. I'd collected two children who would be able to provide minimal contributions while consuming much needed supplies in addition to needing to be watched over. Toss in the fact that I'd been teamed up with a woman I couldn't stand right off the bat for no real reason. Also, there was no way I could ignore the fact that I'd basically led a psychopath back to our compound.

I walked back up to the master bedroom and looked out the window. If the breeze blew right, the trees would flutter and I could see the roof of the house where Carl, Betty, Michael, Selina, that new girl Amanda, and my Chewie were safe and secure. Leaving them was probably the only thing that I'd done right since this whole nightmare began.

And that brought up another thought. My grand plan was to walk basically across the street and wait until I was so sick that I would take my own life—sure, it was down a hill, across a four-lane road, and then up another grassy expanse. Carl might not be the touchy-feely or warm-fuzzy type, but I was willing to bet it would still be an unsettling day when he stumbled across my rotting corpse...my brains splattered all over some wall. Worse still would be if I chickened out and he encountered the zombie version of me.

"I need to get out of this place." The words sort of echoed off the walls.

It took me a few hours, but eventually I'd set aside and then pared down what I considered a proper amount of supplies. When I thought about it, Carl was more than capable of clearing

10

this place. Heck, even if he had to do it alone, I was willing to bet he could pull it off.

I slipped out the back door of the house. I was about to take off when I recalled that my axe was still out front in the middle of a zombie's head. I crept to the gate and peered over it. I spotted it jutting up from a body near the foot of the driveway of the home I'd just exited. There weren't any walkers close by so, after taking a few deep breaths, I took off at a sprint. I heard a few moans as I grabbed the handle and wrenched my weapon free. As soon as I had it liberated from its impromptu skull sheath, I bolted back to the gate and into the backyard of the house.

From there, I used the series of yards to make my way to the wall. Once I reached it, the wall was a struggle to climb up onto without any sort of ladder, but I made it. I glanced back in the direction of where I knew the others to be.

"Take care of my Chewie," I whispered into the wind.

With that, I slipped down to the other side. I paused at the edge of an open park. A small sign identified it as Altmont Park. It wasn't much more than a flat section of land with grass, not much of a park in my opinion. There were a few lone zombies staggering about. Nothing I didn't think that I could slip past even if they did manage to see me and start in pursuit.

As I reached the other side, I noticed the first houses all showed signs of hasty evacuations. All I needed was one with a car in the driveway. That would become my target. I would slip in, look for the keys, and hit the road.

If not for the fact that I would be abandoning this vehicle once I had it loaded with supplies from the veterinary hospital, I would try for Mount Hood. I couldn't think of a better place to end it. I'd always loved the mountains. My hand absently patted my bag. Inside it was my single memento of the world before: my picture of Stephanie and I on a ski trip to that mountain.

I was disappointed to discover that apparently most of these people had either left no vehicle behind, or the closed garage doors hid their second or third vehicles. I was not about to peek in and search every one of them for something that I knew would eventually reveal itself to me in plain sight. I was just starting to rethink that idea as I arrived at the end of the street I'd started down.

I reached the tee-intersection of Southeast Bristol Park Drive and Southeast Bristol Park Terrace. From here, I could see another neighborhood. I recalled spotting it on the map and being somewhat amused by its unique spiral shape. I didn't realize that it was another gated community until I got closer. But that wasn't what was so humorous. Who designs a neighborhood where the street wraps inward with a distinct spiral shape?

Southeast Bristol Park Drive was the street that led up to the gate of this spiral-shaped townhouse duplex community called Graystone. Honest to God, I'd had no idea there were so many gated communities in the entire city of Portland…much less in just this little region.

I was about two houses away when I started to notice something. The gates had been left open, which is what had me heading this direction in the first place. I wouldn't have to worry about how I would escape the neighborhood. Only, just past the first set of duplexes on each side where the road split and led into the heart of the community, there were a series of vehicles.

From here, I could see that they spanned the road all the way into the yards on each side. There were even cars that sat parallel to the fronts of those first houses. It was as if they'd been placed in a defensive position. I paused, looking around at what I was now certain was some sort of created barricade.

Maybe this isn't where I need to be looking, I thought. I took a step backwards, not wanting to turn my back on this area.

"That's far enough," a voice called down from the upper floor of the house on my right. This house was still outside of the walls of the gated community.

"Damn," I breathed.

"On your knees and lace your fingers with your hands behind your head."

"I don't want any trouble," I called out. "I'll just go back the way I came and you won't see me again."

"A week or two ago, I might've believed you," the voice replied. "But I think I've seen enough these past ten days or so to erode any degree of hospitality or trust that I might've had in my heart."

"Yeah, well, I was just across the way and saw it as well. I understand, but I ain't asking to come in. I just want to go about my business."

I was greeted by silence. A moan from behind me ended my attempt at being patient.

"Look, I'm not gonna stand here and be eaten. I'm gonna turn around and walk away. If you are gonna kill me, you're gonna have to shoot me in the back." I spun on my heel and took a few steps when a gunshot rang out and the road just to my left erupted in a puff of grit.

I drew my Glock and turned, diving to that side of the road. My thought process was to get as close to that building as possible. That would make it more difficult for this person to get another shot at me. Of course, if there was another individual in the building across the street, then my actions were all for naught.

"I said I didn't want any trouble," I shouted as my eyes scanned the area for any approaching zombies. The first one rounded the corner of the house I was pressed up against.

One zombie didn't pose much of a threat, but when five more rounded the corner, my mouth went dry. I was caught between a rock and a hard place.

Funny thing about knowing you are going to die soon...you think you are going to become magically fearless. You believe that you will adopt the mindset that, since you are about to die anyway, you can act boldly and charge into the teeth of danger because you know you'll be croaking soon.

I stood rooted to the spot. My brain was trying to send my feet the signal to run, but one way was into a small mob of zombies and the other was into a potential piece of high-velocity lead. Neither seemed all that appealing.

Still, the thought of being eaten outweighed all other options in the degree of how much it would suck. I backed up and looked down the length of the house. Looking up at the second floor, I saw a shadow in one of the windows. Just as I spotted it,

I caught movement and ducked back as a shot was fired and a bullet ripped through the siding right by my head, sending flecks of metal flying.

A look over my shoulder revealed that the approaching number of zombies had now reached well over a dozen. There was no choice. I would make a run for the front door of this house. Real people were not as good at hitting a somewhat fast-moving object. Sticking to the house as close as possible would reduce what this person could see and get a clean shot at. Once I reached the front porch, I would be under cover. After that, all I needed to do was get inside. I doubted this person left the front door open.

Taking a deep breath and holding it, I took off at a sprint. I heard cursing come from above and a volley of shots were fired hastily, but I didn't feel anything, so I was going to assume he'd missed. I dove onto the porch and then hurried to the front door. I wasn't surprised when I discovered that it was locked.

Backing up, I went to the large front window. Using the butt of my pistol, I gave the window a solid rap, jerking away as glass shattered. I could hear something inside that sounded like a herd of buffalo stampeding above me. Looking inside, I spied the stairs just down a semi-dark hallway. I brought my Glock up and waited.

Silence fell and I guessed that this mystery person had just realized that running down the stairs might not be the best thing to do. Very cautiously, I swung my leg up and over the sill of the busted window. I winced when my boot came down with an audible crunch as the shattered glass broke into even smaller bits underfoot. A bit hastily, I ducked down and swung my other leg inside. I certainly didn't want to be caught half in and half out.

I could hear the moans from behind me as the zombies neared the corner I'd come around. I'd come in at the side of this porch and had to throw myself up onto it. The stairs were around in the front. Zombies were not known for their powers of reason, so I was hoping that they would just shamble on by. Of course, if there was any noise made, they would turn and come for the house and make their way up the stairs. Since I'd busted the window, they now had easy access to this home.

I wasn't doing well on my first zombie apocalypse.

"You idiot," the voice from upstairs hissed.

I crept to the hallway and made my way to the stairwell. As quiet as I dared, I called up, "You started it by shooting at me."

"You were supposed to run away."

I guess I could see the logic in that. Most people just a few weeks ago would have bolted like a jackrabbit the moment they were shot at. So why hadn't I? I'd rushed over to a spot that basically pinned me in a corner and then had to choose between a shooter and some oncoming zombies. I could've just as easily taken off up the street and left this place behind. It wasn't like there weren't literally hundreds of other options for me to seek out and spend my last days.

"I told you I didn't want any trouble and that I was willing to walk away. You shot at me," I reminded.

"Again...just trying to get you to move faster." Just as the person stopped talking, I heard a noise. There was a scurry overhead and muffled whimpers.

A baby? This person has a baby up there. No wonder he is so jumpy.

"Listen, I am coming up, I won't hurt anybody." I took a step for the stairs and heard an even faster scurry as the person upstairs rushed back to the top of the stairwell.

"Don't even think about it. If you put one foot on those steps, I'll shoot you."

I could hear the tremor in the man's voice. He sounded young. My own adrenaline overload had ebbed to the point where I was now able to start picking out details. This was a young man. I would guess him to be in his late teens.

"I'm not going to do anything, I—" I started, but was cut off.

"You're right, because if you try to come up here, I'll shoot you," the voice warned again.

I pondered for a moment if a young man could kill somebody in cold blood, or if it was all just a bunch of bluster. I decided that I didn't care enough to test the hypothesis.

"Okay, I am going to slip out the back. Zombies out front and all," I added that last part just to clarify.

"Whatever, but if I hear a single squeak on the steps, I will just start shooting."

Wow…this kid was seriously jumpy. I rushed past the open stairwell just in case and then made my way down the rest of the hallway. I passed a bathroom and then eventually emerged into a kitchen.

I paused at one of the open cabinets. The place looked to have been cleaned out. I imagined anything worth a damn was probably upstairs. I reached the back door and was just slipping out when I heard a clatter, a thud, and the sound of crunching glass. Right on the heels of all that was the very identifiable sound of a zombie moan.

They'd come up the stairs to the porch and were getting inside.

I paused. Part of me said to go back inside and help. The other part of me said that I wasn't wanted. That had been made clear.

I closed the door and started across the backyard. This house bordered the gated community. I could just hop the fence and venture inside. To the left was the street where I'd been approaching. To the right was another backyard.

In a matter of a second, my brain had come up with a theory. If that kid hadn't gone into the gated community, chances are that there was a reason.

I turned right.

Just as I climbed up onto the fence that separated these two properties, I heard a series of gunshots from inside the house. It wasn't too late. I could hop down and run in there. Maybe I would save the day. It would be one good deed to put on my resume just in case a pair of Pearly Gates awaited me on the other side.

I was still struggling with what to do and finally lowered myself to the ground and prepared to run back inside when I heard that terrible scream. I was too late. I sighed and fell back against the fence I'd just started to climb.

"I'm sorry," I whispered.

16

I wasn't sure why, but I felt that I might've been able to do something. If I was so sure that person was younger, maybe all I needed to do was break out my authoritative voice...like a teacher taking control of a classroom of rowdy kids.

A second later, I heard another sound that made me weak in the knees. It started as a cry...a simple baby's cry. It was just different enough from what I'd heard from those creepy zombies to let me know it was the real thing. Then that cry changed to something else. Something terrible. Something no person should ever have to hear. It raised in register to a point where it hurt my ears. Maybe I was imagining it...but I don't think so.

I felt a stabbing pain in my heart that was so sudden and severe that I looked down expecting to see a knife or an arrow jutting from my chest. There was nothing...nothing physical at least.

That terrible cry amped up for another second and then went silent with a wet gurgle. I'd slid down and was now sitting on my butt in the grass. It was a struggle to make it to my feet, and I wasn't sure my knees would hold. Somehow, I climbed up and over the fence and lowered myself down into the next yard.

I repeated that move another couple of times before reaching the end of this block of houses. I was now on another road with what was apparently the other entrance to the spiral shaped gated community. Straight across the street was a tree line. I could tell that those woods went on for at least a little way. I headed into the gloom of the woods still fighting back the tears that wanted to spill from my eyes as my brain tormented me with the sound of that tiny shriek.

DEAD: Alone

2

The World is a Graveyard

I emerged from the woods and stopped abruptly, my heart pounding in my chest from the sudden shock. I was on the edge of a massive cemetery. It took me a moment to realize that this would not be some gender-swap remake scene from *Night of the Living Dead.*

"They're coming to get you, Evan," I mocked and then laughed.

My pulse slowed back to normal, and I stepped out onto the rolling slopes of whatever graveyard this might be. It was still a bit eerie as I strolled through all the memorial marker plates planted in the ground. I stayed on the paved path and eventually emerged from this tree-walled alcove to discover a series of buildings that at first I mistook for lockers. The names and dates etched on the squares told me these were just more memorials. Each had a metal ring jutting from the lower left corner, and a couple still held long-since-dead bouquets of flowers. There were three tiers of these little structures; this is where the path forked. I took the top path and momentarily paused. For some reason, it fascinated me to discover that the granite or whatever stone that faced these little memorials was of a shinier, better quality stone.

"Even in death we are separated by class," I mused.

I began to imagine the ghosts or spirits of these structures engaged in a class war of sorts where the upper-class ghosts on this top tier sneered and made faces at the ones below them. Once again, I had to ask myself if madness was perhaps an indication that I was turning. What I wouldn't give for a mirror so I could check my eyes.

I just wanted to get out of here and find a new neighborhood where I could snag a car. I still had some unfinished business to attend. I wanted to make that run to the vet and drop the supplies off for Carl and the others to find before I died.

Next, I passed by a series of neatly spaced tombstones in even, straight rows. Several were empty of any sort of writing. That creeped me out a bit, but when I rounded a bend in the path and emerged from a naturally made arch of tree branches, I saw something that almost set my heart to racing as much as when I'd first discovered that I was in a graveyard.

In the distance, a green canopy sat over an open hole in the ground. A pile of dirt off to one side completed the scene. My steps slowed involuntarily. I immediately tried to tell myself that this was nothing, but it was still too creepy for my tastes. I skirted wide of the open grave and almost gave myself whiplash as I snapped my head in a new direction every single time I heard even the slightest sound.

When I was finally able to see inside the gaping hole, I saw a single zombie just standing there. She'd obviously fallen in and was now stuck down there. She hadn't spotted me yet and was just staring at the earthen wall that would've been the head of the grave. She was dressed in all black and had some damage on her left shoulder. As I slipped away, I could hear her soft moan carry on the air. For some reason, it made me a bit sad.

Eventually, I entered another section of this massive cemetery that was just trees on either side. I was almost to the clearing when I stopped dead in my tracks again. I looked back the way that I'd come and then faced the direction that I was headed.

"What am I so creeped out by in this place?" I asked the breeze. "The whole world is a graveyard now."

With that thought actually lightening my apprehension, I continued along the narrow and paved pathway until I emerged again to the rolling, grassy hills dotted with small memorial markers. I could make out the exit now as well as the large building that sat at the entrance. Apparently, I'd just traversed the Lincoln Park Memorial Cemetery. I reached what the sign told me was Southeast Mt. Scott Boulevard and took a look in each direction. To the left, the road bent out of sight and gave me no real clues as to what might be in that direction. To the right, I could see what looked like a collection of houses. Directly across the street from me was yet another massive looking cemetery. The number of flags that I saw planted in the ground told me it might be some sort of military memorial site.

I headed to the right and could not believe I was seeing another damn wall. As an added bonus to screw with my day, it transitioned into one of those pointy-topped wrought-iron fences. Eventually, that pointy section soon vanished behind a wall of tall evergreens.

I considered climbing over the wall since it would be less treacherous than the pointy-topped fencing, but then reminded myself of how that last encounter ended. Also, my arm was really throbbing. I paused long enough to root through my bag and produce a bottle of some over-the-counter pain reliever. It wouldn't do much more than take the edge off, but it was better than nothing.

After I shoved the bottle in my pocket where it would be available for use much sooner than a doctor would probably consider prudent, I returned my attention to the situation at hand. If there were survivors inside, I might be seen as some sort of raider. It would be best if I walked to wherever the entrance to this place might be. Also, it would suck to find a car, get it going, and then reach the exit only to find it barricaded.

I was patting myself on the back as I strolled along the two-lane road. I was actually feeling relatively safe. On my left was that massive memorial cemetery with nothing obstructing my view for perhaps a hundred yards or more as well as the fence acting as a safety measure. On my right were all the trees and what I figured was that pointy-topped fence that ran along behind the trees. The road ahead was straight and relatively flat. I was going at a slight incline, but I still had the ability to see well ahead of myself.

If not for what I knew to be a harsh reality, this could be a normal day. I might just be out for a stroll. Of course, every so often, I could still hear the moans of the undead or a random gunshot. Those single instances would pop the little bubble, but every time it popped, this casual stroll would re-inflate it.

At last, I reached the entrance to this community and discovered that there was no gate. The fancy script on the brick wall on either side of the entrance told me I was entering the community of Lincoln Heights. Since I saw no need to venture into the heart of any neighborhood, I hugged the wrought-iron fence and ducked into the backyard of the first house. This choice was all that much easier since I could see a few wandering undead up the street from me as well as one crossing at the first intersection.

The back patio was covered by a deck above and had a few pieces of outdoor furniture scattered about, all of it knocked over haphazardly. A small propane barbecue grill sat up against the wall where the house jutted back out and I paused to check it. I was thrilled to discover a small bottle of propane and even more so when it proved to not be empty.

I'd taken time to notice that all the windows—at least those I could see on this side of the house—had their blinds down and shuttered. Once I had the small bottle of propane stuffed into my pack, I slung it back over my shoulders and gave the sliding glass door an experimental tug. It resisted for a moment and then gave way with an audible pop as the seal of what was apparently a well-insulated house finally broke.

I sniffed the air and then slipped inside. I had to imagine that a house that appeared to be fairly airtight would trap the stench of the undead in it and make it easy to detect. All I smelled was rotting garbage and a bit of mustiness.

I stood in a dining room and could see into a nice kitchen. The cupboards were all thrown open and I could see that a lot of what were probably dry and canned goods had been taken. There had been a bag of flour dropped which was then tracked all over the place. I saw footsteps of at least three different sizes spreading the mess in every direction.

I picked through what remained and was surprised to discover a half-empty jar of peanut butter. I unscrewed the lid and opened drawers until I discovered the one containing utensils. Plucking a spoon, I dug out a glob of the chunky, sweet goodness and stuffed it into my mouth.

I continued to roam through the house as I ate peanut butter, my eyes taking in the details and assembling how I thought things had gone. Since I didn't see any blood, I had to guess (or hope) that nobody here was infected. They'd probably seen the news broadcast and chose to make a run for it. I poked my head into the garage and felt a strange surge of optimistic hope for these people.

It was obvious that they'd cleared out some camping gear. This was one of those two-car jobs with an additional space for recreational vehicles like Jet Skis and such. I say Jet Skis because the trailer with two of them strapped in place was sitting in that extra space. I could see a lot of gaping holes around the garage on the shelves that were built into the walls on the near side as well as the rear of this garage where I assumed outdoor equipment had been stored.

There was a plastic tub on the floor that was obviously scrounged through for specific items. I saw a broken lantern cast off to one side as well as a heavily stained sleeping bag. I was sort of surprised that they'd taken the time to close the garage door in their obviously hasty departure. I was willing to bet it was out of habit.

There was no vehicle inside, but I could see a dark stain where one had been parked. I exited the garage and went to the front room. Again, the shades were down and shuttered, but on only two of the three windows that faced the front of the house. I looked out and spotted what I was pretty sure was a Subaru wagon parked in the driveway.

I started my search from there, checking the walls for a

hook where keys might be hung, opening drawers and scanning all the table tops. Once I was certain that there was nothing to be found downstairs, I headed up to the bedrooms. The first thing I did was check every item of clothing on the floor to see if there might be keys in the pockets.

It looked like this would be a bust. I had plopped down on the bed and was staring up at the ceiling when the thought hit me that I hadn't looked in a mirror. I forced myself to my feet and stood slowly, almost as if against my will. I remained staring into the bathroom that sat off of this master bedroom for a moment. It was dark, and there were no windows. I used that as my excuse for a few heartbeats until I forced myself to stop delaying and trudge in there to take a look. Just my luck, there was enough ambient light that allowed me to see. I had to lean forward, close to the mirror, in order to confirm my assessment.

"Still nothing," I muttered.

It would be just my luck. I would take that full seventy-two hours. On the plus side, I should be able to make that run on the veterinarian's office before I turned.

"Provided I can find some damn keys," I cursed.

I exited the bathroom and my eyes landed on the two nightstands beside the bed. That would be the last place I would look here. If I still didn't find any keys, I would have to move on.

The first drawer was a bust. The second revealed nothing more interesting than a tiny women's "neck massager" stuffed in the back.

I headed down the stairs and had my hand on the sliding glass door when movement made me pause. I blinked my eyes and then rubbed them. I was frozen in place. My eyes were the only visible part of me that moved as I scanned the road that I used to enter this neighborhood.

When the burning in my chest began, I realized that I was holding my breath. I let it out slowly. As I was sucking in that next batch of much needed oxygen, I saw it again. This time, it was directly across the street from me. I watched as a heavily clad individual pulled him or herself up and over the tall wooden fence that shut in the entire backyard.

I continued to watch as this stranger craned his or her head first back up towards the entrance of this neighborhood, and then down into its heart. The person started to head into this residential area, but paused, and I swear they looked right at me. That was when I realized that I'd been just standing in the frame of the sliding glass door…in plain sight.

The stranger's head turned away and then snapped back to me in an over-exaggerated doubletake. Apparently, I wasn't the only person surprised at this chance encounter. As we both stood there, I had an opportunity to at least make some basic observations.

He or she was fairly short. That led me to think the likelihood was high that this was a female. They wore pistols holstered on each hip and had a shotgun jutting up over one shoulder. In one hand was a wicked looking curved blade. During this momentary close look, I was able to tell that wetness dripped from that blade. The main reason I could not confirm the gender, besides all the heavy clothing, was that this person was wearing what looked like a riot helmet with a dark face shield.

The two of us were both obviously frozen due to shock and surprise. I shook it off first—at least I am going to make that claim for now—and raised one hand in a wave. The person raised the helmet's visor to reveal a face that didn't do much to help me determine the gender. It was sort of squished, like perhaps the helmet was a couple of sizes too small, and the features were distorted.

Since this individual had made the effort to expose themselves to me to at least some degree, I decided that I could step out onto the patio. I waved feebly. The person waved back and started in my direction. I took a few steps toward the individual out of habit.

"You from around here?" she asked. Hearing her voice, at least now I had a gender.

"Not exactly," I answered.

"Looting?"

"No…well…" I thought it over. In truth, I was when you

got right down to it. "I guess so."

I started and looked around abruptly. When I'd entered this neighborhood, there had been a few zombies visible. I had this sudden fear of being set up. This person would distract me as a pack of zombies came up from behind and grabbed hold.

"You okay?" she asked, suddenly catching my visible fear and looking around just as frantically as I'd just done.

"Is anybody these days?" I shot back with a nervous laugh.

"A bunch of the infected just came out of this place around ten minutes ago," the woman said after we both ensured that we were alone for the most part. "I was across the street in the Willamette National Cemetery when they all strolled out onto Mount Scott and eventually turned to the left. Did you just get here?"

"Yeah, just about…ten minutes ago," I acknowledged.

"A couple of 'em probably saw you and started for ya. Of course, if they lost sight, then they just keep moving in whatever direction they were headed."

That fit with everything that I'd observed so far as well. All except for the kid versions, but I didn't feel like bringing that up at the moment.

"Name's Evan," I said by way of introduction. "Evan Berry."

"Miranda Swells," the woman replied.

"Out here on your own?"

As soon as I asked that question, I saw her expression change. The curved blade she held down at her side drifted up a few inches.

"Oh crap…sorry," I exclaimed, holding my hands up with them open to show that they were very empty. "I was just surprised to see anybody out running around all alone. It's pretty nasty out and about. And if zombies were the only problem, I'd say it was awful, but they aren't even half the problem."

"Look, Evan, you seem like a nice guy." Miranda took a step back. "The thing is, I don't really wanna hang with anybody. I think I'll be better off by myself."

I could understand her to a point, but it was not a decision I would've supported if not for my current condition. How could being alone in the apocalypse be a good thing for anybody? And it isn't as if I'm sexist or anything like that, but a woman least of all.

"I guess you gotta do what you think is right for you." I gave a shrug.

"If you aren't minding, then I'd sorta like to give this place a good look around. I'm trying to locate some decent supplies before I head out to the river and make my way to someplace like Elk Rock…or maybe even Sauvie Island."

"Good luck to you," I said. And I meant it.

She gave me a nod and headed up the street, pausing to take down a lone zombie that had wandered out from some thick shrubs acting as a natural border between two houses. I was both sad and relieved to see her go. The sad part was just in the simple fact that it was crazy how nice it felt to talk to a living human being for just that brief few moments. The relief came from knowing I was about to be a dead man in the not-so-distant future. I wanted to use that little bit of time left to find and get those supplies to Chewie and the others, not to mention that I could turn at any time. Lonely or not, it wasn't the time to pick up a traveling companion.

I glanced back at the car I'd failed to find keys for and sighed. Looking up the street, I saw the next few houses on the same side of the street as the home I'd just searched all had cars in the driveway. I would just continue going from house to house until I either started feeling sick, or I found a set of keys.

As I approached the second home, I mused inwardly about all those shows where people found cars still running or with the keys in the visor. I had to question if people even did that sort of thing anymore.

It got so bad that I was almost up the front steps of the next house when I just had to run back and check the Subaru. It ended up being a bust, but I soothed my ego by telling myself that they would've been there if I *hadn't* gone and checked for sure.

I tried the front door and discovered that it was locked. It had skinny windows on either side of the front door, so I used my elbow to break the glass. Once I cleared an opening, I stuck my hand in, found the deadbolt, and unlocked the front door. I was pulling my hand back when I realized how monumentally stupid I'd just been.

Cracking the door open, I was hit by a smell, but it wasn't zombie. I stepped inside and shut the door behind me. Down the hall, I spotted a stairwell going up as well as a kitchen at the end. I decided to check out the kitchen first, but as I passed that stairwell, the smell was at its strongest. I decided to take a detour and head up to investigate.

I reached the top of the stairs and the smell became over-whelming. There were three doors up here, all of them shut. The first one was almost directly across from the stairs. I opened it very cautiously and was almost knocked back by the force of the stench.

Once I recomposed myself, I opened the door the rest of the way. Sitting in the bathtub was a man—at least what remained of him. The shotgun between his knees and the clumpy dark stain that grew up the side from where his head had once rested on his neck told the story.

Stepping inside, I saw the box of shells sitting on the bath-room counter. Even though I was not long for this world, I could still use the firepower. Plus, I could leave it with the veterinary supplies when I made my drop at the old sanctuary. I scooped the box into my bag and then wrenched the shotgun free, sling-ing it over one shoulder.

There were two other doors to check. I was almost afraid of what I would find, but I could not suppress the curiosity that welled up inside me. I went to the door on the left. I listened first. Even though I couldn't smell a zombie, there was no need to be foolish.

That was what I told myself, but the sign dangling from a small hook on the door that read "The Princess is in!" probably had more to do with my hesitation. I opened the door and was very surprised to find the room empty. I had to guess that the former occupant of this room was a pre-teen. There were plenty of animated princess faces looking at me from the posters that adorned the walls, as well as a red-haired mermaid bedspread and pillowcase.

I entered very cautiously, not convinced that I wouldn't find something terrible. After checking the closet and even looking under the bed, I was satisfied that the room was indeed empty.

I gave the room one more glance just before I closed the door. That left just one mystery door to be opened and have its surprises revealed. I paused, but once more, I could not smell that very distinctive zombie funk. I opened the door slowly and saw what had to be the master bedroom. It looked like a fight had taken place in here. The lamp on one side of the bed had been knocked to the floor and broken. The bedding was wadded up in the center of the bed and I saw the dark blood stains in some of the folds.

I entered the room and searched for any signs of keys, but I was already deciding that I could move on to the next house and so did not search that intensely. I exited the master bedroom and shut the door behind me as I had the others. Something terrible had happened here and, while I didn't believe in ghosts, I hadn't believed in zombies until very recently either. Something was nagging at me and giving me a chill.

I went to the front door, prepared to leave this house and simply move on, and paused. A trio of zombies were making their way down the road in the same direction that I was headed. I didn't see the need to tempt fate and try to take them down. I could just as easily slip out the back, hop the fence, and enter the next house from the back door.

I ducked back through the house and ended up in the kitchen. I felt my heart leap when my eyes fell on the keys sitting out in the open. They were on the counter in plain sight. It was almost funny. I'd already given up on this place, consigning myself to searching the next house...and there they were for the taking.

I scooped the keys off the counter and stopped short as I was about to exit. I sniffed the air, almost certain that it had been just my imagination. Nope...I could smell the very distinct odor of the undead. It wasn't strong, but it was there. I turned to the door beside the refrigerator. It had to be the door to the garage.

I stepped to it and paused. The smell was there. It was faint, but it was definitely not my imagination. If there was something trapped in the garage, I guess I could just leave it. It wasn't like I needed to go in and see for myself. I turned away and got three whole steps before I returned to that door. I gave it an experimental knock. There was no response. If there was a zombie in there, I was certain it would come to the door and start pawing at it after I'd knocked.

I rapped on it again and literally jumped back like I thought the stupid door would transform and attack me. I was being ridiculous. The only problem was that I really needed to know. I'd equated that certain smell with the undead. Could I be wrong? It didn't seem likely, but this was still so new...and who knew what sorts of assumptions were being made only to eventually end being debunked.

I turned the knob slowly and gave the door a little nudge. It opened and the smell was stronger, not overpowering, but it was definitely present. I listened, but it was silent.

Opening the door further, I spotted a black sports car. As I opened the door a bit more and was able to fully take in the entire scene, things made immediate sense. At the same moment I was connecting all the dots, a meaty slap of a hand on glass made me jump a little.

I'd been staring at her just as she stared at me. The little girl was perhaps eight years old. Her curly red hair was now a fright wig fouled with clumps of dried gore. Her mouth still bore the old stains that had faded to the point that they could've been from dark cherry Kool-Aid if I didn't know the awful truth. Her skin had probably been very fair before she'd turned. Now it was almost the blue of a robin's egg. The multitude of freckles had darkened to nearly black like she'd been flicked at with a paint brush. Her hideous, filmed-over eyes stared at me and I stared back. She cocked her head first one way, then the other as she continued to observe me. Once again, she reached up and slapped the window. Just that one time, but it was almost plaintive in nature.

She wanted out of the car.

I took a step into the garage. It was almost as if I was hyp-notized and she was willing me to her. I knew that to be false, but my curiosity more than made up for my lack of being under some sort of mind spell. I could see another figure in the car, and I was almost certain as to what I would discover, but I'd come too far to walk away now.

Next to the little girl, in the passenger's seat was a woman who was obviously the mother. Her hair was red and very curly. Now that I was beside the car and looking in, I could see a single bite on the mother's arm. I could also see the dark hole in the middle of her forehead from what was obviously a very small caliber weapon. I was willing to bet it was a .22. If I searched this residence more intensely, I was almost certain that I would discover that weapon.

From this vantage point, I was also able to make another discovery. The wrists of the little girl were an awful mess. A strand of twine dangled from one wrist. The hand at the end of that wrist reached up and slapped the window again. I focused my attention back on the child zombie in the car and was stunned to see that she was making no other moves. So far, just those few slaps on the window had been her only action. There was no sustained effort to get at me. It was so strange. But none of it as strange as how the child simply continued to stare at me. Every so often her head would twitch or cock to the side. It was giving me the creeps to no end.

"I can't leave you like this," I said to the zombie. Once again she twitched. It was almost as if she understood. "A stupid person would be fooled by whatever this little trick of yours might be."

I wasn't stupid.

I reached down and pulled my hand axe from my belt. As soon as I did, it was as if a switch had been thrown in the child zombie. Suddenly, it was trying to bite the glass and slapping at it with both hands instead of just the one.

I retreated, just a bit spooked by the sudden noise. The child zombie continued her futile attempts to get at me. Concerned that the noise would bring other curious zombies to the front of the house and put a kink in my escape, I exited the garage. I wasn't two steps away when the slapping suddenly stopped.

I continued a few more steps, but again found myself drawn back to the garage. If this was something relevant, perhaps I could write it down. I could include the notes in this supply drop I was intent on gathering for Chewie, Carl, and the others. Of course, there was the very real possibility that they would dismiss it as the ramblings of a loon, but maybe they would read it, laugh it off, then see an example of what I shared that would get them to take it more serious.

I glanced down the hallway to the front door and didn't see anything that gave me cause for alarm, so I returned to the garage. I opened the door and peeked inside. It was almost like stepping into a time loop.

The girl regarded me, her head cocking first one way, then the other. I slipped my axe back into my belt and re-entered the garage. The child zombie continued to regard me with what was almost pathetic curiosity.

I walked all the way up to the car again. A single hand came up and slapped the window. She studied me just as she had before—those creepy, blackshot eyes boring into me. I had to take this to the next level. I reached for my axe and pulled it free. Once more, the child immediately reverted to what I would now consider "standard" zombie behavior. I tucked the axe back into my belt, but that did nothing to alter the slapping and attempted gnawing at the glass.

I left the garage and was rewarded with the return of silence a few seconds later. Since I'd been in the child zombie's presence longer than the first time, I hurried up the stairs and chanced a look out front. There were a few shambling corpses in the area, but none seemed to be headed my way.

I returned to the garage and ran my little experiment four more times. The results were almost identical. The only glitch I could discover was that the child zombie basically saw anything I picked up as a trigger. I knew that somebody smarter than me could probably make real sense of this information, so I was determined to try and take the time to write it down.

At last, I was done with my study and decided that it was time to give the child peace. I reached over and opened the car door. The child was no more coordinated than any other zombie and fell out gracelessly. She landed hard on the cement pad of the floor and I stepped in quick, my axe burying itself in the back of her skull.

I pulled my weapon free and then scooped the child up and placed her in the car beside her mother. It wasn't much, but the gesture made me feel good inside for the first time in a while. Recent events and thoughts had gotten me to question my own moral fiber.

I exited the garage and looked outside to see that I'd lost most of the day. The sky was changing as the sun sank in the west. A few of the clouds were capturing and enhancing the reddish glow of sunset.

"Red skies at night...sailor's delight," I mumbled.

I decided that, if I stayed quiet and didn't do anything to draw attention to myself, it would probably be in my best interest to ride the night out here. I went to the bathroom on the ground floor and looked into the mirror again.

Still nothing.

What the heck was taking so long? It was becoming a bit ridiculous. Even worse, I was beginning to feel a glimmer of hope. One of the advantages as well as the disadvantages of the zombie apocalypse that is seldom addressed in any of the fiction would be the horrendous boredom. It is in that boredom that the mind sort of caves in on itself. I worked very hard to keep from letting memories of Stephanie overwhelm me. Maybe once I knew it was over, perhaps then I could sink into her one last time before ending it.

Right now, my mind was trying to focus on the task at hand. No tracers at the moment meant that I still had a little while before the turn would occur.

Chewie had been bitten early on when this nightmare began. That was how she'd lost more than half of her tail. I'd seen with my own eyes a zombie version of a dog. That confirmed one of

Carl's earlier observations that dogs turned. I've yet to see a cat or any other animal that turned.

To date, all the way up until I'd walked away from the group, my Newfoundland showed no signs that she was any worse for the wear. I was now wrapping up my second day post-bite.

Only…it wasn't really a bite. It was just a nasty scratch. And while I had no doubt as to the origin of the scratch, this lack of any black tracers in my eyes led me to believe that perhaps the rate of infection was different depending on where a person was injured. Also, perhaps the scratch and the bite had different rates. There had been an announcement that bites and scratches were equally fatal, but I wondered if the powers-that-be had taken the time to monitor the separate cases and see if there were differences.

And that was how I drifted off to sleep; my mind racing with the possibilities that I was perhaps turning slower due to the nature of my injury. I only woke once before the sun rose and began to bathe everything in soft golds. I was not able to roll over and return to sleep until I ventured into the bathroom once more to see that my eyes remained their normal selves.

As soon as I woke to discover that it was morning, I hopped up, collected my things, and made my way to the front door after one more look in the mirror. Peering out the window, the coast looked clear. I opened the door just a bit and gave a look up and down the street. I saw a few zombies stumbling about as well as a couple lying dead in the street. There was nothing close enough to be considered an immediate threat.

Remaining cautious and alert, I crept to the car in the driveway; I could smell the undead. I couldn't see any close by, but there was definitely one in the area. The vehicle was a Dodge Durango. From the outside, it appeared well taken care of and clean. I opened the driver's side door and smiled. The first thing my eyes lit on was an old french fry. It had the size and shape of Mickey Dees. Back before the madness, I'd often joked that I was pretty sure every car came with one as a standard feature. It didn't seem to matter the social status or income level; you could climb in just about any car in this country and feel that your odds were good when it came to finding an old fry somewhere on the floor. Maybe under a seat, or wedged in between the lip of the floor mat and the actual floorboard of the car...but you would find one.

The rest of the interior was in fantastic shape. I tossed all my stuff on the passenger's seat and climbed in. Closing the door carefully, I stuck the key in the ignition and held my breath. I didn't think that enough time had passed for batteries to lose their juice, but I still had to worry all the way up until the engine turned over.

This baby didn't disappoint. It ran so smooth that I initially thought nothing had happened. Of course, I saw all the zombies in the vicinity stop and turn in my direction if I had any doubts. I could still smell them, but I didn't see any that were so close that I might hit them.

I put the vehicle in reverse and backed out of the driveway. I had to swerve to avoid a single zombie when I reached the inter-section and the left turn that would take me out of this place. I was up the slight incline and at the tee-intersection when I realized that the map I'd located was folded up and in my bag.

Checking the rearview and the side mirrors, I saw that I had a few moments before the closest one would be on me. I coasted to a stop and reached down, plucking the map from my pack and opening it to find the traced route I'd marked. What would've taken hours on foot and been like trying to navigate a minefield would only take a few minutes in this vehicle. Even better, I could load it with plenty of supplies. I could be useful all the way to the end.

I cranked the wheel and turned right onto Mt. Scott Boule-vard. Out of curiosity I turned the knob on the radio. Static was all I got, so I hit the 'SEEK' button. It skipped through the entire FM band before I even got a block. I tapped the button for AM and again engaged the 'SEEK' feature.

Two things happened at almost the exact same time. The first was that a partially garbled voice came through the static as the numbers on the dial froze at 1550AM.

The second was a strange grinding noise followed by the sudden jerk of the vehicle, next was the sound of at least one of my tires exploding and the Durango starting to skid to the right. I hopped the curb and the nose of the maroon-colored SUV collided with the trunk of one of the many trees that lined the side of the road.

3

Who Can I Trust?

I wasn't going that fast. Despite that, my collision still activated the airbags. It was like being punched in the face. Not wearing my seatbelt probably made it even worse. I imagine if you were going fast enough that death was likely, and the airbag exploded and busted your nose, you would be thankful. A busted nose is way better than being dead, I guess.

I flopped back in my seat. The bag was deflating in a whoosh and I was doing my best to see past the stars dancing around my head. I glanced up in the rearview mirror and saw the blood streaming from both nostrils. Still no dark tracers in my eyes, though.

"That sucked," I said, my swollen and clogged nostrils making me sound like a goon.

My brain started screaming that maybe I was in danger. If somebody shot out my tires, then it made sense that the next bullets would be slamming through my window. I laid flat on the seat, hoping that I was not visible from the potential sniper's vantage point.

I fumbled for my Glock and checked it to make sure it was ready to shoot. Lying on my back as much as I could with the armrest, shifter, and cup holder between the two front seats, I got my breathing under control and listened. Realizing that I would be somewhat hampered with all the windows up, I reached over my head and hit the button on the passenger's side. Since the key was still turned, the electrical system of the Durango was still active and the window whirred as it lowered. Once it was down about half way, I let go and returned all my attention to being as silent as possible as I listened for the crunch of somebody walking up to the truck. I wasn't going to pause for even a second. I kept telling myself that it would be okay to kill anybody that poked their head into this vehicle.

I waited.

And I waited.

It seemed eternal, but nothing happened. Were they waiting for me to get out? Had they seen me flop down?

Another long period passed, and at last I heard the approach of feet. The unsteady dragging noise led me to believe that this was not one of the living. Perhaps that had been the plan of this sniper. They would let the zombies flush me out or kill me.

A hunched over figure limped past the driver's side window. Definitely one of the undead. It kept walking. I saw no reason to draw attention to myself and stayed as still as possible. Eventually, it disappeared from view. I let out a sigh of relief and risked a peek up over the dashboard.

I could see the back of the zombie as it continued along its way. Looking back the way I'd come from, I didn't see any zombies close. There were a few on the road almost all the way back by where I'd exited the graveyard. Over in the other cemetery, there was nothing.

I scanned all the way around my surroundings, but I still didn't see anything that might be my sniper. I tried to keep my eyes peeled for any possible reflection off of metal. After all, wasn't that how snipers were always detected in the movies?

Still nothing.

I sure as hell couldn't just stay in this truck forever. I would have to climb out sooner or later. Having run off the road, I couldn't tell which side had the blown tires. I decided to get out closest to the trees that shielded the neighborhood that I'd left. That meant exiting from the passenger's side.

I twisted around in the seat and eventually wormed around so that I could open the door. I eased it open slowly, still worried about exposing myself to the mystery shooter.

Crawling forward, I saw the right front tire was destroyed. Craning my neck around, the back one was flat as well. The smell of the undead drifted up my nostrils, and I decided that being on my belly, and hanging partway out of the door of this vehicle, was not going to enhance my chances of survival. I slid out and managed to get to my hands and knees with very little difficulty.

I still had my Glock in my hand and used it to assist as I scanned my surroundings. The undead back up the road were closer, but not so close that their stench should be that prevalent.

When I glanced to my right, I could see underneath the carriage of the Durango. And that was when I discovered my mystery shooter.

Of course, my first reaction was to scoot away from the vehicle, my hands and knees getting all gouged up by the sharp gravel barely registering on my consciousness.

"How the…" I gasped, my voice trailing off.

As best I could tell, the child had crawled under the Durango. His clothing had gotten snagged on something and then managed to get caught in the drivetrain. Most of his right side was just gone. It had been ripped away in the violence of being jerked and dragged along under the vehicle. I could see what looked like a piece of bone embedded in the rear wheel and had to assume that I'd discovered the culprit behind my two flats.

A shiver rocked me and I moved away from the useless vehicle. It was done for just as much as that pathetic creature underneath. My last image of the child was its head rotating towards me slowly, its mouth opening and spewing some sort of dark sludge. It might've not actually been black, but since the zombie was underneath the vehicle, everything had a darker hue.

I got to my feet and slung my pack over one shoulder. The zombie that had walked past had obviously heard all the ruckus and had turned to face me. I had my axe in my hand as I approached and gave him a single strike to the face. I snapped my arm back reflexively and paused long enough to wipe my blade off on a patch of grass beside the road. It wasn't long before I passed by a lone house on the left. I stopped cold in the middle of the road. If the last home I'd been in was luxurious…well, to put it plainly, this place made that one look like zombie scrapings.

This house had a massive wall that I had to assume surrounded the property. The driveway was barricaded by a sturdy iron gate, which was shut, and an old, beat-up pickup truck was parked just inside. I saw a lot of what looked like garden tools in the back of that truck. I didn't find that too crazy; after all, many of your common yard implements made pretty good weapons for killing zombies. What did strike me as peculiar was the body of the naked man that was impaled on the spikes that topped the entry gate to this place.

Since the slumped over figure wasn't moving, I was confident that he was simply dead. As I drew near, initially out of that same curiosity that used to cause us to slow down when we passed a terrible accident on the road, I was also convinced that this guy had been thrown onto this fence while he was still alive. There was a lot of dried blood splatter all over the driveway that looked like it came from somebody who had thrashed about quite a bit.

I reached the body and knelt down to look up at the man so I could see his face. The eyes would still have the tracers if he had been one of the infected. Sadly, I wouldn't get any help here; the eyes had been plucked or gouged out. However, there was a large wad of cloth stuffed in this guy's mouth. That was strangely fascinating. It had soaked up a good amount of blood and then dried so that it almost acted as a seal for this man's open mouth.

I got up and was trying to decide what to do when something hissing arced over my head. I ducked instinctively, then I jumped when a loud series of pops and bangs sounded from behind me. I spun just in time to see the last of a strand of what was easily a few hundred firecrackers going off in a storm of blue smoke and paper shreds.

"*Lagarté, pinche vato!*" a male voice called. "*Los muertos están llegando.*"

"And me without my English-to-Spanish dictionary," I muttered.

Looking up, I saw a short man standing on the balcony of the second floor. The man had black hair that looked like perhaps it hadn't been washed in a while. It was matted to his forehead. He was easily a hundred pounds overweight, so maybe walking all the way to the balcony had worn him out. He was leaning on the rails for support, and I now realized that his voice had sounded just a bit strained.

I looked around. Sure enough, coming up from what was apparently another entrance into that neighborhood that I'd just left behind were a small mob of the undead. They were about the equivalent of a half a block away and turning in my direction. Back from the way I'd come, the road was still sort of clear, but I had a feeling it wouldn't stay that way for long.

"You speak English?" I called.

"Yes…just not to you, now go," the man replied, surprising me.

I really wanted to argue with this guy, but there wasn't time. I considered just climbing over the fence. He must've seen the intention in my eyes, because the man pulled out a wicked looking shotgun and laid the barrel across the rail of the balcony. Sure, a shotgun was crap from distance, and I had my Glock, but I wasn't ready to get into a firefight just yet.

I resorted to giving the man the finger before I took off at a jog back in the direction that I'd come from. I heard him laugh, and I admit that it felt sort of good when I heard his laughter fall apart and become a series of painful sounding coughs.

I was now halfway between the two roads that led down into the neighborhood that I apparently was destined to never leave. That was when several zombies began to appear in that direction. So now I had them in front and behind me. Glancing over at the open vista of the Willamette National Cemetery, I even saw a few stragglers coming from that direction.

My only choice was to make it over the wrought-iron fence and then vanish into the trees that acted as the border to this place. I was pretty sure that I would come out in a backyard. It would suck that I'd have to go back into a house and repeat my search for keys once I located another car, but it couldn't be helped.

I was almost up and over when I heard a scream back in the direction of that nice house with the not-so-nice Hispanic man and his shotgun. I briefly considered returning. I credited that feeling to the part of me that still survived from the Old World. *How long would that part of me have been able to survive if I wasn't on borrowed time?* I wondered.

I threw one leg over and prepared to jump into a currently empty backyard so that I wouldn't be ripped apart and eaten alive by the two approaching zombie mobs. Another piercing scream clawed its way into my ears. I stopped. I was confident that I knew the sound of a young person's screams versus those of an adult. I'd just walked away from one poor defenseless infant. Those shrieks still rang in my ears, even now. While this was no toddler, it still had a younger sound to it. Could I make the same decision twice in as many days?

"Nope." I reversed my position and dropped back down onto the road that was becoming very crowded with the undead at an alarming rate and jogged back to that closed gate.

The height was an issue that I could work out, but the main problem was in the spiked tops of the wrought-iron. I really hated what I was about to do. Grabbing hold, I had to rely heavily on my good arm to pull myself up. As soon as I could, I threw one leg up, planting my foot in between two of the spikes, using the cross bar that ran the length as my support. Next, I hauled my body up the rest of the way, using the corpse that was impaled on a series of those spikes as a bit of a buffer so that I would hopefully avoid the same fate.

I was amazed when I landed on the other side and appeared no worse for the wear. I scooted along the side of the truck, my eyes glued to that balcony where I'd been warned away.

Another scream sounded, and I was certain it belonged to a man. And when I heard that same scream hitch for just a moment and change into *the* scream that I now knew so well, I hurried to the front door.

I tried the knob and cursed when it proved to be locked.

"So much for the element of surprise," I grumbled as I used my axe to shatter a window just to the side of the door. This one was actually about the size of the living room picture window of my old house. On this place, it looked deceptively small. The noise quickly reminded me that I was acting like an idiot as glass cascaded down in a sheet of potential pain and suffering. I danced back out of the way until the last large shards tumbled free, then I moved forward and cleaned off the bottom of the pane so I could climb in. I gave a quick inspection to ensure that I wouldn't end up being stabbed by a glass stalagmite...or was it stalactite? I never could remember which was which. My college geology professor would be very disappointed in me right now.

It's funny how the mind works. All these random thoughts were whizzing by in my head as I climbed into this gigantic home in the hopes that I might be saving somebody.

Naturally, the first thing that hit me was the stench. Only, there was more than just undead funk going on. I got whiffs of sweat and human waste mixed in. Also, there were other smells that I could not nail down. But it was as if somebody had collected the worst funks possible and created a massive scratch-and-sniff.

I gagged and threw my arm across my nose. That might help in fiction, or less stinky places, but it did very little for me in the here and now. I decided that the gate out front was going to have to serve as protection from the walking dead and stuffed my axe back in its little loop on my belt.

I drew the Glock and ensured that I had a full magazine ready for firing. I wouldn't be screwing around.

Another terrified scream came from upstairs. The problem was that there were two staircases that I could see that made their way to the second and third floors. One of them was a wraparound job that left me wide open to any attack from the extensive walled landing above. The second set was this retro-cool spiral number that offered almost no room to maneuver, but was also at least mostly obscured until my head would emerge on the next floor.

I chose the spiral one and tried to be as quiet as possible while I climbed the steel steps. A few stairs from the top, I paused.

I could hear muffled sobs as well as whispered dialogue. It sounded like it was all in Spanish, so it did me little good even if I could overhear what was being said. There was also an irregular thumping sound. I was already pretty certain that I knew what that would prove to be.

I continued my ascent and stopped again as soon as my head came up to floor level. From this vantage point, I discovered that I was in the middle of some sort of upstairs rec room. A pool table was to my left, and on one wall were three classic pinball games. It was strange, but I'd always dreamed of owning my very own actual pinball machine. Not some cheesy one-off, but an actual arcade-style classic.

The exit to my left led down a hallway. On the bad side, all the doors along its length were shut. That made it a very dark corridor. Also on the bad side was the lone zombie that was clawing at the door just about halfway down the hall.

She was a short, portly woman. Her hair had been in a bun when she died; but that bun was coming loose and long strands of hair floated around her head as she tried to gain entrance to whatever waited on the other side of that door.

Of course, I could also see that lone zombie as a plus. One zombie wasn't that tough to take down. That was always one of the issues I had with zombie films. Groups would run into one lone zombie and get all crazy-scared. Maybe I was becoming desensitized already, but to me, a single zombie was no real threat. Of course, if they sprinted *a la* Danny Boyle or Zak Snyder, then I imagine things would be much worse and a single zombie could truly be a threat.

I climbed those last few stairs and paused to draw my trusty hand axe. If I struck quickly, maybe I would have a moment to actually catch my breath and figure out what the hell was going on. At least that was what I told myself as I started up the hallway towards that single zombie.

I was a few steps away when it realized that I was there. It turned to me and opened its freshly bloodstained mouth to let loose with a low mewl. Something wet and meaty dropped from its open maw and I lunged forward. My axe struck her just to the right of the center of her forehead. The force of the blow was enough to crash through the bone and partially dislodge the eyeball from its socket.

The body collapsed to the floor and I took a step back so as not to get tangled in its sprawled-out legs. Sure, they were kinda stubby, but in a confined space, tripping was a much easier possibility to have happen.

I barely had time to congratulate myself when the door the zombie had been pawing at flew open. I recognized Mr. Firecracker instantly. His gut was even more pronounced up close and without the rail of a balcony to conceal it. His shirt was perhaps two sizes too small, so I could see bare belly drooping down and folding the tops of his jeans over.

I could also see the big, scary machete he held in one hand. My gaze flicked from that weapon to the ugly bite on his left arm. He'd wrapped the wound in what looked like a gray tee-shirt but the amount of seeping blood oozing from the saturated cloth along with the fresh smear that had been dripping around the mouth area of the rotund female Hispanic zombie added up to that being a new bite.

When the man stepped towards me, I guess I half-expected a word of thanks. Maybe even an invite to stay which I would politely decline considering my current infected condition. What I did not expect was to have to dance back and away from that damn machete as it came slicing through the air in my direction.

"What the—" was all I managed to say as I scuttled away from a blade that missed me by what I was certain had to be less than a centimeter.

A stream of profanity came at me in Spanish. I knew it for what it was from working construction. Plenty of my co-workers were Hispanic. Most of them were great guys. After a while, you pick up a few things.

"Whoa!" I yelled, putting my hands up for a split second

and then yanking them away just in time to avoid having them hacked off by that nasty machete.

The man swung wildly a few more times, but it was clear that he lacked the energy to continue the assault as he staggered a few steps and then sank to his knees. He buried his face in his hands and I could hear him sob. I wasn't fool enough to go forward and try to offer any form of consolation. I stood where I'd retreated to, which happened to be a few steps away from the spiral staircase I'd used to get up here. If I had to, I could plunge down that rabbit hole and be gone.

"I-I-I'm sorry," I finally stammered. "But you have to know what she was…you said it yourself out there about *los muertos.*"

When the man looked up at me, I almost ended up falling down those stairs. His eyes were laced with blackness. He was infected. He must've understood my reaction because he moaned and smacked his fist against his leg.

I didn't have time to process what was unfolding in front of me before another sound caused me to look back up the hallway. A small figure was emerging from the open door where the man had come. It paused at the figure on the floor. I was willing to bet that I'd not just killed this guy's wife, but the child's mother.

I was starting to feel bad. Not physically; no, it was my in soul. It was almost as if I could feel it dripping with the tainted blood of the woman I'd just killed.

She wasn't a woman, I reminded myself. *You know that. She was a zombie just like all the others you have put down.*

But that was a lie. She was nothing like any of the others I'd killed. This one had a family. I'd killed the matriarch of this little clan, and now they were being forced to accept what they apparently could not until I stuck my big foot in the middle of this crap-fest.

The small figure stepped all the way out into the hallway and I felt my mouth go dry and my heart drop through my stomach. As that shadowy shape took one unsteady step and then another, I didn't need it to reach the light to confirm what I already knew beyond a shadow of a doubt.

What I wasn't quite prepared for was the whole visual package. If I had to guess, I would put this little girl at seven or eight years old. She was not chunky like her parents. This child was rail thin. Her long black hair was pulled back into a braid that was too fresh and lacking signs of coming undone for it to have been done while she had been one of the living.

The wounds on her shoulder and the nasty rip in her throat were old and dried out. I'm no medical expert, but I was certain that the wounds on the child were several days old.

All of that was bad, but if you added in the thick leather strap tied around her head and wedged into her mouth, the scene went up another few notches in the "Disturbing sights" category. It wasn't a stretch to figure out what was going on here.

I looked over at the man and saw that he was watching the little girl make her way down the hall. His face said it all. I could see the love, the fear, the heartbreak, and the sense of failure. All of those emotions were etched clearly on his face. Then he started and his gaze returned to me. His eyes flicked to my Glock and then back to the little girl.

"Please," the man whispered.

The thing is, I wasn't entirely certain what he was asking. Was he asking me to spare her? Or did he want me to do what he obviously could not? I was going to go with the latter. The thing was, his fate showed in his eyes; he was just as dead as the girl. The only difference was that he was still breathing, but that didn't make him alive.

I considered ending the man first and then the child, then it hit me. Who was I to make that kind of decision? If I was so intent on putting infected people down, why hadn't I taken my own life yet?

I turned my attention back to the little girl. She was now at the end of the hall and had stopped her advance. Her head cocked first one way, then the other as she regarded me, then her father.

"*Venir a mí, hija,*" the man whispered, his arms going wide to accept her in his embrace.

The girl shifted her body and turned to the man. My mind raced back to when Stephanie had first opened her eyes. I could have saved myself from all of this by just giving myself to her then, but something had triggered my desire to survive.

Or maybe I'd just been afraid.

This man had obviously been keeping his daughter long after she'd turned. He had no fear of her as she took one slow and unsteady step after another. At last, she stood right before the man.

She stopped and regarded him. Her head making an occasional twitch or jerk, but her feet had stopped moving. Again, I was witnessing behavior that reinforced my theory that the child versions of the undead were just a bit different.

Why wasn't she attacking?

Of course, with that strap in her mouth, she would not be able to inflict much damage. Then the man leaned forward and released whatever was holding the gag in place. It slid away to the floor, a thick strand of milky goo stretched out and eventually broke, leaving a wet trail down her chin. But still the girl did not move.

The man looked at me, tears streaming down his face. I saw something in his eyes, but didn't know what it was until he reached down to his boot and drew a knife.

As soon as he did, the girl switched into just another zombie. Her hands came out and she dove at the man. I was frozen in place as I watched her lunge in and bury her face in the man's throat.

He cried out in pain, and his cry quickly ramped up to that same scream I'd heard so many times. The merciful thing was how short it lasted before becoming a gurgling sound.

At last, whatever spell had kept me rooted to the spot melted away. I moved in with my axe and drove it into his temple with all the force I could muster. Before the girl could react, I yanked my weapon free and brought it down on the crown of her skull. Surprisingly, it took me three swings to put her down for good. I staggered back from the carnage and collapsed on one of the couches that ringed the room.

Time began to lose all sense of meaning. I could hear the moans of the dead, but I knew I had a fence between me and them, so my brain dismissed those noises and tried to find very secure corners to shove the memories of the past several minutes.

I have no idea how long I'd been sitting there with the soundtrack of zombie moans before I realized that one of those moans was coming from down that dark hallway. I ran my free hand down my face as if that might wash away the dread.

Getting up, I ventured into the gloom and felt that very darkness try to wrap its tendrils around my heart. A part of me said to run away. There was no need to expose my already battered spirit to whatever fresh horror was at the end of this hall. Yet my feet chose to ignore those sentiments as I took the last few steps to the doorway.

The door that the man and then his daughter had emerged from was wide open. There would be no suspense of a creaking hinge sounding. I looked into the room, my feet straddling the dead woman sprawled on the floor.

The figure that stared back at me from where it was lashed to a chair opened its mouth and made what was almost a snarl as its teeth chomped together with an audible click. Unlike the girl, this boy was a fresh turn. The blood drying on his shoulder was still damp and reddish. I was confident that I'd just discovered the source of the scream that had brought me here in the first place.

Another difference was the age. This boy was in his teens. He was just like every other zombie. There was no curious cock of the head as it studied me. It simply wanted to get its teeth into my flesh. The head lunged with each snap as I entered the room.

As I had with the rest of his family, I put my axe to use. I cleaved the boy's head, wincing at the familiar tingle as my weapon bit into the skull. I had no idea what the hell had gone on here. It didn't seem terribly nefarious, but it was certainly tragic and sad.

An idea struck me.

Twenty minutes or so later, the mother, father, and both children were laid beside each other in the king-sized bed that dominated the room I'd found the boy in. I even found fresh linens in the closet that was at the very end of the dark hallway. I draped a large, red comforter over the family and then bowed my head for a moment of silence.

With that done, I started searching the residence for anything substantial. Apparently the former residents were neither hunters nor fishermen; if they were, they'd cleaned out every single scrap of gear. They liked to ski, though. Their garage had three empty bays, and it looked as if these people had taken quite a bit of stuff when they'd departed. Something told me they didn't head to a FEMA station.

I was still able to find a case of sports drinks and a few canned goods in the cupboards. I moved the supplies to the front door and then ventured outside. Even before I reached the truck that was parked just inside the gate, I could hear a few moans and even a baby cry from the street.

I reached the gate and was greeted by about a dozen undead that had gathered and were all reaching through the bars in a futile attempt to get at me. For the first time, I noticed the decal plastered to the side of the truck: Jose Reyes and Family Gardening Services.

Well, now at least I had a name to go with the people I'd put to rest upstairs in the house. That also explained all the yard tools in the back of the truck. Heck, they probably worked for the family that used to live here. I bet they ran here thinking that this would be their sanctuary. I had to wonder if maybe the little girl had been bitten before they arrived and everything just went to hell from there. I imagined that there were probably plenty of stories that ended this way. Heck, we'd simply gotten lucky. At least that had been the case until I'd gotten scratched or whatever by one of those things when Carl and I had been making our escape after killing that bastard Brandon Cook.

The sounds of the zombies just a few feet away brought me back to the present. I needed to get moving. There was no telling how long I had. I'd just seen one person show the telltale symptoms of the black tracers in his eyes probably minutes after being bitten. I did my best to ignore the little flock of undead as I looked inside the pickup truck's cab.

Keys dangled from the ignition!

"Maybe my luck is starting to turn," I said, glancing over my shoulder at the zombies. "Shall we see if there is any gas in this baby?"

One of the zombies made a mewl and smacked its lips. I was going to take that as a yes. I opened the door and turned the key just enough to activate all the gauges.

"Woo hoo! I yelped.

My little zombie audience increased the intensity of their moans and other assorted noises, obviously sharing in my good fortune. A half of a tank of gas would be more than enough to get me to that vet's office and then back to where Carl and the others were holed up.

Just to make sure I wasn't putting the cart before the horse, I climbed in and turned the key. The engine turned over on the first try.

"Hot damn!" I smacked the steering wheel, feeling better than I had in quite some time.

I looked up, my gaze skimming the rearview mirror. I froze, every bit of that happiness evaporating in an instant. It had only been the briefest of glimpses, but I was pretty certain that I knew what I'd seen.

Steadying myself, I took a few deep breaths. I closed my eyes and tilted my head up, turning just enough to where I thought my gaze would meet that of my reflection's. I stared into the eyes that stared back at me. I blinked.

Once.

Twice.

Three times.

I let out the breath I'd held in anticipation of the terrible eventuality becoming real. I smiled, then I started laughing. Tears filled my eyes and I leaned back in the seat of the pickup.

I didn't know whether to feel relief, sadness, anger, or any mixture of all of the above. I wiped my eyes and leaned forward again. This time, I used my fingers to pry my eyes open as far as possible.

"Still nothing," I chuckled.

What I'd been sure was that first black tracer was nothing more than a small crack in the rearview mirror. The eyes that looked back at me were, in truth, a bit bloodshot. I hadn't managed to get much quality rest since the night or early morning that I'd left my fellow survivors behind and struck off to die in relative solitude. The capillaries were very visible against the whites of my eyes, but the color remained a healthy red.

I think it was the first time in my life that I celebrated bloodshot eyes. That thought made me chuckle again as I hopped out of the truck.

"You guys are gonna have to wait a little longer," I said to the zombies gathered outside the gate.

I turned back to the house and stopped only a few steps away from the truck. I returned to the group gathered outside and pursed my lips.

"…seventeen, eighteen, nineteen, twenty, twenty-one," I finished counting out loud.

I was certain that the number had grown just in the short amount of time I'd been out here. If too many more stacked up outside, my chances of escape would be greatly reduced. As it was, I had to wonder if there were already too many.

I'd been the passenger in a car that had hit a person who crossed the street. They hadn't been in a crosswalk. The speed limit on that stretch of road was thirty-five miles per hour. Granted, we'd been in a little Ford Escort wagon, but the damage to the car had been massive. I also recalled kneeling in the street, holding this guy's hand as the light in his eyes dimmed. While I was in no way concerned about the damage I could do to the undead gathered out front, I was still very concerned about the possibility that it would incapacitate the truck. There I would sit, trapped in the cab of the pickup with a bunch of those things outside, banging on the glass and wanting to get in at me. I'd end up having to blow my brains out in the cab of that truck.

I applauded myself for thinking the situation through. It would be a big pain in the ass to have to search yet again for a vehicle and the keys to start it, but I'd waited this long. My eyes were still clear. No sense in acting desperate until the situation became as such.

I jumped out, grabbed my gear and headed back inside. It took me the better part of an hour to whittle everything down again to what I could carry in my pack. A few times, as I sat in the sumptuous living room and watched my discard pile grow, I considered just ending my days here.

If not for Chewie, I probably would have given up. My idea of cruising up to Mount Hood to off myself was a touch on the overdramatic side. It would be a pretty picture. The beautiful mountain scenery. Maybe the sun setting and just starting to paint the face of the snow-covered mountain in soft pinks and purples as I leaned back against a tree. I would stick the Glock in my mouth just as the last sliver of that giant yellow orb slipped below the horizon. There would be a muffled 'pop' and a flock of birds would take flight.

"Roll credits," I scoffed.

Yeah, I needed to get over myself. Being a drama queen was just not my style.

Once I had what I would be able to carry without too much trouble loaded back into my pack, I went around to the back of the house. I'd taken the time while I was inside to climb to the third floor and get a better look around. The backyard was this massive expanse of manicured lawn that was bordered on three sides by lush pines.

I could slip into the woods and eventually emerge in yet another neighborhood. From there, I would again try to locate a car and make my way to the vet's. Only once had I paused and asked myself if maybe I was fixating too much on that idea.

I decided that I didn't care. Plus, it wasn't like I had anything else to do.

DEAD: Alone

Sunday Driver

It was a strange walk through the woods. I'd gone to my share of haunted houses over the years. In fact, Halloween was almost as big of a deal in my house as Christmas was for most people.

I can't recall having ever been so jumpy in my life…so afraid of every little sound. As I made my way through this fairly dense little patch of woods, I got turned around more than once. In fact, at one point, I ended up back outside the rear of the property I'd recently escaped.

Sense of direction was never my strong suit. I was the last person that you would ask for directions. I had friends that you could drop off in the middle of nowhere, or in a strange neighborhood. They had the innate ability to just figure out where they were and how to get back to their location of choice.

By the time I did emerge from the woods, I was sweating like crazy and feeling feverish. I was desperate for something to look into because I was almost certain that the infection must've finally taken hold.

I emerged at the edge of a large field. I could see houses on the other side. Even more encouraging was a car parked in the driveway of the house right across the street from this wide-open expanse of grassland.

And goats.

The first bleating sound from one of the animals caused me to pee just a little. I don't think I'd ever looked a goat in the eyes. Maybe back in grade school on some field trip, but it hadn't made that big of an impression. This horned creature bent down and nibbled on a patch of grass as I approached. I didn't see any sign that it might be a zombie goat, but I almost reconsidered when that horned head rose and I saw the eyes. The pupils in a goat's eyes are creepy. No wonder people equate them with Satan.

"Nice goaty-goat," I sing-songed.

I had no idea if goats were mean. I made an effort to give it a wide berth, but once I encountered a half-dozen more of them spread out across this field, I knew I would have no choice but to come into close proximity with a few of them. Fortunately, they appeared far more interested in the grass than me. I reached the other side of the field and climbed the fence.

The tightness in my shoulders and the budding headache told me that I had tensed up a great deal. That made me laugh again. Here I was, all alone in the middle of the zombie apocalypse, about to die from the infection, and I'd been traumatized walking past a small herd of goats.

"Evan Berry…action hero!" I crowed softly.

This was basically a dead-end road. There was a house beyond some trees to my left. If I couldn't find what I needed here at this first home, then I would consider ducking in and checking that place out. I really hoped that I found keys to the little Audi parked in the driveway of this place. I felt like I'd paid my dues when it came to searching. So far, I'd found a few perfectly good vehicles and had not been able to use any of them. It was time that I caught an actual break.

I reached the front door and froze. "Aww, screw this nonsense," I growled.

Staring out at me from the window just to the right of the door was a small child. She looked to be around ten or eleven. Honestly, I was guessing. At a certain point, kids all looked basically the same age: young. This one was doing that creepy zombie-kid thing where it just stared at me. It wasn't even slapping on the window.

I considered just passing on this place. Maybe the house beyond those trees or one of the other ones up the road from here would be an easier target. Or...maybe it would be even worse. This was the freaking zombie apocalypse; if I was expecting things to get easy, then I was fooling myself.

I walked up the pathway to the front door, the entire time, I had my eyes locked on that kid staring out at me. Her filmed over, blackshot eyes reciprocated.

My hand gripped the front door and gave it an experimental turn. *Damn...locked.* There was an additional door with decorative windows on the top half that was right beside the garage. I'd glanced in when I passed it and saw that it did indeed open to the garage. I'd already tried that one and that would be where I would attempt my break-in if it came to that.

But first, I decided that I would at least go around back and see if the back was open before I started breaking windows. There was a little rock trail that looked like it was supposed to mimic a creek or something, so I followed that. When I reached the backyard, I was looking out across another massive, open field. Across the way was another gorgeous home. A minivan sat parked in front of it and I glanced back at this residence.

"You've got to be kidding," I breathed.

The zombie child inside had made its way to the sliding glass back door and was standing there...once again staring out at me. I decided that I would take a pass. I still didn't know what the deal was with the child versions of the undead, but the fact that this one knew enough to come to the back of the house where I'd headed told me that there was something very different going on with them.

I started across the field. I refused to look back even though I was certain I heard a tiny hand slapping on glass.

I was almost halfway across when I spotted the first dark figures emerging from the trees to my left. There were five of them. I gauged the distance between them and the other side of the field. Seeing that it looked as if they would possibly cut me off if I didn't pick up the pace, I broke into a jog.

There were some trees off to my right, and it figured that a handful of the undead just so happen to be simply standing around. It was as if they'd all decided to just hang out in the shade. Once more I had a spoofing reel play in my head as to the conversations that zombies might be having, but I shoved it aside and changed my jog into a sprint.

As I got closer, a new sense of dread and uncertainty arose in my gut. This house was almost like all the others. I say almost because it is fancy and well outside of any price range that I could have ever hoped to acquire.

The differences were subtle, but, at the same time, very obvious. For one, this one had a reinforced fence that ran all the way around it. A detached building off to the side had the door open, but that wasn't where my attention was drawn. On top of it was a recent addition in the form of what could only be described as an encased turret—almost in the shape of a chess set rook.

I was just reaching the far side of this field and would soon be at the fence that bordered the house. That was when what looked like a bed sheet unfurled from the top of the turret.

IF YOU TRY TO ENTER WE WILL KILL YOU.

Okay, that seemed pretty basic and easy to understand. My only problem was that the zombies that had come through the trees on my left were now directly behind me and had cut off my retreat. Also, their numbers had quadrupled.

The ones up ahead and under the tree still just looked to be standing there. And then I realized that they were all staring up into the trees they were under. That was when I noticed movement in the branches.

I was already making up my mind to break right and follow the fence until I was past the visible property border of the house I'd hoped to target when a voice called out.

"Hey, mister!" a man rasped. "Can I get a little help here?"

That caused the zombies gathered below to suddenly start reaching up into the tree. For whatever reason, they'd stayed put, just basically standing there doing nothing; but it wasn't until the man in the tree spoke that they started reaching. I was sort of bummed that they hadn't been doing so from the beginning. Had I seen that, I would've probably jumped to the conclusion that somebody was trapped up in that tree. Maybe I wouldn't have continued my approach. But I doubted it.

I still had a fence between me and the zombies gathered around the tree, so I didn't see the harm in at least taking a closer look as long as I didn't dawdle. The zombies that had come through the trees behind me were making their slow and continuous march in my direction.

What I saw was absolutely disgusting and pathetic. The best I could guess, that poor fella had been up in that tree for a long time. Days.

"Them sumbitches in that house over there chased me off and right towards a bunch of zombies. I figured I could get up in this tree and they'd eventually lose interest." He was becoming more difficult to hear. His voice was ragged and raw sounding; and the zombies beneath him were starting to kick up quite a racket.

I considered the scene. Glancing back, I saw three people now on the roof of that house that warned me off. One of those people was a child that came up to about waist height. I thought back to my incident with Brandon Cook. I'd had a bad feeling in my gut about him almost from the moment that we'd met. He turned out to be a real piece of garbage as far as humans are concerned. Trusting strangers was not going to be easy. If that child was theirs, then they were probably being even more protective and would not hesitate to end anybody foolish enough to ignore the warning.

I returned my attention to the man in the tree. You only get one chance to make a first impression. Unfortunately for this guy, he'd been up in a tree for who knows how long. He was filthy and bedraggled. Not to put too fine a point on it, but he looked like a scum bag.

I changed course and headed away, making my path up the street from the warning sign, the family with at least one child, and the man in the tree that began to hurl obscenities at me. Fortunately for me, his voice was drowned out after just a moment.

Maybe it wasn't the right thing to do. The problem I faced at the moment was that my time was limited. I didn't have forever—not that anybody did in a world where the dead walked. I just wanted a vehicle so that I could make this one final run for some supplies that would benefit my Chewie. Also, I'd gathered at least a few notes on what I'd witnessed with the child zombies.

Luck taunted me from the field just one house away from the one I'd left behind. The car sitting in the driveway was an older model Jeep Cherokee. It looked to be in fine shape. It struck me as strange that this house and the rest I could see up this street all appeared to be a bit older and more...lived in, I guess was the term I was looking for.

That house at the end of the street looked like it might belong in *Better Homes & Gardens* or something. These houses just looked like...well...houses. Nothing rundown, but certainly not as fancy.

I cut across the lawn and stopped at the series of five windows that sat just to the right of the door. There was a bench on the patio that I climbed up on so I could get a better look inside. I was momentarily grateful for the shades that at least partially obscured my view.

I almost fell over and busted my ass. Scrambling back from what I'd just seen, I looked back towards the direction of the house that had warned me away, and then over to the tree where that man was trapped.

Steeling myself for what I now knew was inside, I climbed back up and looked in. When I was in high school, I'd gone through a phase where I'd been fascinated with reading about the likes of Charles Manson and Ted Bundy. I don't know why. What I do know is that, even reading about it and knowing that what I was reading was based on something that actually happened...it just did not seem real. No human being could commit the acts that were described in the pages of those books.

Yet, what I saw inside this house had not been done by zombies. The bodies inside had been brutally murdered. Butchered in a way that would make even the most stalwart horror fan shake their head in disbelief if they saw it enacted on screen.

Tied to one recliner chair was a man. The attacker had used fishhooks through the eyelids to keep them pried open. He was lashed to the recliner with wire that had obviously cut deep into his flesh. My guess was that he'd struggled a great deal. Considering what was laid out, I had to assume he'd been made to watch as his wife and two sons were murdered in ways worthy of torture-porn movies like *Saw* or *Hostel*.

The wife had been opened up surgically on the dinner table where both sons had been tied to chairs. Only one of the boys still had his head. I was about to give up and move on to the next house when I spotted them.

Tossed casually on the island counter that sat at the entrance to the kitchen was a jumble of keys attached to a large rope monkey fist that acted as the key ring. I glanced over at the Jeep Cherokee and decided that, while it would no doubt be unpleasant, this was the opportunity I'd been waiting for.

I made the decision to go around to the back of the house and break in on that side. While there was very little zombie activity in my immediate area, I saw no sense in bringing them down on me. As I walked around the house, I had to wonder. Had it been that man in the tree that had committed this horrendous act? The family up the road? Or just some random passerby getting a sick thrill?

I'd often doubted what I saw in the typical zombie tales when it came to how people behaved. Surely we were not that bad of a species. But then I realized that it was illustrated clearly in our history. Genocide. Slavery. Human trafficking. Murder. Rape.

For such a supposedly evolved being, we were capable of some very nasty things. I wondered briefly if maybe this whole zombie apocalypse thing wasn't for the best. As soon as that thought crossed my mind, I scolded myself. How on earth could anybody consider themselves a good and decent person and think that an extinction-level event was okay?

I reached the back door and gave it a try out of reflexive

habit. The door opened, and I was instantly driven back by the smell. This was not the stench of the undead. What I was hit full-force with was the smell of actual death. The rank and bitter smell of feces mixed with the lingering coppery smell of blood and a fetid hint of decay.

That was also when I heard the buzzing sound. At first, I thought that maybe I'd been struck just a little bit dizzy. It wasn't long before I wished that to be the case.

As I ventured inside, taking a deep breath first and holding it so that I would not breathe too much of that smell into my lungs, I could see the bodies a bit more clearly.

The open cavity of the mother was rippling with movement as maggots writhed inside her splayed torso. Flies buzzed in the air everywhere in numbers I'd never been witness to in my life. In places, they almost created a grayish curtain that swished and undulated. I realized that I was standing flat-footed now, just at the edge of the kitchen where it opened to the dining room. My body had shut down at the shock of what I was witnessing.

Deciding that I just wanted to get out of here, I swiped the keys and exited in a hurry. I made it to the back porch and had just congratulated myself on how I'd handled the situation when I doubled over and vomited all over the back patio. I barely had time to toss my bag aside to avoid being sick all over it. The fit was so violent that it drove me to my knees.

I had just taken a second to wipe my mouth when I heard the crunch of feet on gravel. I'd followed that fake stream made of rocks, and now it seemed that someone or ones had followed me. The dragging sound told me what it was before I saw or smelled the zombie that rounded the corner.

She was the poster of a soccer mom. Her hair was cut short, and even in death, it seemed to be gelled in place. Only now, dried blood was her product. At some point she must've buried her face in the belly of a victim because she didn't just have a smear across her lips. Her face looked like she'd just been hit in the head with a rancid blackberry pie. There were even dried chunks of meaty bits on her cheeks and chin.

I was still a little weak in the knees as I stood and drew my axe. I shoved her back so that I could get a clean shot and then ended her with a swift stroke. Her body crumpled and I stepped back so that I could catch my breath and gather myself before I finally got into a vehicle and headed for my ultimate destination.

I rounded the house and returned to the front yard to discover that about a dozen or so zombies had apparently picked up on me at some point and were now trudging up the driveway. I hurried to the Jeep and was thankful that the keys had the logo emblazoned on them.

I tossed my bag into the front seat and hopped in just as the closest of the undead reached me. Its hands slapped impotently on the window as it attempted to get at me. I gave it a wave as I slid the key into the ignition, then I made a gulping noise in my throat. Already, the Jeep Cherokee was surrounded.

I said a silent prayer and turned the key. The thrum of the engine almost made me want to cry in relief. Instead, I settled for a whoop of joy and punched the overhead enthusiastically.

I popped the vehicle into reverse and slowly began to back out of the driveway. Zombies fell to the ground and I could not help but wince as the vehicle lifted and fell as it rolled over the downed bodies. I was really hoping that I didn't blow out another tire.

When I finally reached the road and cranked the wheel around to facilitate my departure, a new rush of adrenaline dumped into my system. I now knew where my latest undead arrivals had come from. The end of the road was clogged with more zombies than I could count.

I fumbled for my bag and pulled out the map that I'd used to highlight the route I needed to take to reach the Happy Valley Veterinary Clinic. Since I knew that the way behind me was not only a dead end, but also being guarded by people who had banners stating their intent to kill, and the exit to this road was clogged with more zombies than I was willing to try and drive through, my only option was to allow this four-wheel-drive vehicle to be put through the paces.

I was mostly clear of the zombies in the driveway. That being the case, I goosed the accelerator, heaved the steering wheel to the right, and bounced my way across the massive open lawn of the house across the street from the murder scene I'd just left behind. As I drove through the grass, I felt a surge of hope starting to bloom in my gut. It was either that…or gas.

I reached the far side of the yard and had to swerve just a bit to avoid a sapling that looked like it might not just fold over if I tried to drive through it. The last thing I needed at the moment was to damage this vehicle. Glancing in the side view mirror, I could see a seething wall of the undead coming my direction from up the road.

My problem now was that the route I'd traced required me to turn left at the tee-intersection of Ridgecrest Court and Ridgecrest Road. The zombies coming up Ridgecrest Road forced me to turn right. Once I had all four wheels on the road and had cleared the yard that I cut through, I cruised ahead a good distance and then slowed to do some manual recalculating.

Once I had the first couple of stages committed to memory, I took off again. Glancing in the rearview, I slowed when I noticed that a group of the zombies were branching off to the left towards a large, white house. I hoped that I hadn't just led that mob to the doorstep of some poor unfortunate.

"Still no damn tracers," I muttered.

It was good news in that it was starting to actually look like I might be able to make this run. Granted, a million things could happen between now and the moment that I pulled up to the gates where Carl and the others remained—hopefully safe and sound.

I remembered something from one of my earlier attempts to obtain a vehicle and turned on the radio. I recalled it being somewhere towards the end of the AM dial, so I clicked it until a static-filled voice finally came through the speakers.

"…repeat, stay away from downtown Portland. The fires along the waterfront in the industrial district are burning out of control." There was a pause, and the man's voice continued. "We will be abandoning our position here now. We've heard gunshots in the area, and they seem to be drawing nearer. Danny says that there is a convoy consisting of civilian and military vehicles rolling through the streets of Mill Plain and opening fire on anything and everything that moves. They are not attempting to save survivors, and it is our belief that this group is nothing more than an organized group of raiders out for themselves."

There was another pause, and I was almost convinced that the person had indeed abandoned his place. I couldn't blame him, if what he was saying had any lick of truth to it, and I had no reason to think otherwise after what I'd seen for myself, then getting out of Dodge was probably for the best.

"If you are listening, then I want to urge you to just hunker down for a bit. I know we have all seen terrible things these past several days. But I believe that these wicked elements that remain will come undone. Just stay hidden a while longer. We will get through this…we must. Stay safe out there. This is Rick Taylor, signing off."

There was a hiss, and then nothing but static. I hit the button to scan for any other possible stations that might be live, but the numbers simply scrolled through over and over again. I turned down the volume and concentrated on where I was going.

My route took me back over to Mt. Scott Road where I would follow it until it made a bit of a dogleg bend and turned into Southeast King. Fortunately for me, most of the way to the veterinary center allowed me to just follow the bends on what looked on the map to be the main road. The only two streets that I needed to remember were Southeast Misty Drive where I would turn left, and Southeast Blackstone Avenue marking the location that I would hang a right into the complex where the vet's office should be.

I was moving down King Road at a good clip. It almost felt strange moving so fast after being on foot so much the past several days. I passed by many of the walking dead that were roaming through yards and some of the open fields on either side of the road. It just seemed so overwhelming to see this so widespread in such a short amount of time.

All of our advances in science and technology had made the world smaller. I believe it is what led to our undoing. Couple that with people refusing to believe what was happening until it was too late, and all the ingredients were right there.

I'd become so engrossed in looking all around that I wasn't paying attention to what was right in front of me. I looked ahead just in the nick of time and slammed on the brakes, causing the tires to squeal their protest.

Directly ahead of me was another large mob of the walking dead. They were just spilling out onto the road. My eyes drifted to the left where they were coming from and I felt my blood chill just a few degrees.

"Happy Valley Middle School," I said out loud.

I heard the metal clang to my right and looked over to see a series of houses—none of them looking all that remarkable. My eyes were scanning the area when I heard the sound again.

CLANG.

This helped me focus on the source and I felt my jaw drop as my eyes tried to make sense of what they were seeing. He was standing on the hood of a car that had hopped the curb and come to a stop with its nose buried in the hedges that acted as a fence between two homes.

As I watched, the boy lifted the garbage can lid and brought it down on the car's roof with a loud clang. Looking back to my left, I saw even more of the undead that were roaming the parking lot of the school as they turned towards the sound and began to move.

"You have got to be fucking kidding me," I gasped. "That sonuvabitch is trying to clog the road and block my way."

The zombie child banged the garbage can lid down again. The entire time, his eyes were locked on me. Occasionally, his head would tilt to one side or the other.

This would be something that certainly deserved some intense study and consideration; unfortunately, I had time for neither. It was going to be close, and there was no way that I could make it through this without clipping at least one or two of the zombies now flooding down onto the road, but I was not about to try and backtrack and figure out another way to reach my goal. There was no telling what would be waiting down each road I took.

I gripped the wheel tight with both hands and stomped on the gas for all I was worth. The Jeep Cherokee didn't so much as launch forward as just make a steady and constant speed increase. I did my best to be sure not to hit any zombie head-on. The ones I did hit made a loud meaty bang or slam as their bodies crumpled and spun.

At first, I didn't think it possible. It had to be an illusion brought on by the odd spectacle that I'd seen with the boy and the trash can lid. I blinked as I shot an anxious glance to both the left and right. It was no trick of the mind.

Children by the dozens peered at me from windows of several of the houses on my right, and even more lined the top of the ridge where the school sat to my left. All of them were between the ages of maybe five at the youngest and perhaps twelve being the oldest. Their filmed-over gazes were locked on me as I drove past. A shiver rippled through me as I emerged on the other side of the expansive school parking lot. The second entrance to the school had been blocked by a nasty crash between a school bus and a pair of cars that looked like they'd tried to force their way out to no avail.

Right next to the school was a continuation of the horror. The modern looking building announced itself as a Baptist Church. The words "God is DEAD" were smeared on the once white siding of the church in what I had to assume to be blood. A man was dangling from a crossbeam that had been wedged in the open archway of the entrance.

I had to figure the man had been alive when the hanging took place. He was struggling and squirming at the end of the rope like a fish on a line. He was gone from the waist down, and strands of what was left of his insides dangled from the gaping hole that was the bottom of his torso.

The actual doors to the church had been ripped from their hinges and I could see inside the church. That struck me as odd until I realized that I could actually see *through* the church. It looked like the place had been gutted on the inside by a fire. I was curious how the exterior still appeared okay, but as I passed by, I saw that the other side of the building was blistered and smudged. There were also two more makeshift scaffoldings erected with another five bodies hanging from each.

I sped past and reached the sharp corner that was the first of the markers I'd made myself remember. The hard right on Southeast 145th Avenue made the Jeep fishtail just a bit and I backed off the gas. I wouldn't be that idiot that lost control of his vehicle and crashed on an empty, open road.

On my right was a fence that ran along the backsides of a line of houses. On my left were older but more luxurious homes with long driveways that ran up to them. The funny thing about the zombie apocalypse was that it didn't discriminate. I saw the undead on both sides. The road I was on made a long but gradual climb uphill which began to put me closer to eye-level with the upper floors on the homes behind that long, wooden fence.

I was just about to a series of trees that would totally obscure the houses from view when I saw a window open on the last house before those trees. A person's upper torso jutted from the open window and began to wave wildly.

I forced myself to look away as the person obviously tried to get my attention. Just as the person vanished behind the curtain of trees, I could hear the shouts and pleas for me to help.

It probably didn't get me any points in the cosmos that I would've kept driving if the voice hadn't been obviously feminine. Even when I heard what was undoubtedly a woman screaming and begging for help, I continued driving for about another ten seconds. By the time I stopped, the house was out of sight and well behind me.

Could I do it? Could I drive away and just leave that person to whatever fate was waiting?

Carl and I had spoken at length and on more than one occasion about how the apocalypse was going to show us who we really were down deep. So…who was I at my core?

"Dammit," I hissed as I did a big U-turn and shot back down the road.

I pulled up just after I passed the trees that blocked my view. I opened the door to the Jeep Cherokee and could hear the low moans of the undead coming from the other side of the wooden fence.

"Thank God!" a voice cried.

I looked up and saw her. She had climbed out on the overhang that I guessed covered the back patio to the home. She was certainly in a bad situation. I climbed up on the fence and saw that the entire backyard was shoulder-to-shoulder zombies. Adding to her troubles, a pair of them were reaching out the open window that she'd climbed from which meant that they were obviously in the house as well. One of them reached too far and tumbled out, sliding down the eave and landing on the sea of undead gathered below with minimal effect.

I studied the scene and could not figure out for the life of me how I could be of any assistance. I scratched my head and tried to find a way that I could extricate this woman safely.

When the thought came, I almost shoved it away as being ridiculous. I'd once been to a seminar on brainstorming. One of the rules they had insisted upon was that no idea, no matter how crazy it might seem, should be dismissed during that phase of problem solving. The idea was that sometimes it is the most far-fetched ideas that offer the solution, and they are never tried because of people dismissing them as ludicrous.

"I want you to stay put. Try to duck behind that outcropping," I called out, pointing to where the house had a bit of a natural wall around the corner of the window she'd used to escape. "I'm not leaving, just coming from a different angle. You will know if or when this works…and you need to be ready."

Before she had a chance to say anything or ask questions that I probably didn't have the answers to, I took off. I made the left that took me back towards the church and the school. I was so set on getting to the woman that it took me a moment to realize that the road was clear again. Just as I turned into the neighborhood where the house and the woman in distress waited, I spotted two clusters of regular zombies. One was up in the school parking lot just milling about. The other group was gathered around the house where I'd seen the child zombie on the car with the trash can lid.

"They've reset the trap," I gasped. The thought of that gave me a chill that went to the core of my soul. That indicated at least some sort of rudimentary ability to…think?

No, that was impossible, I thought. *Just like the dead rising and a zombie apocalypse wiping out humanity.* That second thought came right on the heels of the first.

I shoved it away and hoped that I would remain cognizant long enough to include this all in my notes. For now, I had to focus on the task at hand. I turned up onto what the sign declared to be Southeast 144th Loop.

I pulled up a house short of my destination, and it was very apparent which house was my target. The front of the house was a mess. There were smears of vile fluids all over the façade, and the front door had been destroyed. I imagine the force of so many undead smashing against it had simply been too much for the frame to handle.

I took a look around and saw that the road ahead was basically clear. Apparently, all of the zombies in this little area had converged solely on this one residence. That seemed strange, but then, so had most of what I'd seen today.

I rolled just past the house and then laid on the horn of the Jeep Cherokee. It wasn't an impressive sound for such a supposedly rugged vehicle, but in the relative silence where the moans of the undead provided the greatest part of the ambient soundtrack, it was enough.

Some of the undead that were milling about along the sides of the house and just inside the front door turned my direction. It was an agonizingly slow process, and I was doubting that it would work, but pretty soon, more and more of the undead turned in my direction and began to come after the new stimulus.

I pulled a few houses ahead of the pack and opened the door. "As soon as it is clear, make a run for the street you saw me on, I will come around and pick you up." It seemed almost like it didn't need saying, but I hastily shouted, "And keep quiet or they will come back for you."

I hopped back in and rolled up the street, laying on the horn like I was in the worst traffic jam in the world and stuck behind an idiot who was too busy texting to notice the line had moved forward. Once they all made their way out onto the street—there were obviously still a lot of them—they didn't look as imposing now that they were all strung out in a stream versus clumped together in an enclosed area.

I guessed that I'd created a window of opportunity for the woman and then sped away, making the turns like I was a NASCAR driver on the final lap. I reached the exit of the neighborhood, putting me at the tee-intersection where the church sat directly across from me.

A small pack of the child zombies had gathered under the body of the half-man hanging in the entry way. They all just stood there watching me. As I eased into the street and made my right turn, they just continued to observe me as I rolled away.

Removing the fact that I was infected and not long for this world, I really wished that I could stick around a bit longer and try to figure out why the child version of a zombie acted so differently. Sadly, that would not be. I glanced up in the rearview mirror and still saw nothing more than my regular eyes staring back at me.

Still no sign of the tracers.

I turned right again, putting me back on Southeast 145th Avenue. I rolled up the long, gentle incline, my eyes scanning everywhere for a sign of the woman. I breathed a sigh of relief when I confirmed that she had at least made it off the roof.

I was almost even with the house I'd spotted her on when a figure burst from the trees on the side of the road. It was her and she was waving her arms wildly.

I slowed to a stop and opened the passenger side door. She hopped in, filling the cab of the vehicle with the stink of sweat and fear. I hadn't known that fear had an actual smell until just this minute.

"Thank you so much," she gushed as she locked the door and reflexively strapped the seatbelt across her body and clicked it in place. I started away as she gave a long exhale and then turned to face me. I glanced over to see a pistol pointed at my head.

"Seriously?" I barked.

DEAD: Alone

5

Stranger Danger

"Just get us out of here," the woman demanded. I could hear her voice tremble slightly. Also, the arm holding the gun was bobbing around like we were driving over a bumpy road. The thing was…we hadn't moved an inch yet.

She was scared.

I didn't know if she was afraid of me, or if she might be part of some nasty scheme. I also knew that I didn't like having a gun pointed at me by somebody who was just as likely to pull the trigger by accident as she was on purpose.

I was gonna hate myself for what I felt I had to do. And at the same time, I had serious doubts that it would work. Again…this was some sort of action-hero crap. I think I'd already made it clear that I was not one of those.

I pictured what I had to do in my head, and then took a deep breath. *What the hell*, I thought, *I'm dying anyway. If she puts a bullet in my head, it will save me the trouble.*

I turned back to face front and put the truck in drive. I gave it just enough gas to start us moving, then I slammed on the brakes as my right arm lashed out and smacked the woman in the wrist. The pain that went all the way to my gut was a reminder that my arm was injured and that I needed to stop being an idiot if I didn't want to lose the use of it completely. Her arm flew away and I heard a metallic *click-click-click.*

Huh, I thought as I spun in my seat and smashed the woman in the face as hard as I could with my balled up left fist, *an empty weapon.* I felt her nose crumble under the force of the blow and her head snapped back, smashing into the window on the passenger's side.

As fast as I could, I threw the truck into park and then lunged over and caught the dazed woman by the throat with my left hand as my right caught her wrist before she could recover. I gave her arm a good shake and heard the gun land on the floor of the truck.

"Please," she begged through a bloody nose. "Do what you're gonna do to me and just get it over with."

The woman was crying now, and her hitching sobs were causing her entire body to shake. I loosened my grip just enough so that I wasn't actually choking her.

"Why would I pick you up only to hurt you?" It seemed like a logical question.

"Because…umm…well…" her garbled response came between hitching sobs.

"How long have you been on your own?" I asked.

"Th-th-three weeks," she managed as her sobbing ebbed.

"And has anybody tried to…" I found that I struggled to even say the word that hung in the air like an evil spirit.

"I've managed to stay hidden." She sat up straighter in her seat as I let go and moved back into my own. "But I've heard terrible things happen. I've heard people begging and crying and screaming. At first I thought that it was all just more zombie attacks, but there is a difference." She shuddered violently. "That one scream." Her gaze got far away, and I could tell she was reliving a bad moment.

"I call it *the* scream," I said, emphasizing the word 'the' when I spoke.

"It's so terrible. Like nothing I've ever heard."

"Yeah."

I eased the truck into drive and started away as I saw a group of zombies heading for us from around the corner in the direction of the church and the school. After a moment of driving in silence, I came up with an idea.

"Listen, I'm headed to a vet for some supplies for my dog. I can bring you with me if you don't have any place else to go. After I get what I need, I am taking supplies back to where this nice little group is holed up." I sensed her tense and heard her breath catch. "One of the people there is this nice lady named Betty." Yeah, that was a big fat lie, but maybe knowing there were women present would ease her mind. "Also, there is this other girl who we just rescued. I think her name is Amanda. There are two kids, Selina and Michael. Then there is Carl. He's a good guy, and pretty smart about this whole zombie thing."

"You said something about getting supplies for your dog?" she said in a whisper. "So, you guys have a dog there, too?"

Now we were getting someplace. She wasn't crying anymore, and even better, she wasn't pointing a gun at my head. I was actually starting to feel bad about punching her in the face. Then my brain would replay that moment that I was literally staring down the barrel of her pistol, and the guilt would ease up.

"Yeah, a Newfoundland named Chewie."

"Like from *Star Wars*?"

Wow, this was a girl after my own heart if I still had any of mine left—which I very seriously doubted. Still, it was a plus in my book about her that she got the reference. I'd honestly believed when I chose that name for my girl that everybody would get it. The first time I met somebody who didn't, I think I was in a bit of shock.

"Yeah…just like that. Besides how big and furry she is, she makes a lot of the same noises."

That earned me a tiny giggle. "And you're out here all by yourself?" she asked, a hint of disbelief creeping back into her voice.

This felt like a moment of truth. I could tell her about my condition and then let her out if she didn't feel safe, or I could just make something up. It only took me a few seconds to make the choice. I pulled over and stopped the truck once I was certain we had nothing close by that could pose a threat.

"Sort of my last gasp...one final act and a chance to do something good," I said. I hiked my sleeve up to reveal my scratch. The redness and inflammation made it very visible on my skin. "Chewie is all I have left. I figure if I grab a few things for her, the group will have an easier time taking care of her and then maybe she'll be allowed to hang around."

"Holy Jesus," the woman breathed. I noticed that she inched just a little further away from me despite the fact that we were in the front seat of a Jeep Cherokee and there really wasn't very far she could go.

"I want to make this run and drop it off at their gates before I go off to die," I said hastily.

"Y-y-you're infected."

"Yeah, thanks for stating the obvious. Like I said, I want to make this run before I reach a point where I swallow the business end of my pistol and end it. You don't have to come along if you don't want to. I get that it might not seem safe."

"Not safe?" she barked a cold laugh. "I'm in an SUV with a man who punched me in the face, choked me, and then tells me that he is going to become a zombie sometime in the near future."

"You left out the part where you pulled a gun on me *after* I risked my ass to save you."

"You're dying anyway," she retorted. "What risk did you take exactly?"

"Whether you know it, or even realize it, I still could've been grabbed, ripped apart, and eaten alive. Just because I am infected and about to die any day now doesn't mean I relish the idea of being chowed down on by a mob of zombies."

There was a moment of silence, and I put my hand on the lever to shift the vehicle into drive. If she was going to take her time to think it over, then I was going to get just a bit closer to my destination.

"Listen," she said hesitantly, "I'm sorry. I think I just sort of dumped all the fear and tension I've been experiencing these past several days right on you. You have enough problems. And I owe you a thanks for saving my butt back there."

"You're welcome," I replied, keeping my eyes on the road.

"And you're really doing this for your dog?" she asked, sounding more curious than doubtful.

"I love her more than any person walking the face of the earth," I said. The thing was, I could make that claim and be certain that it was the God's honest truth. The only other being that I'd really loved was now one of the living dead.

"And everything that you said about the people?" I heard the hope seeping into that question.

Her reaction was also something that was resonating with me. Despite how things would eventually play out, I was realizing that I missed the company of living human beings. It might seem all macho to strike out on your own and be some sort of solitary warrior, but normal humans were not meant to be isolated and by themselves. It isn't part of our makeup.

"Every last word."

We drove in silence for another moment. I was feeling fairly confident that she would come along and want to at least try to make a go of it with Carl and the others.

"My name is Ariel," she finally said. "Ariel Mannheim."

"Evan Berry." I looked over and gave her what I hoped looked like a friendly smile.

"And I'm really sorry about your situation, Evan." She sounded like she truly meant it.

That almost brought a tear to my eye. Seriously, how often can you go from having a gun pulled on you, punching somebody in the face, to exchanging names and pleasantries in under five minutes?

I zoomed through a residential neighborhood and heard Ariel gasp. Several of the houses were nothing more than charred, skeletal remains. A nasty fire had wiped out well over what I would guess to be a hundred or more homes. The one bonus was that it created an open line of sight where we could see the few zombies in the area as they staggered and stumbled around.

At last, I made the right turn on Southeast Blackstone Avenue. The Happy Valley City Hall building was on the corner to my left as I turned and I felt my heart skip a few beats as I realized where it was exactly that I was headed.

"The Happy Valley Outdoor Mall?" Ariel breathed. "I thought you were going to a vet's office? This mall thing seems a bit cliché," she snorted.

"Excuse me?" I said through clenched teeth as I saw a parking lot with countless zombies roaming and shambling about amidst all the abandoned vehicles.

"Just seems like you're heading into a bad remake of a Romero movie." She sounded simultaneously skeptical and amused.

As for me, I was now just more than a little impressed with Ariel. She got the *Star Wars* reference, and now she was hitting me with classic zombie lore. I bet I would've liked her if I'd gotten the opportunity to get to know her.

"The vet hospital is supposed to be right here." Just as I said the words, the building and the sign popped into view.

The thing was, the complex was a damn gold mine. Not only was the vet hospital here, but there was a grocery store and a couple of restaurants, not to mention a walk-in emergency clinic for humans. I could really hook Carl and the group up if I played this right.

"You aren't seriously thinking about going out into that place," Ariel squeaked when I pulled the Jeep around in a circle and rolled to a stop in front of the building that held the veterinary hospital. "There are hundreds of those things out there in the parking lot."

It was here where I would have to make my choice. Trust was something I didn't have much of, but I would have to hope that this girl was as smart as she appeared. She obviously knew enough about zombie stuff to realize that she would have a better chance at survival with others.

"If I jump out and then you race around the lot blaring the horn, you will lead them away. I can get in, get what I need, and then get out," I said in a rush.

As I told her this, I continued to prowl the parking lot. The zombies were all turning toward the Jeep as it rolled past. Add in the horn and I was willing to bet that they would be cleared out and lured away from the vet so that I could get inside.

Despite how it might've looked to an outsider, I wasn't being a total idiot. I was also searching the lot for an older model vehicle. The Volkswagen Bug in front of the New Seasons natural foods store was a prime candidate if I needed to make an attempt to hotwire a car and escape on my own. Ariel didn't need to know that; all she needed to know was that it looked on the surface like I was trusting her. If she did take off, then I would simply make do.

"Are you stupid?" she scoffed. "You are just gonna jump out of this car, leave it to me, and then trust that I'll stick around to pick you up when you are done?"

"Yeah, that's about the size of it." I gave her a shrug as I looped back around towards the entrance of the veterinary hospital.

"You are either crazy, or you have a death wish." As soon as those last two words came out of her mouth, she clamped her teeth shut with an audible click. "I'm sorry, Evan," she blurted. "I didn't mean it like that."

"I know." I turned and flashed her a smile, trying to let her know that it really was okay. "So, will you do it?"

"I guess." She wasn't very reassuring, but I doubted anything would give me even a shred of comfort at the moment. I also knew that, if I didn't jump out of this car right now, I probably wasn't ever going to.

Without another word, I opened the driver's side door and stepped out as the Jeep rolled along at a snail's pace. I was smart enough to grab my bag just in case she took off, as well as have my axe drawn before both my feet even touched ground.

I was two steps away when the door to the Jeep slammed shut and the vehicle sped off. I instantly felt a lump in my throat.

"Yep," I grunted as I chopped into the only zombie that had been close when I exited, "I'm an idiot."

A few seconds later, as the Jeep banked hard around one of the parking lot's many light pole fixtures, the horn began to blare. A few of the zombies that were within less than twenty feet from me continued for me, but most of them stopped advancing and turned to this new stimulus.

I took advantage of my window of opportunity and bolted for the doors of the veterinary hospital. I was moving so fast that I had to use my arms as a cushion to stop myself when I reached them. I gave them a tug and spit out a string of obscenities when I discovered the doors to be locked.

I didn't have time to mess around and used my axe to stave in the bottom half of the glass door. While it wasn't foolproof, I hadn't seen many zombies crawling around unless they were missing their legs.

With a glance over my shoulder, I noticed that only a few had broken off from the Jeep and turned towards me. Seconds later, when the horn bleated again, they were already starting to turn back away from me.

I crawled in, ignoring the pain in my hands and knees as I crawled over the busted cubes of safety glass. As soon as I was inside, I knew there was going to be trouble. I could smell it on the air.

Coming to my feet, I drew my hand axe, but before I took a step, I made sure that the Glock was sporting a fully loaded magazine. I jammed it in the front of my pants and then pulled the headlamp from my bag out and put it on. Once I was past the ambient light of the lobby, it would be pitch black. There were no windows that I could see and that meant darkness.

I started down the hall and paused at the first door. It had a tiny window and I peered inside. It looked to be some sort of exam room. There was a stainless-steel table and a counter with a few odds and ends along with walls plastered with posters that sang the praises of various flea medications.

I edged further down the hall, stopping at each door and peeking inside to discover the same basic setup. I noticed that the smell was growing stronger as I ventured further into the building. By the time I reached the end of the hallway, the smell was almost gag-inducing. I gripped the metal doorknob and held my breath as I gave it a turn.

The smell hit me even stronger and made me stagger back. I was fighting the urge to be sick when a woman stepped into the beam of my headlamp. She had shoulder-length brown hair and looked like she'd been athletic in life. Sadly, she also looked like she'd been the victim of a pack of wild dogs or wolves.

The rips and tears in her skin were jagged and nasty looking. Also, her left cheek appeared to have been nibbled at, and the meaty flap was shredded at the ends.

When the three dogs moved in behind her, I was getting my first up close look at a zombified dog. The eyes were filmed and tracer-riddled just like a human's which made these nightmares an even more sinister visage to take in.

I made out what I was almost certain had to be a Lab, a German Sheppard, and the most pathetic Pug in the world. The poor thing had obviously been savaged by one, if not both, of the two larger dogs and had lost both its eyes. Its head swung back and forth as it followed behind the other two dogs and the woman who I guessed to be a vet here.

She was wearing the filthy remains of what had once been a white lab coat. Although, now, you would be hard pressed to find anything white about it. The zombie vet led the group towards me, her low moan almost echoed eerily by the dogs to a varying degree. I was stunned by the odd sounds that came from the three zombified dogs, but now was not the time for an in-depth study.

I backed up the hallway I'd just travelled down to keep them all in front of me. If they flanked me, I knew that I wouldn't last a minute. At the last second, I decided the knife would be best in such close quarters. I timed my attack, and as the vet staggered forward, I jammed the tip of the blade under her jaw like I'd seen Carl do countless times.

She fell so fast that I almost lost the knife as her weight was suddenly entirely supported by my wrist. I managed to yank it out and kick her away from me as the German Sheppard stepped into range. I drove the blade into the top of its head and almost broke my already aching wrist as the handle wrenched free.

I was all the way back to the lobby where I caught the sound of a horn honking over and over, coming closer, then moving away. I think I breathed a sigh of relief as I drew my hand axe. It hurt my heart to end the Labrador, but when that pathetic Pug wobbled out into the lobby and swung its head one way and then the other, two dark, empty holes where its buggy eyes had once been, I had to fight back the tears.

My axe came down with a final thud, and I headed back up that hallway. When I first heard it, I wasn't sure that it was not my imagination; but then the mewl of a cat came from somewhere in the darkness and I froze.

"Cats too?" I moaned.

My headlamp had a lone feline in the cone of light, its eyes shining a hideous green. It regarded me in that way that cats have. Basically, it was acting like I was intruding on its peace and quiet. I guess I sort of was when you got down to it. The thing that got my attention was that it did not seem like this creature was zombified. For one, when the headlamp hit the eyes of zombie humans (or dogs for that matter), there was no glow. It landed on lifeless eyes that you could see clearly. I don't know why that stood out to me, but I somehow knew that this cat had not been turned. I knew because of the glowing green eyes.

While I had no intentions of taking on a pet, I could at least let this little thing out. But that brought up a new series of questions. For one, how had this thing managed to avoid being eaten? Also, what had it eaten in all this time?

The question of water was answered when I spotted several open cages, each with gravity-filled water dishes. A few were empty, but I also saw several of them with water still in their reservoirs. When it made another meowing sound and hopped from where it had been perched on top of a series of wall-mounted kennels, I jumped back out of reflexive fear.

It landed with what seemed like normal cat-like grace—further advancing my theory that this cat was no zombie. I was happier and more satisfied with that assessment when it strolled past me and swished its tail. I promised myself that I would rip open a few bags of cat food on my way out and lead this animal to its freedom. Granted, I was letting it out into a world overrun by the walking dead, but it would at least have a shot at survival.

With the sounds of the Jeep's horn growing nearer and then

farther, I headed into the back area knowing my ride was still close at hand. I still had to fight the desire to be sick as the smell lingered thickly in the air and seemed to coat my throat with its vile foulness. I didn't know where to begin my search, but at last I found a room with all sorts of plastic boxes that had neat rows of packaged creams and ointments. Also, I found the pill dispensary. Since I didn't know what to look for specifically, I just started grabbing things and filling my bag.

Once I had my bag filled, I realized that I'd only made a dent in the medications available. I would need to bring everything to the front of this place and then have Ariel stop the Jeep and allow me to load it up. I knew it would be tricky, but I also knew it could be done if done right. I sprinted to the front and spied a display of decorative tote bags with the name of the veterinary hospital emblazoned on them. That would help, I decided, and quickly rushed into the back again with the collection of empty totes and the sounds of a blaring vehicle horn rising and falling in a Doppler symphony that was strangely comforting.

I loaded up five of the totes to levels that had them bulging in the middle. I was now feeling like I'd done something significant. The added bonus came in the form of the stacks of dog food in a display against one wall of the lobby. I would toss all that in the back and feel good that I'd provided Chewie with as much of an opportunity to survive this madness as any of the people. Heck, maybe better.

I stopped at the door and then remembered that I'd promised myself that I would do what I could for the cat. Looking around, I didn't see him (or her) at first. When I did, I didn't know whether to gag, scold it, or just add it in with all the other madness I'd witnessed since this terrible event began. The cat, an orange and white tabby, was hunched over the downed body of the zombie vet I'd ended. It was currently tugging at a piece of loose flesh on the side of the neck.

"Shoo!" I finally barked, clapping my hands to try and spook the cat. It turned, looked at me for a moment, and then returned to its feast.

Maybe it was just really hungry. After all, what could it possibly have been able to eat while it had been trapped…

That thought died in my mind as my gaze went to that shredded cheek of the female veterinarian. I cocked my head as I considered it and then quickly shook it when I realized that I was mimicking the study pose of the creepy zombie children.

"Maybe you just need a more palatable option," I said to the cat as it gulped down the piece of meat it had managed to tear free with its tiny, sharp teeth.

I grabbed a bag of the cat food from the display beside the dog food and unceremoniously ripped the bag open, letting the dry kibble pour out on the floor in a rush. The cat paused, another strip of neck skin in its mouth. Its eyes flicked to the dry food all over the floor…and then returned to tugging at the piece of meat in its teeth.

"Suit yourself," I said with a shiver.

I didn't have any more time to fool around with this cat. I looked outside and saw the Jeep Cherokee just as it went into a spin and did a series of donuts in an open section of the parking lot, blue smoke pouring from the tires.

I had a pang of regret that I wouldn't be able to get to know this Ariel better. She seemed like a great gal. Shaking off the melancholy before it could sink its grips into me, I started shoving everything out the busted square in the front door that I'd entered. I had to push the bags of dog food with my legs, but I didn't mind.

I chanced one more look back at the cat and then climbed through myself. Standing out on the sidewalk, the sun suddenly looked brighter. The air smelled cleaner.

And I was out in the open.

That fact became clear when the three zombies rounded the corner of the building and began to shamble my direction. I realized in that moment that I'd never made any sort of arrangement for a signal to get Ariel's attention. I did the only thing that I could think of. I pulled my Glock 21 and dropped all three zombies in relatively rapid succession. The second one took the bullet in the face, but kept coming, and I had to adjust for a shot that smashed into the forehead and exploded out the back in a dark spray of chunky gore.

I looked over my shoulder and saw the Jeep Cherokee weaving through the lot and right for me. It braked hard and skidded sideways with a squeal of rubber.

"What the hell took you so long?" Ariel yelped as she jumped out of the vehicle after popping the rear hatch. I was actually surprised when she started grabbing my haul and throwing it all into the rear cargo area alongside me.

"Besides the undead veterinarian and the three zombie canines?" I replied with a grunt as I scooped up a bag of the dry food over one shoulder and then collected a pair of the heavy totes.

"Zombie dogs?" Ariel came to a sudden stop. She looked at me as if she waited for me to tell her I was only kidding.

"Three of them." I dropped my load into the Jeep and nodded for her to get in as I rushed around to the open driver's side door.

We both pulled our doors shut and I hit the gas just as the harried undead that had been engaged in the fruitless chase around the lot were almost on us. With a jerk on the wheel, I veered left and then made my way for the main street that ran along the front of this shopping center.

I was just turning right to speed off down Southeast Sunnyside Road when two people sprinted out into the street from the bushes across the way where the charred remains of a Taco Bell once stood. For some reason, I had a sudden craving, which is funny, because I'd never really liked that particular fast food chain in the past.

I was seriously considering just speeding off and leaving the two people behind when something made me slam on the brakes. Ariel hadn't put on her seatbelt, and certainly had not anticipated the sudden stop. She was thrown into the dash hard and made an audible grunt of pain.

"What are you doing?" she managed as she struggled to inhale.

"That woman is pregnant."

"Did you learn nothing from picking me up?" she grumbled as I hit the button to unlock all the doors.

"So you are saying that I should just leave them behind?"

I watched anxiously as the pair hurried over to where I'd stopped. As I took those few seconds to see everything a bit more clearly, I realized that the man was moving fast, but the woman had a limp to go along with her pregnancy. Her right leg had a strip of bloody cloth wrapped around it just below the knee. He had an arm around her waist and was almost carrying her as they scrambled across the divider between the north and southbound lanes of the road.

Coming through the row of tall hedges where they'd emerged were perhaps dozens of the walking dead. In fact, just as the couple reached the Jeep, one section of the hedgerow folded down as zombies appeared to be almost vomited out onto the road.

The man was tall and slim, his dark skin reflecting the sun with the added boost of the sheen of sweat that coated his face. His head was clean shaven, which was impressive considering that we were weeks into the zombie apocalypse now, and things like shaving had become a bit of a luxury. He was wearing jeans, a very worn and heavily stained tee-shirt, and high-top basketball shoes. Not what I would consider your typical post-apocalyptic apparel.

The woman looked to be of Asian heritage, but not exactly. She had a slight tilt to her eyes, and jet back hair that actually looked to have been sawed off around shoulder-length versus having been cut. She barely came up to the man's armpits and her petite frame probably made it a much easier task for the man to be practically carrying her at the speed they were moving. Her skin tone was very pale, but I didn't know if that was her natural pallor, or if perhaps she was showing the effects of blood loss from that leg injury.

The door flew open and the man practically threw the woman inside before jumping behind her and slamming the door shut behind them. By now, this newly arriving mob of the walking dead were just reaching the raised divider between the lanes.

"Everybody hang on," I called, and then floored it.

While not terribly impressive, the big SUV lurched forward and then began the steady acceleration. I knew this area, and I also knew the best way to get to where Carl and the others were staying. As the zombies vanished in the rearview mirror, and we topped the steady and gradual incline in this section of Sunnyside Road, I breathed a sigh of relief.

I was almost ready to allow myself to believe that I would make this happen. Okay, so I hadn't managed to gather a bunch of supplies for the humans, but my dear Newfie would be taken care of, and that had been my real priority. Also, I was perhaps about to deliver something to Carl and Betty that was better than supplies: people.

"Look, I wanna thank you for stopping." The man leaned forward, his hand reaching over into the front seat. I reached back and shook it despite the awkwardness of the position. I think I saw Ariel tense up as I did so. "My name is Franklin Murphy, and this here is Joan Kioki."

"Evan Berry, and this is Ariel Mannheim," I replied as we barreled along past residential neighborhoods, apartment complexes, and small shopping malls.

I looked up in the rearview mirror and my foot slipped off the gas pedal. I blinked twice to be certain, and once I was, I felt sick.

"How long ago were you bit, Joan?" I asked, doing my best to keep my voice even. I didn't want to sound freaked out or like she was in any danger from me. I wasn't entirely sure how to make that happen with my voice, but I was making a point to sound as calm as possible.

"L-l-last night," she answered.

"It was my fault," Franklin blurted. "I was supposed to be on lookout. I had to piss really bad. I just slipped out for a second…" His words had come out in a hurry at first, then slowed as he laid out his guilt.

"It wasn't your fault," Joan insisted.

"I left the door open," Franklin almost wailed. He had a low voice that sounded strange emoting such sorrow.

There was a long silence. Ariel was staring at me, and I saw something in her eyes that I couldn't read. I was almost certain that she was trying to will me to say something. There was only one thing I could think of that might be relevant to this conversation.

"I was scratched a couple of days ago," I admitted.

The odd thing was how I was losing track of time. I could no longer pinpoint the exact period that I'd been infected. Was it two days? Three? I was puzzling over it when Joan interrupted my inner musings.

"So what are you doing out here just rolling around? And what was all that nonsense in the parking lot?" She paused for a moment and then added, "That is how we found you guys…all that racket with the horn and the screeching tires."

I explained about the injuries to my dog and how I was out to gather her some much-needed supplies. I told them about how I was now taking this Jeep to their gates and leaving it there. I told them about Carl, Betty, the new girl, and the kids, as well as how the house was a pretty good spot to ride this thing out as far as locations went.

"If you want, you and Ariel could probably stay there," I offered. "Joan, you and I can drop them off and then I will leave with you. We can ride this out together."

There was only a moment's pause before she said, "I would like that."

Monsters

"What now?" I gasped as we came around a gentle bend in the road.

Many of the books and movies about the whole zombie thing tried to capture what the creators thought might be terrifying. Sometimes I would see or read a scene and think, *That's a bit over the top*. What I saw ahead would have garnered just that sort of response.

The entirety of Sunnyside Road was barricaded in a manner of speaking. Bodies were stacked at least three feet high all the way across what amounted to several lanes. There were left *and* right turn lanes on each side, as well as the two lanes going north and the two for heading south. In addition, there were bike lanes on each side and then sidewalks bordering it all.

The way was blocked by the wall of bodies. I could not wrap my mind around who or what would do something like this. We could turn around and try to find our way using the back streets, but I was so shocked by what I was seeing that I just sat there with the vehicle idling. We were on just enough of an incline that the Jeep did not roll forward of its own volition, and so we were all still sitting there when I heard the dull pop sound.

My eyes flicked to the hole that had just appeared in the

windshield at the same time everybody else figured out what was happening. The vehicle erupted in shouts as all three passengers started hollering or screaming about how we needed to get out of here.

I shifted into reverse and stomped the gas. As we began to gain momentum, picking up speed as we raced backwards on the downhill slope, two more holes appeared in the windshield.

"Hang on!" I yelled above the other screams as I stomped on the brakes and turned the wheel hard to put us into what I hoped was a bit of a spin.

It wasn't a full hundred and eighty degrees, but it was most of it, and I changed to the accelerator and now had my foot pressed to the floor on that pedal as I corrected enough to bring us around the rest of the way. We had a bit of a hill going down and then another easy slope headed up. I just wanted us up and over that ridge as soon as possible to put whatever the hell was going on behind us as far away as I could manage.

"Anybody hit?" I called out.

"No," Ariel answered first.

"Nope," Franklin said next.

"Not me," Joan added, and she almost sounded disappointed. We could deal with that later, right this moment—

The Jeep jerked wildly to the left and we were now rocketing towards the curb. Before I could correct, we bounced up onto the sidewalk and then slammed into a tall streetlight post with a big, circular concrete base.

I heard the airbags go off…and then everything went black.

**

The sounds that filtered into my consciousness were muffled at first. I thought I heard screaming, then it sounded like laughing. It took me a few minutes to realize that it was both. When I tried to open my eyes, things appeared to be a bit fuzzy. At first I thought that I was maybe seeing through gauze or perhaps a very thin blindfold.

"Looks like another one of them is awake," a voice said

from just to my left.

"So, that's the last of 'em?" a female voice asked.

"The last one that matters," came the cryptic reply.

"Go tell Don *they* all survived," the female's voice said, and it was with a tone of authority, but there was something in the way she said the word "they" that had me on edge. There was a meaning behind it, I could tell by the way she emphasized it. "See if he wants any of them brought in."

"Sure thing, boss," the male voice said, and then I heard a door open and shut.

I was trying to look around, but my head wouldn't move. It actually took me a bit to realize that it was held in place by some sort of strap or band around my forehead. Also, I was in the upright position, standing with my legs wide. A bit of deductive reasoning told me that I was strapped to something that was 'X' shaped. My feet were on small ledges, but I was a good six or so inches off the floor and there was a single beam that split the 'X' up the middle which dug uncomfortably into my back, but at least gave my head a place to rest.

With what little that I could see of the room, it seemed to be a classroom. I didn't see any desks, but there was a large Dry-Erase board directly in front of me and an old file cabinet. The way the shadows danced across the wall in front of me, I could tell there were windows behind me and that it was still daytime. I was guessing that I was seeing the shadows of trees blowing in the breeze.

I heard what sounded like a chair scooting across the floor, and then the distinct sound of boots or heavy shoes on the tiled floor. A moment later, a hazy figure stood before me. I felt a hand cup my chin and lift my head up.

"You look like shit," the female voice I'd heard earlier said.

Now I was realizing that I wasn't blindfolded or anything of that nature. Apparently, my eyes were just extremely swollen. I was beginning to waken more completely, and that is when I began to feel pain. It was centered in my face, but my ribs felt like they'd gone ten rounds on the losing end of a cage fight. Also, I could not breathe very well. In fact, I was breathing solely through my mouth at the moment.

"I am guessing you have a busted nose, maybe a few cracked ribs. Your arm came through surprisingly well considering it appears to have been injured prior to the wreck."

When she stepped into view, she was nothing like her voice. In fact, I almost started laughing. It reminded me of that classic Aerosmith video when the guy thinks he is on the phone with this hot chick…and she is shown with a kid on one hip, cigarette dangling from her lips as she stirs something on the stove, and is easily over three hundred pounds. It is all topped off with a face that was beaten by a forest of ugly sticks.

I'd heard this woman talk, and already pictured what I would see. Especially when the guy she'd been talking to referred to her as 'boss' before he left. The thing is, this woman had sounded like she might be some sort of longshoreman.

She was maybe five feet tall. If she weighted ninety pounds, I would guess that she had a few rocks in her pockets. Her blonde hair was actually styled fashionably and her blue eyes were shiny. She looked and *smelled* amazing, particularly in contrast to me who hadn't shaved in a few weeks, had hair that was greasy and matted down, and probably smelled like the north end of a southbound moose.

As soon as I realized that her smell registered, I felt my heart skip a beat. Was that the start of my spiral into undeath? The living would start to smell good?

Then I realized that she simply smelled good…not tasty.

As she came into focus a bit more clearly, I saw what might be the cause for her rough voice. She had a nasty scar across her throat. It looked horrible; but it also looked old, so it had nothing to do with the zombie apocalypse.

"You got a name?" the woman asked as she grabbed a chair and pulled it around to sit in front of me.

I tried to speak, but my mouth was dry, and only a rasping sound came out. I tried to swallow, but not much was happening.

The woman stood up and pulled a canteen from her shoulder, stepping onto a stack of pallets in front of my stanchion. "Open your mouth," she said. I was confused, and it must've shown on my face. "You don't seriously think that I will let your mouth touch my canteen, do you?"

She had a good point.

I opened my mouth and let her pour in a trickle. It was just enough to clear away the grit. It hardly came close to quenching my thirst, but at least it was something.

"Name?" the woman insisted, sounding more like a bored receptionist than some sort of evil captor.

"Evan Berry." I didn't see how it could hurt to at least answer the most basic of questions.

"And what is your relation to the people that you were brought in with?"

I noticed that she avoided or simply chose not to use the word "captured" in describing the situation. Of course, this contraption that I was lashed to told a much different story.

"And you?" I tried, not expecting a response. "What is your name?"

"Natasha Petrov," she answered without hesitation. The reply caught me by complete surprise and I just hung there with my mouth open until she looked up at me and cocked an eyebrow of visible disapproval.

"Now, I will ask you again, what is your relation to the people you were found with?"

"Just survivors that I ran across."

"And…" She glanced down at the clipboard in her hand, but I think it was more perfunctory than anything else, I had a feeling that she knew exactly what she was doing and what she planned to ask. "You were carrying a great deal of medical supplies. If not for a few of the things we catalogued, I would've guessed that you raided a medical center, but I am told that it is apparent that you raided a veterinary clinic? Since no animal was found, is it safe to guess that you were transporting all of that stuff to someplace specific?"

"Yeah, that would be a safe bet."

"And you say that these people with you were just people you willingly picked up?"

I didn't like how this was starting to change. Her tone was

hardening with every word and the look on her face was starting to remind me of what a shark would look like if it had blue eyes.

I stared back, but I was already wondering how much torture I could endure before I spilled anything and everything she wanted to know. It wasn't that I was a big sissy, but I didn't really owe anything to Betty or Carl. As for the kids, I did not wish them harm, but being that guy who gets fingers snapped or hooked up to car batteries and answers the interrogation with witty quips through gritted teeth was fiction.

The woman stood up, and I braced myself for something terrible, but she walked out of my line of sight and a few seconds later, I heard the door to the room open and shut. I held my breath, trying to discern if maybe she was still in the room, but I couldn't hear anything.

I waited, and at some point, must've slipped out of consciousness. My eyes snapped open when the sting of a slap brought me back around.

"Mister Berry," a low voice grumbled.

The man standing in front of me was a giant. He was looking down at me as he stood flat-footed *on* the floor and I was mounted on this 'X' with my feet several inches *off* the floor. His brown hair was shaved on the sides, but the strip he kept on top was long and pulled back into a ponytail. His skin had a coarse ruddiness like he spent too much time in the sun without sunscreen.

"Jesus," I gasped.

"No…not even close," the man said with a dismissive wave. He leaned in close and gave me a salacious wink, "But I have made a few of the ladies see God."

I was too caught up in the minty freshness of his breath for a moment to actually catch his little jibe. It was a running theme with this group from what I was seeing. They were all so fresh and clean; you would be hard pressed to believe that the undead were wiping out humanity. Had I missed something during my spell of unconsciousness?

"I hear you are some sort of good Samaritan," the man said after I continued to stare at him with no idea what to say at this point. "You were found with a carload of people that you just scooped in off the street. Maybe you haven't realized it, but these are dangerous times. The thin veneer of law and order are gone and people are becoming rather base and crass."

I listened to this man speak, but the words coming out of his mouth did not fit. I was expecting some kind of gorilla, a buffoon perhaps in the mold of Biff from *Back to the Future*. Despite his deep voice, he was soft-spoken. The book was definitely not matching up with the cover. If not for being lashed to this stanchion, I might consider this person to be a potential ally. This would be the kind of guy I would be able to join up with and follow.

"You know my name," I finally managed, "but I have no idea who you are or how I should address you."

"Where are my manners?" the man laughed heartily. "Don Evans...Diamond Donnie to my friends."

"So, what should I call you?"

His tone was still friendly, but I was seeing something in his eyes just as I had Natasha Petrov's. There was a hard coldness that hinted at something dangerous. His smile was real enough, but it was one of a sadist in the thralls of torturing someone or something.

"You can call me Mister Evans. Kinda funny that our names are so similar." His words made it sound like a joke, but his tone said otherwise.

He moved around behind me and I tensed for something terrible. I heard the rasp of metal on leather and knew well enough by now the sound that a blade makes when being drawn from its sheath.

Here it comes, I thought.

I heard another sound and then felt the strap around my forehead fall away. Next was the twine that had bound my left ankle to this 'X', and a moment later, my foot went hot and tingly as the blood rushed back to the extremity. This process was repeated with my other leg, and then each wrist.

I eased down from my perch and felt the pins and needles in my feet for a moment. It took everything I had not to crumble to the floor. As I regained full feeling in my hands and feet, Don Evans walked back around to regard me. The knife was still in his hand and it took everything in my power not to stare at it. Instead, I glanced around the room. I noticed three more of the large 'X' structures shoved to one side of the room.

"So, where is everybody else you found with me?" I dared to ask, almost afraid of what I might be told.

"One of them is being processed just like you," Don replied. "But the infected one was put down."

"Joan...her name was Joan Kioki." That left one person unaccounted for. That was a matter of concern, but at the moment, I was focused on my own problems.

"Does it really matter?" the man scoffed. "She was infected and soon to become one of *them*."

He was not saying anything that I didn't know, but it was the total lack of feeling that galled me. Despite her eventual fate, she was still a human being.

"Was it at least merciful?"

I had no idea why I was asking all these questions. Maybe I was just curious as to how I would be treated as soon as I started to show the symptoms. I felt confident that I was still not displaying the tracers in my eyes considering how I was being treated.

"Is there really such a thing?" Don laughed. "I have yet to meet anybody who was just okay with dying. They all want that last few minutes. The problem with that is that resources are finite these days. The delivery trucks have stopped running."

"Was it quick?" I clarified. "I mean, you didn't make her suffer or anything, right?"

"Wow, you sure seem to care an awful lot about somebody you supposedly just picked up off the side of the road." Don crossed the room and grabbed a chair, spinning it around and straddling it as he took a seat. "And I am told you had a bunch of animal supplies and dog food in your vehicle. Unless you are just that desperate for food and medicine, or you have a giant invisible rabbit companion...that has me thinking that you are part of another group. That would also make me doubt that you were just driving around with a group of strangers."

And there it was. This guy—and by extension, his group of survivors—thought that we were all some small team from another group.

"That why your people attacked us?" I asked bluntly.

"That's the funny thing about perspective."

Don rose to his feet and I tensed. He still had that knife in his hand, and I didn't have a thing to defend myself with if he attacked. Of course, as big as he was, I had serious doubts as to my ability to offer up more than token resistance. I was fully aware that bigger did not always mean badder, but this guy had an air about him that sizzled with danger.

"One of your people shot at us. We were trying to get away when we crashed," I said, taking a step back and trying to figure out the best way to prepare for the attack I was sure had to be coming at any moment.

"That is your way of seeing it," Don said with a slight shrug of his shoulders. "Or…maybe we were defending ourselves from a group of people out raiding. You don't think we haven't heard the screams at night, or seen the people skulking around, watching us from all angles like they are trying to figure out a way to get to us…take what we have started."

"If that was the case, why did we turn around? Why did we go the other direction?"

"Testing our defenses."

I could already see that there would be nothing to come from this circular argument. This guy had his mind made up. I was the bad guy in his scenario. Honestly, I wasn't so against the whole dying thing. I've had the past few days to come to grips with it. I just wanted it to be on my terms. Something told me this was going to be painful and anything but the way I'd envisioned it. Even worse, I'd worked so hard to gather some stuff for my dog, and now it was all for nothing. I'd failed her.

Unless…

"You asked about all the animal supplies. The dog food and other things from the veterinary hospital?" I blurted. "If I tell you where that stuff was going and why, maybe you might believe me. You would easily be able to check it out for yourself."

"I'm listening." The man looked down at the knife in his hand with an expression that almost looked like regret.

I opened my mouth. I could tell him about Chewie. Hell, I could explain about how we'd faced off with our own bad guy in Brandon. Maybe if I told him about the kids, and about Betty and that girl Amanda that I didn't really even know...and then I could tell him why I was out by myself. Maybe then he would see that I wasn't a threat. I had no bad intentions when it came to him and his people.

The scream that pierced the moment of silence between me and Don sounded close. It sounded horrible. It was *the* scream. I'd heard it too many times not to know it for exactly what it meant. Somebody was being ripped apart and eaten alive by one of the walking dead.

Don's gaze returned to me from examining his knife, and that evil glint was replaced by something predatory. Something...evil.

I always believed that true evil was a very abstract idea. I'd written a paper in my college psych class about how evil was only defined as such by people of different belief systems who might not agree with the actions of another person or group. The discussion in class after my paper was shared had almost caused a miniature riot.

Eventually, I'd admitted that I might have made some foolish jumps from one ledge of faulty logic to another in order to support my thesis. There was such a thing as true and universal evil. I was looking it in the eye this very moment, and it made me want to shrink inside myself and vanish. I had no doubt that I was about to feel real pain for no other reason than to satisfy this man's sadistic wants, needs, and desires.

The scream changed to a gurgle and Don closed his eyes, his lips curling slightly as if he might be hearing a favorite song.

"I think Joanie is awake."

I hadn't known him long enough to recognize his voice, much less the sounds of his screams of pain, but I was now certain that I knew the fate of not only Joan Kioki, but that of Franklin Murphy as well. It didn't make any sense.

"Why?" the word slipped out almost involuntarily.

"This is a new world, Evan Berry. The slates are clean and it is only those who choose to reach out and grab the rudder of this ship that will have any say in the direction that it will take."

Just that fast, this guy had gone from regular scary to cuckoo-for-Cocoa-Puffs. I had no idea what he was talking about, but when he opened his eyes, I felt my blood chill.

"You think all this is an accident, Evan?" Don asked as he brought his knife up and made a shaving swipe down one side of his already clean-shaven head.

"I think it is a tragedy."

The wet sounds died out mercifully and I felt terrible about just how much relief I found in that few moments of silence where the only sound I could hear was that of my heart pounding in my temples and my blood racing through my veins.

"We brought this on ourselves. We've allowed our government to take far too much power. We've sat back while this nation became the world's toilet. All the shit that no other country wanted just floated into our bowl. We spent billions of dollars having all our welfare applications printed in a dozen languages so that the human waste could sap our resources..."

Oh great, I thought. *This guy isn't just the garden-variety crazy. He is one of those racist types.*

The irony came around and slapped me right in the face. I still remember when one of my classmates had used the term racist to describe the type of mentality it would take to write that very same paper about evil that had just resurfaced in my memory mere moments ago. I'd been so full of myself when I wrote that paper that I truly believed I was sharing some sort of existential piece of wisdom that would make everybody sit up and take notice. What I had failed to do was look at the human events that I had managed to gloss over or simply ignore: slavery, the Holocaust, and a host of other human atrocities that were the simplest examples of evil, and impossible to be seen as anything else.

"...and now we can wipe it all away and start again. This

time…we can make sure that those who don't truly belong here never get the chance to pollute this nation again." Don brought the knife down and I saw a thin line of red well up on the side of his head. A single ruby bead eventually lost the fight with gravity and rolled down to vanish behind his ear, leaving a crimson trail in its wake.

I'd been concerned for my well-being before. Now, I was trying to figure out a way to go out and take this creep with me. This was the shining example of exactly what Carl and I had spoken about. This was a person who no longer had the restrictions of a civilized society to keep him in check. Without the social structure and deterrents in place, this was one of those fringe types that usually made the news when they were under siege by the ATF or some other multi-lettered branch of law enforcement.

Now, people like this could band together and embark on whatever their warped and twisted minds could manage. I also knew without even having to think too deeply that this would likely be just the tip of the iceberg. I was willing to bet there would be worse out there just crawling out from whatever rock they had managed to live under.

"So, Evan, you need to answer one question. It really is simple, and there is no reason to put any pretty words around it. You in…or out?"

I looked at the man, my eyes flicking to the blade in his hand. There was no way I would stand a chance the way things stood. If I opted out right here, he would kill me. On the plus side, my worries would be over.

An image of my beloved Newfoundland popped into my head. I'd always heard people say that we—and by 'we' I mean Stephanie and I—treated our girl better than most people did their children. I thought that was stretching things a bit, but here I was, about to determine my own fate, and at that same moment, if I simply gave up, I would be leaving my dog to rely on the mercy of others.

The infection could express itself any moment now. If I didn't get away from this lunatic and his band of evil minions soon, her fate would be sealed as far as I saw things. I would probably have one chance, and it would have to be soon. If I died in the attempt, at least I would do so knowing that I gave my last effort trying to care for my dog.

Not for the first time, I questioned my own mindset. All my thoughts were about my dog first and foremost. There were three adults and two children that I imagine a normal and more well-balanced person would be placing higher in his or her thought process.

I decided that I really didn't care. Chewie truly did represent all that I had left from that old life.

It was in that moment that another revelation hit me. This one came like a punch in the gut. My bag containing my picture of Stephanie had obviously been confiscated along with everything else.

"I'm in," I said, hoping that my voice didn't give away the contempt that I felt for this guy and anybody who would follow him.

"And you have to know that it isn't quite that easy. I mean…anybody with their feet to the fire would probably say the same thing." Don paused and pursed his lips in consideration. "Unless they were trying to go out as some sort of bad ass."

I saw his eyes flick to me. He was obviously checking my reaction. I would have to play a role for as long as possible if I was going to have any chance of pulling this charade off with even the slightest chance for success. As long as he didn't ask me to murder some poor person they had captive, I felt that I would be able to maintain the fragile façade for a short time.

"So, where is your group holed up?"

The question came so quick that I didn't have a chance to check myself. Good or bad, at least I'd already told myself that I would give up the location if it meant that I gave my dog a better chance to survive. I really didn't owe Carl, Betty, or the others a damn thing.

I was hoping that they would not see the kids as a liability and simply kill them out of hand. Yeah…I got the irony of how those very thoughts about their lack of usefulness had been my own to some degree.

I gave them the general location without pinpointing the specific house. I did my best to put them in the area and tried to play it off like we'd just picked that spot to hunker down and that there had been no concrete plans to make it permanent. It was close enough to the truth that I didn't think I gave away any hint that I'd been less than a hundred percent truthful.

"You get that, Natasha?" Don called out once I was done.

"A team is gearing up now," the woman said as she entered the room.

"And how did your questioning of the woman go?" Don slid his knife into its sheath and turned his back on me.

I imagine that was easy for him to do since Natasha was standing just inside the door with one hand on the grip of a pistol holstered to her hip. Add in the fact that I didn't have anything I could use to inflict any harm except my bare hands, and it was less like Don was being bold and more like he'd simply dismissed my presence entirely.

"Her story matches his almost verbatim, and both versions match what that other couple said before we took care of them," Natasha said with no more emotion than if she were discussing the weather despite what I knew to more or less be the fates of Joan and Franklin.

"Who do you want running point with the team?" Natasha asked.

"Well, he says that there are women and children in this little group if he isn't yanking our chain, so why don't you go? I think they might be a bit more receptive to letting a woman in. I am willing to bet your sweet little ass that these people are still clinging to the old ways. They will probably think that you are perfectly harmless."

I had to almost bite my tongue. They hadn't met Carl. These people were going to be in for one hell of a surprise. I was almost feeling smug until Don continued his instructions.

"And if there is a dog, you know to leave it behind, right?"

"Of course," Natasha said with a nod.

"But—" I started to protest.

"No buts, Evan," Don interrupted. "We are doing well enough taking care of our own. A dog is a waste of resources."

"Then I will take care of her. I will make sure that my dog has everything she needs, just...don't leave her to die."

"Is that the kind of monster you think me to be?" Don snorted. He even sounded offended. "We would not dream of leaving your dog to suffer. Natasha will shoot her right between the eyes."

"Why?" It barely made it out of my throat as it seemed as if my ability to speak was suddenly a near impossibility considering how it felt as if it had constricted to a pinhole.

"Haven't you been paying attention?" Don walked to the door, opening it for Natasha who ducked through without even casting a glance over her shoulder. "The old world is dead. I am the phoenix that is rising from its ashes to usher in a new world...a new era."

"What does that have to do with my dog? Why kill her? She's just a dog, and I'll—"

"That's the point, Evan. She is *only* a dog. If you are out making supply runs or tending to some stupid animal, then you won't be doing your share for the greater good of the humans. Haven't you been paying attention? Our society crippled itself with a bunch of frivolous crap and worrying about shit that didn't matter instead of taking care of ourselves first and foremost."

I opened my mouth to protest, then closed it. It wasn't that I didn't think he was crazy. I had no doubts that this guy was much worse than the walking dead and as mad as a hatter, but what if I did manage to buy Chewie a reprieve? How long could that last? Just like I knew my own fate the moment my eyes gave away my condition, I knew that she would be executed the instant that I was no longer able to care for her.

I'd failed.

Not just my dog, but I'd also just reduced Carl, Betty, and the others' chances of survival. And on the off chance that Carl bought into this madness, I knew Betty would have no part in it. I have no idea why I was so certain in regards to her reaction to this, but I was.

"And the kids?" I finally managed. I braced myself for the response, not sure of how I would even feel when he declared their fates would be the same as my Chewie.

"Jesus, man!" Don snapped, spinning on me with a look of exasperation on his face that was echoed in his tone. "You really do think I am some sort of monster. Those children are our future. They will be taken into our care and molded into proper citizens." He paused and arched an eyebrow. "They are white…right?"

"Yes," I managed to say without being sick to my stomach as I considered the full measure of this walking pile of human excrement.

Okay, it wasn't like I had lived my life with blinders on. Of course I was aware of things like racism, sexism, and all sorts of societal prejudices. Still, to witness this degree of extreme disdain for any sort of person, then just maybe this whole zombie apocalypse wasn't such a bad thing. I realized it was the idea of "cutting off the nose to spite the face" sort of mentality, but I saw no world that could thrive or flourish with somebody like this allowed to walk free and unopposed in it.

I followed Don as he exited the room and headed down a long hallway. It only took me a moment to figure out just exactly where I was. We'd seen that stack of bodies across the road at the intersection where a big church sat. It had been on our left and was one of the larger churches that I think I'd ever seen.

Super, I thought.

Some of the most over-the-top lunatics in most zombie stories were either military or religious. I'd always been bothered by that. I had friends who were either in the military or had served. Also, while not much of a church-goer myself, I had friends who did. They were no better and no worse than any other friends or acquaintances that I'd made over the years. Every demographic has good and bad. Yet, here I was, walking behind one of the more common stereotypes.

We came to a stop at a door and Don turned to me. "Before we go meet some of my people, there is a little something I need you to take care of first. You see, you arrived here with some undesirable sorts. Now, I could've dispatched of them myself, but then what would I do for fun later?"

I had no idea what he was talking about, but as soon as he opened the door, the stench hit me like a wave. I couldn't see past his enormous frame, but I didn't need to in order to know what was inside this room. He stepped to the side and revealed a pair of zombies. One of them was staggering towards us. The second was trying to get to its feet, but one leg had been gnawed down to the bone at just above the right knee and he was having difficulty standing.

I guess somebody had come up from behind us at some point. I'd been so caught up in my head...or they'd just been that quiet. Whatever the case, this person (or maybe there was more than one, I had no idea) shoved me into the room and the door slammed behind me.

DEAD: Alone

7

One of Us

"Franklin," I gasped involuntarily as my eyes flicked from Joan to the man making his way to his feet, only to fall again when his injured leg buckled.

By now, Joan was only a few steps away. I reached out with both hands, checking her in the shoulders and sending her tottering backwards. She staggered twice, almost managed to correct and keep her feet, then she fell hard on her back. There was a vicious crack of bone slamming into and then bouncing off the checkerboard pattern-tiled floor.

The moment she hit, it was as if a switch was thrown in my head. This was not Franklin or Joan. These were zombies. The walking dead. Whatever had once been human in them, it was now long gone. I searched the room and my eyes paused on the chair behind what I figured had to have once been the teacher's desk.

I darted across the room, hurdling the zombie version of Joan on my way. I reached the desk and slid across it like one of the *Dukes of Hazzard* boys. I turned and knocked the chair onto its side. I was still a bit surprised to discover such a relic. I didn't know any teacher that still sat on a wooden chair. They all used the kind with back support, wheels, and that lever that let you raise and lower it with ease. Whoever had been the teacher in this room, he or she had been old school.

I stomped down on one of the legs and it made a loud, wooden crack, but didn't break all the way. By now, Zombie-Joan had managed to regain her footing and was turning to face me. Zombie-Franklin was on his hands and knees and had made the unlikely leap that crawling after me would meet his needs much easier than continuing to try and stand up.

Another stomp and the leg gave with a nasty breaking sound. I grabbed the chair leg and brought the broken and jagged end around just as Zombie-Joan reached the desk. She swiped at me impotently, her mouth opening and an ugly moan escaping. It was made all that much worse by the hissing noise that came from the long slice across her throat.

These bastards had to know that slicing the throat would not be enough. They'd intentionally wanted her to become one of the walking dead. They'd probably already decided how they were going to kill Franklin.

I stared into the blackshot, filmed-over eyes of the thing that had once been Joan. I knew I had no choice, but that didn't mean I would enjoy it. I would do what had to be done in order to survive.

"Rest in peace, Joan Kioki," I mouthed, making it a point not to say it out loud just in case they were somehow listening in. I shoved the pointy end up and under her jaw. The wood pierced the flesh easily, but hung up as it broke through and ground against the roof of her mouth. A grunt of effort forced it up and through. She collapsed, and my arms jerked a bit despite how tiny she had been in life. I pulled the piece of wood free and winced when Joan's body landed hard on the floor one final time.

That left Franklin. By now, he'd managed to haul himself to the desk. He was coming up the side closest to the wall. It would be impossible for him to turn around without a considerable amount of effort, so I stepped around and came up behind him.

I raised the chair leg and drove it down and into the back of his head. The jagged bits splintered and broke off for the most part. The skull was simply too much for a wooden chair leg. I was left with no choice and changed my grip. It took five swings but eventually, the skull cracked open and my blows pulverized brain and bone into a dark slurry of gore.

Sure, I hadn't known these two for more than a few minutes, but that didn't ease my pain. These were two senseless deaths brought about by the worst sorts of people. Part of me wished that, if I was unable to secure my escape from these lunatics, I could turn in the middle of the night and rip into Don at the very least.

"I don't know how...but I am going to end you, Don Evans," I whispered to the empty room.

I felt my heart skip a beat when the door flew open. "That's a pretty good start," Don's voice crooned. "Nice bit of creativity using that chair's leg. Almost a shame that one there didn't figure it out."

I turned to see Don staring past me and down at Franklin's inert corpse. I fought to wipe away any sort of emotion that might be lurking in my expression or leaking through my eyes. He gave his head a shake like he was honestly sad that these two people were now truly dead, then his eyes swept up to me and locked on mine again. I saw his expression change just a bit and felt my stomach drop. It had finally happened. I was certain that he was seeing the tracers in my eyes.

I wondered if he'd been the one to slit Joan's throat, or if he'd had somebody else do it. I wondered, if it had been him, did he take joy in what he'd done even more knowing that she was pregnant?

"You have something on your cheek." He pointed at me with a look of revulsion turning his lips down into an ugly frown.

I brought up a hand and wiped at my cheek. When I looked down, I saw a chunky bit of what I guessed to be brain now smeared across the palm of my hand. I was equally parts revolted and relieved. Of course, it took a few extra seconds for the actual relief to slip in and make itself known.

I brushed my hand on my pants, still struggling with all of the emotions swirling around in me. My eyes were drawn to the walls where a board was adorned with a collection of drawings done by children proclaiming, of all things, "He is Risen" in the newest touch of irony.

I glanced over my shoulder and saw three people, two men and one woman, walking a good distance behind, but obviously following. I wasn't sure what they believed that I could do; even my chair leg zombie-killing weapon had been taken from my hands after I'd exited the classroom containing Joan and Franklin's corpses. I had nothing but my bare hands.

"So," I tried to sound casual as I began to try and wrap my head around my most recent predicament, "do we have regular services we are supposed to attend? What is the schedule?"

Don stopped and turned to face me. I was going to nickname this guy Billy Idol. He loved to flash that sneer of disdain. It seemed to be his go-to expression.

"What are you talking about?"

I gestured to the hallway we were in, then my eyes lit on the door ahead with the ornate cross hanging over it. "We are in a church. I assume there to be a reason...a significance that you have chosen this spot."

"For now, it is in a spot that allows us close proximity to a few markets and neighborhoods that we are using for supplies. Also, we have found a few survivors that have joined our numbers. We have a team out right now that is scouting a new possible location for us to relocate within the next few weeks." He cocked his head in a way that reminded me of the creepy zombie children and then a smile crept across his expression. "You thought we were some sort of religious group." His laughter was loud and echoed off the walls of the long hallway. "That was just another societal opiate that numbed people to the ways our government was slowly destroying the nation. All this crap about being inclusive and opening our borders and communities to these people who swoop in and suck up all our welfare while good American families go without. The ones who take all the jobs while our nation wallows in unemployment?"

Once again I was hit by the astonishment that, despite the fact of seeing these sorts of claims being tossed around on tabloid television and some of the more sensationalist broadcasting trying to pass itself off as news, I could not come to grips with the fact that I was hearing a person spout this right in front of me with such a degree of conviction that it told me this guy had been living with just that kind of ideology for a long time.

I decided that I could not trust my voice or the tone that would seep through if I spoke, so I just continued to stare at the man. He waited for a moment. His smile actually grew broader as I maintained my silence.

"Yeah, if you were one of them church going types, I'm pretty sure you'll get over it," Don finally continued. "If not, just make sure that you keep it to yourself. Believe what you want when you are alone, but when you are around others, keep a lid on that crap."

With that, the man turned and opened the door to what had once been a massive chapel or whatever they called the room in a church where all the people sat, stood, and kneeled while the priest or preacher or reverend stood at the podium and did his thing. The room was huge, and there were still several rows of pews, but they had an assortment of sleeping bags spread out either on them or on the floor in between.

As my eyes took everything in, I actually breathed a sigh of relief when I spotted a few children in the mix. Perhaps Carl and Betty and the others would stand a chance. That thought simply drove the idea in deeper that they planned on killing my dog...my Chewie.

"This is where we all stay." Don held out an arm, ushering me inside. "If you continue to show that you are one of us, then you will be allowed to stay here as well."

It took me a moment to actually process what he'd just said as well as hear the shift in his tone that had become almost out-wardly threatening. I turned back to him as the trio that had been following us came up and took positions behind him, effectively blocking my way. I'd noticed another set of double doors across the room and opposite of the pulpit that sat at the bottom of the long, sloped rows that ran between the sections of pews. There'd been a flicker of light and shadow that hinted at outside. There were also armed guards at those doors as well as a barricade of long tables turned on their sides and stacked up against them.

"So, where exactly will I be staying?" I asked, trying not to sound nervous among other things.

"In the daycare wing."

At first I wasn't sure if he was joking or not, so I just smiled and nodded. Don stepped back and the trio of escorts moved in close. I tensed, uncertain if they would simply escort me, or if there might be something more physical and violent in store for me.

In a moment of inspiration, I blurted, "What about my bag?"

"Anything of value was added to the stores. Your weapons were inventoried and marked down as well. You have no need for any of that right now." Don gave my query a dismissive wave and started away.

"There was a picture." I did not want to sound desperate and perhaps give these people even more leverage against me, but I was certain that my death was not only imminent, but very near. If I could have nothing else, I just wanted that picture of me and Stephanie. I would weep and mourn Chewie's loss once I was alone, but I needed that picture now more than ever.

Don glanced at each of the people around me who all gave non-committal shrugs or shakes of their head. I felt my heart sink as my anger rose.

"Sorry, Evan," Don said with a tone that did not come close to matching the words.

"But—" I started to protest, however, Don was already walking away.

"You should get some rest, you'll be joining a team in a probationary role tonight. You don't wanna head out there and not be well rested," Don called over his shoulder.

"Let's go," one of the three guards said, giving me a shove.

"Maybe you should lead the way," I managed with a wince as some of the aches and pains from my accident began to assert themselves.

"Just shut up and get walking," another of the trio, the woman this time, said with a sardonic snort.

"And when exactly will I be heading out?" I asked as I started toward the wooden door that they herded me towards.

It wasn't a real surprise when I didn't receive any answer. The woman edged past me and opened the door, moving aside and ushering me in. We were in another hallway, this one much narrower than the one with the classrooms. It was also very dim. The only light came from the frosted skylights in the ceiling.

I was marched down to the second door on the left. Again, the woman was the one to step forward and open my door.

"Right inside there," she snapped.

I did as I was told and saw that this was little more than a small office. There was barely room for the one desk and trio of metal filing cabinets. There were no windows or any source of light, but just before the door was shut behind me, I saw a figure sit up from where it had been curled up on the floor in the corner farthest from the door.

"Evan?" a familiar voice whimpered in the darkness.

"Ariel?" I said, moving forward in the absolute black with my hands out in front of me to hopefully keep from running into anything or stepping on the woman who sounded absolutely terrified.

"I didn't think any of you survived the crash," she hiccupped through her sobs.

"It seems just the two of us made it," I said. There was no reason to drop the fates of Joan and Franklin in her lap.

"Are you certain?" she sniffed.

"Yes." I let that word hang for just a moment before continuing with just a slight change in subject to get her mind moving in another direction. "So how long have you been in here?"

"I have no idea." I heard her shift and move. A moment later, her hands found mine and gripped them tight. "In case you haven't noticed, it's kinda dark in here."

"Oh…good," I tried to force a laugh into my voice, "I thought maybe I'd taken one hit to the head too many."

"There is this man…" her voice faded as she spoke and I remembered back to when she'd drawn a pistol on me right after I'd rescued her just hours ago. Now I felt even worse for having punched her in the face. She'd been afraid. Considering all I knew and much of what I'd read in books or seen in movies, perhaps she had good reason.

"Did he hurt you?" I asked, almost afraid of the answer.

"No, not with his actions, but the things he was saying, maybe it is better that those two didn't make it. Something tells me that they wouldn't have been welcome, and there is no telling what that might mean." There was a moment of silence, and then she began to speak again, this time even more tentatively. "Do they know about your...condition?"

"Not that I know. I have to assume that my eyes still haven't given me away."

"If you start to turn in here with me—" she started, but I saved her the trouble.

"I will let you know the very moment that I feel the least bit sick. As soon as I lose consciousness, just tip one of the filing cabinets over on top of my head or something. I wouldn't worry too much, though, supposedly I am being taken out tonight with a team of foragers. If I don't feel anything, but they open the door and my eyes have changed, I imagine they will take care of me then. In any case, I won't turn and attack you," I promised.

We both sat down on the floor. For a while, we just sat in silence. I spent that time trying to search myself internally for any sign that I might be turning. It had to happen soon, I was certain of it. I would not allow that to happen in here since I doubted that any effort would be made to rescue Ariel if she started screaming for help.

As I sat there thinking, I felt her hands seek out mine again and grip one tightly. I couldn't begrudge her this small measure of comfort. Whether due to exhaustion or the darkness, it was not more than a few moments before I heard the steady breathing and soft snores that told me Ariel was asleep.

I sat in the dark and fought off an onslaught of emotions that, if I let them leak through, might very well consume me beyond my ability to recover. I shoved away the sadness and the sense of loss as I waited for the door to open and my captors to summon me.

One of Us

I started going over a variety of possible scenarios in my head that might lead to my escape. Of course, by the time I was brought out, whatever team they'd sent to retrieve Carl and the others would probably be back. My Newfie would be dead, and I would officially have nothing left to live for. Maybe once that moment came, perhaps that would give me the strength to just go out while attempting to take that maniac Don Evans with me.

I have no idea how long I sat in the darkness with Ariel slowly relaxing into my side, but eventually I heard a bit of a commotion out in the hall. I eased away from her as the sounds of footsteps grew nearer. If I was about to get snatched up, I didn't want her caught in the madness or possible scuffle.

The door flew open and four figures rushed in with rifles, each with a high-powered flashlight mounted on the barrel. I just made out a fifth shape that had to be Don Evans standing behind his little goon squad.

"Get his ass out here!" Don snarled.

I was yanked to my feet as Ariel began to stir awake. Somebody gave me a nasty shove and sent me sprawling into the hallway where I landed on my stomach with a loud 'oof' as the air exploded from my lungs. A boot caught me in the ribs and put me almost onto my back. Before I could process that attack, another set of hands reached out and snatched me to my feet, spinning me around and slamming me hard into the wall.

"You set us up?" Don's voice hissed in my ear. "Now three of my people are dead because of you. I've a good mind to take your ass over to that church and string you up with some of the other idiots who were fool enough to try and cross me."

"What?" I managed as I fought to get air back into my lungs. "I have no idea what you're talking about."

"My people were drawn in and then some sort of noisemaker was employed that brought in zombies from behind. They had snipers picking my people off from one side and a wall of rotten flesh from the other."

Despite my pain, I had to struggle to keep a smile off my face. It seemed that Carl and the others had been busy in my absence. I just wish I could've seen it all play out.

"I don't have any idea what you're talking about," I wheezed.

"You said there were just a few people and a couple of kids." Don put his face right in mine as he spoke. "According to the one person who managed to make it back alive, there are quite a few more people than you led us to believe."

"And they are using the undead like shock troops," a familiar female voice added as Natasha stepped up beside Don. She had a few strips of cloth wrapped around her upper left arm and I could see a bloom of fresh blood already spreading across the fabric.

"That is all news to me," I said honestly. "You sure that you were at the right place? That doesn't sound like my people at all."

All of this had me wondering exactly what was going on back there. Had more survivors been found and allowed to come inside the walls? And what about these so-called zombie "shock troops" that Natasha mentioned.? There had been no mention or discussion of such a thing. Whose idea had it been? How had they implemented it so fast?

"I think he's telling the truth," another voice offered up. I glanced over to see a man dressed in a combination of leather, heavy denim, football shoulder pads and several bits of equipment that you would find on a baseball catcher.

Don let go of me and was right in the face of this person before I could blink an eye. "And what gives you such incredible insight to human nature?"

To his credit, the man didn't bat an eye as he flipped up the grill that was covering his face. "Not that it makes me an absolute expert on the subject, but I was a cop for one. I have had a bit of experience reading people. I was watching his face as you were relating what happened and he was absolutely surprised."

Don stepped back from the man and returned his attention to me. I saw his eyes flick to Natasha with what I almost believed might be suspicion. Maybe there was a fracture here that I could use to my advantage. Of course, at the moment, I didn't have any idea how to even begin to go about that, but I could at least add it to the list of things to ponder if I was shoved back into that dark room.

"Get him fitted for a collar and assemble the group that was supposed to take our newbie here out on his first foraging run," Don announced. "Natasha, I want you cleaned up and with them as well. You guys are going back to this stronghold with Evan. He will be the one to broker the surrender of his friends or they can watch as we feed his miserable ass to the undead."

I felt a hand grab me by the arm and I was surprised to see that it was the supposedly former policeman who had me just above the elbow. He pulled me down the corridor to another one of the empty classrooms, stopped long enough to open the door, and then shoved me inside.

"You wanna get yourself and your little girlfriend killed, you just keep screwing with Donnie," the man snarled as he turned on a small battery-powered lantern to reveal a room that had several heavy collars hanging on the walls. Each had a coil of what appeared to be nylon boating line attached to them.

"Is it true that you used to be a cop?" I asked as the man reached up and grabbed one of the collars.

When he turned to face me, I took the time to really look at this guy. He did sort of look like a cop. His haircut was of the high-and-tight style, but I could tell that he had dark hair that was changing over to gray as those lighter hairs glinted in the light cast by the lantern. He had hard eyes that looked at me with equal parts distrust and disdain. They looked to be a dark brown and a bit squinty which made the wrinkles around the edges of them seem that much deeper. I guessed him to be right around six feet tall and maybe a shade over two hundred pounds making up his muscular frame.

"You don't get to ask questions, newbie," the man said as he nodded at his choice of collars and then turned back to face me.

"So, I get to wear a collar and be treated like an animal. Is that what you guys do with every new arrival?" I asked as the leather strap was fastened around my neck.

"No, most of the people we've found so far have not made it past the indoctrination process," he answered flatly as he clipped something in place with an audible click.

"And you're okay with all this?"

"You don't have any idea what you're talking about, kid," the cop said as he grabbed one of the coils of nylon line and attached it to my collar.

"Is that right? You think I am missing some part of the bigger picture? Well then, why don't you fill in the gaps."

"That's not my job," the man said as he stepped back and gave me a look up and down. "And this conversation is over. Here's how things are gonna work. You are going out into the local neighborhood just a couple of blocks away. We have been collecting resources from the area, but with it looking like we will be moving to someplace more permanent, we want to grab a few select items that will make the trip easier. On our way to your friends' place, we will be stopping in a few of the homes and marking them if they have anything worth grabbing on the way back."

"So I will have some sort of shopping list?"

"In a manner of speaking." The man stepped closer to me and I seriously doubted that you could slide a piece of paper between us at the moment. I was about to step back and try to reestablish some of my own personal space when he grabbed me by the arm again. "You need to keep your mouth shut and refrain from making any statements that question what Don has going on here. If you want to have any chance of surviving, you will fall in and do what you're told without question."

"And you're okay with what is happening?" I challenged.

I saw something flash behind the man's eyes for just a moment. It was just a fleeting shadow, but his hard façade had cracked for a split second. I was certain of that much.

"There is a new rule book being written. If you are trying to live, you are going to have to adapt."

With that, he jerked the door open and shoved me back out into the hallway. Apparently, the conversation was over. I staggered forward and then skidded to a stop.

"What the hell," I yelped.

"You say that you just met this person, but something tells

me that you are either lying, or that you are the sort of person who forms quick attachments." Don leered at me over Ariel's shoulder. Her arms were lashed behind her back and she had a gag tied tightly around her head that looked like it might be cutting into the corners of her mouth. She was crying, and tears ran down her cheeks, carving tracks in the dirt and grime.

"What are you going to do to her?" I demanded.

"Nothing, as long as you come back from your little run with my team. I don't buy anything you've told us. I think you sent my people into a trap, and now I imagine that you've been churning things over in your mind as to how you might be able to slip away from my team instead of doing your part and contributing to the community." Don jerked back on Ariel's hair, causing her to let out a muffled cry around the gag. "So, we will take your little friend here down to the basement. She will be waiting for your return, but if you should somehow not make it back for whatever reason, then we allow some of the current residents we have staying down in that basement to come out of their rooms and pay your friend here a visit."

"You're keeping zombies in the basement?" I blurted.

"Well we sure as hell don't want them up here with us," Don snorted.

I opened my mouth and felt a nudge in the middle of my back. I shut my mouth and then locked eyes with Ariel.

"I will be back. Don't you worry about that at all." I saw her give a shudder that might've also been a nod. Then I returned my attention to Don. "What if something happens to me out there and I get torn apart or something? Hardly seems fair to kill her if I die trying to help."

"If you die, what do you care? You'll be dead." With that, Don yanked Ariel around and shoved her up the corridor, around a corner, and out of sight.

I spun on the man who now held the end of my leash. "And you're okay with this?" I asked again. "What the hell sort of cop were you?"

"Just shut up, do what you're told, and everything will be fine." He gave me a nod, indicating that I needed to start moving. "This is a milk run. We've been to this neighborhood a dozen times or more. Haven't lost a soul since the third or fourth time. And if these friends of yours care about you at all, they will come out when we arrive and just surrender. Easy-peasy, lemon squeasy."

I headed up the hallway, my mind churning over any way that I could take these people down, get Ariel out of here alive, grab the stuff for my dog, and then go someplace to die in peace. It didn't take me long to realize that I had zero chance of accomplishing all these goals.

As I walked outside into the cool air of the late afternoon, I sent an unspoken apology to Ariel. If the chance to get away from these lunatics presented itself, I would absolutely take it. I was pretty sure that meant I was now officially going to Hell. I could perhaps soothe my conscience about it later by reminding myself that she'd put a gun in my face right after I'd saved her ass. Somehow, I didn't give myself much of a shot at convincing myself of that lie.

Now that I was outside what had once been a massive church, I could see the measures that Don and his people had put in place. Besides the wall of corpses out on the road, they'd parked a few dozen school busses end to end around the perimeter of the parking lot. Also, the street on one side was jammed with cars. The thing is, it looked like they'd been on their way here. There were a few fender benders in the mix and the driveway entries were a disaster. In a few of the vehicles, I could see movement.

It took about five minutes, but eventually, it seemed that the team was assembled. Including Natasha and the former cop, five more followers of the megalomaniacal Don Evans joined us. I was surprised when two more people on leashes were brought out to be part of this as well. Natasha was the last to arrive and she had three wire cage-like boxes containing what looked like, of all things, some sort of MP3 player. I was confused as to what they were for until one was attached to each of the collars of those of us with leashes.

"Here is how it works," the woman said, a nasty edge to her

voice that intensified when her eyes stopped on me. She produced a small device and held it out. There were four green indicator lights showing. "If you try to run, I will simply activate the devices that each of you is wearing. Any zombie for miles around will hear them."

To make her point, she pressed a button on the small device that I had already assumed to be the remote activator. It was confirmed a moment later when music blared from each of the cages. The unholy aural onslaught of Britney Spears, Josh Grobin, and Barry Manilow erupted at volumes none of those musical artists should ever be played. I had what I considered the worst of the draws as an overly processed voice begged me to "Hit me baby one more time…"

A few seconds of the torture was enough to make the point and Natasha shut them off. The silence flooded back like the tide, and seconds later was shattered again by moans of the undead coming from several locations.

"It has been observed that the zombies are attracted to sound. If you try to escape, then I will activate the devices. And I should probably share here and now that we don't have it figured out yet so that each of the MP3 players has its own remote. The one I have is paired to all three, so, if one of you makes a run for it…you basically condemn the others." Natasha smiled that evil shark smile of hers again like she'd just sighted an injured seal and was moving in for the kill. "Each of the buckles closes a circuit that is displayed here as being intact by these little green lights. Any attempt to unfasten the device will open the circuit and the light changes to red."

I felt the stain on my conscience already starting to grow. My escape was now condemning three living, breathing human beings to a terrible death.

"Let's get moving," the former cop said, giving me a shove.

Our group headed down the side of the church. There were a variety of well-manicured bushes that were evenly spaced in the strip that ran between the building and the sidewalk, but I noticed that a few of them had been scorched pretty bad and were already starting to wilt.

We reached the end of the building and I discovered what was the likely culprit. There was a burn pile with more than a few skulls and charred bone. Currently, a trio of zombie children had been torched to the point that the bodies were almost totally blackened. Their various limbs were stiff and jutting from the bodies at odd angles as they continued to smolder.

"I thought those bodies were supposed to be disposed of," the former cop groused as we reached a brick wall that was just a little bit taller than waist-high.

"How about you just grab them and toss them over the wall before we leave, Arlo?" Natasha said as she threw one leg over the brick wall.

A few of the other members of the group made poor attempts at hiding their smirks and chuckles. I saw the former cop's face flush just a little. He locked eyes with Natasha as he picked up one of the two small bodies. I heard it make crackling noises as he handled it, and then tossed it over the brick wall just a few feet away from where Natasha was now straddling it. The sound it made when it hit the ground almost made me want to be sick.

"That's right," Arlo said as he grabbed the second body, "your little pet Tommy was tasked to do the job." Now it was Natasha's turn to have her face flush. "Wasn't he with your task force earlier today? I guess he probably won't be able to do his job now."

In a flash, the woman was in the much larger man's face, but it didn't seem that she cared a whit that he had so much of a size advantage. The knife that appeared out of nowhere in her hand and up to his throat with a flash might've had something to do with it.

"Casualties happen out here in the shit," she snarled, reaching up on her tiptoes to get as close to in his face as she could manage. "You not making it back wouldn't be that big of a deal to anybody."

"Save your threats for somebody who gives a crap, Natasha," Arlo said with a degree of coolness that I would not have been able to manage considering the situation.

I took the time and momentary distraction to get a better look at my fellow shackle-mates. Their reactions were a range of fear and astonishment. For the most part, they just seemed like cattle being led to the slaughter. Of course, they had no idea that I would be the reason for their demise.

I felt a trickle of guilt try to seep into my conscience again and I shoved it aside. There was no place for such things right now. I was going to do what I needed to do in order to finish what I considered my final mission. My only allegiance was to my dog, Chewie. After that, I felt a certain degree of camaraderie with Carl, Betty, and the kids. I had to keep reminding myself that we'd just added another member to our ranks right before I left. Also, if the reports could be believed, perhaps they'd bolstered their numbers even more in my brief absence.

"Get moving," a voice barked as a hand shoved me forward.

We headed into the adjacent neighborhood and my eyes paused for just a moment on a wreck that I managed to get a glimpse of through a perfect degree of open yards and our current angle of the main road. The upside-down Jeep Cherokee in the distance made my stomach tighten at the memory of what had happened.

We turned right and ventured into the neighborhood. I was given a list of items that I was made to recite back to Arlo, and then my leash was unclipped.

"You have exactly five minutes," Arlo warned. "That might seem like an eternity, but I assure you that it isn't." He hung a stopwatch around my neck and held up a similar one. "I am going to give you a countdown. We will both activate our stopwatches at the same time so that there is no excuse. If you are even a second late, Natasha pushes the button on her remote."

I glanced back at the house I'd been tasked to search. My eyes did their best not to drift to what waited beyond. I saw no reason to waste a moment. I would go in and shoot right out the back door. There was a wooded field beyond that I should be able to duck into and stay out of sight long enough to give myself a good head start.

"And just in case you are thinking of doing something stupid," Arlo's voice cut into my scheming with an edge that caused my head to whip around to him, "that same green light that signals the connection is intact will also turn red if you just happen to *accidentally* start drifting out of range of her remote receiver. If that red light comes on, she will activate your MP3 player as a warning. Since we can easily hear where the sound is coming from, she will know whether or not you are just becoming difficult to keep a fix on, or if you are indeed slipping from her range. If it is the latter, the device will remain active."

"And what will you guys do about the zombies coming down on you?" I challenged. "It isn't like they will just ignore you guys and go just for those of us with your little collars on."

"We return to the safety of our base. Anybody who tries to climb the wall wearing an active noisemaker will be shot in the knee or some equally disabling location."

"Not just killed outright?" I couldn't help but shake my head at this display of inhumanity. They were going to ensure that their captives were set upon by the undead.

"Once the zombies have done what is needed, we retrieve the bodies before they reanimate. They are taken to the basement."

My mind flashed on Ariel being led away. Don had warned me that she would be taken to the basement where she would be kept until my return. I was not dumb to the reality that I was sacrificing three human lives in order to hopefully resume my quest for Chewie.

"Time to go," Arlo said.

I glanced around and saw my fellow captives obviously just finishing up with getting the same general spiel. I wondered briefly if any of the other two had the same thoughts as me. Perhaps for different reasons, but maybe they were also contemplating the idea of making a break for it.

"On my mark…three…two…one…go!"

I turned and sprinted for the house I'd been assigned. I had no weapon and no way of really knowing if it was empty. I also had no intention of staying long enough to really find out.

The Guilt of an Executioner

I reached the front door and only paused long enough to take a big sniff. Despite the likelihood that these houses had been at least given a cursory search, I would not trust these people as far as I could throw their collective asses.

I tried the door and was only marginally surprised when I discovered that it was unlocked. I pushed it open and sniffed again. The stink of decay hit me hard, but nothing indicated that the walking dead were present.

I made it up the hallway when I almost tripped over the first corpse. The man had most of his head blown off. All that remained was a beard that was stiff with dried gore. I hopped over it and my eyes went to the sliding glass door. It opened out to a backyard that was just starting to show signs of the slowly approaching spring. The grass was starting to grow and the stalks of a few dandelions could be seen holding court over the emerald landscape. The trees had tiny buds displaying the faintest hint of light green, and one rose bush was already sporting a few small nodes that would open to a world that could care less.

I could hear my own voice as I'd recited the items I was tasked to locate and identify for the scavenger teams: blankets, sleeping bags, personal hygiene items. I was admittedly impressed by their approach. Instead of just ransacking the houses

125

without rhyme or reason, they were making a systematic assault on the supplies. I had to imagine that it made cataloging what they brought in an easier task. I had no doubt that they were keeping close tabs on everything. Don didn't strike me as the sort that left things open for the masses to consume as they wished.

I reached the back door and paused. Once I walked through it and made my way to that fence, I was sealing not just my fate, but that of three other people. It seemed so easy as the scheme unfolded in my head, but now that I was about to commit the act, I was having trouble silencing my conscience.

Why not just wait until we reach the house? a voice that I dubbed 'Reason' asked inside my mind.

You think leading these people to the doorsteps of Carl and the others doesn't end with you being killed by either side? the voice that I dubbed 'Pragmatic' shot back.

That was the hard reality of it. I had to figure that Carl would do whatever he needed to do in order to protect those living behind the walls with him. He would know my condition, and so he might even consider it a mercy to put a bullet in my head before things even managed to reach the negotiations stage.

My hand gripped the handle of the door and I made a hasty apology to the cosmos and the soon-to-be-departing souls of the people that my actions would condemn. I tugged at the door and cursed when it didn't open. I looked down, found the lever, and unlocked it with an exasperated sigh.

My hands went to my collar. I would need to find something to cut that off my neck as soon as I could manage. I would be on the run, and I would be drawing the attention of everything living and undead for hundreds of yards in every direction until I could ditch it.

The next moment, I was sprinting across the yard with all the ability I had. The first surprise was how tired my legs were. It was too late to consider it now, but I hadn't eaten in a while. The body does not hold an infinite supply of energy—another fact that I think is often ignored in most zombie stories.

"*...oh, bay-bah, bay-bah...*" The MP3 player erupted in

sound. No matter how hard I tried, my brain would not equate this noise with music.

I reached the rear fence as the sounds of voices shouting from the street in front of the houses the three of us captives had been sent into began in earnest. There was a shout, and then gunfire erupted along with a scream that I was willing to bet came from one of the other MP3 wearers. I landed on the other side of the fence and took off across the field in the direction of the grove of trees ahead of me.

The field that I was crossing was anything but even, and twice, before I'd made it halfway across, I almost sprained my ankle. Once, I did end up sprawling on my belly with a painful thud.

As I reached the trees, I could hear the shouts behind me growing more angry than surprised. I risked a look over my shoulder just before I vanished from any eyes that might still be tracking me. I could not help but being astonished when I saw no sign of Arlo, Natasha, or the rest of the team. I was even more amazed when I spied one of my fellow captives running for all he was worth across the same field I'd just crossed. I was glad that this person decided that he had nothing to lose and had chosen to at least make the attempt to survive.

My relief was short-lived when I saw the person veering my direction with some sort of weapon in one hand. I didn't know if it was a baton or a long and slender blade, but I had no doubt that this individual was coming after me. Whether to join me or take me down, I had no idea. I wasn't in the mood to wait and see as I also heard the first of the moans of the undead coming from somewhere in front and to my right.

I was surprised that I could hear anything with this hellish pop music blaring from just under my chin. It wasn't at ear-splitting levels, but it was well beyond plenty loud enough to grate on my nerves in addition to alerting zombies of my presence.

I was bounding through the knee-high grasses and dodging downed tree limbs, partially hidden trunks, and a variety of vines, as well as the odd clump of blackberry bushes. More than once I was able to just barely keep myself from falling again.

As I got deeper into the woods, I spied a few dark figures drifting in and out of the shadows of all the lush pine trees. I kept getting hints of the stink of undeath as I pushed on.

When I emerged from the relatively shallow wooded lot— much shallower than I would have liked when it came down to it—I saw another row of houses all with fences marking their backyard borders. I also saw something else, something that took a few seconds to comprehend and truly appreciate what it meant to my situation.

The little creek cut through the grassy field that bordered this side of the small wooded area. I was already determining if I could jump it cleanly when another idea struck. It wasn't going to be pleasant, but it was the solution to at least one of my problems.

The closer I got to the ribbon of water, the more I dreaded what I needed to do. The water, despite having a current that I could see in the forms of ripples and eddies, looked absolutely foul. I saw sludge drifting on the surface in places as well as beginning to be able to smell it and all the decaying whatever that made the muck give off its own pungent funk. At least it was a smell I was slightly familiar with having grown up just down the road from a cow pasture.

Without hesitation, I did a belly flop into the water. Pressing my lips together tightly kept the fetid liquid out of my mouth, but that did nothing to prevent it from managing to make its way up my nostrils. I almost gagged on the bitter fluid as it oozed down the back of my throat, but, as I made my way to my knees, I was at least thankful that I hadn't gone into that water with my mouth open. Small victories.

The MP3 player had gone silent. Obviously, it was not of the waterproof variety. I could worry later about removing the collar, as well as the wire mesh cage hooked to it, off me. For now, I would allow myself to be thankful for this tiny stroke of luck as well as the presence of mind that I'd displayed in sabotaging the noisemaker. It was also a huge blessing that I no longer had to endure Britney's caterwauling.

Getting to my feet, I could now see a few dozen of the walking dead emerging from the woods at my back. What I didn't see was my pursuer. I had just taken a few involuntary steps back the way I'd just come when I heard *the* scream.

"Sorry, man," I whispered as I turned and ran for the fence line.

I reached it, struggled my way over, and prepared to vault when my brain caught up to what my eyes were seeing. This particular backyard was a diorama of horrors with at least four dogs and as many children. Additionally, there was a lone adult. All of them were zombified, and the dogs were limping along with the adult in my direction. One of the dogs was already at the fence, and had it been a larger breed, might've been able to grab the cuff of my jeans by the time I recovered, reacted, and withdrew.

I landed back on the ground, but my mind was still filling in the picture I'd just seen. The children had been huddled on the back porch and they'd made no effort to move towards me.

"Creepy-ass zombie kids," I wheezed as I reached the next yard and hauled myself up enough so that I could see into it. The yard was blessedly empty, and I double-checked before throwing my leg over and then dropping down into it.

I heard a pounding sound and located a female zombie on the second floor of this house. She was slapping at a window and doing a great job of coating it from the inside with a vile slime that was dark enough that I doubted very seriously that she would be able to see anything from that vantage point before too long if she kept up her assault.

I cut across the yard and exited to discover a street that looked like a war zone. There were bodies sprawled in the road and in yards. A few of the homes had at least partially burned up, and one of them had a car jutting from where I imagine a large living room window once existed.

I spied a car that had run up on a curb. It was missing the driver's side door, but the driver was still very present and squirming in the front seat, unable to escape the safety harness that held her in place. Other than being up on the curb, having the airbag in the steering wheel deployed, and missing a door, the vehicle looked fine. It was close enough, and at a good angle that allowed me to see keys dangling from the ignition.

"It's worth a shot," I whispered as I hurried to it.

As soon as I did, I became committed to my objective. Zombies were emerging from numerous yards and open doors. It was almost as if my noisemaker was still active. If I had a weapon, the situation would still be dire. Without one...it was beyond horrifying.

I reached the car and took a second to figure out how I could undo the seatbelt without the zombie woman being able to grab hold of me. As soon as the clasp came free, the zombie's struggles sent her tumbling from the car. There was a sickening squelchy noise as the belt apparently ripped free from where the dried blood had welded the fabric to the skin.

Before it could recover, I moved in and stomped hard on the back of its head. It was nowhere near as easy to do in real life as it appeared in movies and video games. At last, the female zombie ceased its struggles. In the time it took me to do all this, several of the zombies had begun to stir with my arrival and homed in on their potential prey...me.

I dreaded climbing into the filthy seat, but now was no time to be squeamish. I hopped in, ignoring the crunchy noises. Holding my breath, I gave the key a twist and almost cried with relief when the engine turned over right away.

I had to back up, and as I did, I glanced in the rearview mirror. A pair of zombies had come up and were just about to the bumper of the older model Buick. If I had to guess, I would say it was an early Eighties' model, which made it pretty close to a tank.

I felt the frame of the vehicle give a shudder as I hit, knocked over, then rolled on top of the pair of zombies that had stumbled into my path. With no door, I could hear the snapping and cracking as bones were crushed. There was a loud, wet popping noise just before I shifted into drive and cranked the wheel around. My eyes lit on an insignia on the dash.

"Never heard of a Buick Electra," I mused as I came around

and started up the street, doing my best to avoid as many of the approaching zombies as they came at me with arms out and no fear of being hit by this vehicle. The ones that I couldn't avoid, I tried to simply catch with as little of the nose of my car as possible.

I passed one yard and felt the hairs on my arms and the back of my neck start to prickle. A pair of zombies stood in the middle of a small rose garden. The boy looked to be around ten or so and the girl maybe four or five. The pair were actually holding hands! To add to the surreal scene, a German Sheppard edged past them, doing its best to join the rest of the standard zombies as they shambled towards or after me. The entire rear of the dog was dragging along on the ground and I could see that both of its back legs were practically gone.

If all that wasn't bad enough, a pair of calico cats wove in between the legs of the zombie children. The kids didn't seem to notice, and if they did, they were showing no interest in attacking the pair of felines.

"What the hell is going on?" I gasped.

There was too much that I could not explain, and my mind was reeling with questions that I could not even form properly, much less try to figure out a way to get at the answers. I now had one purpose. I did not care how, but I was going to do what I'd set out to do.

Glancing in the rearview mirror, I could not believe that my eyes still showed no sign of my being infected. It had to be that scratches took longer. That was the only possibility...unless...

"Don't even let your mind start down that road," I cautioned myself as I made a right turn just before a three-car crash involving a pickup, a minivan, and an ambulance. All of them had zombies writhing in the front seats.

As I got all the way beyond the accident, I could see the rear of the ambulance was open. There was a body strapped to a gurney. The blood of that poor unfortunate soul had dried long ago after spraying the interior of the ambulance's cargo area. I caught a hint of movement and was not surprised when the head rose and the zombie on that gurney moaned its frustration.

"There could be a strong case made for this being Hell," I muttered as I sped along this street that cut through a decimated residential neighborhood.

I began to scan the streets as I drove. There had to be something familiar sooner or later. Also, I was fairly confident that Sunnyside Road was to my right. If I could get to it, I was certain that I could find my way back to that veterinary hospital. While I had taken a hefty amount of supplies, I'd by no means emptied the place.

Of course that would mean circling back and past the church where Don Evans and his band of followers were no doubt already hearing of my escape. As that single thought flickered in the back of my mind, I felt the searing sting of guilt as it sliced into my conscience. The report of my escape (whether they believed me dead or not at this point did not matter) would mean that Ariel would be given to the zombies held in the basement.

"I'm sorry," I whispered, feeling my throat close up around the words.

The outline of a large campus loomed ahead and I hoped to use this to get a better idea of where I was driving. Once again I was struck by how the stories never seemed to have its characters get lost. While I was a native son of Portland, Oregon, that by no means meant that I had a grasp on the entire city. There were many places that I had never been.

The sign on the reader board read: Clackamas High School. I knew *of* the school, but I don't believe that I'd ever actually been there. I drove past the collection of buildings. The football stadium looked like perhaps some effort had been made to secure it. Signs of a nasty battle remained as a testament to the failure of that attempt.

I was also noticing that the undead were starting to become a bigger problem. I needed to get out of this once heavily populated suburban neighborhood. I hooked to the right at the next opportunity and found myself on Southeast 122nd Avenue. If my memory served me correctly, the veterinary hospital was in the hundred and sixty something range as far as streets were concerned. Don's church stronghold was in the one-forties.

The Guilt of an Executioner

Something so simple just a few weeks ago was now potentially an epic adventure worthy of a Grecian odyssey. I wish I had the time to write it all down.

If this zombie thing ever eventually resolved itself somehow in the favor of humanity, it would make one hell of a story, I mused inwardly. The only problem I had was that I was becoming less and less of a hero with my actions. I'd willingly condemned three people to death so I could try to get supplies for a dog.

Was Don correct? Not about the whole race thing, but about how our culture had allowed meaningless stuff to take up too much room in our lives. When had the life of a dog, or any family pet for that matter, become more valuable than another human life?

I had to force down the sick feeling that grew inside me with exponential force as each second...each heartbeat that I pondered what I'd truly done began to manifest itself in my soul.

I was trying to deal with my guilt when a green road sign hanging from the defunct power line just to the side of a now useless traffic signal got my attention. I'd found Sunnyside Road. My destination was to my right. Almost smack in the middle was Don Evans and his band of racial zealots.

I decided that I would follow this street for a ways and then circle back to the veterinary hospital. After all, it wasn't like I had anything else to do. I wished that I knew where another one might be, but having lost all my stuff, I was sort of stuck. If I did happen across one, I would happily give it a try, but at this point, I was sort of limited unless I wanted to venture into the Southeast Portland neighborhood that I was more familiar with. Considering what I was encountering out here in the suburbs, I did not think that was a good choice.

As I drove, it allowed me to distract myself from my guilt while I took in more of the extent of the damage that had been done to the city and its surrounding neighborhoods.

The first thing I noticed was that, while I still caught glimpses of zombies here and there, I could now drive for good distance without seeing a single one. Also, there was a lot of loose garbage blowing around. I passed by houses that looked perfectly fine, then I would pass a few that had caught fire and been allowed to burn themselves out. I even passed a few that still smoldered.

I caught glimpses of hastily made signs that hung like so many useless banners. All of them making the same basic plea.

"HELP!"

Help had not made an appearance, and now those people were likely part of the shambling masses. I slowed once when I thought I heard actual shouts for help, but after idling for what seemed an eternity but had been less than a minute, I continued on my way.

The road made a bit of a dogleg to the right and I had to figure that it was bringing me closer to my goal. I'd passed a few side streets, but they all turned into little communities with brick or rock walls at their entrances with names like "Willow Creek", "Eagle Glen" and "Vista Woods".

The next road sign that I passed told me that this street had somehow become Southeast 129th Avenue. I was coming up on yet another junction and entrance to a subdivision when a figure erupted from the dense foliage and stumbled out onto the road. The figure tripped, rolled twice and landed on its back. I started to swerve, almost ready to write it off as just another zombie when it went from being flat on its back to vaulting to its feet like something out of a Bruce Lee movie.

My brain was screaming for me to step on the gas, but old habits and reflexes made me stomp on the brakes instead. The Buick squealed to a stop just about five yards short of the heavily garbed individual. There was something strangely familiar about this person.

The figure flipped up its visor on the riot helmet. "Evan? Evan, is that you?" the person asked, then cast a glance to her left, back the way she'd come before sprinting to me.

"Miranda?" I wasn't trusting my memory to be certain that I had her name correct. It didn't seem to matter as she reached the passenger side door and gave it a tug.

"Please let me in," the woman said with a strained urgency

to her voice.

I leaned over and flipped up the door lock. She wasted no time folding herself into the car and turning to me with what seemed to be fear in her eyes. With that helmet a bit too small, it was impossible to be absolutely certain, but her voice was more than making up for her smooshed facial features.

"Go! Go! Go!" she urged. "Get us the hell out of here now."

I stomped on the gas and the Buick lurched forward. We were headed up a gradual incline and a bend in the road was perhaps a quarter of a mile ahead. We covered over half the distance when I saw three figures come running out onto the road back by where I'd just picked up Miranda or whatever her name was.

I was still watching them in the rearview mirror when I saw a flash. A heartbeat later, the rear window of the car exploded inward.

"Holy crap, they're shooting at us," I yelped.

"Nothing gets past you," the woman quipped.

I shot her a look. She was leaning back in her seat like nothing was wrong. I had no idea how she had suddenly become calm to the point of glib after being so frantic just seconds ago.

"You wanna tell me what that was about?" I asked as we rocketed through a set of S-curves that had me using most of both lanes as I drove well in excess of the posted twenty-five miles-per-hour limit declared on the sign we shot past.

"Pretty much why I declined your earlier offer," she said cryptically.

I eased up on the gas and allowed the car to slow to a more reasonable speed. I kept shooting a glance at the rearview mirror, but there was no sign that we were being pursued by anything more than the occasional zombie that stumbled out into the street in our wake as the car continued to be the only real noise source in the area.

When I wasn't actively looking behind us, I kept stealing glances at the woman in the passenger seat out of the corner of my eye. After all, the last one I'd rescued had pulled a gun on me. Of course, if this one did anything like that, something told me I would not fare as well if I tried to disarm her. She didn't strike me as the type to hesitate in pulling the trigger. Nor would she be aiming an empty weapon.

"I was taking a break in a house that I'd cleared out. They had food and water actually stacked by the front door like they'd been loading out when one of them obviously turned and did in the others." She paused and I saw her shake her head like she was trying to clear it of a bad memory. "There was a kid…"

That statement hung in the air. Her calm demeanor was crumbling and being replaced by sadness, and uncertainty. I looked over and saw a single tear overwhelm the grime on her face as it sliced its way down her cheek.

"At first I thought it had managed to survive. Maybe all that dried blood was masking him. It was a stupid idea, but it was the only thing that made sense as to why he just sat on the floor and stared at me when I opened the door to his room."

Again Miranda paused, but I wasn't going to interrupt now. She obviously needed to get this out of her system. Once she was done, maybe then I would share some of what I'd seen.

"Then one of those things came crawling out from under the bed. It looked like the older brother, but I knew it for what it was and pulled my blade to end it before it could get me or that boy who was still just sitting on the floor, watching me, holding a toy truck in his hands like maybe I'd walked in while he was play-ing." She took a deep breath and sniffed. "As soon as I drew my weapon, that kid on the floor came at me just like any other zombie. That was when I really took notice of him. I had some-how ignored his eyes. They told me what his actions didn't. I drove my blade into one of those glazed orbs and he dropped. But right before he did, he made that damn baby cry sound. I know what he was, but that whole scene just seemed so wrong. Then I killed his brother."

She finished that narrative and then took a deep breath like a huge boulder had just been rolled off her chest. I continued to drive in silence, and when I looked down, I was surprised to dis-cover that I'd slowed to just over ten miles per hour.

"I cleared out a room, brought up some of the food and water, and then had probably the best meal I'd had in days." She laughed at this bit. "I don't think I'd eaten food out of a can in years before all this madness. Now I actually get excited when I come across canned food. Soup is like gold." She shook her head again. "Anyway, I fell asleep after eating. I woke when I heard somebody moving around downstairs. I tried to slip out the window. It was fine until the damn gutter tore free and I landed on my ass."

"And they just came after you?" I blurted. It wasn't that I was shocked at the behavior exhibited by some of the men lurking about, but it just seemed more widespread than I would've imagined.

"Yeah, that's exactly what I'm saying. And one of them was making it very clear what they planned to do with me once they caught me."

Had we really spiraled to these depths so fast? It seemed so unlikely, but what I was seeing with my own eyes was telling me otherwise.

"So how did you come about having a car? And what happened to your door?" she asked. She cocked her head and gave me a strange look. "And can you please tell me what in God's name it is that you have around your neck?"

I was about to give her my story, but my eyes locked on something and I brought the car to a stop. Miranda started to protest until her eyes followed mine.

We'd reached a tee intersection. We sat at the junction of Southeast 122nd Avenue and Southeast King Road. I knew that I was probably not too far from some familiar territory, but that wasn't what had me stopped. Sitting side-by-side was a Happy Valley Firehouse and police headquarters. I wasn't thrilled or impressed by the firehouse, but my mind was racing with the potential of what we might find inside the police building.

I turned right and then let the Buick creep along the front of the building. There were a few zombies in the area, and all of them were turning towards us. That wasn't great, but I was willing to bet that I would find some good stuff inside if it hadn't already been ransacked.

"What exactly do you think you're doing?" Miranda asked as I pulled into the parking lot beside the big, white police station.

"You were mentioning how you now saw canned goods as gold," I said, turning to her with a smile. "Can you even imagine what might be inside there? If it hasn't been hit," I gave the exterior of the building a glance, "and it doesn't look like it has been. I am willing to bet there is an arsenal inside that place."

"Are you actually suggesting that we walk into the police station and just take whatever weapons we see lying around?" Miranda asked, her voice dripping with doubt and skepticism.

"No," I corrected. "I'm saying that we should go in there, find their weapons locker and take whatever we can get our hands on." I paused to let the subtle differences in our statements sink in. "If we just grab what is lying about, we may only come away with a pistol or two. If we can locate their locker, I am willing to bet we find not only more firepower than we know what to do with, but also some body armor..." I pointed to the helmet that had her head in its vice-like grip. "Maybe even a helmet that fits."

She seemed to ponder things for a moment before giving a slow nod. "That might not be the worst idea. And while we are there, perhaps we can locate the keys to a car with all its doors intact."

I drove up to the entrance of the building, cutting across the manicured lawn to actually pull up right in front of the main entrance. To our right was an open expanse of field that gave us a clear view of anything coming from that way. To the left was the firehouse with an equally large and open field beyond it. Our only blind spot was right across the street—basically at our backs. That was an area that was tree-lined with houses at regular intervals and a turn-in to yet another neighborhood. Currently, there was absolutely nothing moving, at least as far as we could see.

I climbed out of the car and waited for Miranda to join me at the base of the steps that led up to the front door of this tiny little police station. I shot a look down the length of the building and saw that the parking lot was almost totally empty. I counted five cars scattered about with none of them parked next to the other.

"If there is anybody inside, and we can use that as an indicator…" I pointed to the cars, "…then we might have five zombies tops to deal with once we get inside."

"And you plan on using your wit and charm to render them defenseless?" Miranda snorted.

At first I was puzzled. It took me a second to remember that I wasn't carrying any sort of weapon. I opened my mouth to say something when she laughed and unsnapped a leather strap on her belt. She drew a knife that would've impressed the hell out of Carl. The blade was almost the length of my forearm.

"Before we go in there, let me get whatever that thing is off of you."

"Did you have all this stuff just lying around your house?" I said as she made short work of the collar, demonstrating the knife's razor sharpness when it cut through the strap with ease.

She stepped back and held out the blade to me. I accepted the weapon with a bit of awed reverence. Just looking at the blade was almost enough to cut me. I was willing to bet I could shave this scraggly beard that was starting to itch if there ever came a time when I did not have my mind occupied with a million other things.

"Not all of it," Miranda said with a wink as she stepped up to the door and peered inside. "And you may want to have that knife ready."

Before I could draw a blade, she grabbed the door and yanked it open. Fighting back the urge to gag on the thick stench that rolled out at us, I moved past her and met the first figure that was just stepping out into the narrow hallway from a room to the left of the doors. When his arms came up and he reached for me, I almost felt sorry for the guy.

I slapped away his cuffed hands and then stuck the knife into his eye. The ease in which it slid in and came back out was not lost on me, but I didn't have time to marvel as three more of the walking dead emerged from the room at the far end of the hallway.

Once more, I was going to take on zombies that were cuffed. I hadn't taken this possibility into account when I'd counted the cars in the parking lot. When four more came on the heels of the other three, I heard Miranda curse under her breath.

"Maybe we should take a pass on this place," I suggested as I wavered between advancing on the zombies or retreating back out the door.

"Are you nuts?" Miranda scoffed as she stepped over the first zombie I'd dropped and promptly ducked into the room that he'd just exited.

I didn't have time to ask her what exactly she was doing, since it was obvious that she wasn't helping me. If she was going to commit to this, then I guess I was going to do so as well. I started up the hall and had not gotten three steps when Miranda yelled at me to get back. I turned to see her emerging from the doorway she just vanished through. In her hands she had a black, pump-action shotgun.

I rushed back as she advanced, bringing the weapon up to her shoulder. She closed the distance, passing me to get to within the most lethal range of the weapon. I actually dropped the knife in my effort to try and cover my ears before she pulled the trigger. I was perhaps a second or two late as the loud boom of the weapon sounded and caused my ears to instantly begin ringing. I didn't even hear the knife as it clattered onto the floor.

She adjusted her position and aim a few more times, firing for maximum effect and practically blowing entire heads off. The walls beyond her kill zone were now gooped with brain, bone, and dark fluid that ran with the consistency of maple syrup.

When the last zombie fell, I counted nine bodies. Only one ended up being a police officer. It also looked like he might be the one who brought the infection inside. He was the one who was the most gore-covered out of the bunch. He was also the only one of the bunch that Miranda took the time to walk up to and stick in the temple with one of her numerous blades.

The smell of spent gunpowder and zombie stench finally won out and I had to stagger back to the front door, throw it open, and then heave over the railing that bordered the porch. When I walked back in, I had to wade past the carnage to the main room in back where I found Miranda. I discovered her in a small room just off what I had to assume was the booking area. It was sort of difficult to tell, but all the busted furniture looked like it had once been a series of desks and chairs. Of course, now it was splintered wood and bits of metal.

"In here," Miranda called shining her flashlight out the doorway towards me and hitting me in the eyes with the beam.

I joined her, and when I reached the open doorway, I could only whistle in appreciation. There were two open lockers that were totally empty, but the third one held our prize.

"The keys were on the floor right in front of this closet," Miranda explained. "When I opened the door, I thought we'd come in here for nothing, but then I looked past the second open locker door and discovered the third locker was still shut."

As her flashlight scanned over the contents, I spotted shot-guns, a few rifles, a half a dozen handguns, one of those handheld door busters, and a tear gas launcher. I was about to ask the million-dollar question when I heard something scuff along on the floor. I glanced down to see her shoving a large metal crate away from the wall with one of her booted feet.

"I hope that is ammunition," I said, kneeling down in front of the box.

"There are four more exactly like it just to your right."

I followed her flashlight beam to see a stack of identical metal boxes sitting neatly up against the wall. That was in addition to a row of four helmets that sat on a shelf. Under each one was a Kevlar vest. The thought briefly flashed in my mind that a Kevlar wetsuit would be amazing considering the situation. Of course, that thought was quickly followed by the realization that none of it made a bit of difference when it came to my fate.

"I thought you'd be a bit happier," Miranda said, giving me an almost playful elbow in the ribs.

"What?" I snapped out of the depression that was trying to gain a foothold in my head. "No...this is great."

"Umm, okay," she replied with a shrug before taking off her

helmet with a grunt. She scanned the ones on the shelf and set-tled on one that went on much easier.

"How about we see if we can locate a set of keys that might start up that police car in the back lot?"

I exited the closet and went over to a window that looked out onto the rear of the building. Only one police car was left. I imagine it had to most likely have been the one driven by the officer that lie dead just a few feet away. I also saw a lone zom-bie emerging from the trees on the far side of the field that stretched out behind the building.

Just over thirty minutes and a dozen dead zombies later, we had everything loaded into the police car. The keys had been on the belt of the dead policeman just as I'd suspected.

"Next stop…Happy Valley Veterinary Hospital," I said as I pulled out of the police station's parking lot and turned left on Southeast King Road.

"Say what?" Miranda asked with a laugh, obviously think-ing that she had not heard me right.

9

A Ray of Hope

The raid on the veterinary hospital was much easier the second time. One reason was because the zombies that had been wandering the parking lot last time appeared to have wandered away. My guess was that they followed Ariel and I when we made our escape from this place right before we picked up Joan and Franklin.

We had the police car loaded in no time at all. Miranda was a whirling dervish when it came to tossing the bags of dog food. Twice I almost ended up on my ass when the bag came hurling at me and I did my best to catch it and throw it in the trunk. By the time we were done, I was actually feeling pretty good.

"Since we have a bit more room, why not give that walk-in clinic a look?" she suggested as I placed the last case of canned dog food on the floor behind the driver's seat.

I shot a look across the expanse of this shopping center's lot. The permanently darkened red neon sign that read "URGENT CARE" beckoned from across the way. I'd been so fixated on doing what I could for Chewie that I'd completely ignored the fact that a clinic was within striking distance. To my credit, things had been a lot more dicey the last time I'd been here. Not to mention the fact that I'd entrusted Ariel, whom I'd only met a few minutes prior, to drive my car as a diversion.

That was a risk I had to take, although I hadn't been sure if she would stick around or drive off with my vehicle.

"I don't see why not," I replied with a shrug.

We drove over to the entrance of the clinic, rolling up onto the sidewalk to park within feet of the glass fronted entrance. I was about to stave in the bottom of the entry door when Miranda stepped up and grabbed my arm. She pulled yet another of her big knives and showed me a little pointy knob at the base of the handle.

"Glass breaker," she said as she gave the pane a solid rap. It went white with a myriad of spider web-like cracks. A push with her booted foot sent the entire bottom section of the glass door collapsing to the floor just inside the clinic.

We crawled inside and did a visual sweep, but it was pretty obvious that the place was surprisingly empty. Miranda hopped the counter and we searched for some sort of dispensary. What we ended up finding was a lot of basic first aid gear. Antiseptics, bandages, and basic generic pain reliever in foil packets. Just like the veterinary hospital, we brought everything we found up to the doors until we were confident that we could not fit much more into the car.

"Can I ask you something?" Miranda said as we took a break in the waiting area's seats. With the lot still clear of any undead, and nothing in here to bother us, there was nothing preventing us from catching our breath for a moment or two.

"Sure," I replied as my eyes continued to scan the lot outside.

"What are you doing out here all by yourself? I mean, I know why I am out here alone. I didn't start off by myself, but after I lost the rest of my friends, I made the choice."

She paused and examined me to the point where it was becoming uncomfortable. I was about to suggest we get moving when she continued.

"You've been out here on your own for at least a few days, but you are gathering up all these supplies for your group. I get that part. What doesn't make sense is why you are alone. Unless you guys are all idiots, and I don't think that is the case, then you should have at least one other person with you. Also, you don't really talk about getting back to your people. You keep saying you just want to make this *last* run."

I hadn't really thought about how it would look to a stranger. She was exactly right. I guessed that it wouldn't hurt to let her know what was up.

"I got scratched during a run on a small medical center near where my group is staying. I decided that I didn't want them to have to be burdened with putting me down when I turn." That was probably a much shorter explanation than was merited, but I saw no reason to give all the details.

"But your eyes are still clear."

"Yeah, best I can figure, the scratches might take longer. I've seen people who were bitten start to show it in their eyes within minutes, but the last reports I heard on one of the emergency broadcasts was that the infection could be transferred through bite or scratch."

We sat in silence for a moment. Miranda hadn't made any move to put distance between us. I'd seen an almost involuntary reaction from people when I revealed my condition. Granted, there hadn't been many, but it was like back when somebody used to show up at work and say that they had a cold or something. People always did stupid stuff like cover their mouth and nose with their hands...like that would block any germs that might be swirling in the air.

"You ever consider maybe that scratch came from something else? Maybe during your little raid, perhaps you snagged yourself on something," Miranda suggested.

I hiked my sleeve up to reveal the ugly scratch. The skin around it was still inflamed and it looked much nastier than any little scratch I'd ever received before. Working in construction, I'd had my share of snags. It was part of the job. After a while, you could go days and not notice until perhaps you were taking a shower or something and your hand brushed over a flaking scab. I could say without a doubt that this was not just some ordinary snag. It wasn't as definitive as...say...teeth marks. But I was certain.

"I'm sure," I finally answered with a cold finality. I didn't like this topic.

"What about..." Miranda began, but her voice trailed off. She appeared to wrestle with something as a flurry of emotions crossed her face. Finally, she seemed resolute and turned to me with the softest gaze I'd ever seen from her in our brief time together. "Have you considered that maybe you won't turn? Like perhaps you have some sort of immunity?"

I had, but it was like going to the store and grabbing a lottery ticket when the jackpot would reach some unthinkable amount. Stephanie used to crack me up when she would make all these plans for what we were going to do when we won a half a billion dollars. At first I used to just tune her out. After all, I knew damn good and well that we were not going to win, but eventually I didn't see the harm in playing along for a day until we would log in and confirm that we had not won.

"Yeah, I gave it a thought, but it is hard to start getting your hopes up. I just know that the moment I do, those damn tracers will show up in my eyes."

We sat in silence again for another moment. I was starting to believe that this dreadful conversation was over. As with many of my life's assumptions when it came to women, I would be wrong.

"You ever read that book, *The Stand*? It was one of the earlier books by Stephen King," she said in a voice that was barely a whisper, like maybe she didn't want to travel down the road of hope any more than I did.

"Read it a few times," I admitted. "It's one of my favorites. What does that have to do with this situation? I'm not having weird dreams or anything like that."

"Maybe not, but there was a point made early on about how lots of people have natural immunities. Not everybody is hit the same way." She turned to face me again, looking deep into my eyes like she was trying to penetrate the surface and burrow in to see what might be hiding underneath.

I considered her words. I weighed it with some of the facts that I had collected over the past several days. Chewie had been bitten way back when this all began for me. She'd lost over half of her tail. She still showed no signs of turning. I'd encountered a few dogs that had not fared nearly as well. I knew for a fact that dogs suffered the same fate as humans when it came to this infection, virus, or whatever was turning people into zombies.

The supposed turn time was reported to be as fast as just a few minutes, but up to seventy-two hours. I'd passed that mark at some point. Could it really be possible that a person could endure a scratch and not turn? Could I allow myself this small glimmer, this ray of hope?

"I suppose anything is possible, but it is really tough to grab onto something like that. It is like a nightmare where you know the big, bad monster is right on your heels. You manage to stay just ahead of it...but you can almost feel it breathing down your neck," I admitted.

"How about if I promise to stick right by your side for the next several days. We go back to your people...if your dog is still there, then maybe you and your group are some of the good guys."

I thought it was interesting that she would equate a dog's presence as possible proof that Carl and the others were the so-called good guys. I considered her offer. What did I have to lose? Besides, I could not deny that I was curious as to how Natasha's group had been repelled and her entire force wiped out.

"Just do me a favor," I finally agreed as I climbed to my feet.

"Kill you quick?" Miranda offered.

"Okay...two favors. The other is that I want you to say something the moment you notice the change...if it comes." It felt strange saying the word "if" when talking about the possibility that I might turn.

"Cross my heart." She made the physical gesture and I nodded.

We crept out of the clinic and loaded what we had gathered into the back of the squad car until it was so full there would be no way that I could use the rearview mirror. That entire time, not one single zombie shambled our way.

147

I should've known it would be too good to last.

***

"This was a stupid idea," I grunted as I jerked the wheel hard to the left and we rumbled up onto the curb, barely making it to where the driveway was flush with the road.

We skidded just a bit as the tires fought for traction in the grass. Just as I managed to straighten us out, I had to jerk the wheel to the left and then back to the right as I made it past a tree sitting in the middle of the front yard. I heard as well as felt the crunch as the right rear of the police car clipped the trunk of the tree.

"I told you we should've taken 152nd Avenue. It would've brought us down to Highway 224. We could've followed it back to the interstate and avoided these damn residential areas," Miranda snapped as she grabbed the little handle just above the door that I'd always called the "Oh shit!" handle.

"We still would've had to drive through residential areas," I shot back as I swerved in order to avoid slamming into a zombie woman that had suffered the misfortune of turning while she was naked.

"Yeah, but that road goes through the more urban parts of town. It is a lot of farms and stuff. Not this postage stamp yard microcosm of houses that all look alike and are stuffed in tighter than Vienna sausages."

The police car launched off the curb and hit the pavement with a nasty jolt. I hooked left to put us back on the road and shot a glance into the side view mirror. The mob was wheeling around to re-orient itself on the only major sound source in the area: us. I saw a few of them pinball off each other as some made the turn easier and sooner than others.

Up ahead, I saw a dozen more zombies come staggering out from the right-hand side of the four-way intersection. They would be too spread out by the time I reached them and there would be no way past without hitting at least a couple. I tapped the brakes to slow us down in hopes that it would lessen the impact, and thus, the damage to the car. There was simply no way that I was going to lose this vehicle and its cargo. I would not start over. Period.

I edged over to the right-hand side of the street at the last moment since the zombies had mostly migrated to the middle. Rolling up with the passenger side coming up onto the curb that ran alongside the road, I made it by, only hitting one of the zombies before emerging in the clear. As soon as I could, I stomped the gas and smiled as the police cruiser's powerful engine sent us speeding away.

"If you turn right at the next street, it will take you out of this subdivision and towards 152nd Street. Hook a left and just follow it until you reach the highway where you take a right. From there, it is a straight shot to I-205."

I grunted in acknowledgement and eventually came to a stop at the Highway 224 junction. I heard Miranda gasp just before my own breath caught in my throat. Dangling from the power-lines right across from us were four bodies. Each was riddled with bullets, but they continued to struggle. They'd obviously heard our approach and their hands were reaching impotently for us.

"Why?" was all Miranda could finally manage.

"I got nothing," I said as I eased onto the mostly empty highway.

With two lanes on each side, and no barrier separating the lanes, it would be easy enough to travel this road even with the occasional abandoned vehicle or multi-car accident.

We headed up the road, my eyes scanning the area ahead of us. Off to either side were open areas of undeveloped land, many of them with signs declaring that they were for sale or lease as a business zoned lot.

We were just passing a trucking weigh station when a figure darted out from behind a big rig that was parked alongside the weighmaster's building. I slammed on the brakes and the figure adjusted its course, coming right for us. At first I thought that it was a child. As he got closer, I was able to make out a consider-able amount of facial hair growth casting its shadow on his dark face.

Miranda had a blade in her hand faster than I thought possible from the seated position. As the guy got closer, I could see that he was also an absolute mess. His left arm was wrapped in filthy rags that were dark with dried blood. Was it possible that some of the undead could run?

"Help," the man gasped as he skidded to a stop at the nose of our commandeered police car. "About forty of them biters are coming through the woods. I just can't run anymore."

I glanced at Miranda. She was staring at the man. If she had an opinion on the matter, she wasn't letting it show. I decided that it was just not in me to leave somebody behind that needed help. If I wasn't infected and dying, then being too damn nice was going to be the death of me.

I opened my door and edged out of the driver's seat. "We are pretty packed in there." I hiked a thumb to indicate the back of the car's bounty of supplies.

"He can squeeze in with me," Miranda called. "But he needs to do it now."

I heard the tightness in her voice. Both the diminutive man standing in front of us and I turned to the right to see the undead pouring from the brush that ran several feet in either direction along the edge of the weigh station.

"You heard her." I stepped back and the man scurried around the car and practically dove into the front seat. As I followed him, I heard an eruption of gunfire coming from the left.

"Really?" I yelped as I was in and popping the car into drive before our newest occupant was situated or my door was even shut.

"Shit," the man groaned as he squirmed to try and get his body around to a position that was closer to seated than sprawled.

"Friends of yours?" Miranda snarled as she manhandled the guy around so that they were now sharing the passenger side of the vehicle.

"A bunch of them damn rednecks…so that would be a hard no," the man replied.

"Care to elaborate?" I asked as I wove around a three-car crash and a motorcycle that looked more like it had blown up than simply crashed as bits of it were strewn all the way across not only all four lanes, but I thought I even saw a chunk of it jutting from the mud of the ditch that ran alongside the road.

"Umm...great big slabs of meat with names like Zeke, Billy-Bob, and Bocephus. They prowl the area in a fucking monster truck, and they yell things like 'Yee-haw' when they spot people like me." The man tapped his arm, indicating the color of his skin.

"Another bunch of racist pricks?" I almost moaned.

"You new to the area?" the man laughed. "There's always been a strong fringe element of skinheads and white supremacists around these parts."

"Maybe out in the sticks...but in Portland?" I replied, my voice not doing a good job of hiding the skepticism.

"You keep thinking that, white boy," the man guffawed. It wasn't malicious or even slightly sarcastic. In fact, his laugh was quite pleasant...until he began to cough in harsh, rasping fits.

"You okay?" I asked once he got his coughing under control.

"Not really." The man sat back and shut his eyes.

I shot a worried look over at Miranda. Her lips were pressed together tight.

"How'd you hurt your arm?" she finally asked when it became clear that he wasn't going to elaborate.

"I got tangled up in some damn barbed wire," he replied. I was keeping an eye on him with the rearview mirror and saw his eyes pop open suddenly. "Did you think I was bit?"

"Is that such a reach?" Miranda shot back.

"Umm...you see anything wrong with my eyes?"

"No, but maybe the infection hasn't set in yet."

"Okay...that's fair." The man unwrapped his arm. It was quickly apparent that his wounds were not from a bite.

We drove for a few more blocks when I heard a roar. My eyes went to my side view mirror and I felt my heart do a flip in my chest.

A massive vehicle was closing in on us at a high rate of speed. I could see the hint of what had probably once been a pickup truck, but the body had been transformed into something that resembled a pirate ship. A pair of large black flags with a skull and crossbones insignia fluttered from each side. A man was standing up in the bed and I could see at least three faces peering through the windshield.

"What the…" Miranda gasped as her head tilted so that she could look out the side mirror.

"I guess it is time to see what this baby can really do," I hissed through gritted teeth as I stomped on the accelerator.

The police car lurched forward like a horse that had just been released from the corral and slapped on the butt. I felt my mouth widen into a smile. I just couldn't help it. I glanced down at the speedometer and watched as it crept past seventy…eighty…ninety…

"They won't have to kill us," Miranda scolded as her side of the car brushed very close to an overturned station wagon. "You are going to do it for them if you don't watch what the hell you're doing."

"We missed that car by plenty," I laughed. The sound died in my throat a second later when the monster truck sent that same station wagon careening away as the driver made no attempt to go around, choosing the much more direct 'straight through' approach.

We rocketed through a four-way intersection and it looked like we were starting to put some distance between our car and the behemoth that was probably making enough noise to draw every zombie in a ten-mile radius. An idea began to bloom in my mind and the smile I'd been sporting just a moment ago was replaced by a look of grim determination.

As the next intersection came into view, I warned my fellow occupants, "Hang on tight."

Before they could ask any questions, I let up on the gas just a bit as I wrenched the steering wheel hard to the right. The road started its somewhat steep incline just as we reached a series of nasty S-curves. They would be idiots to try and chase us up this winding road. For one, that truck was not designed to handle sharp corners. It was built to mostly just roll over the top of stuff and drive in a straight line. Sure, they could make turns, but those trucks needed to slow considerably in order to do so.

I rounded the second of the successive curves and glanced in my side mirror. There was no sign of our pursuers. I let my foot off the gas to bring us back down to a more reasonable speed when I heard the echo of a roaring engine. A second later, the truck exploded through some shrubs and brush as it basically cut through instead of taking the curve.

"I hadn't thought of that," I groused as I hit the gas again, rocketing away.

While the truck might be able to cut corners, it was now laboring with the steepness of the hill we were climbing. The police cruiser was easily opening the distance between us and them.

"Everybody grab a gun," I said as I brought us to the top of the slope and to a point where the road straightened out.

I spotted a grassy clearing ahead and angled for it, hitting the brakes hard enough to go into a bit of a power slide. When the car came to a halt, we were perpendicular to the road. I threw open my car door, ignoring all the protests from Miranda.

As we'd started to make our escape, the thought hit me that I'd been making one of the classic mistakes from the stories. I was letting the bad guys get away to live another day where they would undoubtedly resurface at the worst possible time. Also, any terrible act that these wastes of flesh committed after encountering me would be partially my fault since I'd let them live.

It was strange, but I could feel something changing in my head. Up until now, I'd resisted the urge to take another human life. The thing was, I suddenly had this epiphany.

"Kill or be killed," I whispered as I climbed out of my car.

We'd been smart when Miranda and I had loaded the car. It did not make sense to have weapons buried under all the other stuff. We'd made sure to place them, along with all the assorted ammunition, on the top just in case the need arose.

Using a two-handed grip on the Glock, I had my arms extended across the roof of the cruiser when the truck rounded the corner and reached level ground. By now, it was moving slow enough that it was not that difficult of a shot when I sighted on the driver. Taking a deep breath and holding it, I made a very slight adjustment to my weapon, and squeezed the trigger. As quickly as possible, I made one more adjustment and fired three more shots in quick succession.

From this distance, I saw the holes in the windshield appear in a neat pattern. My first shot was a bit high. I'd aimed for the bit of torso that I could see above the steering wheel. The bullet ended up ripping through the driver's throat, but the next rounds found their mark and punched through the man's chest. Not that it mattered after that first shot had done its damage, but I was leaving nothing to chance and had fired reflexively more than anything else.

The truck veered hard to my left and the one redneck that had been standing up in the rear went sailing through the air and landed with a nasty crunch on the pavement. I started for the truck, my eyes looking for any sign of movement.

The truck came to a stop when it collided with a brick wall that announced the name of the community beyond to be Megan Estates. I'd covered half the distance when I heard footsteps coming up from behind. Since I wasn't going to take my eyes off the pirate ship-themed monster truck, I had to trust that it was either Miranda or the stranger we'd picked up.

I was almost to the truck when I heard a moan coming from up in the cab. It wasn't that of a zombie. This was a living person moaning in pain.

I scanned the vehicle and saw a ladder just behind the cab. I saw this as almost a godsend. After all the climbing and hauling my ass up, down, and over things, it would only be slightly awkward to make the climb one-handed, especially since I was still sporting this busted arm. Not that it mattered much anymore. I'd used the arm so much that it was now a regular source of background pain.

"Maybe somebody with two working wings, eh, chief?" the

stranger said as he nudged past me and scurried up the ladder. He peered into the cab and whistled low. "That whole buckle up for safety slogan might've been helpful to these fools." He leaned away from the window and looked down at me. "What are we gonna do with these guys?"

I heard the moans of zombies coming from the neighborhood that we sat at the entrance of as well as an apartment complex at our backs. If they were indeed banged up pretty bad, we could walk away and leave them to their fate, but that would defeat my entire reason for stopping. I needed certainty.

"Are you okay with shooting 'em?" I asked, trying my best to make my voice sound confident, like this was no big deal.

The man looked back into the cab and I saw the hand holding his gun twitch slightly. I couldn't see his face as he looked into the truck, but when his shoulders slumped, I had an idea what he was about to say.

"Shooting back is one thing…but this?" He swung back around to me with a pained expression. "These guys ain't going no place."

"And if they manage to get away from here, lick their wounds, and then go back to what they were doing? You don't see the mercy in granting them this quick death versus leaving them to be bitten, turned, and adding more undead to roam the streets?" I prodded. "Were these the guys that hung those people from the power line back down on the highway near that weigh station?"

"Probably," the man answered.

"Get down," I said flatly.

The man regarded me for a moment and then climbed down. When his feet hit the ground, he moved between me and the ladder. "Be sure that this is what you want to do."

"I was sure the moment I hit the brakes." I edged past the man, shoved my pistol in the waist of my pants, and made my way up the ladder. Since it sounded like the guys in the cab were in pretty bad shape, I wasn't as concerned about having my weapon free.

When I reached the point where I could see inside, I felt my stomach tighten. The driver had been thrown forward and wedged to the side of the steering wheel. The passengers had both been thrown to the floor. The problem with that was that it wasn't really a floor as much as it was an extension of the roll cage. Obviously this vehicle hadn't been designed to transport passengers. That side was mostly open and I had to guess that the two young men had been standing on one of the pipes that ran along the underside.

One of the boys, and that was really the most disturbing part of this since he couldn't be any older than twelve, had gotten wedged in between two thick pieces of metal. What had to be one of his ribs was sticking out of his chest, and his arm looked to be broken in several places. Thankfully, he was unconscious. The other had been thrown onto a pipe that jutted up. I had no guess as to what its purpose had been, but whatever had once been mounted in that spot was gone and now that one inch diameter piece of metal was jutting up through this young man's side. He was staring up at me, and when he opened his mouth, blood trickled from the corners of it and he made a weak squeaking sound that gave me chills. This kid was perhaps in his mid to late teens.

I stared in at them for an indeterminate amount of time before Miranda's voice snapped me out of whatever trance I'd slipped into. "Hey, Evan, we need to get moving…we got company coming from damn near every direction."

I looked around and saw zombies emerging from the streets that emptied onto our particular road. From the sounds of it, there were a helluva lot headed this way. No doubt, this truck had been a giant dinner bell.

I felt the lump in my throat grow when the boy with the pipe through his body opened his eyes and looked up at me with pain and pleading fighting for purchase in his gaze.

It's not murder, it's mercy, the voice in my head said as I brought my pistol up and fired a round into the chest of each boy. I made my way down and saw that our newest member of the group had already turned back and was jogging to the car. I headed after him, swerving wide so that I came up on the other member of the group that had been pursuing us. His body was sprawled in the street and it was clear that he'd suffered some horrible injuries due to being thrown from the vehicle. I didn't even bother to check close; I simply put the gun to the back of his head and fired before continuing on to the squad car.

Without a word, we all climbed in. I'd left the engine running, and so all I needed to do was shift into drive and do a big circle to get back onto the road and continue on the direction we'd been heading.

Nothing was said for a few minutes. At last, the oppressive silence was broken.

"My name is Edmund Gibbons, by the way," the stranger said. "I just realized that we never introduced ourselves."

"Evan Berry," I mumbled. I heard Miranda give her name, but my mind was still back at the pirate truck.

Despite the fact that I had come to grips with the idea that survival in this new world would almost certainly mean that I would have to kill the living as well as the dead, it didn't make dealing with my conscience any easier after the deed was done. It made no difference that those boys were doomed and I'd actually granted them a mercy. Hell, I still was not convinced that I would not be seeking my own brand of mercy soon once the infection took hold.

Sure, I was starting to think that just maybe there was a difference in the real zombie apocalypse and what I'd seen in the movies. As the squad car rolled back onto the street, I was considering the near absurdity of that thought. Zombie movies had been fiction, a fringe element of pop culture and the horror genre. Yet, here I was, trying my best to make it in the middle of the real deal. Miranda had been the one to say out loud the very words that I'd stuffed away any time they tried to rise in my conscious mind. Could immunity really be possible?

That was both wonderful and horrifying. If Chewie and I were both immune, what was the reason? And why us? Why not Stephanie? Why would my dog and I both be spared, but she ended up succumbing to the illness and becoming one of the walking dead?

The car rolled along, zombies wandering out into the street in our wake. My mind was immersing itself in thoughts that I'd refused to allow myself to consider; the possibility that I would survive this ordeal. That Dr. Sing had been very clear that the infection could be passed on through a bite or a scratch. Yet, here I was, days away from the moment that I'd been scratched.

"Evan, watch out!" Miranda shouted, snapping me back to the moment.

Up ahead was a series of spiked strips that were laid all the way across the road. I had no choice but to slam on the brakes. No sooner had I stopped when I heard a voice that sounded like it was being projected from a bullhorn, "We need you all to step out of the car and keep your hands where we can see them."

"You realize these situations never go well," I mumbled to my fellow occupants. "We can do what they say, or I can throw this baby into reverse and see if we can get out of here alive.

Those words no sooner left my mouth when a trio of SUVs rolled out from the street we'd just driven past. They did a very effective job of cutting off our retreat.

I opened my door and slowly stepped out of the car with my hands in the air. "We don't want any trouble," I called out. "We are just trying to get through to where my friends are holed up. We won't try anything if you just let us go."

"If we hadn't seen what you did, we might have been in-clined to just shoot you outright," a man said as he emerged from one of the SUVs that was positioned behind us.

I wasn't certain what he meant exactly. Was he an ally or an enemy of the boys in the pirate truck? The other people coming out of the other vehicles with an assortment of weapons drawn did not offer any answers or comfort.

"We really don't want any trouble," I repeated. "If you pre-fer, we can go back the way we came. We don't have to pass through this area if it is yours."

"Ours?" the man laughed. "I guess we have sort of staked a claim to this little area, but we are actually packing up and head-ing out of here. There is just too much going on between zombies and groups of raiders…which seem to actually be worse than the undead."

The man made a gesture with his hand, and before I even had time to tense up, all the people holding weapons trained on us lowered their barrels. A few of them leaned up against their vehicles, but the gesture seemed too casual. I had no doubts that they would be ready to bring their weapons back up if we did anything they deemed suspicious.

"We have no issues with you folks passing through considering how you took down that little pack of delinquents," the man said, craning his neck to look past me as if he could actually see the scene of our little incident. "The Weatherly boys have been wreaking havoc for the past several days. Rumor has it they met up with some lunatic who was actually paying them to patrol the area in search of..." He paused, his gaze flicking over to Edmund. "Well, it's of no importance now...you took care of them."

"Can I ask why you guys didn't do anything?" I said, my own gaze pausing on a pair of African-Americans and a Hispanic woman who looked angrier than any of the others standing around.

"We tried, believe it or not. A handful of our people went out after them." A woman made a hitching noise and I saw a single tear rolling down her cheek. "And as grateful as we are that you took down the Weatherly boys, they are just the tip of the iceberg. And that is another reason that we are leaving. Maybe we can get far enough away from the city that we can reduce our problems to just the undead."

I didn't want to tell him that the problems were just starting. It would not be long before food became an issue. Raiding homes would only be viable for so long. Anybody who planned on surviving long-term would need to have access to fresh water first and foremost. That didn't necessarily mean camping beside the nearest stream or river. Those would remain polluted for quite a while. That meant the need to filter water or boil it before using it. There were just so many things that would be necessary if survival was going to be a possibility.

"You folks are welcome to pass, just be careful," the man

said, making sure to announce it loud enough that all those around him could hear.

A few moments later, the strips were rolled out of the way to allow us to drive through. We had to go by another set at the next intersection. As we drove past, I saw a woman watching us. She was standing just behind the two people who were rolling the spike strips out of the way.

I hit the brakes so hard that Edmund and Miranda both slammed into the dash. The two of them cried out and began cursing at me as I threw open my door and pointed to the woman.

"You there," I yelled, ignoring all the guns being drawn and swung around to point at me as I walked across the street and up onto the sidewalk where the woman stood. She'd drawn a pistol just like everybody else, but I didn't care. I was staring at her face, my mouth taking a few moments to form words. "How long ago were you bitten?"

The woman looked around at the others and shook her head when one of the ladies standing at her side began to protest. She stepped up to me, her own eyes going up and down my body as if she might be looking for something. At last her eyes met mine.

"Probably the day all this started," she said. "I guess that is over a month ago now."

10

Proof

The woman had probably been a beauty before the attack. She had shoulder length hair that was that perfect shade of strawberry-blonde. I guessed her to be just a shade over five feet tall with a very curvy figure that made me instantly think of Marilyn Monroe. She had a tiny nose that came almost to a point, her eyes were a soft, crystal blue with flecks of gold, and I could see a hint of pouty lips under the scabbing that marred her skin.

It looked like she'd been bitten on the face just at the edge of her mouth. The flesh was puckered, but it was obviously healing…and it was apparent that it was a bite.

"How can that be?" I gasped. "Oh…sorry." I threw my hands up when the group around her all closed ranks and brought their weapons up, all of them leveled at me. I can say from experience that those tiny holes that the bullets come out of look a whole lot larger when you are staring into them.

"I can assure you that I am not one of…them," the woman said with a hint of annoyance. "And before you ask, no, I don't have any idea what or why. I do know that I barely escaped from the FEMA center that I'd been staying at when the doctors got wind of me. They took me to a room and before I had a chance to ask what was going on, they strapped me onto a table and started taking my blood, hair samples…they sliced out a piece of my skin." She hiked up her sleeve and showed me a near perfect square that was also obviously several weeks old and healing.

"Why did they let you go?" I blurted, not even realizing until after the words were out of my mouth how that could be taken a number of ways that would cast me in a less than positive light.

"You mean how did I escape?" she corrected, very gently easing down the rifle beside her that was pointed at me. "I didn't. I was rescued."

A woman that was easily a good six inches taller than me with her dark hair shaved down to a crewcut stepped up beside the woman with the bitten face. She was wearing military camo clothing and had her name stitched above the pocket over her left breast: Kolowicz.

"I am sorry, I know this is coming across all wrong," I hastily apologized and went to hike up the sleeve on my shirt. It was like a John Wayne movie. All of a sudden, I heard a variety of clicks as every weapon was readjusted to be aiming at my face.

"Oh, c'mon," I yelped. "I just want to show you something."

Much too slowly for my liking, the guns gradually lowered once more. I noticed that the female soldier, Kolowicz, had stepped just a bit closer and was glaring down at me with a scowl that was more than a little intimidating. Doing my best to ignore her, I showed my scratch. I heard a smattering of titters and giggles.

"This was done by a zombie just a few days ago," I snapped, trying not to sound like their derisive attitudes bothered me in the slightest. "According to all the reports before the world shut down, I should've turned any time these past few days, but so far—"

"Your eyes are clear and you feel fine," the woman with the bite on her face interrupted.

"Yeah." I took a step closer to the woman. "Hey, I'm not trying to be rude, I just haven't met anybody who was bitten and didn't turn. I was starting to wonder…get my hopes up. But it didn't seem possible until just this moment."

"There is another one of us in the group," the woman said. I caught a whole bunch of looks that passed around the rest of the people standing here. I doubt she was supposed to be offering me up that kind of information.

"I won't tell anybody." I made sure to make eye contact with Kolowicz. Her glare hadn't lessened. "About anything," I added when her eyes narrowed.

"What's your name," the woman with the bite asked.

"Evan Berry."

"I'm Katy Joplin."

"You have no idea how nice it is to meet you, Katy," I gushed.

The relief that was flooding me was enough to almost make me want to cry, scream, and just plain laugh. All the hope that I'd been stuffing down was now free from its bonds.

"I understand that you guys are rolling out of here," I said. "And I have no idea where you are headed, so if you are still carrying some sort of concern about me saying anything that could possibly endanger you, hopefully that will lessen things." I continued to make eye contact with Kolowicz.

There was a moment of silence that passed. I felt Miranda step just a bit closer to me at the same time I felt Edmund put a bit of distance between us. I filed that away for later—provided we got out of here alive.

"Here is how it is going to work," the towering woman said as she stepped in front of Katy and folded her muscled arms across her body. "You are going to come with us back to the group. We are just about loaded up, and since we were already planning on leaving today, you are going to remain here until we leave. Then you are free to go." She leaned closer to me, her eyes reflecting a coldness that made me take an involuntary step backwards. "If we get wind of anything following us, we shoot first and ask questions later…you understand what I am saying here?"

I had to bite back my anger as well as a few sarcastic comments that bubbled to the surface. As soon as I was confident that my voice would not betray me, I answered that I understood her meaning perfectly.

"So we're prisoners now?" Miranda whispered to me as I followed behind Katy and her apparent bodyguard

"It's no big deal," I assured her. "Consider this a brief break in the action." I saw her flash me a dubious expression. "I'm not any happier about this than you, trust me. I want to get back to my dog and the group I left behind that apparently took out Natasha's little squad. I am pretty sure that Carl couldn't handle and repel an assault all by himself. And while I won't discount Betty's ability to handle her business, it still seems unlikely that those two were able to do what is rumored to have been done."

Edmund remained silent, but I noticed that he was looking around with more than just a little bit of concern etched on his face. I had to wonder what he'd been through up until running into me and Miranda. He'd been running for his life when we met. Apparently there were some who had taken this collapse in the fabric of our society to allow their prejudices to assume control.

I was suddenly struck by his remark about my ignorance of such things in those first few minutes of our having met. It wasn't that I didn't believe that racism didn't exist before the dead got up and started chomping on people, I guess I just thought it was a very minor and extreme fringe portion of society.

"You know that you're safe with us," I whispered, leaning close to Edmund as we walked down a sidewalk that was strewn with debris.

We were well into this little neighborhood now, and I was getting a better look at just how bad things had gotten. Bodies were sprawled in the street, in yards, a few hanging partway out of vehicles with violent trauma to the head by a variety of ways. One corpse still had a hand axe jutting from the top of its skull. Seeing that particular image gave me a pang in my gut as I realized that I'd lost so much in that encounter with Don and his gang. I'd lost my weapons, but that was no big deal. I'd also lost my picture of Stephanie: the one thing I had left from the old world and a life that was as dead as the landscape around me.

At last we reached some sort of neighborhood community center. Not the kind that I was used to in my old neighborhood in Southeast Portland. This was like some sort of country club. The perfectly manicured lawn and surrounding flower beds were not yet showing too much growth to have lost their meticulous appearance. The bushes were all trimmed into fancy geometric shapes and just starting to show the first buds of spring.

The building itself had not fared as well. The huge window beside the main entrance had been shattered, and the glass showed hints that it had been splattered with an awful lot of blood. The door had been chopped in or beaten in with a large axe or sledgehammer and the frame was splintered.

I could see the top of a swimming pool slide on the other side of the textured stone wall that surrounded the courtyard or whatever lay beyond the proper building. I could also see smoke curling up in thin tendrils. The moment I saw the smoke, I also caught a whiff of cooking meat. I hoped to God that my mouth was not watering at the smell of charred human remains.

We entered the building and I saw at least a dozen people scurrying about, stuffing things into plastic containers. Other people were snapping on the covers as the boxes became full and then hustling them out the side door. I was able to catch a glimpse of a few trucks and a small regional commuter bus that was undergoing a bit of a post-apocalyptic options upgrade packages complete with what looked like metal siding being bolted to the sides and even the front windshield.

"No gawking," Kolowicz snapped, moving over to give me a slight shove in an effort to encourage me to resume walking.

I continued on and we eventually were led to what looked like a small reception room. There were groups of long folding tables on pushcarts and folding chairs stacked in rows along the walls.

"You will remain here until I get back," Kolowicz said flatly before exiting the room and shutting the door behind her to leave me alone with Miranda and Edmund.

"I don't like this," Miranda sniffed. She grabbed a metal

folding chair, opened it, and flopped down with her arms entwined across her chest.

"Yeah, why are we still here?" Edmund added.

"What happened to you being in such a hurry to get to your dog?" Miranda rattled off.

I felt like I was being grilled by the pair. The thing is, they were making a good point. We could have just driven away and put this place behind us. Of course, if we had, then I wouldn't have met Katy Joplin and seen with my own eyes the possibility that being bitten or scratched might not be a death sentence. Then again, I could see how my companions might not consider this verification as worthwhile as I did.

"We'll be out of here in no time." I brushed away their comments and slid down the wall, taking a moment to just catch my breath and process the revelations of the past few minutes.

It was not long before the door opened and Kolowicz and the man I'd first spoken to after dispatching the troublesome Weatherly boys entered. The man shot me a look, and a scowl crept across his features for just a moment before he could smooth it away and resume his air of impassive calm.

"Any reason why you folks decided to stop and interrogate one of my people?" the man finally said after edging past the large woman who looked like she wanted to just kill the three of us and be done with the whole situation.

I explained about my own scratch and made it clear that my only intention was to confirm the possibility of what I was making assumption on in regards to potential immunity. As I spoke, I made it a point to maintain my eye contact with this guy and do my best to ignore Kolowicz. I had no idea what I'd done to her in this life or another, but it was pretty clear that she wanted nothing to do with me.

"That seems pretty reasonable to me." He turned to face the woman. "Jesus, Abby, the guy wasn't trying to heist any of our stuff or hurt anybody. In fact, it was that guy and his people that put down the Weatherly boys…which you failed to do on three occasions I might add."

I didn't think that he needed to add that last bit. I was already at the top of her shit list as it was. Pointing out something like that would only make things worse.

"Is that what's been up your ass this whole time?" Miranda snorted. It took all my self-control not to bury my face in my hands and just hide.

"How about I shove something up your—" Abby Kolowicz started, taking a menacing step towards Miranda, her fists clenched.

"Abby!" the man snapped. He shot a withering look in Miranda's direction. "And I wouldn't antagonize her if you know what is good for you."

"Is that right?" Miranda remained seated and looked like she didn't have a care in the world. Now it was my turn to intervene.

"Hey, Miranda, let's not antagonize our hosts. I am sure that things can be resolved here and everybody can be about their business."

"Actually, my people and I are just about ready to roll. So here is my request, I am going to ask that you and your two companions remain here for thirty minutes."

Miranda started to open her mouth in protest and I raised a hand to silence her. I doubt anyone was more surprised than me when she shut her mouth. I nodded for the man to continue.

"We don't want to be followed, and I am hoping that you and your people will respect us in that regard. Since we will have a good head start, and you say you are returning to your people with some supplies, this should not be that big of a deal." The man put a hand up when Abby Kolowicz began to say something. "We won't take anything of yours and we will even have your vehicle brought to the front of the rec center here. It will be waiting for you when you leave."

I nodded and the man pointed to a clock hanging on the wall. "Battery is good in that baby, and it is still running. It is currently just after three. At half past, you people walk out of here and we just wish each other well."

It all seemed sort of convoluted, but if it gave them a sense of peace, then I didn't see the harm. Heck, we didn't even really have to stay for the full half hour. They should be well on their way within about fifteen minutes or so. We could head out and I could get back to Chewie, Carl, and the others. I had a feeling that we had a lot of catching up to do.

The man stepped up and shook my hand. "This should make us square."

I wasn't sure what sort of math he was using where our having taken down a deadly band of raiders equaled him making us sit in a room while his group slipped away. Heck, it wasn't like I had any interest in them beyond the fact that I was now able to say with almost absolute certainty that the infection was not a hundred percent communicable through bite or scratch.

The door shut and Miranda started in about how she could wipe the floor with Abby Kolowicz. I'd watched a few of the UFC fights featuring women and was not about to discount either lady's ability to dole out a solid ass kicking. Edmund had grown silent and sullen, but the truth was that I didn't really know either of these two people well enough to be that tuned in to their moods.

As we sat in the large, open room, I decided to just let my mind clear. It had been full of worry and so much other garbage the past few days that it was time for a bit of a purge.

"Hey, Sleeping Beauty," a voice snapped me back to the present with a jarring degree of discomfort. "We gonna seriously sit here for a half an hour?"

I opened my eyes to see Miranda standing over me, her own expression twisted into a fair impersonation of what I assumed to be the norm for Abby Kolowicz. The thing that I noticed now that I was even minutely more relaxed was that Miranda had a face that I could not describe any other way than to say she was a homely woman. In contrast, Abby Kolowicz was certainly not conventionally pretty, but she still had a certain attractive quality about her.

I looked over at the clock to see that it had barely been ten minutes. I wanted to ask her if she had someplace that she needed to be, but instead, I just groaned and got to my feet.

"Any input on the situation, Edmund?" I asked the man who had retreated to a corner and remained seated with his eyes shut.

168

"You two go on ahead." The man made a settling motion with his body like he might just go to sleep.

"I don't like the idea of leaving you here by yourself," I said, brushing Miranda's hand from my arm as I approached the man. "Safety in numbers."

"Yeah, I don't think that did me any good last time…no reason to think it is gonna change if I hitch myself to your wagon."

"Nobody is hitching themselves to anything. We are together. For lack of a better word, we're a team," I insisted.

"I don't remember the *team* saying we should slam on the brakes and get into it with those people."

"Get into it?" I had to fight not to blow up. Did he miss the whole part about me stopping because I saw something that literally meant life and death to me? "I just stopped to confirm that woman having been bitten and it being outside the so-called seventy-two-hour window we'd been hearing about, had not turned into one of the walking dead."

"Good for you," Edmund replied with a dismissive wave of his hand.

I was confused.

"Why would you want to be alone in this madness?" I asked.

"Did you even ask me where I'd come from when we met? Did it occur to you to maybe ask what I'd been running from or what had messed me up so bad?" Edmund opened his eyes and looked at me with such a profound sadness.

"You said a bunch of zombies were on your tail," I finally said once I managed to remember. "And something about a fence?"

"Yep. That is part of it." Edmund closed his eyes again and took a deep breath. "I was running because the last place I thought was safe turned out not to be. I lost my entire group…including my cousin…the last family I had left in the world."

"Yeah?" I shot back, suddenly not feeling all that sympathetic. This guy was sinking into some sort of funk because he was finally allowed enough time to process what was going on.

Basically, he was having an experience that was the opposite of mine. The thing was, everybody had lost someone they loved. I doubted there was a single family in the world that remained intact at this point. "Okay, you lost somebody. You think that makes you special? I watched my fiancée turn and try to take a bite out of me."

"But it was my fault!" Edmund finally exploded. "If I would've listened to everybody instead of thinking that I knew best…that I had all the answers when it came to keeping us safe, then maybe he would be alive today and I wouldn't still hear his screams…hear him begging for me to help him, then for me to kill him."

"So your answer is to just quit? You found us, we stopped and picked you up, and now we can go someplace where there are others. We can band together and survive this. But I can tell you from experience that trying to go it alone is a mistake."

"Maybe I don't want to try and survive, maybe I don't see the point." Edmund's tone had gone flat, his voice barely above a whisper.

I considered his words for a moment. I'd wrestled with that very idea not too long ago. If not for Grady Simons reminding me that Stephanie would want me to fight, and to not give up, I might have thrown in the towel a few times when things looked their bleakest. The thing was, I didn't know this guy. I certainly did not believe that I had any sway over his life or possessed the type of motivational energy to get him to change his mind.

"Okay," I finally said. "Well, I wish you the best."

I gave him the basic description and location of where Miranda and I would be heading. More than once, I told him that he would be welcome if he chose to join up with me and the people that I was returning to.

Miranda and I exited the rec room and crept to the front of the building just in case they'd left somebody behind to take us down if we chose to leave before their half hour request/demand elapsed. The parking lot was empty as far as I could see. The lone exception being our police car.

I was almost to the door and ready to leave when the smell

of roasting meat tickled my nostrils again. I did an almost military-perfect about-face and headed back across what had once been some sort of game room where I made my way to the huge glass doors that opened out to the outdoor area that included the pool and a fenced-in tennis court through an open gate.

"No way," I breathed, daring to hope that my eyes were not, in fact, playing tricks on me.

I had discovered the source of that smell of roasting meat and was thrilled to see a variety of steaks off to the side of one massive outdoor grill. A garbage can beside the barbecue was stuffed full of discarded grocery store meat packages and a bunch of recognizable cardboard carriers that almost made me giddy as my eyes tracked to a pair of large coolers. Both of them were open and had several bottles of assorted beers submerged in an icy, watery mix. I had no idea where they'd discovered ice, but I was not about to look a gift horse in the mouth.

I looked around and didn't see any signs of a utensil so I gave one of the steaks a tentative poke and discovered that it was still warm, but not too hot to handle. That settled, I grabbed one with my hands, held it firmly, and then tore off a big bite.

"That could be poisoned, you know," Miranda scolded, staring at me with arms folded across her body and one foot tapping in agitation.

"Then I better hurry up and down a couple of those beers so I can go out happy," I managed around a mouthful of well-seasoned and tasty meat.

Since I was already acting like a total heathen and probably looked like a complete animal with grease from the meat trickling into my facial hair growth, I decided to finish off the look by staggering to the cooler like one of the undead.

"Beeerrr," I gurgled in a horrible aping of a zombie moaning for brains in those gawd-awful *Return of the Living Dead* movies.

Seriously, was I the only person who saw the problem with zombies that talk? That franchise of movies had almost ruined the genre. As soon as somebody would mention zombies, you'd always get some clod who had to moan "braaiiinsss". Did they not understand that it was a headshot that killed a zombie, so if it actually ate the brains of its victim, there would be no new zombies spawning?

I laughed so suddenly that beer came out of my nose in a stinging spray. I also lost the bit of steak that I'd still been chewing with the beer chaser to wash it down.

"What the hell is wrong with you?" Miranda snapped, jumping back to avoid my foamy spray, dropping the steak she'd just settled on.

I considered telling her about the string of thoughts that had just whizzed through my mind, but decided that I didn't want her thinking I was an even bigger idiot than she already probably did.

"Nothing, just enjoying the irony of a post-apocalyptic barbecue," I lied.

She eyed me with suspicion and then reached tentatively for a steak to replace the one she'd dropped on the ground. That got me to thinking of the day no doubt on the horizon where it won't even be a thought to reach down, pick food up off the ground and maybe not even dust it off due to the overwhelming hunger gnawing at your belly. That thought was a big buzzkill and I quickly dismissed it.

"You wanna bring some back to Edmund before we go?" I asked after consuming two good-sized steaks and a couple bottles of wonderfully cold beer that had me experiencing only a mild but pleasant buzz.

"Not really," Miranda said after taking a huge pull from the bottle in her hand and emitting a belch that would impress a trucker.

I shrugged, grabbed a steak and a couple of beers, and headed back inside to the rec room where we'd left Edmund. I paused with my hand on the doorknob. I had this terrible thought that something awful would be waiting for me on the other side of the door. It took me a few seconds and a deep breath or two, but I finally opened the door and poked my head inside.

Edmund was still sitting against the wall where we'd left

him just a few minutes ago. His eyes were closed and his hands were resting limply in his lap.

"Hey, Edmund?" I asked, my voice cracking as a tendril of fear wrapped itself around my throat just as the words came out.

The man opened his eyes and regarded me. I could tell that he'd been crying. His eyes were red and puffy, and now that I looked a bit closer, I could see the smudges on his face where he'd wiped at the shed tears.

"I said I don't want to go anywhere," the man croaked.

"Yeah, and that's fine, but those folks left a few steaks on the grill for us as well as some honest-to-goodness cold beer." I held out my offering.

The man stared at me for a moment, and I thought he might refuse my offer. At last, he reached out with his hands and waggled his fingers for me to bring the treasures forth.

I handed him the meat and the sweaty bottle of liquid gold. He stared at it with an expression of wonder and then gave the meat a sniff.

"You sure its beef?" he asked skeptically.

I gave him a smile and a nod. "Saw the packaging myself."

I watched him take that first sip from one of the bottles. He made a very satisfied moan and then promptly bit into the steak.

"Take care of yourself," I said as I headed for the door. "And you know where we are if you change your mind."

I was met just outside the door by Miranda. Together, the two of us exited the community center. Looking around, there were no signs of any mobile walking dead. I had to imagine that any still in the area had likely wandered off in pursuit after the folks who'd just left.

I was climbing into the driver's seat when I heard the distant but all-too-familiar sound of gunfire. Lots of it. I had to focus to get a fix on the general direction.

Jumping into the car, I turned over the engine and dropped it into drive as I jerked the wheel and stomped on the gas as soon as Miranda had shut the passenger side door. We did a squealing turnaround in the parking lot and I rocketed to 132nd. By then, I had the window rolled down.

"What are you doing?" Miranda snapped as I yanked the wheel again and took a hard right at the intersection.

I had a feeling in my gut that I knew exactly what I was hearing. It didn't take a rocket scientist to put things together. Sure, I might be wrong...there could be a number of crazy fringe groups that got a kick out of ambushing people and taking their stuff. Actually...come to think of it, there probably are dozens. But I was feeling fairly confident that I knew what I was hearing.

"Evan?" Miranda repeated, her tone taking on a bit of a desperate quality.

"Get whatever gun ready that you feel best about taking into a fight," I said through gritted teeth. "Unless you want out. If that is the case, speak up now."

"Are you seriously doing this?" she pressed.

My mind was spinning with a jumble of thoughts that were like rocks in a dryer. For too long I'd sat back. I'd willingly let people die as I sought to meet my own selfish needs. Sure, I was doing something for my beloved Newfie, but that did not excuse how I'd allowed people to die so that I could have or get what I wanted. In my book, that, made me just as bad as the individuals that I considered to be the "bad" guys.

My actions had led directly to an awful death for Ariel. She did not deserve what happened, and I could've prevented it. Maybe that bastard Don was lying, maybe he'd already planned on killing her, but I'd basically assured her of that fate. I'd sat with her in the dark and convinced her that things would be okay.

It was time that I start acting instead of reacting...or worse...doing nothing. If I was immune like it now seemed possible, then I had an advantage. Not that I wanted to be bitten. That sounded painful, and I am not a fan of pain.

I glanced over at Miranda and discovered that I wasn't all that surprised when I saw her brandishing one of the police rifles. If my guess was correct, it was an M4. I hadn't really taken time to fully inspect the weapons that we'd acquired at the police station, but I was fairly confident in my guess.

"I'll take one of those," I said.

"You sure that is a good idea?" She glanced at my arm.

"How about you get one ready just in case," I suggested. Of course she was right. I wouldn't admit it out loud. That would just confirm my weakness. It was polite of her not to mention it and simply play along.

As we sped down the road, Miranda grabbed a second rifle, loaded it and rested it between her knees. She also prepped a Glock for each of us.

I could hear the sounds of gunfire in fits and starts. It now had the sounds of a standoff. The barrage of a moment ago was now replaced by more sporadic firing. I just hoped that we arrived in time.

As I took a corner, our rear end fishtailing a bit as we came around it at a speed that was bordering on unsafe, I had to slam on the brakes to avoid a small cluster of the walking dead that were trudging in the direction of all the noise. The tires screeched and I heard Miranda curse as she threw her hands on the dash out of reflex—I was glad she'd made the effort to put on her seatbelt in all the chaos.

Edging to one side of the road, I made it around them as they all bounced and bumped off each other in an attempt to change their direction to face this newest noise. Once we were past, I stomped on the gas again and rocketed onwards toward the firefight.

When I was confident that we were within a couple of blocks, I brought us to a stop. Miranda didn't need to be told, she was already climbing out of the car before I shut off the engine. A lone zombie wandered from the open front door of a house to my left. I winced as I recognized the MP3 player in the protective cage fastened to the person's neck. He had been one of the people brought on that ill-fated run with me.

This person was a walking indictment of my culpability in the death of another human being who did not deserve to die. I mean, maybe the individual was a complete ass hat, but I would never know for sure. The dried blood all down his right side acted to cement his shirt to his flesh, making it difficult to see the actual injuries. That was little consolation as I stared at the pale flesh and tracer-riddled eyes.

Miranda shoved past me and drove a knife into the man's temple. She shot me a sour look and then hurried down the side of that same house the zombie had emerged from. I shook off the emotions that were threatening to paralyze me at this most inopportune time and followed.

We reached a backyard with a tall fence that enclosed it. I heard a quick flurry of shots from just the other side. Since I had no idea who was who, I wasn't sure how to go from here. I'd rushed in to do something, and only now was I realizing that, with the exception of Katy, Abby, the man who I was assuming to be the leader, and maybe one or two other faces, I had no idea who was on what side. It wasn't as if they would be wearing signs or special uniforms that identified them. They would all be regular people.

Miranda crept over to the fence and crouched down. She glanced back to see me still standing there trying to figure out what to do next and waved me over to join her. I crouched down, probably more out of reflex since there were really no bullets flying in my direction.

"…two of them just made it behind that van," a voice hissed from the other side of the fence. "Cover me and I will go around to catch them from behind."

"Just remember, Don said to bring at least a couple back. We need some bodies to do the heavy lifting for the move tonight," a second voice replied.

Problem solved, I thought as I brought my rifle up. Miranda reached over and put a restraining hand on the barrel of my weapon. She gave a curt shake of the head. I raised my eyebrows in question and she leaned in so close that I could feel her lips brush my ears as she spoke.

"As soon as we shoot, we give ourselves away. We need to know more before we just start going off, guns blazing."

It made sense. The problem was that I had no idea how we would find anything out from the confines of this fenced-in backyard.

Pointing at me and then gesturing for me to stay put, Miranda moved down the length of the fence and then ducked behind a small shed that was in the corner. A moment later, she hurried back, staying low and moving quietly through the yard with almost catlike stealth.

Once more she leaned in close. "The yard next to this one is open...no fence. I am going to go over and try to move up behind the person on the other side."

When she pulled back, I mouthed the words, "What do you want me to do?"

"Stay put and be ready to cover my ass," was the silent response.

I wanted to object. After all, wasn't it my decision to stop being a spectator to all this madness and start doing something? Those deaths were on my head, not hers. She didn't know Ariel, Joan, Franklin, or that zombie that had wandered out of the house just a moment ago with the MP3 player around his neck.

Before I had the chance, she had spun around and scuttled back to the shed, vanishing behind it in a bubble of silence as the sounds of more gunshots came from my right, returned by shouts and return fire from the left. It seemed like we might be in the middle of all this madness.

I heard a yelp and what sounded like laughter. A moment later there was the deep boom of a shotgun. As soon as that noise rolled away, I could hear crying...begging...pleading. Then I heard a familiar voice.

"I'll rip your fucking throats out, you pieces of human filth!" It was Kolowicz, and she was close.

Not more than a heartbeat later, a strangled gurgle came from the other side of the fence. That was enough for me. I got up, grabbed the top of the fence and peered over. I could see down the length of it, as well as through the mostly burned down house on the other side to the street beyond where a group of familiar vehicles were all stopped. The van in front had spun sideways and made an effective barricade of the street. At least three bodies were sprawled on the ground near it.

"Don't just stay there gawking, get over here," Miranda

hissed.

"C'mon, somebody else try me!" Kolowicz bellowed from just out of sight to my left beyond the house.

I threw a leg over and landed beside the dead man staring lifelessly up at the sky. The ground under him was darkening as blood leaked from someplace on his back.

Another volley of gunshots and return fire sounded. And then I heard another familiar voice.

"If you insist on you and your people all dying, continue to resist." It was Arlo. "If you surrender now, I can promise that most of you will be allowed to live. Of course, our boss has final say, but from what I've seen, many of you would make good additions to our group."

"You think I am going to believe anything you people say?" Kolowicz snorted, a sardonic laugh coloring her words. "Why would I even consider your offer?"

"Because," Arlo replied solemnly, and then paused. At first I thought he'd simply decided to give a single word answer.

The crack of a rifle came from my immediate right, not too high above me. My head jerked around and I saw a figure crouched down behind the chimney of the neighboring house. The person had a scoped rifle pressed against one shoulder, the weapon adjusting just a fraction, and then spewing lead once more. It was followed by two shots from the left. My neck almost snapped as I jerked around to see a second sniper on the roof of that side as well.

"I can have every single member of your group picked off one by one." There was no emotion in Arlo's voice. He was stating a simple fact.

From all the commotion I heard out in the direction of the street, it was clear that there had just been multiple fatalities. I heard a mix of angry shouts that were almost drowned by wails of despair.

Miranda looked at me. This time I saw hesitation in her eyes. I felt nothing of the sort. I pointed to the roof on the left, and then her. I hiked my thumb to the right and then tapped myself on the chest.

There was a moment where I thought she would balk. When she nodded once, I let out a little sigh of relief. We clasped hands and then moved away from each other. Arlo was speaking again, but I was no longer paying attention. I was about to kill somebody…or die trying.

DEAD: Alone

11

Survivor

Maybe later I could take the time to analyze everything that I'd done these first weeks. For now, I would not allow my conscience to get in the way of what I knew had to be done.

I'd only been getting it partially right up to this point. I'd had no problem with the *idea* that the world had changed and the old rules no longer applied. When it came to putting that into practice, I'd been very selective. While I don't believe that I will ever embrace this new reality...I must accept it fully. That would certainly mean doing things that I would've never imagined just a few weeks ago—hell, even a few hours ago most likely—but I would survive.

I slipped into the backyard of the house on the right and heard something snuffling in a cluster of nearby rhododendron bushes. I barely had time to think of any good expletives when what was left of a brindle colored Boxer crawled out, its head lolling my direction as its tongue licked at the air in anticipation of just how tasty it figured me to be. One of the legs had been gnawed down to the bone, and its belly had been savaged so that all manner of viscera spooled out behind the poor thing as it fought to get free of the large rhododendron and make its way across the small expanse of lawn that existed between us.

Reaching down for the large knife sheathed at my hip, I

drew it and drove it into the head. At least that had been my intention. Apparently the skull of a dog is a bit harder than I anticipated and the point of the blade did little more than dig a furrow down the side of the canine's head and ended up plunging through the upper lip. I jerked back fast and drove it into the filmed over left eye.

The dense base of the budding bush gave a shudder and then vomited out another zombie Boxer. This one did not seem to have any visible injuries, but I seriously did not have the time to give it a thorough inspection. I hastily repeated my actions of sticking it in the eye socket with my blade.

Deciding to stay low, I crawled on my hands and knees until I reached the actual house. As my little dilemma was unfolding, I think two more shots were fired from each location. I heard some return fire, but it was disturbingly minimal. I began to wonder if there would be anybody left to save by the time I got up onto the roof and took out the sniper.

I scurried to the small back porch. It had a sturdy railing all the way around it. I winced twice when a board creaked as I crossed the porch and then climbed up. The next part would be tricky. It would also be the point where I had the greatest chance of being spotted. Considering the fact that I would be completely helpless as I got up onto the roof, I was about to launch myself into a live-or-die situation. It wasn't as if life didn't exist in that state now, on a constant level, but I would be upping the ante.

I peeked up over the lip of the roof and was relieved to see that the sniper was very focused on whatever was happening on the street below. I considered just pulling my handgun and taking this guy down, but that would eliminate any chance Miranda and I had of surprising these people. Since I had no idea how many others were part of this task force, I was going to try to save using the gun as a last resort.

I was smart enough to draw the weapon, give it a quick visual check, and then set it quietly in the trench of the house's gutter. Holding my breath and gritting my teeth against the pain I knew would come from using my still-injured arm, I planted my palms on the roof and then swung my right leg up. Like an idiot, I reflexively glanced down. That almost cost me as I felt my heart begin to thunder in my chest. It suddenly seemed like a long way down if I were to fall. That was an aspect of myself that had never gone away despite my years in construction. I knew some guys who would just bound around up on a job. Not me...despite the amount of ribbing I usually took from the fellas.

Shoving those thoughts away, I pulled myself up just as I heard Arlo begin hollering out another series of threats and ulti-matums. That masked the small amount of sound I was making as I heaved myself up onto the roof and laid flat. I grabbed the pistol in my off hand and once more drew the big knife that I'd just used to put down those two Boxers.

I got to my feet, but stayed down in a crouch. The sniper was sweeping to his left, and then he fired. That almost made me fall back as it startled me just enough to cause my footing to slip. That was also enough noise for him to realize that there was somebody on the roof with him. He started to turn and I did the only thing that I could think of—I adjusted my grip on the knife I was holding so that I had the tip pinched between my thumb and fingers, then I whipped it at him as hard as I could without upsetting my balance too much.

That always looked so cool in movies and television. Unfor-tunately for me, my blade simply thudded into the sniper's shoulder...handle first. It clattered to the sloped surface and slid almost halfway back to me as I stared like a deer in the head-lights at the business end of the rifle pointed at my chest. Luckily, the man was caught just as off guard as I was and was staring dumbly down at the impotent weapon that slid away from him after causing absolutely no damage.

Okay, maybe it bruised his shoulder a little, but that would be about the extent of things. I recovered first and did the only thing left for me to do in this situation: I raised my pistol and fired. My shot rang out and the bullet slammed into the center of the sniper's chest. He didn't go flying, but simply slumped over backwards, his body folding back on his knees. Just as my knife had done, the sniper began to slide down the sloped surface of the roof. His rifle clattered on the shingles and slid by much too fast for me to adjust and grab it, but I was able to retrieve my knife and jam it into the sheath on my hip. Just as the rifle hit the deck below, I heard a scuffle and looked over to see Miranda pulling her knife out of the lower back of her target. Unfortunately, I'd just committed a mistake by taking my eyes off the body. In that brief moment, the situation had changed dramatically.

At first, he'd merely slumped down and began a slow slide, then, it was as if gravity had changed because suddenly he was rolling at me like a human bowling ball. I had to move to my left in a hurry and got out of the way just in time as the body tumbled past and careened off the deck with a nasty cracking sound that might not have been wood splintering.

I scurried up to the chimney and peered around it. At first glance, I counted seven bodies sprawled on the street, obvious victims of the twin snipers. My eyes did another scan and easily discovered where at least Arlo and a few of his party were hunkered down.

There were five people besides Arlo and they were all crouched down behind a decent looking RV. It was sitting parallel to the street and offered maximum coverage from Kolowicz and the others.

Now that I was getting a better look I made a discovery that punched me in the gut. Katy was one of the bodies sprawled on the street in a dark pool of blood that was staining the asphalt. It didn't seem fair. She'd been terribly injured and disfigured; she defied the odds and proved immune to the infection that turned people into the walking dead only to be taken down in a senseless killing by a bunch of narrow-minded ass hats.

Pistols are not really designed for long range. They are capable of hitting distant targets, but their forte is the up-close attack. If I had to guess, I put the distance between me and Arlo to be at about forty yards or so. That would be close to the edge of my effective range.

Up until now, at least it did not seem as if Arlo was aware that he'd lost his snipers. I would probably only have one shot. I was confident that he was at the upper end of the chain of command with Don. Killing him now would save me doing it later. I was not going to commit the cardinal sin of letting one of the important bad guys get away.

I brought the Glock up and took careful aim at the man's body. Part of me hated the idea of shooting a man in the back. It seemed a bit cowardly, but that was quickly snuffed when I watched him gun down one of the people they'd ambushed as he or she tried to sprint across the street to one of their downed companions.

It was just one simple squeeze of the trigger, but in that moment, everything changed for me. I felt a sliver of icy coldness take root in the deepest part of my heart. There was no nausea or regret flooding me. I felt no trace of remorse as I saw the man twitch violently as the bullet pierced his body. Before he could react, I fired twice more. The second shot went just a bit wide, but I corrected for the third and saw his body jerk again.

I had no idea where my round scored until he flopped onto his back and began drumming the ground with his feet as his hands clutched at his throat. Even from this distance, I could see the darkness of his lifeblood trickling through his fingers as he clutched at his neck.

I didn't have time to watch any longer as the people around him were all leaping to their feet and searching frantically for the source of the gunfire that had just ended one of their own. Another squeeze of the trigger caused one of them, a woman, to stagger back as my round caught her in the middle of her chest.

The report of a rifle to my left let me know that Miranda was now joining in the slaughter; and that is exactly what it was. It was the very massacre that Arlo had threatened; the big difference existed in the targets. It took Miranda and I just a few seconds to put an end to all those who had been gathered around Arlo behind that RV which was now splattered with blood that ran in rivulets down its exterior.

The brick of the chimney suddenly exploded right next to my head. I felt a stinging sensation bloom on my right cheek and then felt a much bigger pain erupt around my right eye socket.

The first thought was that I'd just lost my eye.

I dropped to my knees and slid partway back down the slope of the roof. My free hand went to my face and I felt a flap of meat dangling just above and to the side of my right eyeball. My hand came away soaked with blood, but I was cognizant enough to be at least temporarily thankful that my eye still seemed to be intact.

I wanted to get back up and join Miranda in the fight, but the pain had me struggling with the simple act of standing. To make things worse, all the blood was screwing with my ability to judge things like distance. This became clear when I reached up for the chimney in order to pull myself back up to the top of the roof. My hand swiped through the air and caught nothing except for my knuckles which grazed the sharp corner of the brick structure enough to cause me to let loose with a very undignified yelp of pain.

I jerked my hand back, amazed that I had any pain receptors left to send signals to my brain or that I could hurt myself enough to feel it past the white-hot agony already emanating from my right eye.

Another shot was fired from Miranda's direction and I heard her swear which made me believe that she must've missed. I scooted on my butt to reach the crown of the roof and tuck in behind the chimney as best I could.

"Evan!" Miranda hollered.

I looked her direction, but the blood from the injury was now stinging my good eye which was already seeing through a bit of a blurry haze to begin with. I was about to ask her what she wanted when I saw a hand come up onto the lip of my roof from pretty close to the same spot that I'd climbed up.

Before I could ask Miranda if it was friend or foe, she fired another shot off, this one sending up a chunk of the section of shingle where her round hit. "It's one of the bad guys!"

That seemed a bit pointless considering her most recent action. Still, I brought my Glock up and fired at the arm attached to the hand that had just come into view. I have no idea where that bullet went. It didn't hit anything close to where I was aiming.

My depth perception was worse than I thought.

I adjusted down a bit and fired again. Nothing. However, the person trying to climb up onto my roof apparently decided that was a bad idea and the arm snaked away from view.

"I have no angle on that guy!" Miranda called, and then fired again.

I was about to ask her why she was wasting ammo when I glanced over and saw the blurry outline of her profile with the barrel of the rifle definitely pointing out towards where the rest of the bad guys were apparently organizing their counterattack. I made that assumption based on the sounds of bullets slamming into the chimney that I was hiding behind. I was guessing that Miranda was coming under fire as well, but until I could get my eyes cleared, I would have no real idea as to the extent.

I jerked the bottom of my shirt free and cut a big piece of it off using my knife. I wiped at my face to get as much blood cleaned away as possible considering the circumstances. Next, I shoved the wadded-up cloth against where I figured my injury to be. There was a stinging sensation that told me I'd most likely hit the mark. Not having any better ideas, I stuck my knife into the roof and shoved my Glock behind my back, then I just yanked off another big strip of cloth and wrapped it around my head, cinching it as tight as I could stand.

As I did this sloppy bit of field triage, I kept my eyes glued to where that arm had appeared. Nothing reappeared and I snatched my pistol from behind my back and kept it at the ready. I knew I still had a few rounds in the magazine and decided to point my weapon down a bit further than my earlier attempts. I pulled the trigger and got a bit of good news mixed in with the bad. On the good side, at least I'd hit the roof this time as a section of shingle erupted in tar paper, wood, and grit. On the bad side, my shot was still way above where I'd figured it to be...and a few inches to the left.

A wave of relative silence suddenly washed over the scene. I glanced over to see if Miranda was okay. She seemed fine, crouched behind her chimney and fiddling with her weapon. I continued to watch as she patted down the body of the individual that she'd killed on her roof. She produced a box and I figured out that she was reloading. I risked a peek around the corner of my chimney and saw nothing more than a few zombies staggering down the street. They were all veering towards the house that Miranda was on top of, but I didn't see any signs of a living person.

Had we gotten here too late? I wondered.

"Evan? Is that you?" The relative silence was finally broken by Kolowicz.

"Yeah. You guys okay?" I called back.

"No...no we are very much not okay." I heard her voice break up a bit. It was hard to imagine anything that could cause that woman to choke up, but it was clear that she was on the verge of tears if she hadn't already teetered over the edge. "Katy's...dead."

Of course I already knew that, but it still took a bit of air from my lungs to hear it confirmed. I'd been pretty sure that I recognized the body I'd seen sprawled on the street.

"Wait...she's moving. I think she may be alive!"

That caught me by surprise. I almost lost my balance as I hurried to my feet. That was all it took to renew the attacks from the remaining survivors of Arlo's squad. A barrage of gunfire erupted from several locations almost at once as if they'd been just waiting for a target of interest to appear. I ducked back down, but not before I caught a glimpse of Katy's body stirring. She was trying to get up to her hands and knees. I'm no doctor, but I didn't think that was a good idea with all the blood it looked like she'd lost.

I looked over to Miranda and saw her kneeling, her head tilted just a bit as she peered into the scope and swept the area for a target. The moment she found one, the rifle bucked in her grasp and a coil of smoke rolled from the barrel.

As fast as it had started, it was over. The sound of gunfire had completely ceased. All that remained were the moans of the dying...and the undead. I risked another look from my perch behind the chimney, holding my breath as I waited for another round of gunfire. Nothing came and I got to my feet.

"Oops, big mistake," I groaned as a wave of dizziness and nausea rolled through me. I pressed my back against the chimney as I slid back down to my butt.

My vision was already horrible, but when you coupled it with the blurriness from the sick feeling that was washing over me, I was going to end up falling off the roof and dying from a broken neck if I wasn't careful. From where I was sitting, I saw Kolowicz kneeling beside Katy. It looked as if, despite the terrible injuries, the smaller woman was trying to get to her feet.

"Should she be moving?" Miranda called, voicing the very thoughts that were bouncing around inside my own head.

I was starting to struggle with my focus. I sure as hell didn't want to pass out. Once again, that was likely to end up with me falling. I'd come too far to die this way. I wanted to call out for help, but at the moment I felt like Katy was in a more dire predicament than me. I could hold my tongue for another minute or two at least until they got her out of the street and to relative safety.

I saw a few of the other members of this group starting to emerge from wherever they'd hidden during this confrontation. A thought flashed in my head that these people were certainly ill-equipped to survive this apocalypse if their big move during a fight was to run and hide. I was stunned as I saw at least twenty people emerge and start trying to help those who were injured.

The scream snapped my head back down to where Kolowicz had been attending to Katy. I had to rub my eyes because I was having a hard time processing what I was seeing. Katy was immune. I knew that to be true. Yet, if that was true, why did she have her face buried in Kolowicz's throat? A spray of blood shot skyward as Katy pulled free, leaving a nasty wound behind that was spurting a crimson jet in time with its owner's heartbeat.

Miranda wasted no time bringing her rifle up and firing. I saw Katy's head snap back as the bullet entered from the rear and exit the front in a slurry of brain and bone.

Meanwhile, Kolowicz had pushed away and was trying desperately to staunch the flow of blood from her throat. I could do nothing but sit and watch as she struggled from her knees to a standing position. She took a step, staggered first to the left, then the right before crashing back to the ground. I winced when she hit. Her hands had made no effort to break the fall, and when her face slammed into the street's surface, it bounced off it with an audible crunch.

Another round came from Miranda. Kolowicz jerked and then was still. A series of shouts came from everywhere and when I looked around, I saw many of those who'd just emerged from hiding in a furious sprint to get back to their hiding places. Shouts and screams came from several of those who were diving back behind whatever cover they could reach.

"Another attack!"

"Those strangers are in on it!"

"Somebody get them!"

I found that last one to be almost entertaining. Much faster than they'd emerged, this group had vanished from sight. It looked as if they'd even left behind those who were injured that they'd come out to help.

"Wait!" Miranda was shouting over the din. "I was only taking down that girl who just turned and attacked Kolowicz." She paused and then continued. "Katy...her name was Katy. She just took a chunk out of your friend. All I did was put her down and then end the other one's suffering."

"Liar!" somebody screamed. "Katy was immune. She's practically healed up from an attack that happened weeks ago. She doesn't have the infection."

And that was true. I'd seen it with my own two eyes, but I'd also seen her rip out Kolowicz's throat. Something wasn't clicking. I tried to resolve the discrepancies in my head, but my brain was still too fogged over from the pain and the blood loss.

"I'm telling you, that Katy girl was dead. She'd been shot...only she started moving and your friend Kolowicz tried to help her. She got her throat ripped out for her troubles. If you don't believe me, then inspect the bodies," I called down, my voice weak, but at least audible in the relative quiet.

"Yeah, I bet you'd like that," another voice challenged.

I looked around and saw surprisingly few zombies starting

to arrive on the scene in response to first all the gunfire, and now way too much hollering coming from up and down this whole block. I doubted that would hold for long. We needed to resolve this and clear the area.

"Screw 'em, Miranda," I croaked, surprised at how weak my voice sounded—it was as if it might be getting worse. "Most of those idiots hid while a couple of people tried to fend off the attack. They're scared, and are probably not ready to listen to reason. We need to get out of here."

"If you are just going to walk away, then why the hell did you drag us here to help them in the first place?" Miranda snarled in response.

"I made a mistake. I thought the group wanted to survive. I had no idea it was just a select few and that the rest were mere lambs ready for slaughter."

"That's bullshit!" Miranda stood up and moved out from behind the cover of her chimney. "You people want to sur-vive...right?"

There was a long silence. The few zombies that arrived on the scene had turned and were now staggering towards the cor-ner of the roof under where Miranda stood, a few already clustering below with their arms extended, hands grasping futile-ly at the air.

"Of course we want to survive," came a tentative and almost whiny retort. "What kind of question is that?"

"I believe my friend misspoke," I corrected, drawing on whatever strength I could muster. "She made that sound like a question. It is a statement. And if you are going to be a survivor in this new world, then you are going to have to put aside every-thing from the past. You must understand that there won't be any cops coming to save you when you are attacked. And in this new world, a lot of folks have just one thought...to survive at all costs. That means they will kill you to take what you have. That means you need to be prepared to respond...with violence if it is called for. You can't think of it as murder. You are simply doing what the situation calls for, no matter what the old social norms might've been."

I used the chimney to help myself stand up so that the people hiding in the area could perhaps see me better. I saw a few bushes rustle, but as of yet, nobody was willing to be the first person to step out into the open.

"This is happening, people," I continued. I felt a little of my strength returning as adrenaline seeped into my being.

I glanced down at the bodies sprawled everywhere. I spotted Arlo still slumped where I'd killed him. Katy and Kolowicz were almost side-by-side in final death. There were several others that I didn't recognize, as well as an assortment of the walking dead. So far, the relatively small group clustered under Miranda were the only ones still mobile. They were shifting around and trying to wade through the hedge that ran between our two houses now that I was the current noise source.

"You have to accept that things are never going to be the same again. I intend on surviving this madness. I am going to carve out something and make the most of what we have. If you want to be a part of it, then I invite you to join me." I paused again, and a few bodies emerged from hiding. A couple of them glanced at the zombies now starting to gather under me. One of the women pulled a hammer from her belt and advanced. That acted as some sort of catalyst and a few others pulled weapons to help put down the remaining zombies.

"But this won't be easy." I decided that now was as good a time as any to test these people's resolve. It would not do me any good to have them fall in with me and Miranda, only to seize up again the next time we faced opposition. "I am returning to my people, but first, I want to try and put an end to the group that your attackers came from. They are not far away, and it would not do us any good to allow these people to continue with what they are doing. I've seen it firsthand, and now so have you. They are some of the worst sorts that humanity has to offer. And with the end of civilized society, there is nothing to stop them from pursuing their agenda."

I saw faces looking up at me; some with expectation, some with fear, and some with the grim determination I felt would be necessary if humanity was going to avoid extinction. I believed that these people needed to be reminded about Don Evans and his agenda. "They want to wipe out anybody who is not white."

I saw a few faces shut down. The woman who had been the first to take down one of the zombies with her hammer now had a look of open skepticism. But there were a couple that made me nervous. I tried to commit them to memory. Those would be the ones I would expect to be the most likely to turn on me if I could somehow convince these people to join me in what I had planned.

"Here is the situation, people." I glanced over at Miranda and was encouraged when she gave me a nod. "This group is no more organized than you all are, I am willing to bet." Okay, that was probably a lie, but if I was going to have them follow me, I needed to give them a reason to think we stood a chance. "But every single day that we let them be, they will gain strength. There are a scary number of people who subscribe to the type of gospel they are preaching. I was blind to it before. It was just a story that flitted past on the news every so often. But it was there…here. It exists around us. And now, these people don't have any repercussions if they decide to embark on a campaign of terror. Maybe you won't ever cross their paths in the future. But then again, who knows where these people will settle down. I can tell you after recently escaping from their camp that they plan on relocating. What if they just so happen to end up going in the same direction as you people?" I let my gaze linger on a young man who looked Hispanic and the woman beside him who was African-American. "If you're lucky, they'll just kill you where you stand. They let two people I was travelling with get bitten and turn, then they threw me in a room with them and made me kill them. That is the sort of mentality that you will be letting go if you choose to do nothing. And if they don't find you, then can you be okay with knowing that they will do that sort of thing to others?"

I knew I was pushing it. These people had all hidden during the attack. They had demonstrated that they were cowards…or just followers. Either way, I was now asking them to take a huge step off a ledge. I was encouraging them to kill other living beings. That was something I'd struggled with myself until basically just a few minutes ago.

"If you want to live, then follow me," I implored. "Otherwise, I wish you luck, but it will take more than that."

I turned back and made my way off the roof. By the time I reached the ground, Miranda and a dozen others had all come to the back porch of the house where I'd given my speech.

"You look horrible," Miranda gasped.

"Jesus, it looks like most of your eyelid is gone," a male voice added, stepping forward into my field of vision and then physically grabbing me and peering under my makeshift bandage. He was the one I'd assumed to be the leader when we'd first met. "You need to get that cleaned up or you will lose your eye…if it isn't already too late."

"What are you, a fucking doctor?" Miranda spat as she elbowed the man aside and leaned in to take a closer look.

"No, I was a nurse," the man shot back as he reasserted himself in front of me and gripped my chin in his hand so he could turn my head and resume his inspection.

That seemed to be good enough to shut Miranda up, but the rest of the group gathered around all began to fire off various questions about what we were going to do next.

"We are going to go up the road a ways and assess the location where the man who sent those people to attack you are holed up. If possible, and it seems like we have even the slightest chance at success, I plan to attack his group and put an end to the threat they represent." I pulled away from the man inspecting me as I spoke, but I noticed that he didn't move away from me, but instead crossed his arms and waited.

"You aren't doing anything until I at least clean that up properly," the man said once I was done talking.

"We don't have a lot of time to waste," I countered.

"Be that as it may, you will lose that eye if you don't get it cleaned up."

"And how do you propose I do that? Do you have antiseptic in your pocket, or are you just glad to see me?"

"No, but we do have some supplies in one of our vehicles.

The people who chose not to follow you might not want to part with anything, but they are not going to put up a fight if we demand it."

"We won't take everything," I said. "Leave them their share, otherwise we are not much better than those people who attacked you."

"I am gonna check inside this house while you get cleaned up," Miranda huffed, shoving past me and heading up onto the back porch.

Great, I thought, *I have no idea what has her panties in a bunch, but obviously something has pissed her off.*

A few of the other people who had chosen to join me looked back and forth between the nurse who was now heading out to the street where the remnants of their convoy still sat, me, and Miranda's back as she set to breaking the sliding glass back door in order to get inside the house.

I shrugged my shoulders and followed after the male nurse. I caught up to him just as he threw open the back doors of a white utility van. A few of those who had opted not to join me were standing aside and just watching. As I scanned their faces, I saw the same thing on each of them: defeat, hopelessness, emptiness. I tried to imagine a state of mind where I watched people rifle through belongings that might be mine or belong to those travelling with me and doing absolutely nothing about it.

The reality was that those people were already dead. Whether by zombie or raider, it was just a matter of time for them. I edged past them and sat where the nurse indicated as he opened a box and produced a dark brown plastic bottle along with a pouch of cotton balls.

"This is gonna sting," the man said as he pressed a wad of the cotton balls against the opening of the bottle.

"Then maybe you could tell me your name so I know who to properly curse," I quipped.

"Marshawn King."

The man flashed me a smile and nodded his head. He was tall and looked a bit like Denzel Washington. The stubble forming on his head led me to believe that he probably kept it shaved once upon a time when razors were handy and showers weren't a luxury that I would just about give my left nut for at the moment. I saw a variety of tattoos on his dark-skinned arms and he had an ugly scar on the left arm that looked like somebody had tried to cut it off just below the elbow. I bet there was an interesting story to go along with it. His eyes were a chocolate brown, but there was a worn out look to them and I briefly wondered if we all had that same affliction…then he swabbed at my eyelid with the cotton and the only thing left in my mind was the desire to punch him square in the face.

I let loose with an impressive string of profanity and tried to jerk away, but Marshawn had my arm in a vice-like grip that kept me in place. His eyes met mine and a look of concern was there for just a second before he resumed cleaning the area.

"Stay put," he muttered as he pulled out another bag and rifled through it until he found what he was looking for.

A few minutes later, he'd doused some gauze with more of the stinging solution he'd used to clean me up and then pressed it over my eye and wrapped an Ace bandage around to hold it in place.

"Am I going to lose my eye?" I asked once I was sure I could do so without my voice cracking.

"Not sure…it looks pretty bad." Marshawn stepped back to admire his work for a moment. "Okay, that should do it."

"Then we need to gather Miranda and the others. Daylight is burning." I stood up and glanced around at the people who had chosen to join me. "Last chance to change your minds. It is going to likely end with one or more of us dead."

12

Delaying the Inevitable

Marshawn leaned over to me and whispered in my ear, "If you aren't careful, you will absolutely lose that eye. Are you sure you want to do this now?"

I thought it over. I really didn't want to lose my eye. That would really suck. I had just faced my mortality and I was not at all proud of how I'd acted. My selfishness and narrow-mindedness led to the deaths of people that might not have been murdered by me directly, but I could not say that my hands were clean.

I'd read enough books and seen enough movies over the years. If you left the perceived "bad guy" alone instead of attacking when you had the chance, he would come around and make your existence a living hell. Your friends would die painful deaths and you would end up finding yourself taunted by semi-clever quips. Like, for instance, if I did end up losing my eye, he (or she to be fair) would say something like, "I bet you didn't *see* that one coming."

"We are doing this now," I insisted.

"We got a shitload of undead coming this way!" a voice called from the roof of the house that Miranda had been on.

"How about you hang back for this," Marshawn said as he took a look at his bandaging work and then glanced at my wrapped-up arm. "And what's the deal with that." He gave a nod at the offending limb.

"Supposedly its broken," I replied. "The people I am heading back to helped set it. We didn't have any proper cast material, so Betty, one of my friends, she wrapped it up pretty good and showed me how to keep it secure."

"And you're running around, doing all this crap with a busted arm?" the man replied dubiously. "You trying to end up with just a single of everything? I mean, should we lob off one of your legs and maybe remove a testicle so you are uniform?"

"Jesus!" I gasped. "What kind of question is that?"

"The one that seems logical considering the amount of extra strain you are putting on that busted arm. There is no way it is healing properly. I wouldn't be surprised if you haven't done permanent damage to it."

"Yeah, well, to my credit, I didn't think I would live to see it heal."

"We have them coming from every direction!" the same voice called down, this time sounding a bit more frantic.

"We can discuss my health later," I groaned as I stood up.

Maybe it was all the talk about my so-called condition, but I was suddenly feeling really beat up. My arm felt like it had been run through a meat grinder from the inside, and the stinging around my right eye was almost worse. Almost.

"There won't be much to discuss," Marshawn grumbled as he pulled a small caliber pistol from the waist of his pants.

"You sure about that?" I nodded to his weapon.

"You don't need to blow their heads away, just put a round in the brain and switch 'em off."

"Doesn't seem big enough to do the trick," I snickered as I pulled my Glock and made sure it was fully loaded.

"Why is it you white boys always start worrying about size when you're around a brother?" Marshawn deadpanned.

I felt my jaw start to ache from my mouth obviously opening so wide. I'd just met the guy, and not under the best of circumstances. I had no idea how to take this comment. Finally, his mouth split into a wide grin.

"And y'all are even easier to mess with," he chuckled, giving me a careful pat on the shoulder. "Now, let's go kill some zombies."

"Did you ever think you would say those words without a video game controller in your hands?" I said, an ironic laugh rumbling in my throat.

I took two steps and pulled up. Marshawn stopped as well as several of the others who had opted to join me. Now that we were all together, we started towards the approaching wall of zombies that were just rounding the corner at the end of the next block.

"I'm still not convinced that I won't wake up in my bed with all this rattling around in my head. If I do, I'm writing it down. I bet writing about zombies is a much easier life than dealing with their funky asses."

"Make sure you name a character after me." I switched my pistol to my injured arm. I reached down and yanked the rusty and heavily stained machete that was jutting from the head of a downed zombie lying in the gutter. The smell of the horde was just starting to stain my nostrils with its foulness.

You could see it happen with an almost comical slowness. The first zombie to notice we were near came to a stop and began to slowly turn its body to reorient on us. One by one, the other zombies did likewise.

"What'd you do to your eye?" a familiar voice said from a few steps behind me.

I turned around and would've rubbed my eyes in disbelief if I didn't think that would hurt enough to bring me to tears. "Edmund!" I managed around the lump forming in my throat. "I thought you had given up."

"I had, but then one of those damn things stumbled in and I've seen and heard enough people go down to those things to know it is an unpleasant experience." Edmund shrugged his shoulders. "What can I say? I hate pain...it hurts."

That earned him a snicker from the few people standing close enough to hear. Quick introductions were made between Edmund and Marshawn as we all started for the pack of undead that looked the thinnest. There was no need to say it. We would fight through the smallest cluster and then regroup. I noticed Miranda arriving as this little reunion was taking place. If I didn't know better, I would swear that dour expression she apparently had plastered permanently on her face softened just a bit.

The variety of injuries that had turned all these poor souls were varied and gruesome. Seeing these incarnations of the undead as they marched towards us without the ability to feel fear gave me a dose of two very distinct emotions. One was envy. I could only speak for myself as we moved closer to the zombies and began to veer towards our own individual targets that we'd each picked for whatever reason, but I was ready to piss my pants. The other was a dose of shame. I'd been so caught up in myself and never once considered that I was quite fortunate for only having experienced a slight scratch.

It might seem a strange thing, and I can't say I ever heard of such nonsense in any zombie story I'd ever watched, read, or heard. Of course, it wasn't normal for people to ever have the chance at being immune. But I'd probably been infected in one of the most mundane and painless ways possible.

Those thoughts are the only reason I can think of as to why I started to laugh as I reached my first target, such as it was. As soon as my eyes fixed on her, that moment of laughter evaporated and my mouth went dry.

She had probably been a mom. I guessed her to be in her early thirties. She had dark brown hair, and was just a shade over five feet tall. She was neither fat nor skinny. She was just average. There was nothing remarkable about her in any way based on appearance, but I could not help but wonder what had been special about her in life.

That was something I'd picked up from my fiancée, Stephanie. Anytime I lost my temper over being cut off on the road, or cut ahead of in line, those moments when the food I ordered in a restaurant arrived and turned out to be cooked poorly or just plain wrong she knew just what to say. It was as if she could see my anger start to manifest. In those moments that seemed so important back then, she would lean over to me and tell me that he or she was a person with flaws and faults just like me. They might have a reason, or, in the case of a waiter or waitress, no control over what had me so worked up.

"Every single person has something about them that makes them special," she would say.

The first time she did, I asked her what that had to do with anything. Her answer was, once again, beautifully simple.

"One of the things special about you is your heart. The compassion that you have for others. You will say something that you will regret later. Long after that person has forgotten the incident, you will be beating yourself up for how you acted."

I have no idea what made her see me on such a deep level so early in our relationship, but it was that reason and a million others that made me love her. She was just such a good human being that I often wondered what made her pick me.

As I brought up my big knife and prepared to plunge it into this woman's eye socket and end her existence as one of the walking dead, I wondered what had been special about this woman in life. That spell was erased as she moaned, her mouth opening and her bloodstained teeth snapped at the air in anticipation of biting a chunk out of me.

I stepped into her as I struck. The knife went in easy and I jerked it back just as her body went limp and crumbled to the ground. The next couple were a blur and there were no deep thoughts about what they had been like when they were living.

I ducked under the sweeping arms of a man I guessed to be in his fifties. He'd been ripped open and his insides were hanging from the tear in his belly. Even more disgusting was the fact that he'd been more than slightly overweight. A piece of meat from his abdomen was still dangling and the inches-thick layer of fat had turned a nasty grayish-black.

I stuck him in the temple and felt a surge of relief when I realized that I'd somehow fought my way through the worst of the crowd. There were still more zombies trudging my direction, but they were spread out to the point that I might be able to make it past them without having to engage any.

Then I heard *the* scream.

I spun to see some woman that I didn't know as a trio of zombies dragged her to the ground. I also saw what appeared to be the likely culprit of her situation. Standing just back from the scene were two children.

Zombie children.

The pair were still hanging back as if they might simply be observing the scene. The woman vanished under her three attackers, and that seemed to be the signal for the children to pounce and move in. Just like any other zombie, the two children staggered forward and fell on the downed woman.

Amidst the thrashing of the woman's arms and legs, I could see hands clawing and mouths tearing into her flesh wherever they could. At first, the zombies were struggling to get past the layers of clothing, but once they tore away her coat, one of the adult zombies leaned in and buried its face in her belly. If the sound was muted, it could have been something as innocuous as a bunch of people holding the woman down and tickling her and then one of them being so bold as to blow a raspberry on her stomach.

I shook away the shock and the screams flooded back. There was a squirt of blood as the flesh was torn away. I rushed forward with only one objective.

My advance went unnoticed as one of the children now had its mouth fastened to the poor woman's neck. The only positive thing in that moment was that it strangled her screams. They were now wet gagging noises as blood likely filled her throat.

I stopped just a few feet away and brought up my pistol. There was a single moment. It was likely no more than a second. In that instant, her eyes locked on mine. At first, there was that flash of fear as she saw a gun pointed at her face. Maybe it was just my imagination, or maybe my own mind was in overdrive as it tried to re-write what was happening in order to give me some sense of peace that I would likely still never experience again in my life. The next thing to make its way through the ocean of pain that was consuming her was a look of longing. It was as if she reached out to me telepathically and pleaded for me to end her suffering.

I pulled the trigger.

It felt like time slowed down. My eyes recorded every moment like it was being processed frame by agonizing frame. I saw the dark hole appear just above her left eye. Her head snapped back with the violent force of the bullet slamming into her skull.

And then she was still. Her scream ended suddenly and completely, but her mouth remained open and part of me felt like maybe her tormented soul would echo that sound for eternity.

The zombies feasting on the woman took a few more swipes and bites, but it was obvious that they were losing interest very quickly as they began to push away. Their slowness was my only advantage and I hurried in, punching my knife into the side or back of the heads of each one. Oddly enough, the children were still acting just like their adult counterparts.

My mind flashed back to the little zombie girl inside the car in that garage with her mother. Each time I left the room and then returned, she acted in that peculiar manner that I was seeing from the children until I would draw a weapon. These children were not resetting. Just more information to process if and when I ever got the chance.

Around me, I heard the sounds of people fighting off the undead. Some were working in tandem, but most of us were just trying to get through the main group any way possible. As soon as I finished off the last one that had been gathered around the downed woman, I turned to sprint out of the main kill zone again.

"That was a good thing you just did," a voice said from my left.

I turned to see Marshawn and two others—a young man and woman who looked to be barely out of their teens—wade out of the melee. If I looked anything like them, there was not a shower in the world that was hot enough to scour the gore from me.

I turned back to where the others were fighting their way through and searched for Miranda. I felt a trickle of panic when I didn't spot her. I know I'd heard a few screams of people being pulled down, but they all had a very similar quality in their pitch. I doubted that I would've recognized hers or anybody else that I actually knew well in this situation. One was pretty much like the other. Also, I still didn't really know Miranda that well. We'd simply been traveling together for a while.

"Evan!" a voice shouted, causing me to snap my head around to look behind me.

I turned to see Miranda pretty much clear of the mob and almost a block away with a few others. I guess I shouldn't be surprised.

With Marshawn, his two companions, and another man who had just fought clear of four of the undead, we took off and did our best to get completely free of the horde. By the time we reached the end of the next block, there were a handful of undead that had turned to pursue us, but the screams from those that were not yet clear and fighting for their life—a few that were obviously in a losing battle—caused those to stop and then turn unsteadily back towards the main body of the herd.

We stood as silent sentinels over a scene of terrible carnage. It was made worse by our inaction, but it was clear that each of us knew there would be no attempt to wade back into the fray. We'd made it. Each of us had survived this far and would only continue to do so by taking care of ourselves first.

"This is the new world," Marshawn whispered. "Every man and woman has to consider self-preservation first."

I wasn't sure if his whisper was so quiet in order to avoid detection, or if he hadn't intended to be heard. I glanced around and saw a few of my new companions nodding. Miranda was simply staring back at the last of the skirmishes. It was then that I realized that Edmund was missing.

I scanned the scene, my eyes drifting from one cluster of zombies attacking a survivor to the next. At last, I found him. He was shoving an elderly male zombie away with one hand as he brought a machete down with the other to cleave into the head of a young woman still wearing the tattered remains of a bathrobe. In fact, it might've been that robe that was saving him at the moment. It was all twisted and torn and the tie had miraculously gotten tangled around her like a blue boa constrictor. The woman's arms were almost pinned to her sides, but that still left a very dangerous mouth that snapped at him. I was too far away to actually hear it, but I swear I could hear the teeth gnashing together with an audible click each time they came together just inches from his face.

Then he went down and I lost sight of him. There was a part of me that wanted to rush forward and try to help, but I knew that getting out once had been a feat...almost a miracle. To tempt fate twice so soon was asking to die.

But I'm immune, I thought.

Yes, it would absolutely suck to be bitten. Even worse would be the fate of the mob dragging me to the ground and ripping me apart.

I had the desire to survive, but I'd already sent too many people to their deaths by my actions, or worse, my inaction. I was perhaps five or six steps towards the madness when a hand grabbed my arm. I spun to see Miranda standing there with a look that was equal parts concern, anger, and fear.

"You can't go back there," she hissed. There was a tremor to her voice that caught me off balance and made me hesitate.

The entire time this was playing out, Edmund was back there—possibly fighting for his life. He'd made the choice to join me. That meant something. I could not ignore it.

Pulling away, I blocked Miranda's attempt to grab me again. "I have to," I said.

It was not anything special, but it said everything in tone that was lacking due to the brevity. I turned back and started for where I'd last seen Edmund.

"You don't want to live," a voice growled from my left and just behind me. "You have some sort of crazy death wish."

I looked to Marshawn striding fast to catch me and fall in beside me. He had a pistol in each hand, apparently forgoing the peashooter that I'd seen him with moments before. He swerved slightly and shoved the barrel up against the back of a zombie's head and fired. The blast was only slightly muffled and all the zombies closest to us that were not already occupied with rending and tearing apart the handful of survivors that hadn't made it through turned to face us.

I stepped to my right with my Glock in hand and dropped two in a hurry. I saw a flurry of activity in the midst of the writhing pile of arms and legs where I was pretty sure Edmund had fallen. If nothing else, he deserved a permanent death.

There was a shout. It wasn't a scream. This was like somebody at the gym pressing a heavy weight. There was real force and energy behind it. When the figure stood, he was covered in gore, but I recognized Edmund. He pushed a body aside that was draped over his shoulder and stepped over another corpse. The problem was that for each one he got free of, it looked like two more took their place.

I brought my pistol up and fired at one that was just about to get ahold of one arm. Edmund was slashing with two knives now. He'd apparently lost his machete at some point. He would jab first one, then the next as his face became a mask of rage.

His eyes found mine and they lit up. Maybe it was just relief that he had not been abandoned. Whatever the reason, a smile spread across his features as he renewed his attacks and counters to the undead still trying to feast on him. Marshawn had managed to get ahead of me by a few paces and shoved one of his pistols into the waistband of his jeans as he pulled a long knife from a sheath at his hip.

I rushed up beside him as one zombie on the ground reached up to try and grab his legs. I kicked the thing in the side of the head. While it had no outward effect on it, the body had shifted enough to end up on its side. It now turned its attention to getting back onto its belly and I took that moment to plant my foot in the middle of its back. I followed Marshawn's lead and drew a blade which I promptly slammed into the base of the zombie's exposed neck in an upwards thrust aimed at the brain pan.

I was now just a few steps from Edmund. He reached out for me as yet another zombie tried to pull him down from behind. My fingertips brushed his and he staggered back as two more zombies grabbed his shoulders and tried to yank him back. He thrashed and jerked, but they showed no signs of letting go as they moaned in apparent anticipation of their upcoming feast.

Edmund was starting to lose his footing now as the fifth and sixth zombies fought for position like a litter of puppies. If he went down again, I had no doubt that he would die the horrific and painful death that only being eaten alive can offer.

There was no time to think, and no other option, I dove forward. The only thing I did have the presence of mind to do in the process was to turn my body so that I collided with Edmund using the shoulder of my good arm.

We went tumbling and I felt a foot connect with my jaw hard enough to make me see stars. My vision began to tunnel as darkness tried to close in, but I forced it back with everything I had left in me. I landed on my side and found myself staring into the filmed over eyes of a girl in her early teens. The face of some blonde pop star named Shari—I know because it was visible through the bloodstains in big glittery blue letters—stared back at me from the shirt. Her half-lidded eyes trying to ooze sexuality but managing nothing above basic sluttiness.

I realized that I still held my knife. Somewhere in the madness, my Glock had spun away. It probably hadn't helped that I'd been holding it in my bad hand; the ace bandage on that arm becoming unraveled as I had seemingly lost the fasteners in the chaos.

I brought my good hand up and jabbed the blade into the eye of the girl as I rose to my knees. Edmund was untangling himself from a pair of the undead. He was down to one Buck knife, but he was using his arm like a piston as he jabbed at the zombies close enough to be a threat.

Like a guardian angel sent down to sweep up his charge, Marshawn grabbed Edmund and physically slung him away from the melee and in the direction of safety. He turned to me and his expression changed to one of grave concern. He hopped over one downed corpse and kicked away another to reach me. I was stunned when he made the adjustment that allowed him to grab my good arm and yank me past him.

I wasn't foolish enough to pause and staggered forward with the momentum he'd provided. Once I was confident that I was clear, I slowed to look back…just in time for Marshawn to race past me like the devil himself was in pursuit. Taking the hint, I joined in the run.

We rounded a corner and the group began to slow now that danger was behind us. I took that opportunity to work my way to the lead of the group. As I did, I counted. There were eleven of us—seven men and four women. I had no idea how many people had been lost back there, but I was buoyed by being around this many living beings. It was the most I'd been in company with since the Franklin High School FEMA center.

"Hey…this is back the way we came," somebody called out after we'd gone a few blocks.

"I have a car back towards the rec center that you all abandoned," I said as I continued on.

"That's super for you, but that doesn't do anything for the rest of us," the person insisted.

I turned to see a man stopped with his fists on his hips, his feet planted in protest of moving another step. I didn't know this guy from Adam, but I had an instant disliking for him. After my encounter with Brandon Cook, I decided to trust my gut.

"Then stay here and die, I really don't care." I gave the guy a dismissive wave of my hand and turned to walk away.

I breathed a little sigh of relief when first Miranda, then Marshawn and Edmund, and then more of the group hurried to catch up. We passed houses that had been looted, and a few that had suffered from the rash of fires that broke out when all hell broke loose.

I discovered that I wasn't even curious as to whether or not the dissenter had opted to join the group. I had a goal in mind and I was going to see it through.

"You aren't still thinking of taking on this Don Evans and his people, are you?" Miranda whispered as we hurried along the empty streets of a city that was becoming a wasteland.

"I have to at least take a look before we head to my own crew." A voice in the back of my head was arguing against that sentiment. It was pretty foolish considering our situation and current circumstances. Despite that inner warning, I needed to see his camp one more time and get an idea what we would face. If I was fortunate, maybe they would be gone leaving no trace. That would take any further decisions out of my hands. I could simply drive my vehicle loaded with food and supplies for Chewie back to where Carl and Betty were still hopefully safe and sound.

If we made it back intact, I could actually take the time to rest and heal. My entire body felt as if it had been run through a meat grinder. I was sore, exhausted, and ready to put my feet up for a few days and just do nothing but sleep and pet my dog.

My mind was drifting to a good place. We'd gotten clear of that horde and lost a few people in the process, but it could've been worse. We would get to my vehicle, cram as many people in it as possible, and the rest would have to sit on the roof or the hood. I could keep the speed slow, and I didn't think there would be any cops out to enforce the 'Click it or ticket' campaign.

"Evan," Marshawn whispered, pulling me from my reverie.

I glanced over at the man to see that he was more grim-faced than usual. His eyes kept flicking past me and then back as if something just over my shoulder had his attention and would not let it go.

I could not help but turn to look and see what had this man so vexed. I almost tripped over my own feet when I realized what had him so disturbed.

"Hey, Edmund," I said around a throat that was growing tighter and drier with each second.

"Yeah, Evan?" He looked over at me when I spoke so that we were making direct eye contact. My name faded on his lips as he saw my expression.

It was no trick of the light. The darkening of the capillaries was getting more pronounced with each passing second. I was literally watching the infection take root in this man.

"You sure you didn't get bitten or scratched back there?"

The man stopped walking and looked at me. His eyes were growing wide with fear. He knew something was wrong and he had probably already guessed as to what.

"I think I would've been aware."

"No way," Miranda breathed as she stopped beside the man and saw what all of us could now see quite plainly.

"My eyes are bloodshot in black, aren't they?" he asked. The question wasn't directed at any one person and the response he got consisted of a few muttered affirmations mixed in with those who chose to just turn away and end any eye contact with the man.

"But I didn't get bit," Edmund insisted, spinning back to face me with tears starting to fill his eyes. "This is a mistake."

There was a strange crunching sound and the man's eyes went wide. He fell to the ground, his body still twitching in the last moments of final death. A large metal spike jutted from the back of his skull.

Miranda stared down at the man for a moment. Everybody else just stood in shocked and silent immobility.

"Why would you do that?" Marshawn stepped towards Miranda, his hands balled into fists.

"Would you prefer that he suffer? Did you want to wait until he turned into one of those things?"

"I…well…" The man deflated and stepped back from Miranda who knelt down beside Edmund's corpse.

At first I thought that she was simply retrieving the large railroad spike that she had driven into the back of Edmund's head. I was stunned when she bowed her head. I could hear whispered words coming from her as she prayed and then very gently closed the man's eyes one final time.

She stood up and looked around at all the eyes that were now staring at her—mine included. She opened her mouth to speak, but then clamped her teeth together and turned on her heel. Without warning, she stormed away in the direction that we'd been heading.

One by one, the others fell in and we resumed our trek. I considered my options for about a block and then broke away from the group and jogged to catch up to Miranda. Once I caught up, I fell in beside her, matching her stride.

"You did the right thing," I whispered.

She said nothing, but I think I saw her eyes flick towards me briefly. We continued on in silence for a few more steps.

"You could have said so back there instead of leaving me out to dry," she finally said.

"Honestly, it took me a few minutes to get my mind wrapped around it. I doubt I would've seen your side in this as recent as yesterday," I admitted.

"Well you better get your stuff wired in tight if you are gonna lead our group."

"Who said anything about me leading?"

"If you have to tell people you are the leader, then you ain't it," Miranda snickered. "Being a leader is about having people willing to follow you. You sort of put off a good vibe. People are drawn to it. If you want proof, just look over your shoulder at the little flock that you've already built."

"I didn't build anything," I sputtered. "I'm just trying to get back to my people and my dog. Hell, until just a while ago, I thought that I was a dead man walking. The possibility of immunity never crossed my mind."

"Yeah, well, I don't think this is gonna be much like the movies," Miranda snorted. "In fact, if you have this secure compound that you've been talking about, you might need to consider how many people can fit there comfortably. If we pack it in too tight, we will be dealing with illness and hot tempers before long."

"You mean turn people away?"

"If it comes to that." She paused as if considering her next words. "We don't want to let in the wrong sort of people."

I knew what she meant. Unlike that creep, Don Evans, who felt that anybody who did not match his skin tone needed to be eliminated, Miranda was concerned about letting in people like Don. People like Brandon Cook for instance. I'd brought him back to the group despite my gut feeling that he was bad.

"I understand what you mean, but how are we going to know the difference between the good guys and the bad? It isn't like they'll be wearing signs around their necks."

Miranda stopped suddenly and grabbed my arm. I stopped and looked first at her, then let my gaze follow hers. She was perhaps sixteen. Or...she had been. Now the girl was swinging by a noose that had been tossed over a street light. Her feet dangled about two feet from the ground. That was disturbing in and of itself. It was what was scrawled on the sign hanging around her neck.

I'm no saint. I am a flawed human being. I can't say for a fact that I've never uttered a racial slur. One or two may very well have slipped from my mouth in anger. Most likely while I was behind the wheel. But I would not, nor could I ever make racism a part of my life.

Taking a closer look at this poor girl, I could see that being lynched had not been the worst part of her ordeal. Her body was a mess. Both eyes were swollen shut and I could see blood starting to dry around her nose as well as her mouth were her lips had been shredded against her teeth in what had to have been a brutal beating. The fingers of her right hand were still trapped between her throat and the noose where she'd obviously tried to free herself.

"This wasn't too long ago," Marshawn said as he walked up beside me.

"And I have a good idea who the culprits are," I hissed.

I turned to the rest of the group that were all coming to a stop and staring up at the poor girl who had suffered such a needless and cruel death. Most were fixated on the terrible sight, but there were others who could not bring themselves to look. While I was glad they were upset by this scene, I was also concerned. Those were the sort who might freeze up when it came time to take a human life. If we were going to survive, there could be no hesitation. That time was past. I'm sure it had been long ago. I imagine I was feeling many of the same emotions that Carl had felt when I basically went into shock after he and I killed Brandon and his cohort.

Carl had known all the way back on the day he beat down that first zombie in my bedroom. I looked at some of my actions and was almost embarrassed. This was not the time for such things, however, as I stepped towards the group and surveyed them for a few seconds.

"The people who did this are not far from here. As soon as I get my car, I plan on heading back there. They've suffered some losses, but I have no idea what their actual numbers might be. If there are not too many, then I plan on ending them right here and now." I paused and let that sink in. "If we have an opportunity, I fully intend to kill these people."

I intentionally used the word "kill" when I spoke. I thought it had a harsh sound to it, and this was going to be nothing if not harsh. I knew from experience that the taking of another life had a way of taking a serious emotional toll on a person. It was not something that you could erase or undo, and unless some of these folks had actually killed a person (as opposed to a zombie), then they would be in for a rude awakening.

"If you don't feel that you can take part in this, I understand, but from this point on, if you are following me, then you are in this to the end." I didn't want to push any potential help away, but I could not afford to have somebody freeze up if we did make our attack now. "So, I am only going to ask this once...who is in?"

I was surprised when all but two hands went up. I looked over at Marshawn and nodded. "These two trustworthy?"

"I know her," he pointed to a petite blonde girl who looked like a stiff breeze might knock her over. "She was my babysitter. I don't know this guy."

"Name's Stevie Ray Nichols, most folks call me Nicky." The man extended a hand to me—I shook it after I realized what he was doing—then he repeated the gesture with Marshawn. "I joined up with you folks two days ago. I was one of the people trapped in that railroad car."

Stevie Ray Nichols, or Nicky, was a man in his late twenties. It wasn't hard to imagine him tossing bales of hay onto a cart by day and hanging out at some dank and dirty cowboy bar at night. He had blonde hair even whiter than the young babysitter's and a gap between his front teeth that looked like it was seriously missing a long stalk of wheat or straw or whatever it was that cowboys stuck between their teeth. I didn't begrudge anybody for sitting out what was bound to be a nasty fight if one ended up happening, but this was a very able-bodied young man. Maybe I was relying on stereotypes, but this strapping young man looked like he could handle his business in a fight.

"Went hunting with my daddy when I was a youngster," Nicky started to explain, obviously seeing the look on my face and deducing my concern and perhaps more than a little suspicion. "Had a six-point buck in my scope on my first trip…first dang morning even." His face flushed and he dropped his gaze. "Then my hands started shaking."

"Buck fever," Marshawn said with a nod.

"I don't doubt that the people doing all this have to be stopped, but I just don't think I can do it…" His face flushed an even brighter red. "And I don't want to die because I couldn't pull the trigger…or worse, be the cause of somebody else's death."

I glanced over at Marshawn, then Miranda. They both returned my look with a shrug.

"No use delaying the inevitable," I said with a sigh. I pulled out my keys. "But I can't just hand all the stuff I grabbed over to you." I knew I was going to catch a dose of hell for what I was about to do.

13

Stepping Off the Ledge

In the end, Miranda put up almost no argument about not coming with me on this run. I think she saw the logic in her being along for the ride with all the supplies we'd gathered. If it was just the dog food, I doubt anybody would covet it enough to run off with it, but the gear we'd nabbed from the police station was a different story.

She'd obviously not been happy about it, but she acquiesced without so much as a dirty look. I found myself suddenly very relieved with that issue out of the way.

Most everybody had their own weapons, but a few were lacking any sort of firepower and were more than happy to pick up whatever struck their fancy from the police hardware. I limited everybody who chose to scoop up a police pistol or rifle to four magazines worth of ammunition.

They were in short supply, but I decided to don one of the Kevlar vests under my heavy coat. I wasn't interested in the helmets, but Marshawn grabbed one along with a vest and one of the M4 rifles.

After making certain that Miranda knew exactly where to find Carl and the others—which seemed to annoy her more than her relegation to being a watchdog over our procured gear—we all said our farewells. I watched the car roll away and felt confident that it was in good hands. Nicky had been tasked to drive. I assume Miranda made that arrangement so that she would have her hands free. At least that would've been my reason.

"Okay, this place is at the big church on Sunnyside and 142nd," I announced to the group. "They have it barricaded with stalled vehicles around the lot. There is a waist-high brick wall around the back. I am willing to bet that is our best way in. I have no idea what their numbers are, so I think that we would be best served by getting there, finding some good spots to scout from, and then making a decision about whether we hit these people now. If they are simply too much for us to have a reasonable shot, then we can make it back to where I sent Miranda and formulate a defensive plan should they come sniffing about."

"How would they just happen upon this place of yours?" one of the people gathered around asked.

"They already made a run on it once and were repelled. It was only a small scouting group, and only one of their people managed to escape, but that one person is enough to lead them back with greater numbers if they decide to do so."

Okay, I left out a lot of details, but they didn't need to know that I had basically sold my old group out to these assholes. I certainly wasn't proud of my actions, and I doubted I would inspire much confidence by revealing such things. Before anybody could ask any more about the subject, I moved on.

"We don't have any way to communicate, and I doubt any of us will be lucky enough to stumble across a set of fully charged two-way radios, so we will need to rely on signals. As soon as we get close, we will select a good rendezvous point and set a time to meet back where we can share our intel." I glanced over at Marshawn. "You got anything to add?"

"Sounds like you have it all under control, chief," he said with a shrug and a crooked smile.

With that, we started towards our destination. Zombies were scattered along the way, but we only deviated from our course to take down the ones that were getting close enough to be a concern. We did our best to stay quiet which kept too many from tagging along. After a dozen or so blocks, it was suggested that we send a few of our people back to take down the small cluster that was starting to gain in size behind us.

I agreed as long as nobody took any unnecessary risks. That actually got a few raised eyebrows and funny looks.

"We are in the middle of the zombie apocalypse preparing to possibly launch a strike on a racist band of raiders holed up in a church, is there ever gonna be such a thing as an unnecessary risk again?" Marshawn snorted, shaking his head as he motioned for those he selected to go back and take care of our little zombie problem before it became too big to handle.

The area wasn't one I was overly familiar with, but I knew where Sunnyside Road existed in relation to us. And finding Southeast 142nd Avenue was simple mathematics. We were cutting through a neighborhood and at the junction of Southeast 134th Avenue and Southeast Scenic Ridge Drive. I was also seeing a few familiar landmarks. Since this wasn't a neighborhood that I was actually acquainted with, I had to guess that I'd come through here during my escape.

As if fate wanted to do me the favor of making that confirmation, a trio of zombies rounded the corner of a nearby house. I had to figure that the battery had died, but I recognized the contraption strapped to the neck of one of the zombies. The man had been one of those poor people fated to be on that mission where I'd escaped, causing Natasha to activate the MP3 noisemakers we'd each been fitted with. I'd killed mine by diving into a water-filled ditch.

He had bites all up and down his arms and his pants had been ripped off. From the looks of it, his upper right thigh had been tucked into like a Thanksgiving dinner. The entire upper part of his leg had a cantaloupe sized chunk torn away that made me wonder how he could possibly keep his feet. Something had ripped into his right pectoral as well. This guy had obviously been pulled down by a small pack of undead and savaged. It was shudder inducing to imagine such a fate, but it was made worse by the fact that I knew beyond any doubt that I was responsible.

It would've been very easy to skirt this little group of zombies, but I felt I owed something to this guy. I veered away, ignoring the exasperated objections voiced by Marshawn and some of the others.

I stopped just a few feet away from the visible source of my guilt and the fodder travelling with him. There would be no way I could take down just the one. I would have to fight my way through to my intended target. This group consisted of two male and three female zombies, one an elderly lady lacking any visible teeth which struck me as comical. She was the zombie equivalent to an unloaded gun. In fact, slap a set of sturdy gloves on her and she would be about as dangerous as a puppy. I have no idea what set my mind down that path, but it was enough to allow me to basically ignore her as I chose the male that was not my primary target. Two reasons, the first being that he was the closest. The second reason was that he also looked like he'd fed recently. There was a stain around his mouth that still had some of its reddish tint.

I chose a machete to deal with these particular undead and brought it around in a sidearm swing that dug into the temple of my first target. Using my left arm to hack and slash was almost starting to feel natural. That didn't mean that I would not look forward to the day that my right arm was fully healed.

I jerked the blade free and took down a young woman who might've been a banker, an accountant, or simply liked to dress in non-descript skirts and blouses while wearing sensible shoes. Her death had come from having her throat torn open by the looks of things. The blood had long since dried, flaked away, and left little more than a black stain on her now shabby clothes and gray, tattered skin. I ended her with an overhand chop that broke her skull open more than actually cutting into it.

I was stepping up to my intended target just as Marshawn rushed up. He was about to take down the man that I'd sent to his death.

"No!" I shouted, causing Marshawn to skid to a stop.

He backed up a few steps in a hurry and then spun around to face me. "What the hell?"

"That one is mine," I said grimly as I pushed past and lined up my attack.

He had not been anything remarkable. Just a man…a face in the crowd. Yet, our paths had crossed and I'd altered his fate irrevocably. I tried to tell myself that I couldn't hold onto this anymore. I'd made choices, and I would have to live with those consequences. It was not really a form of atonement, but I felt as if it would be important for me to put this man down. If asked, I couldn't really explain why I felt the way I did.

The man reached for me and I shoved him away, but not before his cold, dead hands brushed my face. That sensation caused a shudder. There was an unnatural feeling to having something dead come into contact with your exposed flesh; at least that was the case for me.

"I'm sorry," I whispered.

I used my right foot to sweep his legs out from underneath him. As soon as the body hit the ground, I moved in, planting my heel in between his shoulder blades. The swing was sudden, and the man's ending proved anticlimactic. I felt no sense of closure or ease in my conscience.

"Just as well," I whispered as I jerked the blade free.

Everything had grown blurry and it took me a second to realize that tears had welled up in my eyes. I wiped at them with the sleeve of my shirt and looked around to realize that Marshawn and the others had put down the other few zombies that made up this particular little cluster.

I made no effort to explain, and nobody asked as we resumed our trek. I could feel something building in me with every step that I took bringing me closer to Don Evans and his band of followers. It wasn't necessarily hatred, but it was a type of anger that I'd never felt or even knew existed. At first, it scared me.

My mind was clearing the shelves of anything that might get in the way of what I knew had to be done. Wrapped in my own thoughts, I wondered briefly if this was what turned people into sociopaths. I was on my way to a place where I would be committing acts of murder; there was no nice way to sugarcoat this and take away the reality.

That was another aspect of the fiction that was sadly lacking. I had seen plenty of movies and shows where people killed each other with no apparent mental aftermath. How could anybody take that as even possible with what we'd seen from our troops returning home. Killing another human being is just not an acceptable act for most. I acknowledged as I marched onward that it would happen. Period. That did not make it any more palatable.

"You okay?" Marshawn's voice chiseled into my awareness, snapping me out of the trance I'd put myself in to hopefully steel myself for what lie ahead.

"Nope," I answered simply.

I waited for a reply or a question from the man, but he simply walked beside me in silence for a few blocks.

I pulled up as we reached a grassy expanse with woods on the far side. With my one eye covered, I had to physically stop walking and examine the area to find where I was almost certain I'd come through. I knew there would be a little stream cutting through the area, but that was the only thing that stood out in my memory. In truth, I'd been running for my life. My brain had other things that had taken priority other than committing the landscape to memory.

"We're close," I finally said. "It will be across there, to another neighborhood that they were systematically stripping of supplies. The church will be to our left eventually, and not far. I think now is a good time to solidify our plan."

The rest of the people that had opted to follow were now gathered around. As I looked at their faces, I saw a variety of expressions that mirrored what had been going on in my head. Mixed in were traces of doubt, fear, and the most frightening expression that I saw on a couple of our group—nothing.

We went over the signals one more time to be absolutely certain that everybody had them down. I stressed that I really wanted to make this happen now before they slipped away, but that I would not ask or expect everybody to charge in to their deaths.

"I think we all realize what we are dealing with here," Marshawn said, stepping into the middle of our cluster. "And you might feel like you are ready to go and do what we are asking you to do, but I doubt that any of us has killed a man—"

"Or woman," I blurted, remembering Natasha and feeling certain that she wasn't the only woman in that group.

"Or woman," Marshawn agreed. "I will take three of you with me and circle along the back side of the church. Our goal will be to find any sort of rear exit and cover it."

"My group will be coming in from the north with Marshawn's people to our right," I continued. "That means anything moving in from any other direction has to be considered likely to be hostile. Undead or otherwise, we take down anything and everything." I scanned the faces again and saw a few more expressions void of anything.

"This is your last chance to back out," Marshawn said after a painful silence as we all stood on the precipice of murder. There is no coming back from it, I knew that for a fact.

"We're here to put an end to that, right?" one of the women asked, her voice so hushed that a breeze would have whisked her words away before we could hear them. She pointed past us to a light pole that could be made out through the trees. If it would've been full-on spring, there would've been too much greenery and the example she'd located might not have been seen.

I had to crane my neck, but a gentle breeze helped by giving a little push to the body hanging from the light fixture's metal arm. We were too far away to tell if it was a zombie, and I honestly couldn't make out if the person was of a non-Caucasian ethnicity but, considering the situation, it seemed like a safe bet. I knew for a fact that there hadn't been anybody hanging there when I'd been escorted through on the mission that had facilitated my escape.

One of our group brought a hunting rifle to his shoulder and peered through the scope. He didn't need to say anything; the expression on his face told the story for us. The real giveaway was his inability to look at Marshawn or any of the other members in the group that were not white.

I was suddenly very conscious of my skin tone. I knew that I was nothing like Don Evans and his ilk, but I felt a wave of shame roll through me.

At last, we all gave solemn hugs or handshakes and went our separate ways. Just as we started to split, Marshawn stepped over and clasped my right forearm in a firm grip. "When this is done, we can talk about whatever is bothering you. But I want you to know that I got your back…always."

I nodded. There was nothing else to say. I looked at my team. The woman who'd noticed the hanging body and four other men were with me.

We hadn't gone more than ten yards or so into the sparse woods when the sounds of activity began to filter through to us. To their credit, Don's people weren't making that much noise. All conversations were kept low to the point of only sounding like giant bumblebees. The sliding or pushing of what sounded like crates of some sort being shoved were the most dominant noise source.

We spread out to form a loose line and crept forward through the brush, each of us doing his or her best to stay under cover. I was the center of the line and a step or two ahead of everybody else. When I reached the edge of the wooded area, I came to a halt and got a look at my surroundings. To our right, in the direction that Marshawn and the others would come from was the neighborhood that butted against the west side of the church. It showed signs of several fires that were just starting to grow and consume the houses. If I had to guess, I would think that Don and his people were using that as a diversion. That also led me to believe that they were preparing to roll out of the place now.

As I scanned the parking lot where I could make out some activity, I noticed three school buses in a line. That was where everything was being loaded—both on top and inside. I focused my attention on the buses and tried to discern between the different people that I saw rushing around.

One thing I noticed was that every single one of them was armed with a pistol on their hip. Some also had a rifle or shotgun slung over one shoulder. In addition, each of them had knives in a variety of sizes dangling from their belt.

Across the parking lot, I saw a team of three people rushing about and taking down any zombies that wandered close. So far, there wasn't too much activity. I had a feeling that would change as soon as they turned over the engines on those buses.

While not totally certain, I thought that I counted eleven people. That didn't mean there weren't any more lurking inside the series of buildings, that just meant that it seemed as if they had eleven different people involved in loading up supplies. Since I didn't see Don Evans, I had to assume that he was inside and that he probably had some of his upper-level minions gathered around as he laid out whatever plan he had floating around in his head. I also did not see Natasha.

A flutter of white caught my attention and I glanced over to my right to see Marshawn and two of the people in his group peering over the brick wall. From my vantage point, I didn't see anybody at the rear of the building. That meant it was safe for him to advance and I gave the "go ahead" motion with my hands. I adjusted the bandage on my head a bit, wishing I could just tear it off and be done with it, but Marshawn made is seem like the injury was at least somewhat serious, so I kept it on and did my best to tighten it a little before things got crazy.

I withdrew a few feet and motioned my team over to me. As they gathered around, I made note of who carried what weapons. I had two men with scoped hunting rifles. They would be the shock portion of my assault.

"You two move to the far left and right of our position. As soon as I give the signal, start picking off those closest to the buses. If you can nail one just as they are climbing in so that their body is maybe in the way of people trying to get inside, so much the better."

"We're really doing this," the woman muttered, shaking her head.

I didn't have time to coddle anybody. We were going to strike hard and fast. My only concern was that I had yet to see any sign of Don Evans…or Natasha for that matter. I had a feeling that this would prove to be a prime example of "cut off the head of the snake and the body dies" when it came to the followers. I already knew of at least one person who was simply falling in with the best numbers. Of course Arlo was dead now, but there could be more like him who were not fully under Don's influence and just along for the safety the group provided. It might not be too late for some of them if we could just kill Don.

It was that line of thinking that had me considering the possibility of just waiting until he showed himself, but then we would risk having to take on his entire little army at once. Right now, we had the element of surprise on our side. We could put a big dent in his numbers before they could regroup. That might be enough for us to come away with a win…and minimal casualties.

"The rest of us will attack from this location. Start with those who are closest to the building's entrance so they don't get away. Marshawn and his group will be coming around from that far corner." I pointed. "So watch yourselves if you have a target in that direction."

I doubted that I would be going down in history as a master strategist, but I felt that our best chance was a straightforward attack. The moment you start making things fancy, you give yourself all kinds of possibilities for the plan to go awry.

"Does anybody have any questions?" I scanned the faces staring back at me. I think that a few of them were just now realizing exactly what it was that we were about to do. Maybe it hadn't seemed real for them until just this moment, but I couldn't worry myself with that; I had a mission.

"What if they try to surrender?" the woman hissed, her voice almost loud enough to cause concern.

"That isn't an option at this time," I said, surprised at both the quickness of my response and the conviction of the fact that this was the hard truth.

She opened her mouth, but I was saved having to answer it when a small stone whizzed past. I looked up to see that Marshawn had managed to get up on the roof of the building without being detected. When he'd mentioned that as his goal, I had mixed feelings. It would offer a good overhead view of the killing field, but they could end up trapped up there if things went poorly.

"If we are gonna do this, then we go balls out...no half-measures," was his reply.

I pointed him out to the team. I saw two more individuals up there with him. He'd chosen the ones carrying rifles. That left two of his people on the ground. As long as nothing had changed, they would be coming around that corner I'd pointed out earlier.

"We're burning daylight," I said, drawing my Glock.

Another point that we'd agreed upon was that noise was not a concern. If we had to make a retreat, having a bunch of zombies converging on the location might be a benefit. We all had hand-to-hand weapons, but they would be as a last resort if we ran out of ammo. As for me, with my arm throbbing and my injured eye, the choices were even more limited. If I ran out of bullets, I would have to retreat or charge in to my death. There was no reasonable possibility that I could survive if we had to get up close and personal in the fight.

I shook off the morbid thoughts of my potential for failure and the resulting death that would come from such an outcome. Raising my hand, I extended my fingers and made very exaggerated motions as I ticked down the signal.

Three...

Two...

One...

The sounds of both hunting rifles were like cannons in the relatively silent world of the undead. I saw one person who was just entering the lead bus stumble forward and land hard on the narrow steps. I didn't have time to scout out the second target as I rushed forward, pistol in my left hand. I saw a man spin around about thirty yards away. He'd been carrying a metal case in each hand that I was pretty sure had to be ammunition of some sort. He was quick on the draw and actually had his pistol clear of the holster when I fired off two quick shots.

"Fuck!" I cursed.

I have no idea where my rounds had gone. All I know is that they hadn't come anywhere near the target. My injured eye had thrown off my aim. I pointed my weapon down in the hopes that I would hit the pavement in front of the guy and then be able to adjust my next shot. The problem was that he was now extending his arm and there was nothing I could do about it.

I'd been riding that razor's edge between life and death during those days when I believed that I was infected and doomed to become one of the walking dead. I'd just discovered that I was going to live not more than a few hours ago, and here I was, about to die in a fight that I'd picked. I closed my eyes in anticipation.

Two shots were fired, but I didn't feel anything. I risked opening one eye just a crack to see my would-be attacker lying facedown on the asphalt. A dark stain was spreading from his body, turning the pavement a darker shade of gray. Standing behind him was the woman who'd seemed so hesitant as the fight loomed. I gave her a nod of thanks as she turned and directed her fire at a pair of figures running for the main doors to the church.

I brought my own weapon up and fired in support. I saw wood explode from the solid door beyond my target indicating that I was wide to the left. I corrected and fired again. The body on the right staggered and then made a graceless dive onto the ground. The one on the left got perhaps two steps closer to the door before three rounds slammed into his back. He collided with the door that had been his goal, and then slid down it, leaving a bloody trail in his wake.

I stepped over a body and discovered a person trying to crawl under one of the buses. I brought up my weapon, certain that I would not miss from this range as I planted my feet on either side of the crawling figure. I pulled the trigger just as the person realized that she was not alone and tried to roll over onto her back. Her body jerked once with the impact of the bullet that dug into her brain and ended her struggles forever. My only thought in that exact moment was relief that she hadn't been able to make it onto her back. I hadn't had to look into her eyes and see that plea to be spared. I wasn't sure if my resolve to finish this with no prisoners could hold up to that sort of thing.

All around me, the sounds of battle were now rising to a cacophony of gunfire and screams. From the roof, I heard Marshawn barking something and had to pull back from the conflict to process his words.

"...escaping out the back!" he bellowed.

I looked up to see him pointing frantically. Of course, I couldn't see what it was he was pointing at, but my gut already knew the answer. I started for the corner of the building but pulled up when I saw a man with a machete running up behind the same woman that had just saved my ass.

A voice in my head was screaming for me to hurry, that Don and anybody with him would get away if I delayed too long, but my instincts were to try and help the person I could see that was in mortal danger.

I adjusted my course and brought my Glock up. I tweaked my aim to the point that I believed might at least give me a chance of clipping the machete-wielding man who was now less than ten strides away from being close enough to chop into the woman whose name I didn't even know, and fired. The first shot must've missed because the guy never broke stride. I took a guess and brought the weapon a shade to the left and fired again.

The man's right shoulder snapped back like he'd just been punched really hard. He still took a couple of steps as his brain had to catch up with the information his body was sending. As he did, the right arm dropped and his head jerked around in my direction. The man was halfway between me and his original target and quickly made the choice to alter his course and come for the person who'd just injured him.

His choice was fatal. As he closed the distance, he became a target that I couldn't miss...and I didn't. The first round hit him square in the middle of the chest and sent him backwards. There was no need for another shot, but I did put a round into his head as I passed him just to be certain.

The woman was crouching behind a stack of pallets and never even realized what played out behind her, barely acknowledging me as I hurried past on my way to where Marshawn had indicated. As I ran down the length of the building that was the school if my memory was serving me correctly, I heard something above me.

"They are on the far side, past that dorsal structure just ahead," Marshawn called down to me. "I can't make it over and they are still close enough that we can take them down if we hurry."

I looked up and saw what he was talking about when it came to not being able to make it over. I now also knew why he hadn't just gone over there and taken Don down himself. There was a vertical wall-like structure jutting up from the roof and running the length. It had a slight curve to it, but even at the tapered end, I was willing to bet it was ten or so feet above the surface of the roof. It would be hard enough jumping up to get a grip on the top of that structure, much less climbing over. Add in the fact that anybody doing so would be totally exposed and vulnerable and I couldn't blame him for being "stranded" on this side of the building.

I moved along the rear of the church and school facility, pausing to scan for any signs of movement. From my position, I was at the top of a gradual slope that would take me down to the southwestern entry drive to the parking lot. In effect, I'd just done a lap around most of the building and was coming back to where I'd launched my attack from.

Just to the left of the last house before the entry drive I thought I saw the gate swing shut. I realized that I was on my own since nobody was following me and glanced up at Marshawn.

"How many?" I asked.

"Four." The answer hung in the air as I steeled myself for what had to be done.

"Send anybody you can. If I don't make it…" I started, not really sure what to ask for in the event of my demise.

"I'll take care of your dog," Marshawn called down. "But don't worry, now that you are on the trail, I'm coming down and will be right behind you, so don't do anything stupid."

I wasn't sure that was possible. I was preparing to chase after four people without knowing anything about how they might be armed. I had one arm that was a throbbing mess, my right eyelid may or may not be totally gone and that eyeball could end up being lost *if*—and it was looking like a really big if—I managed to survive.

I gave a weak salute and turned my attention back to the house where I'd been pretty sure that I saw the gate beside it swing shut. I hugged the church building as long as I could until I reached the end and then raced across the street towards my potential quarry.

I arrived at the somewhat pinkish house, only taking a second to observe that there would've been no way in hell that I'd have allowed any house I would live in to be painted that color. It wasn't some "pink is for girls and blue is for boys" thing, it was just that it made for an ugly house.

I skirted an abandoned car that had collided with the small birch tree in the front yard, doing my best to stay low. As soon as I was able to see, I could confirm that the side gate was indeed open. I still couldn't be sure that I'd seen somebody come this way, but this was the moment where luck or providence decided to grant me a favor.

A single gunshot came from beyond the tall fence in the direction I was currently looking. It wasn't so close that I thought it could be in the backyard, but it wasn't that far away, either. I broke into a run, ignoring the way every step was making me hurt. I don't think I'd ever been this close to incapacitated and still mobile.

It's funny what desire, adrenaline, and stupidity can accomplish in a person. I'd heard of people doing amazing things when they were put to the test. Heck, I remember one pro football quarterback that played an entire quarter on a busted leg. As normal people, we had a tendency to limit ourselves based on what society said we could or could not accomplish. Yet, from the warmth and comfort of our couches, we would watch people compete in athletic competitions in a sense of wonder and amazement. While I probably would've never aspired to the X-Games, Olympics, or the CrossFit Championships, I'd prided myself on taking care of my body. As a construction worker, I placed physical demands on my body every single day on the job. That was for nothing more substantial than a paycheck.

This was literally a matter of life and death. And revenge. I couldn't forget revenge. Don Evans had killed people based on their skin color. He'd tossed me in a room with people that he assumed were my friends and made me fight for my life against their zombified versions. In truth, they were people we had just picked up, barely qualifying as traveling companions, but that didn't change the evil in his intent. He'd sent his people to try and either raid, capture, or kill Carl, Betty, and the people I'd left behind when I believed that I would turn.

And during my capture, he'd taken the last thing I had left from my life before the dead rose and started wiping out humanity. To any outsider, it was just a picture…no big deal. But to me, it was the best thing I had left from a life that was starting to seem like a dream.

I crossed the backyard and reached the fence that bordered it. There was a child's toy slide with large, red plastic steps on one end. It would be just tall enough to allow me to see over and beyond.

I stepped up and peered over and into the next yard. A curse sprang from my lips almost instantly. The grove of trees obscured my ability to see anybody. However, I could still hear, and it sounded like whomever had gone this way was encountering a bit of trouble. I heard a few shouts, a sporadic burst of gunfire, and then a single shriek that changed into *the* scream.

From the sounds of it, they weren't all that far ahead of me. With them being occupied by whatever was going on, it was very possible that I could catch them. I was trying to figure out the best way over when I realized that all my focus had been in this one direction and I hadn't been looking over my shoulder at all since I'd gotten here. I heard the footsteps, then a voice from behind that made me almost fall off the little plastic slide.

14

Overload

I spun, my heart in my throat. By the time I'd turned to face the person who'd startled me, my brain was already sending signals that it was okay to settle down. It was only Marshawn.

He jogged up to me as my heart clawed its way down from the triple-digit rate it had just been pounding and I allowed myself a single deep, calming breath. Marshawn had a rifle that I didn't recognize slung over one shoulder, as well as a holster hanging over the other with a handgun and a small pouch that I had to assume held extra magazines. In his hand was a machete that dripped with fresh gore. The dark metal of the blade made it impossible to determine if the fluids were from the undead or the recently living. I winced at the idea of hacking up a living human being. Shooting them was bad enough, but to take a machete to a person seemed a lot more personal to me for some reason.

As he reached me, I realized that the sounds of fighting back in the direction of the church had all but ceased. From what I'd witnessed, unless something drastic had occurred to tip the scales in the other direction, we'd made relatively short work of at least most of those who'd chosen to follow Don Evans.

A moment later, two more people rushed into the backyard. One of them was the woman that I'd traded saving each other's lives with. She was holding a mismatched pair of pistols in her hands and I saw a splatter of blood across her face that looked to have been hastily wiped away.

"They are just beyond those trees," I reported. "Sounds like they ran into a little trouble. I heard one of them go down to zombies."

"That leaves three," Marshawn said as much to himself as those of us standing around him.

I noticed that nobody questioned my report that one of Don's people had been the victim of zombies. It was safe to assume that all of them knew the sound of that particular scream that could only come from a person being ripped apart and feasted upon by the undead.

"We better get moving if we're gonna catch up with this creep," Marshawn suggested.

I turned and looked at the fence with a bit of concern. The adrenaline was subsiding and I was getting the full-on pain experience now from my arm and eye. Basically, my entire right side was betraying me at this point. I was about to say something when the woman trotted over beside a small aluminum shed sitting in the far corner of the yard. She reached up, flipped something and the gate opened. I had no idea how she'd seen it since it was flush and the latching mechanism was basically hidden from view. My questioning look must've been plastered clearly on my face for her to see.

"I had the landscapers install a hidden latch when they scaped the yard and built the fence," she said as I passed. "Stupid neighborhood kids were always sneaking in..." Her voice trembled and I waited for her to continue. "My girlfriend used to home brew beer, and when some of the high school kids found out, it sorta became open season." She nodded to a chest freezer on the back patio with a padlock still fastened to a chain wrapped around the handle and latch, and her voice took on a wistful tone. "I would give anything to have that problem be my biggest concern again."

I decided not to mention that maybe she should've considered a different color when she'd had the house painted. I also chose to just ignore the odds that we were passing through the yards of one of the last few surviving people in the city. I didn't ask where her girlfriend might be. I think it was safe to say that everybody still alive had to of lost at least one significant person in their life to this nightmare.

There were four of us creeping through the tall grass and into the trees as we veered towards where we heard then sounds of some sort of fight taking place. Besides Marshawn, myself, and the woman, there was a short, squat, elderly man who looked like he might be a Pacific Islander. He had an uncanny resemblance to a professional wrestler that I used to watch when I was a kid. He'd been known as "The Superfly" and I could almost picture this guy climbing up onto something and hurling his body at the enemy. All he needed was a band of pukka shells acting as a headband along with a floral print lava-lava and he would have the look down solid.

The lone woman in our impromptu commando squad, the one who had saved me only to have me save her moments later, had straight black hair cut just above the shoulders. It also looked like she used to keep at least part of one side shaved down tight. She was filthy—as were we all—so it was impossible to tell if that was the case or not since her hair was a mix of mats and clumps held in place by the combination of dirt, blood, and just the natural oils that occur after several days of not being washed. I guessed her to be just a shade over five feet and maybe a buck ten on the scale.

We were now just a short distance from the point where we would run out of cover. If my memory was correct, there would be a rather uneven strip of treacherous field with a nasty little stream that cut through it. This was very near to where I'd doused my MP3 noisemaker. I knelt beside Marshawn to try and get a grip on what was going on with Don and his minions.

There were twenty or so undead converging on three people—one of them very recognizable as Don Evans, and another as Natasha. Don was sporting a sword that looked like a stolen prop from the *Conan* movies. It was massive and unwieldy, which was the first reason it made a terrible zombie killing weapon. I watched as Natasha ducked just in time to avoid being clipped by Don's swing as he took down a pair of undead by cutting them in half at the waist. That would be the other reason it made a poor choice. Of course, the outfit he was wearing was also something out of a bad fantasy movie. The fur cape he had over his shoulders looked like a bear skin rug that had been pilfered from the Playboy mansion. His torso was crisscrossed by what looked like a few leather straps you might find in a fetish store. I rubbed at my good eye in disbelief.

"Is he wearing assless chaps?" Marshawn snorted.

"Umm…yeah, it looks like he is," I replied.

"I would give anything to see a zombie bite him on his bare behind," the woman sniffed. "He was always a jerk, and I'm not surprised to see that this is the person behind all this nonsense."

I craned my neck around to look at the woman again. She was becoming more than a curiosity. First it had been her pinkish house where Don's group had slipped down the side of to escape, now it seemed that she'd known the man I equated with evil personified at least on some level before the apocalypse.

She looked over and saw three sets of eyes locked on her. I assumed we all had the same questioning looks on our faces.

"He lived two houses over from Mikki and me," the woman began. "Shortly after we first moved in, signs started showing up on our front lawn saying things like 'Carpet munchers not welcome' and that sort of thing. We finally put in a security camera and caught him. We knew right away who it was since we saw the guy basically every weekend when he would work out in his yard or on his car. He'd usually have some vapid bimbo draped on him. Basically, I knew he was a jerk, I guess I just had no idea to what extent."

I wanted to hear more, but this wasn't the best time or place. "So, what do we do?" I asked the group, cocking my head towards the small battle raging in the field about forty or fifty yards from where we all crouched.

"I say we let it play out and see if the zombies do our work," Marshawn offered. That received a unanimous collection of nods.

I turned back as Don practically cleaved another zombie in half, his sword shattering rib bones as it almost completely sliced through the body. I was reminded of Peter Jackson's *Dead Alive* for some reason as viscera flew, splattering the living and the undead like it was being thrown from buckets.

Natasha had an aluminum bat with spikes jutting from it. I had no idea how they'd managed such a feat, but the damage the weapon dealt was impressive. When she spun our direction, I saw the butt of a pistol jutting from the waist of her jeans. Of the three, she was the only one dressed in what would've been considered normal clothing before the apocalypse. A pair of jeans and a simple black pullover shirt was it for her. I couldn't see her shoes, but most people didn't get bit on the foot, so it wasn't that big of a deal. I couldn't get over how casual she was taking everything. She would swing, drop a zombie, and then move on to the next one. She moved with an economic frugality that screamed fearless confidence.

At one point, I thought her confidence or cockiness—whatever the case might be—almost cost her as she moved in to attack a pair of undead. She hadn't seen the one that stumbled out of a nearby bush almost directly behind her.

It was strange, but I actually had to fight the urge to call out a warning. It managed to get a grip on her shoulder just as she brought her bat down in a ferocious overhead smashing blow that pulverized the top of the head of her target. The one that grabbed her leaned in, and I thought we were about to see one of Don's lackeys bite the bullet, but she did this forward roll move and came up already facing her attacker. With one swing, her bat connected (literally) to the side of the zombie's head, ending its existence in an instant.

"Damn," Marshawn whispered. "Too bad she's on the wrong side of this situation."

"She's kind of a bad ass," I agreed.

She yanked the spiked weapon free and moved to stand at Don's back. Together, the pair began to move towards the broken fence of the house nearest their location. It was immediately clear, at least to me, that they—Don and Natasha—were abandoning the third and final member of what remained of their group.

This poor unsuspecting fool had a machete in her hand and was surrounded on all sides by a tightening noose of the walking dead. I doubted that there was any chance the person could be saved unless a daring and dangerous attempt was made to do so, but I did not believe for a moment that Don even considered that possibility. I don't think an attempt would've been made even if the odds were significantly better.

Just then, it seemed that the woman realized what was happening and called out for Don and Natasha to help her. She received no verbal reply, but Don drew a pistol from its holster. In that single moment, there were a number of possibilities. I was foolish enough to believe that he might at least provide his former minion a quick death. I could not have been more wrong.

The gunshot rang out, and for that single instant, it was the only sound that could be heard. The sounds of the undead and the whispers of those gathered beside me were all drowned out in that one split second. If only it would've stayed that way.

As soon as the echo of the report faded, the woman began to wail.

"My leg...Donnie, why?" And then she began to scream.

It started as a normal scream of fear with a hint of pain, but it didn't take long for that shriek to climb in pitch as it found a whole new register that informed everybody in earshot as to this person's fate—she was being eaten alive.

"If there was any doubt as to how evil that bastard is, I think this erased it," Marshawn muttered.

Of course, I didn't have any doubts what so ever. I knew the man for what he was in just the short period of time I'd been in his presence. He was the face of a new world where people could devolve into their baser selves with little fear of reprisal.

The cluster of zombies around the now helpless victim all started flopping to the ground as they tore into her. Mercifully, one of them obviously found her throat. There was a wet sound, and then the scream was no more.

"Let's move while most of them are occupied," Marshawn

suggested, getting to his feet.

I agreed. As heartless and cold as that might seem, she was one of them.

We started across the grassy clearing, only catching the attention of the zombies not engaged in rending the downed victim. We were almost to the other side, and now passing even with the huddled group of zombies that were all on their hands and knees around the body. I couldn't help it, and had to look. I could make out one leg that was still drumming the ground in erratic, violent thrums. I swear I saw one hand still trying feebly to push away her attackers, but that might've just been her arm being moved about by the zombies gathered around her. What I was certain of was that I heard a wet mewling sound. It was not coming from the undead, of that I was almost positive. That meant that the entire time we'd watched, and then however long it had taken us to cross this much of the field, that woman remained alive and conscious. She was probably watching parts of herself being torn free, chewed, and swallowed by the ghoulish faces clustered over her. The thought of that made me shudder. Part of me wanted to veer just far enough from my current course to end her suffering, but the handful of zombies that remained unoccupied and were still moving towards us, seemingly oblivious to the horrific scene playing out on the ground near them, was enough to entice me to continue moving.

I fell in behind Marshawn as we reached the far side. The moans of undead not too far ahead caused us to slow. Since he was in the front of our group, Marshawn took it upon himself to climb up on the tall wooden fence and peek at what waited on the other side. He scanned the area for a moment before dropping back down.

"Evan, you and Amy follow this fence down that way for two houses." He pointed to our left. "The green house doesn't have any sort of fenced in backyard. Chet, you come with me. It looks like there is a street just on the other side, and from what I am seeing in the zombie traffic, they went to our right."

"Then why are we going to the left?" I asked.

"Because, you look like crap, and I don't think your body,

much less your arm, can take any more of the abuse you have dealt it."

Without waiting for anybody to ask any more questions, Marshawn threw a leg over, pulled himself up, and then vanished as he dropped to the other side. The man, I guess his name was Chet, followed suit.

That left me with the woman...Amy. She was giving me an appraising look as if she'd just noticed that I was a walking mess.

I began to grow uncomfortable under her scrutiny and started off for the green house. I heard Amy start to follow, but she made no attempt to pass or even walk alongside me.

When we reached the green house, I saw that the back door had been smashed in. There were dark stains all around it from whatever had beaten its way inside.

As we slipped up the side of the house, I realized that damn near every residence I passed had its own little horror story to be told. Just this street could probably fill up a few volumes.

When we reached the corner of the house, I let Amy take a look. I figured two eyes were better than one. She spent long enough that I finally tapped her on the shoulder.

"Well?" I asked when she turned back to me.

"I don't see Marshawn and Chet, and I don't see Don. What I do see are a dozen or so zombies heading away from us. There is a little dogleg in the street, so we are going to need to move up a few houses to get a better idea." She paused, considering me with a very critical expression. At last she spoke the thoughts that were flitting around her eyes. "You sure you're up for this? I mean, you look like are about ready to fall over."

She wasn't far off from describing exactly how I felt. In fact, if not for the adrenaline still managing to pump into my system, I did not doubt that I might possibly pass out. I could feel the nausea churning in my gut, and my vision was hazy around the edges like I was looking through a fur-lined tube. Add in that I only had the use of one eye and I was half blind.

I stopped moving and just listened. The zombies were all shambling in the same direction. That seemed to narrow down our choices. Since they were all past us, we could fall in behind this small, spread out herd and follow them. I was certain that it would lead to where we needed to be.

I started walking. At least that was the signal I tried to send to my legs. The problem was that nothing happened. I looked down at my legs to see if perhaps something had hold of me.

"Nothing." I heard that word, but it didn't really feel like I'd said it. Something was wrong...very wrong.

"Evan?" a voice whispered from behind me. The problem now was that I couldn't remember the name of the person attached to that voice.

The fuzzy tunnel began to constrict. Then...everything went black.

***

I could hear voices. They were whispering, but they were close. It took my brain a moment to catch up and catalog them all as familiar and friendly. I opened my eyes slowly and could see the flicker of light on the wall beside me that told me there was a fire burning nearby. There was something wrong, and it took me a moment to realize that one of my eyes was covered.

It was as if that realization woke up all my pain receptors. My right arm pulsed with a dull pain that seemed to start at my fingertips and end at my neck. The area around my eye felt like I'd rubbed that part of my face with an industrial-sized cheese grater. There was a haze in my brain that refused to clear, but it wasn't entirely unpleasant.

The rumble in my belly reminded me that I was hungry. I tried to sit up, but the world tilted and dumped me on my side. Unfortunately, it was my right side and a very undignified yelp of pain escaped my lips.

"I think somebody is waking up," one of the familiar voices said with a chuckle that sounded much too pleasant considering how I felt.

I let gravity roll my head in the direction of the voice and saw Marshawn getting to his feet. He was across the fire from me and his was one of the few faces not cast in shadows to the point of not being identifiable.

"Good, I want to have a few words with the idiot."

I recognized the voice and saw another form rise and start in my direction. It was the man who had initially questioned my decision to circle back for my car after the gunfight with Don's raiders that killed Katy. Nobody else seemed inclined to leave the warmth of the fire, and now that my body was becoming aware of the surroundings, I couldn't say that I blamed them. There was a chill in the air that seeped into my bones now that I'd knocked away a sleeping bag that had been laid on me.

"Are you trying to get yourself killed, because if so, just say the word and I'll finish the job," a man railed as he stomped across the room.

Now that I was able to get a look, I could see what appeared to be the interior of a church. Had we ended up in Don's stronghold? As soon as the name surfaced, I wanted to look around and see where he might be watching all this. Had we all been captured?

"I'm surprised you made it as far as you did in your condition," Marshawn said, easing the seething man aside.

"What happened? Did we get captured?" I babbled.

"You passed out," he answered simply. "Amy managed to drag you into the house that you two were hiding out beside. As for Don, we lost him. Not that we would've been able to do anything had we caught him. I guess he'd already sent part of his people out. Somehow, he was able to summon them back. Three big trucks and a small bus rolled back and picked him and that woman up. They had a damn machine gun turret mounted on the top of the bus. It ripped through zombies and practically disintegrated them. I'm no expert, but I am pretty sure it was a .50 cal. It brought down small trees and devastated the fronts of a few houses. If it would've been turned on us, we wouldn't be having this conversation."

I let that sink in. I'd been to a military demonstration before and seen just how powerful the .50 cal was when put to use. It could almost vaporize a person with just a few rounds.

"Amy?" It dawned on me that I had neither seen nor heard her since coming to and that put a lump in my throat.

"Right here, Evan," a voice said from near the fire.

She got up, and I noticed about half the people joined her to come over and perhaps get a look at the idiot that sent them on a foolish mission when he couldn't even stay conscious long enough to see it through.

"Did we lose anybody else?" I asked.

"Nope. As soon as we saw the firepower they were packing, everybody backed off. We regrouped and took shelter in a church," Marshawn explained.

"Aren't we worried he'll come back here?" I asked.

"Evan, there is more than one church in the area," Marshawn laughed. "Granted, we are only a very short distance up the road from the one he was using, but the building is pretty safe. The windows are high up and there is only the front and rear doors to keep secure. We moved furniture in front of them both, but nothing has come around since we got here, so I think we are okay."

"The fire is probably the only thing that will give us away, and that will probably only attract the living. I didn't see any zombies directly affected or drawn to fires that were not in their direct line of sight. I camped in one apartment building for three days, used the second-floor unit in the corner and kept a fire going in the tub of the master bedroom every night. I went outside once just to see and it was like a freaking lighthouse beacon in the dead of night, but no zombies came." The man who I was really growing to dislike knelt beside Marshawn.

"So he got away," I sighed. The comment was meant more for myself, but apparently everybody heard.

"Did you hear the part about the .50 cal, or how you basically passed out and had to be carried to safety?" Marshawn snapped.

"I know." I held up my hands and discovered that took way more effort than it should. "I just feel terrible that a monster like that is out in the world. He's only going to grow stronger. I fear not only for our lives, but for any group of survivors he comes across."

As soon as those words left my mouth, I had another thought. A terrible thought that almost felt like a punch in the gut. If Natasha was alive, then she knew where Carl and the others were holed up. Her boyfriend—if I could believe Arlo's words during their little confrontation—had died trying to raid them. I had no idea what sort of defenses they'd managed in my absence, but I had my doubts as to its ability to hold up to something as awesome as a .50 cal machine gun.

I tried again to sit up straight but failed. Marshawn put his hand on my chest, but if his intent was to keep me from getting up, his efforts were not necessary. I wasn't going anywhere.

"You need to rest, Evan," the man said tenderly. "Your body just can't take anymore."

"But Carl...Chewie, Betty and the kids," I sputtered.

"Have met whatever fate that has befallen them. You won't make any difference at all even if you could manage to get to your feet and make it there right now."

Never in my life had I felt like such an utter failure. Everything I'd done up to this point had been for absolutely nothing. That thought lasted in my head for all of about ten seconds.

No, there was no way in hell I would accept that as an answer. There had to be something that I could do. I'd thought enough of Carl and the others to want to spare them having to deal with me once I turned. Maybe friendship was stretching it, but there was a bond...some sort of relationship that had grown between us in that short time we'd spent together.

"There must be something we can do," I finally managed.

"Evan, there really isn't," Marshawn said. He looked at me and I could see my sadness reflected in his eyes. I noticed that pretty much everybody had returned to the fire by now. "We have our limits, and so do you...right now, perhaps more so than usual."

I laid back and shut my eyes against the stinging sensation that had nothing to do with the injury my right eye had suffered. I tried to think of any possibility that would offer itself in the form of a solution. I was blank.

Something was pressed into my hands and I felt a warm cup. I looked down to see what looked like chicken noddle soup.

"This church had a room with shelves full of non-perishable items...probably for the needy. I think we meet those standards," Amy said with a weak smile that barely turned her lips up enough to qualify.

I sipped at the soup. It was just a shade past warm, but not quite hot. After another sip, Amy reached out, opening her fist to reveal a couple of pills. "It's only some generic ibuprofen, but it will help keep a lid on the pain."

I accepted them with a nod of thanks and popped them into my mouth. Their bitterness was quickly washed away by the saltiness of the soup as I took another long drink from the cup.

"I guess I owe you a thanks for basically saving my life...again," I said to Amy. "You could've just left me."

"What kind of person would do something like that?" she said, sounding affronted by the idea.

"Somebody who risked being killed by a bunch of zombies."

"There weren't any close by."

"Yeah, but how did you drag me someplace without being noticed?" A person seemed to weigh a lot more when they were dead weight. I wasn't a huge guy, but I wasn't petite either. Amy was on the small side, and it couldn't have been easy to move me all by herself.

"There was a wheelbarrow in the backyard of the house we'd just moved past. Once I got you in it, it wasn't that difficult." She flashed me a smile. "Besides, I used to push wheelbarrows full of manure at my grandma's farm in Sherwood when I was younger."

We both laughed and a few of the people gathered around the fire looked at us and gave us a shushing noise that was louder than our actual laughter. Still, I took the hint and pressed my lips together.

"Well, I still want to thank you. I owe you one."

"I imagine there will be plenty of opportunities for me to collect if we get out of here."

"*When* we get out of here," Marshawn said as he crouched down beside Amy. "I figure we need to give you a few days to get yourself together, and then we will roll out of here.

I wanted to protest, but he'd been right earlier when he said that whatever had happened to my group was done and over with. There was absolutely nothing that I could do for them now. If Don and his followers had indeed returned to finish off or take revenge, or whatever reason/justification they used to motivate themselves, then it was basically history. As I lay in the gloom, my body feeling aches and pains that I'd ignored for too long, I made a silent vow that I would hunt that man down and finish what I'd started, albeit poorly.

The possibility that everybody had been killed, that those innocent children and my beloved Chewie might be wiped out, sat on my chest like a massive weight. This was also my fault. I'd given up their location. I could've been the hero like the kind you see in movies or read about in books and accepted death in any form rather than give up that location. In the end, I'd been weak…human.

I closed my eyes and tried to allow sleep to take me away from the thoughts swirling in my head. All I got were nightmares.

The next couple of days were about as uneventful as any I could ever recall in my life. It was on the second day that the first fight broke out. Surprisingly, it wasn't the guy who still made it a point to blame me any chance he got for our current situation—whose name was Neil Pearson, not that I cared since I always referred to him by either 'hey you'…or 'asshole' if he wasn't around—it was between Amy and a woman named Tracy Gibbons.

I'd never seen two women actually go to blows outside women's boxing or cage fighting matches. Fortunately, neither of the women were so big that Marshawn wasn't able to quickly step in and separate them. Their little scuffle did make enough noise to bring a few curious zombies to our location. Once they were put down, there were scowls, dirty looks, and even a few passive-aggressive bumps of shoulders in passing, but everybody kept their mouth shut.

By the third day, I was able to get up and move around a bit more comfortably. I still hurt, but not enough to require any of the precious and very finite amount of ibuprofen that we had in our meager stores. Twice, a few of our number slipped out to some of the nearby homes to scavenge supplies. Water was the top of the list since the charity cupboard here was doing a good job of feeding us.

At night, we all gathered close to the fire and huddled. It was during that time, when it was the coldest and darkness forced you to be alone with your thoughts, that I didn't care how much I liked or disliked the person beside me, I simply sought warmth. It was also on that first night that I made another discovery.

During the day, we were more mobile and nobody felt the need or desire to really congregate with more than one or two people at a time, but in a group...we stunk. There was no nice way to put it. As we clustered around and everybody shared blankets and packed in tight to share body heat, those first few minutes were almost humorous. Noses would wrinkle and some would even make the initial attempt to move away. The need for warmth would eventually win out and we would all pack in as tight as sardines...although I am pretty sure that the sardines smelled better.

Besides the smell, the other bad part about the dark were the screams. I kept thinking that they would eventually stop. There could not be that many survivors in the area...right? Apparently there were either many more than I believed, or else people were so spread out and scattered in small pockets of just one or two. Either way, for whatever reason, the screams were more common after dark. Some were surprisingly close, and once, I was almost certain that it could be no farther than the parking lot of this church.

On the fourth day, I woke to Marshawn giving me a shake. I forced my eyes open and bemoaned the fact that there had been no coffee in the church pantry. The gloom told me that it was still not quite sunrise, so I was curious as to what this was about.

"We need to move out," he whispered.

I looked around to see a few others waking the rest of the sleepers. We'd kept lookouts posted on the roof in shifts. A few people questioned the need, but Marshawn had said simply that it was a precaution and that it wasn't up for debate.

"We have a band of raiders in the area. They are doing a systematic search of pretty much everything that interests them and setting fire to anything that doesn't," he whispered in response to my unasked question.

We'd been smart enough to load up packs and carry bags with food, water, and other assorted supplies, and stack everything in the dais where the pastor or priest or whoever handled the religious stuff would do the sermons. In moments, everybody was loaded up and hustling out the back door to the church.

We were at the intersection of Southeast 132nd and Sunnyside Road. Just across the street from us was the Sunnyside Elementary School. That location had been very quickly crossed off the list of places to go near. One of the scavenging teams had returned to say that a cluster of zombie children were, for lack of a better term, in control of that location. That report and the resulting shivers from a few of my fellow survivors meant that at least some of them had encountered zombie children and noticed something different.

We were all moving across the church parking lot in the gray of pre-dawn. I was still trying to wrap my head around the report of raiders when a scream that was more of a battle cry came from what sounded like the front of the church. A moment later, there was a roar, and a terrible explosion.

15

New Friends and Enemies

I felt a hand slam into the middle of my back and send me sprawling facedown. Luckily, I was almost to the edge of this section of the parking lot, so I ended up in some bushes that acted as a bit of a border to the property. Oh…it still hurt, but much less than asphalt.

"Coming around from the left," a voice cried just before a barrage of gunfire erupted all around me.

In the days we'd spent recuperating in the church, Marshawn had done a great job cleaning up and checking on my injured right eye. It turned out that I'd suffered a nasty tear of the actual eyelid, but not enough to lose it or the eye itself. I'd also had a big chunk of meat from my eyebrow torn away. That had been the worst injury between the two; it was that piece of dangling meat that had initially been mistaken for my eyelid.

Marshawn had snipped it away with a pair of scissors and then cleaned and bandaged the area. I no longer had a patch over my eye, but it was still swollen enough to hamper vision from that side and make everything seem just a bit blurry around the edges.

At the moment, I was almost blind as I tried to crawl to the other side of the shrub I'd landed in. I could hear somebody just to my right as they racked the slide on a pistol. The distinctive sound snapped me into action as I pulled my own Glock and rolled onto my back as I emerged into the clearing. I got my bearings and started crawling for the fence that separated the backyard of a house from the church. I knew that we'd already checked this house and most of the other ones nearby, so if I could get inside, then I could position myself to fight back against whatever or whomever was attacking.

By the time I managed to reach the waist-high fence, two more loud 'WHUMP' concussions exploded behind me back in the direction of the church we'd just abandoned. I made it to my feet and pulled myself up. Just as I swung a leg over, I heard a yelp from just to my left. I looked over to see Amy stagger forward a few steps and crumble to her knees. An arrow was jutting from her hip and she was now trying to stand while also tugging on the feathered shaft.

Looking past her, I could see black smoke starting to pour out of the back door of the church. One of the ornate stained glass windows mounted up high had busted and there were flames and smoke roiling out of it as well. There were several dark figures moving down each side of the large, brown building and I could see that some of them were sporting bows, a few had rifles and were sweeping the area behind them like they feared a flanking attack—either that, or they were keeping an eye out for any undead that might move in, drawn by all the noise.

As I watched, a pair of the ones holding rifles stumbled and fell on the heels of the reports of what I had to assume were our own high-powered rifles. That made the raiders scramble and dive for cover. That also offered me the perfect opportunity to swing my leg back over and scurry to Amy.

"Put your arm around my shoulder," I hissed when I reached her.

"If we keep saving each other, people are gonna talk," she managed through gritted teeth.

I was on her right side, the opposite one from the arrow. She limped along, still sporting the projectile from her hip as she'd been unable to remove it up to this point. I didn't even bother to look back as I got us to the fence I'd just about been ready to climb over before she'd been hit.

"How are we gonna do this?" she whimpered, and I could tell that the pain was getting worse with each step she'd had to take.

I pulled her to the ground, able to put her against the trunk of a tree. I stayed in line with her so I could utilize as much of the cover as possible. Kneeling, I looked her in the eyes and then glanced down at the arrow.

"Just do it," she managed, knowing what needed to be done.

"Close your eyes," I said over the sound of a volley of gunfire that was exchanged between our group and the raiders.

Amy did as I asked and I reached down. I positioned my hand, making a circle around the shaft of the arrow without touching it yet. I knew this was going to hurt, and I had no idea what sort of damage would be done by me yanking it out.

I was about to do it when the fence shook and a head appeared just a few feet from us. I grabbed for my Glock—I have no idea when I'd put it away—and pointed it at the new arrival. My finger was just starting to squeeze the trigger when I realized who it was.

"Jesus, Marshawn, you want to get your head blown off?" I snarled, setting the handgun beside me just in case. That was when I realized that Amy had shifted just enough to pull her weapon as well and held it in her extended arms. She let her arms fall and her head drop.

"Not really," the man panted as he threw his other leg over and landed on the ground in a heap when the cuff of his pants snagged on the top of the fence. "I try to keep the number of times I get shot per day down to one."

I saw a dark stain on the sleeve of his left arm. That was the one thing about a Kevlar vest, it didn't do a damn thing for the extremities.

"Can we get this freakin' arrow out of my hip?" Amy said, her voice constricted from the pain.

Marshawn got up to his knees and made his way to us. "We need to get moving." He looked down at the arrow jutting from Amy's hip and winced. In a flash, he ripped off a piece of the already bloody shirt sleeve and then yanked the arrow from Amy's hip. In a flash, he wadded up the slip of somewhat bloody material and pressed it hard against the now open wound. Amy made a hiss and yelp. Her left hand swung out and slapped Marshawn across the face...hard.

"Ooops, sorry," she said hurriedly, the offending hand hanging in the air like it was being held up by an invisible puppeteer.

"Not the first time that's happened," Marshawn said after he opened and closed his mouth a few times as if he was making sure that his jaw still worked. "Now, hold that in place." He gave a nod to the wad of cloth and ripped away almost the rest of his shirt sleeve to reveal a small, ugly, puckered hole in the bicep that leaked blood, his black skin now exhibiting a dark sheen.

I watched as he tied the piece of cloth around the wad he'd practically stuffed into the hole on Amy's hip. As I continued to observe, I couldn't help but think of all the cross-contamination protocols that had just been violated. I started to chuckle as we helped Amy to her feet.

"What the hell is so funny," she hissed as she threw an arm around each of our shoulders.

"I'm actually in the best shape out of all of us...it's been a while since that was the case with anybody I travelled with."

"Now?" Marshawn, grunted as we made our way across the yard to the house. "You're thinking that now? We have a band of raiders shooting everything that moves as well as burning down anything that doesn't, and *that* is what you're thinking?"

"You asked," I said with a shrug as we made our way up the steps of the back porch.

I opened the sliding glass door and let Marshawn and Amy go inside first. I followed on their heels, shutting the door behind us more out of habit than anything else. We moved through the house and stopped in the ransacked living room.

"Upstairs would give us the best vantage point to make a stand, or at least get an idea of what is going on behind us," I suggested.

"Or we could just keep moving and put as much distance between ourselves and these idiots as possible." Marshawn adjusted his stance and I could see the tightness around his eyes that gave away the pain he was feeling despite trying to shrug it away and soldier through.

"How about you two wait here just a sec and let me run up to get a look." Before they could say anything in protest, I slipped out from under Amy's arm and started up the stairs, taking them two at a time as I hurried to a bedroom that faced the backyard and would hopefully give me the best view.

I heard Marshawn cursing behind me and almost pulled up and returned to them, but I felt like I had to at least know what was chasing us. It was probably me being stupid again, but I was committed as I hopped over the small bed that had been stripped bare—most likely by one of our supply scavenging teams.

Peering out back, I was really glad that spring was still in its infancy. The trees had little buds forming, but they were lacking the foliage that would prevent me from seeing anything in probably as soon as the next couple of weeks.

"Idiots," I breathed.

The raiders had the church surrounded and were lobbing makeshift Molotov cocktails through the open doors and gaping holes that used to hold ornate stained glass windows depicting the typical assortment of religious symbols and images.

A few had moved the direction our group had fled, but they weren't advancing. They were simply sweeping the area in search of any nearby targets. Fortunately, I could see figures that had cleared neighboring fences and were making their way across the yards. Some were doing like we had done and were ducking into the houses, but others were moving along the sides and continuing past.

A few fallback locations had been selected while we held up in the church. The first was a nearby grocery store. It was far too close to all this madness to be a viable spot. The next location was a house set back from the road about eight blocks away. Funny, but eight blocks were nothing prior to the apocalypse; now, it held the possibility of being an epic journey with death and danger looming ahead of each step.

I hurried down the stairs to find Amy and Marshawn at the

front room window, peering out through the shades. Amy turned at my arrival and I saw a look on her face that I could not figure out. It was like a cross between fear and revulsion. I hurried over and peered out to see what waited for us out front. Honestly, I expected maybe something along the lines of a mob of the undead.

The street was a wasteland of death and destruction. There were zombies and body parts strewn about in a putrefied slurry of bodily destruction. The first thought that hit me was that I hoped all the bits and pieces I was seeing had belonged to the undead. There was an upper torso that had been shattered—that is the best way I can describe it—and consisted of one arm that had been decimated at mid-forearm and the head. If I had to guess, I would say about a quarter of the rib cage remained. This remnant was on the sidewalk directly in front of this house. It was wriggling and the head was turning back and forth just enough to indicate that it was still animate.

"This is what a .50 cal can do to the human body," Marshawn whispered. "Pretty sure your boy came this way and mowed down everything that moved."

"I hope there were no survivors hiding out in this area," Amy added. "Can you imagine thinking that help had arrived, rushing out only to be slaughtered by that bastard?"

My mind flashed on a scene in *Saving Private Ryan*. It was towards the end during the big battle in the ruins of some town. A bunch of soldiers had climbed up on a tank and the Germans rolled out this brutal machine gun that just destroyed the bodies of the American soldiers. I remember cringing in my seat as the men were ripped to shreds. I also recall how that scene had made my grandfather start to tremble. I'd glanced over to see tears rolling down his cheeks. We never talked about it after we left the theater.

My eyes followed the trail of destruction and I realized that I could actually tell which way Don and whomever was still with him had gone. In addition to the trail of bodies that created a path of sorts, there were still more corpses that had been run over and were now flattened like road kill.

"Holy crap," I breathed when my eyes spied a pair of very flattened corpses that had to have been run over by multiple vehicles. It was a landscape of gore and annihilation. The houses had actual chunks missing as well as being sprayed with blood and guts of anything that had been standing in front of them as the hail storm of high-velocity lead ripped through everything like a hot knife through butter.

A flash of movement to the left got my attention and I saw two people hunched over and hurrying across the street. If the raiders were going to waste their time shooting up and torching a church, it was probably best that we leave them to it. Picking our battles would be important. Perhaps now was not the time to fight. There would be plenty of battels ahead. Besides, from what I had seen, these raiders were little more than chaotic morons. It was very likely that they wouldn't last long.

I moved over to the door and opened it and then returned to help Marshawn support Amy as we started across the street. As we headed to our right and followed the trail of destruction left behind, more and more of our little group fell in with us. I was surprised and thrilled to see that we'd come away without losing any of our people. The sounds of senseless destruction continued on behind us which had the negative effect of drawing the undead towards it. That put zombies directly ahead, but a few of our people hurried forward and began cutting them down before they could become a mob.

We reached the intersection of 132nd and this street—which turned out to be Southeast Sagebrush Drive—and briefly debated taking a left to return us to Sunnyside Road. That was the main artery through this neighborhood and would take us on the most direct route to the interstate. It would also give us the most likely chance of running into more unsavory types.

The problem with continuing to the right was that it would take us into more twisting and tightly packed neighborhoods where we were discovering the greatest concentration of zombies. It was quickly agreed that, unless they were in herds numbering over a hundred, they would be easier to circumnavigate and avoid compared to the living which were now a much bigger concern than the undead. In truth, I wasn't sure that hadn't been the case from almost the beginning of this whole mess.

We headed into the guts of suburbia, our team spread out the length of almost a city block. I kept my eye on Marshawn and said nothing when Amy's arm slid off him and allowed him to just walk without supporting somebody else's weight. As for Amy, she winced with almost every step, but never voiced a complaint or asked the group to stop for her.

Twice I had to prop her against an abandoned vehicle to assist in taking down a zombie or three when their numbers became too much for the mobile picket guard of our group to handle.

We'd gone about six or seven blocks when we rounded a corner and discovered a cul-de-sac. It had not registered in my mind until that moment that many of the street signs had been pulled down. I guess it had simply melted in with all the other destruction.

There was this one moment where we were all just standing there looking stupid. We'd even gone about a quarter of the way up the dead-end street because it had a slight hook to it and we hadn't been able to see that the road came to its end with a roundish bubble faced by five houses that were packed in so tight with each other that one of them sat back from the rest and had to be reached by a long driveway that ran directly between a pair of homes that looked almost identical to each other. We had bunched up into a neat little knot that probably made a very appealing target.

The bottle smashed into the asphalt just a few feet in front of us. A whoosh followed by a ball of flame caused us to jump back collectively. In the confusion, Amy slipped away from me and toppled to the road with a yelp of pain.

It was purely instinct that made me bolt away, leaving behind the woman I'd just been supporting. I dove behind a minivan that was resting on its side and shoved the blade I'd been carrying into its sheath, replacing it with my Glock. Being quiet was always trumped by the need to survive.

As soon as I did, my brain started screaming about how I'd just left Amy in the middle of the street. I got to my feet and rushed out to her in a crouch. There was a single gunshot and I saw a spark and puff of smoke or dust erupt from the road just a few feet in front of me. Now my brain was screaming about how I needed to turn around and get my ass back behind the minivan.

I ignored it.

I did a baseball slide as I reached Amy and felt a stinging pain on my left side that would be making itself known with much more clarity as soon as the adrenaline ebbed. I grabbed Amy's arm and threw it over my shoulders, jerking her to her feet unceremoniously. She let out a muffled cry as she tried to bite back the pain, but to her credit, she was already limping along with me as fast as we could manage. The minivan loomed ahead like a burgundy-colored wall of safety as a series of gunshots sounded from in front as well as behind me. I wasn't fully cognizant that the ones in front were from my people until I actually reached the minivan and pushed Amy behind it before joining her.

I had to do a self-examination to make sure that the only injury I'd sustained was what would develop into a semi-bad case of road rash. I looked over at Amy to see that she'd drawn her own handgun and was giving it a quick look to ensure it was ready for action.

Another round of gunfire erupted and I heard somebody cry out, but it was impossible to tell who or what side they were on. I saw somebody run across a yard to my right. The person dove over a downed garbage can that was riddled with bullets a second later. I didn't hear any sort of reaction, but that didn't mean very much considering all that was happening around me as people began yelling back and forth and more shooting rattled on.

The battle was getting intense and another trio of Molotov's exploded on either side of me. One felt like it might've been just on the other side of the van Amy and I hid behind and used for cover.

"We're gonna get picked off here," she shouted to me over

the din of screams and gunfire.

"And where would you have us go?" I yelled to be heard as the boom of a shotgun came from close by.

I will count it as some good luck because I would not consider myself to be some sort of field combat specialist. The shadow that appeared just beyond Amy's shoulder caused me to flick my left hand up and bring my weapon level where I expected the center mass of a body to be located when it came into view.

I had to adjust down, but my brain was too busy sending signals that would allow me the best chance of survival for me to register why. The figure was decked out in what at first looked like some kind of body armor, but proved to be nothing more exotic than baseball catcher's gear. I fired off three quick rounds and the body spun away, landing hard on the pavement.

I heard a scream from somewhere and another shadow appeared suddenly. My weapon was already basically aimed where it needed to be and the person ran directly into my next volley of shots. This time it was easy to tell that I'd just shot and killed a woman. I had no doubt that she was dead considering how she jerked to a halt when my first round hit her in the middle of her chest and acted like a giant fist, putting a sudden stop to her advance. The next round left a crater where her right eye should be. I have no idea where the third round hit because Amy was getting up to a crouch and urging me to do the same.

A second later, I understood why. It was as if the minivan had turned into a bullet magnet. I heard the pings and plinks of bullets slamming into it with a thundering roll. The smell of gasoline wafted into my nostrils and I was suddenly very thankful that cars didn't explode in real life like they did in the movies when they were shot in the gas tank. That didn't mean a spark couldn't ignite what was now leaking from who knew how many holes in the gas tank.

It was time to move. I looked over at Amy and saw tears leaking down her face. She was obviously in pain and every step was only making it worse.

"Just grit your teeth and we'll get out of this," I said above the din.

She looked over at me with a strange expression and then scowled. "You think this is because of the pain?" she indicated her tears.

I nodded, after all, it seemed like a logical conclusion. She glanced over to the bodies sprawled just a few feet away. I guess I'd simply blocked them out. That was the best way to keep my conscience at least partially intact. Killing people was not something I thought I would ever get used to…at least I hoped that was the case. My eyes brought the two bodies into focus and I felt my insides twist. The woman was already occupying a permanent place in my mind so that she could visit me in my nightmares, but now I saw clearly the figure in the baseball gear.

I guessed him to be perhaps fifteen. His light skin and freckles gave him an even more pronounced boyishness to his appearance and I could easily imagine him cruising down the sidewalk on a skateboard or heading up to Mount Hood with a bunch of his buddies to go snowboarding. Basically, he was the boy-next-door.

"We don't have time for this," I said around the lump that had formed in my own throat.

To emphasize my point, one of the Molotov's arced overhead and landed just about fifteen feet or so beyond us. The wall of heat slammed into me and I was pretty sure the scraggly beard trying to come in with its patchy ugliness got singed back a bit.

I threw my arm across my nose as the smell of burning fuel sent a bitter coil of foulness up each nostril and down my throat. I grabbed Amy by the arm and started for the nearest yard. If we could reach the front door to the house and get inside, we would exponentially decrease the chance of being shot and killed than if we remained out here on the street.

To her credit, Amy moved quick and the two of us reached the door. I gave the knob a twist and felt my heart sink. Of course, it was locked. These people were defending the area and it was safe to assume that this was their home or that they were based nearby. We were the intruders. After what I'd encountered out here in what was fast becoming a wasteland, I couldn't blame them for their reaction to our arrival.

I looked around and did the only thing I could think of, I shoved Amy into the tall bushes that ran along the front of this house and I ran for the corner, just beyond the garage door. I didn't dare look back as I heard the sounds of an automatic weapon open fire, quickly followed by the sounds of the wooden garage door I was sprinting past as it splintered from the impact of the bullets.

I rounded the corner and skidded to a stop. Three zombies were lurching my direction from the neighboring yard. The closest one was a good ten feet away so I quickly drew a blade and stepped into it, plunging my knife into its eye socket. I did away with the second one in the same manner and shoved the third one away as I yanked the gate open to gain access to the backyard. It stumbled back a few steps and then jerked once and fell as a bullet tore through its skull and ended it. I had no idea if the shooter had been one of ours or one of theirs, but I didn't care as I slipped into the fenced in yard and pulled the gate shut behind me.

I ran to the steps that led up to a large patio that had probably once hosted a few barbecues and maybe even a kid's birthday party—there was a swing set in the corner of the yard. As expected, there was a sliding glass door that gave entrance to the back side of the house. I fought the urge to rush in and surveyed the interior.

I would be coming in to a dining room with a heavy and ornate table surrounded by six high-backed chairs. That wasn't very remarkable. My eyes locked onto a pair of bowls sitting on the counter of the breakfast bar. The food was still steaming.

I gripped the handle and gave a tug, almost anticipating the door to be locked as well. I was surprised when it slid open. Bringing my Glock up, I swapped out magazines since I'd lost track of how many rounds I'd fired up to this point. The last thing I wanted to do was confront somebody and pull the trigger to discover that I was out of bullets.

I stepped inside and heard something scuffle overhead almost immediately. I hurried past the stairs, my eyes trained on them, and then dashed through the living room to the front door. There was a small square pane of glass set at just about face level and I peered outside.

I could hear the sporadic sounds of gunfire and saw figures popping up and taking shots at not only each other, but also the newly arriving undead that were starting to trickle in; no doubt drawn by all the racket. In short, it was full-blown pandemonium outside that front door.

I shot a glance over my shoulder to be certain that whomever or whatever I'd heard moving around upstairs was not coming for me, then I unlocked the front door. I risked opening it just a crack.

"Amy," I hissed in between the waves of sound that were so much louder just from the simple act of opening the door the tiniest bit. There was no response and I had to repeat myself before I saw the bushes move a bit.

Suddenly Amy exploded out of the glossy greenery. For some reason, my mind picked this moment to inform me the bush was a Green Mountain Boxwood, apparently digging up this knowledge from back in high school when I worked with a landscaper. She rushed the door so fast that I didn't have time to get back far enough. I ended up getting knocked on my butt when I tripped over my feet combined with a small table set just inside the door smacking into me right behind my knees.

She stepped inside and slammed the door behind her. The next thing I knew, she was diving on top of me. At first I thought she had become a zombie. Her speed caused part of my mind to reject that thought, but the other part told me that maybe there were fast ones and slow ones.

Less than a heartbeat later, the door shook and pieces of it flew inward as bullets peppered it. I found myself looking directly into her eyes. That provided immediate relief when two tracer-free orbs stared back. They were showing a lot of the whites, but I'm not sure which of us was more frightened at the moment..

"They're coming!" she managed as she rolled off me and brought her handgun up.

The two of us backed away from the front door, retreating into the hallway that branched off and led to the kitchen. It was also where the stairs were located. The soft whimper from behind us made me spin just as another volley was fired at the front door, swiss-cheesing it.

I spun, bringing my pistol up and applying just about half the pressure needed on the trigger to fire at our potential attacker. The darkness of the hallway prevented me from seeing any details, but the outline of the figure that stepped out from the stairwell was maybe a shade taller than three feet.

I had seconds at the most to determine if this child was living or undead. I can't begin to describe the battle that took place between my adrenaline-fueled self and the finger wrapped around the trigger of my Glock. I raised my arms and retracted my finger just as the shadow made a noise.

"Please don't make me dead," a little boy's voice sobbed.

I rushed to him, just a stride or two ahead of Amy. As I drew near, his features became clearer. The talking was the first clue, but seeing him and once again a pair of eyes wide with fear so that the whites shown very clearly, I knew he wasn't a zombie.

Just as I reached him, the door exploded inwards and three people charged through it. The one in the lead had a pistol-grip shotgun and was swinging it back and forth in search of a target. I also knew right away that he wasn't one of ours.

I jumped past the boy and grabbed him by the shoulders. In a split second, my brain made a decision.

The boy yelped as I shoved him through the arch he'd just exited from. He fell on the stairs and I dove over him, my body effectively shielding his.

I heard a boom and a crash quickly followed by a bunch of yelling. My ears were still ringing from having been that close to the business end of a shotgun barrel that spewed flame and death, so it took a moment for the words to separate from the high-pitched whine in my head.

"...that thing away, you idiot!" a woman screamed at the top of her lungs.

"B-b-but—" a voice sputtered.

A meaty slap came and then there was nothing. I felt the boy start to move under me and could now hear his muffled cries.

"Jimmy!" the woman's voice called. There was a hint of hysteria coloring the edges and my mind made short work of the puzzle.

"He's here and he's safe," I called back.

As the words left my mouth, a new smell made its way through the sensory overload and adrenaline which was now ebbing at a painful rate. There was a coppery hint mixed with the acrid stink of feces. I knew this smell.

"No," I whispered as I pushed up from where I had the boy covered and shielded.

I stepped out into the hallway to the sounds of hammers being pulled back, shotguns ratcheting, and the general shouts of surprise mixed with demands that I not move. I tuned it all out, going so far as to turn my back on it.

My eyes took in every detail of the woman lying face down just a few feet away. The blast from the shotgun had taken Amy square in the middle of her back and sent her flying a few feet past the stairs. A pool of blood was already seeping from under her sprawled figure and I had to imagine that the blast had probably blown her chest out. Despite knowing her fate, I couldn't stop from kneeling beside her. My hand went to her neck to confirm my suspicion.

Just as I pulled away, somebody grabbed my shoulder and jerked me back. "Give me a reason!" the same mealy-mouthed person who I'd just heard get silenced by a slap growled.

I was spun around to see a shotgun just inches from my face. Unfortunately for the wielder, it was pointed at the ceiling since he was also the one trying to yank me to my feet.

"Here's one," I spat.

I had never put away my Glock and it was still in my hand. That is why it was so easy to shove it into his gut and pull the trigger twice. His eyes went wide in shock, and I pulled him to me close so that I could see past him to the figures still standing at the end of the hallway just inside the front door. One of them was kneeling with arms open wide to receive the little boy that was stumbling her direction. The other, a man who looked like he would be much more comfortable behind a desk or the teller window of a bank than holding the rifle he had slung across his body, was staring open-mouthed and in shock at what he knew was about to happen as I thrust my left arm under the right arm of the man who was now leaning limply against me.

I fired three rounds, sending bank teller-man stumbling back through the shattered front door. I dropped my arm and let the shotgun-wielding dead man fall to the floor. As I stepped over the corpse, the little boy reached the woman and threw himself into her open arms.

"Mommy!" the youngster wailed.

At that exact same moment, a lone zombie stumbled through the front door. Its head cocked to the side, drawn to the sounds of the boy's sobs.

16

Small World

The female zombie was strangely fresh. Even creepier were the two relatively new bullet wounds from where she'd been shot in the chest as well as another bullet from something pretty powerful that had blown most of her lower jaw off. Her tongue was dangling from that gory mess, twitching back and forth like an angry cat's tail and her hands were reaching for the woman that still had her back to the situation. The woman's eyes were locked on me and the Glock as her arms wrapped protectively around the boy as he buried himself in her embrace.

I raised the Glock and took aim. I was confident in my ability to shoot…on a range at a stationary target that didn't include a mother and child in between me and it. The woman saw my arm raise and opened her mouth. I imagine she wanted to plea or bargain or whatever it is that people do when they are staring down the barrel of a gun with no chance at escape or defending themselves.

I tuned that out and focused all my attention on the zombie that was about to attack her. My mind was a whirl of thoughts. How could she be that close and not smell it? Was she so dialed in to me and the child she held that she could not feel the specter of death as it swooped in on her in the form of the walking dead?

I pulled the trigger.

There was a single fraction of a second where I considered all the possibilities. The biggest being that maybe I wasn't as good of a shot as I'd led myself to believe.

The bullet smashed into the zombie's forehead and sent it teetering back. It had only been a step beyond what remained of the front door, and since there was nothing but a big gap behind it, the zombie fell back outside.

"Don't hurt us," the woman said, apparently finding her voice at last. "If nothing else...spare my son."

"Lady," I dropped my weapon to my side, "I don't have any desire to kill you, and I certainly wouldn't hurt your boy."

"Evan!" Marshawn's voice sounded like the roar of a cannon. The woman and I both jumped at the suddenness of it.

The man waded through where the front door used to be. He had a shotgun in his hand that I didn't recognize and after shooting a glance at the woman and child crouched just inside the main entry hall, he swept the area with the muzzle of the weapon. Three more people rushed in behind him, all looking like they were expecting a fight. They were from our team and I felt myself relax just a fraction as the fact that I no longer heard gunfire coming from outside registered.

"Hey," I answered with a wave as I slid my weapon into the holster and turned back to Amy's corpse.

"I hate to be a dick, but we have to get moving," Marshawn urged as he approached me and glanced down at the body sprawled at my feet. "We have zombies coming in from pretty much every direction. This is not a good location to make a stand from."

"Sara!" the mother of the boy wailed. "That can't be possible."

I turned to see that the woman had shuffled her son behind her and was looking out at the body of the zombie that still lie sprawled on her back on the porch. Her head had fallen over the edge of one of the steps leading up to the landing which amplified the grotesqueness of her lack of the lower part of her jaw.

"You know this...person?" my nemesis, Neil Pearson, said, sounding skeptical.

"Sara was my neighbor." The woman took a step forward and cocked her head to the side as she studied the corpse on the patio.

"I got news for ya," Neil said with a bitter laugh, "ain't nobody safe from this crap. Neighbor or not, she was one of them."

"But that can't be," the woman insisted more forcefully.

"Why? What made her so damn special?" Neil shot back. Did I mention that I did not like this guy?

"Because she was immune," the woman replied, looking up at Neil, hands planted defiantly on her hips.

The two had a bit of a stare down until the woman knelt beside the body and grabbed her right arm. She hiked the shirt sleeve up and whatever was revealed was enough to make Neil's jaw drop.

I stepped away from Amy's corpse to see what I was almost certain I already knew I would find. I felt more than saw Marshawn's reaction when his eyes rested on the scabbed over arm that had obviously been savaged by a zombie.

"She was attacked over three weeks ago. Her eyes never changed and she has been fine. She wasn't a zombie, so I don't know how this could happen." Her eyes scanned each of us. "One of you had to have done something to her to cause this."

I heard the self-doubt in her voice and made no effort to address her desperate accusation. I turned back to Marshawn who was looking at me now with the most open and raw pain I'd seen him exhibit.

"So then...Katy did turn and attack Abby." The words were a statement of acceptance. He wasn't looking for me to confirm or comment.

"There has to be a mistake." I wasn't surprised when Neil opened his mouth.

"We can discuss and debate this later," I said, my eyes locking on Neil's for just a moment. I hoped he saw in my eyes the fact that I would not have any problem "meeting" with him later one-on-one to *discuss* this issue if he really felt the need. When he looked away first, I counted that as a mental victory, but I had a feeling that Neil and I would have a meeting of the minds in the not-so-distant future.

Unfortunately, the woman was not interested in any of the conversation. Her mind was refusing to accept any alternative other than the one that made us into bad guys. To add more fuel and chaos to this scene, the little boy was now crying uncontrollably. His eyes were even wider with fear than his mother's as he looked from one adult to the next. I couldn't even begin to understand the degree of terror and confusion he must be feeling.

I stepped up to the woman and reached out a hand. "Look, I don't know what I can do to convince you, but I've already seen one person who was immune turn into a zombie after she died from a gunshot wound. I'm no doctor, but my best guess is that this...whatever it is that turns people into zombies...well, I guess it stays in your system. So, if you get bit or scratched and then die later, you come back just like a normal person would."

The woman opened her mouth to say something, but now it was Marshawn who cut her off. "Listen, lady, I don't know you enough to care about you, but if we keep standing around here, the zombies are gonna trap us in this house. I've seen it happen, and it ain't pretty. Once they come in big enough numbers, it don't mean a damn thing about how slow or uncoordinated they are. You got two choices, you can stand here and die, or you can come along with us and we can sort this out later." He glanced down at the boy and frowned. "And make it quick, I don't want to be around if you decide to sentence you and the boy there to death by zombie."

The woman snapped her mouth shut and gave a curt nod. I took that as her acquiescence to come along and started for the front door. The woman who'd gotten into it with Amy put a hand up to stop me.

"We gotta slip out the back," Tracy Gibbons whispered. Although I wasn't sure what good that would do us at this point. I could hear the moans and cries of the undead as what sounded like a good number of them were homing in on the scene of our little fight.

As we slipped out the back and cut across the backyard for a gate, I heard the rattle of gunfire coming from the direction of the approaching mob. In all the excitement, I'd forgotten about the group of raiders that had flushed us out of the church.

I looked around and was stunned to discover that we'd only lost two members of our group. At the moment, not counting the woman and her son, we consisted of me, Marshawn, Neil Pearson, Tracy Gibbons, and seven others that I didn't really know. I'd been sort of pushed aside in the corner and treated like an outsider, which I guess I was when you got down to it. Only, for some reason, Marshawn had made it a point to involve me in a great deal of the decision making when it came to the group. Also, they had all agreed to follow me to confront Don Evans. I wasn't ready to call myself a leader by any stretch of the imagination, but I was definitely on one of the upper rungs of the ladder, that was for sure.

As we kept up a brisk pace, I looked around for any signs indicating that maybe Don had come this way. It seemed as though we'd lost his trail of destruction. On the plus side, I also did not see very many zombies and had to figure that most in the general vicinity had likely started off in the direction of our recent battle.

I made it a point to keep tabs on the woman. She was walking as if in a bit of a haze and I had to imagine it was due to just losing all the people she'd been with and was now basically forced to travel with their killers.

As the day wore on, we saw signs of both the living and the undead. A few times, I spotted people either peering from roofs or even out windows of a few homes. None of them made an effort to try and get our attention which came as no surprise to me. Also, at one point, I glanced back to check on the woman and her son to discover that the boy was riding on the shoulders of one of the men in our group.

By the time we reached Interstate 205, everybody was starting to look tired. It's funny how minimal food intake, constant stress due to fearing for your life, and walking—except for the times we had to run due to large numbers of the undead spotting us and turning our direction—can sap every bit of energy you possess. Most everybody appeared to be running on fumes.

"We got barely a mile or so to go," I announced as we came to a stop for a moment.

Water was passed around and it proved to be the last of what we were carrying. Nobody had bothered to pay attention as we walked along. Everyone simply took pulls from their bottles or canteens as the sun rose and began to heat us all up to the point where we were all sweating somewhat profusely. So, when we stopped as a group and packs were gone through to hand out water to everybody, we got hit with that little sliver of bad news.

It wasn't completely devastating. Certainly we could scrounge some up if it became a pressing issue, but from a few of the reactions, Neil among them which came as no surprise to me, you would've thought that we were halfway across Death Valley when that tidbit of information was discovered.

"Neil?" Marshawn let the last drops from the bottle he held trickle into his mouth and then he cast the plastic container aside.

The man, who had been in mid-rant about how irresponsible some people had been to consume such a precious resource despite my seeing him guzzle from his canteen on at least three occasions, shut his mouth and turned to face Marshawn.

There was just a moment where I thought that the tone in Marshawn's voice had conveyed its message. I figured that Neil would shut up and that would be the end of it. I guess I should've known better.

"What?" the man finally said, his voice dripping with annoyance. He even went so far as to lean Marshawn's direction and roll his hands as to indicate that the man come out with whatever he needed to say. Marshawn obliged him.

"Shut up."

I had to stifle a laugh. It probably didn't help that I put my hands to my mouth and allowed a teensy bit of a snort to escape. In my defense, I wasn't the only one, but I was likely the catalyst for what came next.

Neil's face turned a beet red. He clenched his fists and I was wondering just how much of a beat down Marshawn would have to put on the guy.

Then he spun in my direction.

I had just enough time to dodge backwards as he threw a wild swing aimed at my head. Neil had made two mistakes with that move. His first was missing. His second was having absolutely nothing in his hands. Apparently he had stashed whatever weapon he'd been carrying as we made our way towards our ultimate destination of the home where my original group were staying. I had a stout machete in mine.

I stepped to the side and stuck my foot out as his swing carried him past me. He tripped and landed hard. A deep 'oof' came from him as all the air left his lungs in one sharp burst. I could've done a number of things at this point. He was flat on his belly and completely defenseless. That is probably why I simply stepped back.

He rolled over and started to his feet. I could tell by the way he tightened into a crouch that he was actually considering launching himself at me.

"Ah-ah-ah," I said as I waved the machete like a giant extension of my finger.

I didn't think he could get any redder. I was wrong. Now he was verging on purple. I honestly had no idea why he hated me so much. I hadn't wronged him directly in any way that I could recall. I saw him considering his attack despite his being unarmed. At last, his shoulders slumped and his body relaxed its posture a little.

I used that opportunity to take a few steps back and lower, but certainly not sheathe, my weapon. Marshawn stepped between us, his back to me since he obviously did not see me as a potential problem.

"You need to tighten yourself up, fella," he said calmly, but with a tone that made it clear he was not in the mood for any nonsense.

"We've had nothing but trouble since that guy showed up," Neil blurted.

And there it was. I'd arrived just as the apocalypse chose that same moment to dish out some misery to Neil's group. That made me an easy scapegoat.

"In case you're forgetting, that is also the guy that came and busted us free when we were pinned down and getting picked off," Marshawn reminded. "He made a choice to come to our aid because, in case you forgot, we left him and the two people he was travelling with back at the community center. He heard us being ambushed and came to our defense."

"Why? So he could use us as human targets to throw at somebody he had a beef with?" Neil shot back angrily.

"Those were more of the same folks that attacked us and killed so many of our group." Marshawn took a step towards Neil so that they were almost nose-to-nose.

"Says him." Neil wasn't backing down. "I never heard of Don Evans until this guy showed up. How can he prove those groups were all part of the same bunch of people?"

"Wait!" the woman whose name I still didn't know spoke up. She had her son's hand, but actually let go of it when she took a few steps toward Neil and Marshawn. "Did you say Don Evans?" That made everybody turn her direction. "Head shaved on the sides and sporting a bit of a Mohawk?"

"Umm...yeah," I answered. "Do you know him?"

"No, but my sister came to me a few days after all hell broke loose and told me she'd hooked up with this group led by a guy named Don Evans and that, if we wanted any chance at surviving, we should leave our little place behind and head over to Eastside Church. She said they were using that as a temporary base while they gathered supplies and the vehicles they would need. Ultimately, they were going to head for Sauvie Island and secure it."

"Your sister? So why didn't you go?" I asked what I felt to be the logical question.

"One of the guys went over to check things out and came back saying we absolutely wanted nothing to do with that guy."

"Why is that?" Marshawn pressed.

The woman turned to him, and now she was the one blushing. "He was doing stuff...umm...he was..." she stammered, struggling to say the words.

"A racist piece of crap?" Marshawn offered.

"Yes, but it was worse. They were doing stuff to anybody that wasn't…" Again her voice trailed away and now her eyes went to the ground.

"White," Marshawn finished for her.

"We didn't want any part of that," the woman insisted.

"So you just told your sister no?" I challenged.

"Natasha and I weren't that close," the woman laughed derisively. "She and I held very different social views. I guess now she is free to pursue hers any way she likes."

"Wait." I held up a hand. "What's your name?"

"Darya Kennedy." She paused, her features clouding over. "That is my married name. Before that it was Darya Petrov."

"No freaking way," I breathed.

***

It took a moment or two to get Neil to wind down enough so that he would at least travel. Ultimately, I think it was the threat of leaving him behind and alone that got him moving. My head was still spinning from the revelation that Natasha's sister just happened to be the lone survivor from a group that we'd basically gotten into a shootout with and killed everyone but her and her son as we ran from some other pack of raiders.

It was a lot to wrap my mind around, so I guess that was why it took Marshawn elbowing me in the ribs to get my attention. I snapped out of my trance and shot him a dirty look. His "nudge" was a full-blown strike from a normal person and I swore I felt the bruise blooming over my ribs.

"Is that where we are headed?" he asked, pointing.

I looked up to see white smoke curling towards the sky in the general direction of where I knew our compound to be. I felt my heart constrict at what that smoke implied. Just as fast, my brain began spinning possible scenarios that did not end with Carl and the others being dead. There were other houses in the area. Hell, the neighborhood right across the field from us had practically burned to the ground while we'd basically watched.

I didn't answer and started across the grass, ignoring the

271

wraparound off-ramp. It was mostly an uphill trip, and our group began to get spread out as some of them were unable (or unwilling) to match my pace that was now a jog. By the time I reached Johnson Creek Road, the only person actually beside me was Marshawn.

I passed Biscuits Café and continued up the steepening incline. Next was the medical center. I shot a glance and noticed two of the military trucks were now missing.

Maybe Carl used them to strengthen the barricade, I thought, knowing very well that I was lying to myself as the location of the smoke became clearer.

I decided to jog past 92nd Avenue, opting to hike up the steep grassy hill that would take me to the eight-foot-high wall that surrounded the once opulent home. I rounded the gradual bend in the road and spotted a familiar looking bus that had been reduced to charred ruins. It was just like one of the ones I'd seen Don's people loading in the parking lot.

I started up the grassy hill and twice had to rely on Marshawn to help me keep my feet. The closer I got, the tighter it felt like my chest became. When I reached the summit and stood at the wall, I found my feet suddenly frozen to the ground. I could not bring myself to climb up and see what waited on the other side. If the house was any indication, it would not be good.

I was so fixed on the smoldering skeletal ruins of the house that I didn't even notice the section of the wall that had been busted in a mere ten feet to my left until Marshawn pulled me to it.

I stepped around the rubble and entered the grounds. Right away I saw that the garden Betty and the kids had started had been reduced to a shambles. It looked like it had been deliberately ripped up. Not a single plant had survived. If that was the worst thing my eyes saw, it would've been a blessing.

There were several bodies lying sprawled on the ground. It did not take a genius to figure they'd been ravaged by the .50 cal. Some were missing part of, if not all, of their heads which lent to the possibility that some of the corpses could've been zombies.

Then my eyes landed on a charred pile in front of the multi-car garage. I approached it, pretty certain as to what I would discover. Sure enough, it was sacks of dog food that had been deliberately torched. That told me that Miranda had at least made it this far.

I turned, and my eyes locked on some bushes that ran along that particular section of the wall. I started for it, my steps slow at first, then faster, until I was sprinting across the yard. I reached my destination, legs buckling as my body tried to stop me. Instead, I slid on my knees the last few feet.

My hands reached out of their own volition and grabbed the black fur I'd spotted jutting from under the bushes. A soft whine drifted to my ears.

"Chewie."

Turn the page for a little tale that reveals how the child zombie in the car and her family met their sad fate.

Zombie

The Little Girl in the Garage

"Ashley!" Mike yelled as he ran out the front door.

He skidded to a halt, not from fear, but more due to the shock of what he was seeing. The sweet old neighbor lady from next door, Missus Bentley was straddling Ashley and had his daughter pinned to the ground. His baby girl was screaming like he'd never heard anyone scream before in his life.

There was a nasty rip on her right arm that was bleeding horribly. Just then Missus Bentley leaned down, her blood-smeared mouth open and obviously moving in for another bite. Ashley flailed to little effect and Missus Bentley's teeth clamped down on her left arm this time. The bite was on the forearm, just above the elbow. Ashley screamed again and that was enough to break Mike from his trance.

He thought he heard his wife gasp, but his own pulse was roaring in his ears, drowning out everything almost completely. His only thoughts were to save his daughter.

Rushing in, he dove at the elderly woman, leading with his shoulder just as he had back in school when he played football. There was a heavy slap from the impact and the elderly lady that had been their neighbor since before Ashley was even born crumpled from the blow. Her body made several pops and snaps, and Mike was certain he'd busted some of her frail and brittle

275

bones.

They flew off his daughter and ended up in the strip of grass that ran between the front yard and the sidewalk. Mike landed on top and his eyes locked onto Missus Bentley's.

"How?" he managed as he stared down into her milky white eyes that were riddled with the black tracers just like the woman from the CDC had warned against.

He couldn't understand how Missus Bentley could've contracted this terrible sickness. She never left her home—people on the block and her family even took care of her grocery shopping—and other than what appeared to be an irritated-looking scratch that likely came from one of her nine cats, she did not show any signs of having been bitten.

Her head lolled around for a moment until her eyes locked onto him. As soon as they did she opened her mouth and let loose with a low moan that sounded all the more frightening coming from her tiny body. Her teeth snapped together with a loud click. Mike pushed away and came to his knees, his eyes darting to where Ashley lay curled up on the ground still wailing…and bleeding. He drew the knife that he'd started wearing on his belt and drove the point of it into Missus Bentley's right eye. There was a soft popping sound when he punctured the eyeball, and that, coupled with the horrible smell was enough to cause Mike to lunge to the side and vomit. He heaved twice more before he could get his body to obey his brain's commands.

Scrambling up, he crab-walked the short distance between them and scooped his daughter into his arms. Her wail had ebbed to hitching sobs, but she showed no recognition that he'd picked her up. Her eyes seemed to be looking past him with no real focus.

Mike blinked. The hint of black in the capillaries of her eyes appeared to be darkening as he watched. He had to get her inside and stop the bleeding first. He would worry about everything else later. Starting for the steps, Mike skidded to a halt when he saw Nettie sprawled on the front porch. She must've fainted when she saw what was happening to their little girl.

The Little Girl in the Garage

Casting a quick glance around, the corpse of Missus Bentley seemed to be the only one on the street besides he and his family. Of course, most everybody else had already evacuated to one of the area FEMA shelters. Not Mike Pinkham and his family, though. Nettie had insisted that they wait until Missus Bentley's nephew arrived like he'd said when he called yesterday morning. He was supposedly driving out from Idaho and was due to arrive any time now. That was how Ashley had managed to slip from the house; he and Nettie had been making a list of what they were going to take with them to the shelter once Missus Bentley was safe in her nephew's care.

Mike glanced down at Nettie and decided that his wife would have to wait until he got Ashley inside and laid her on the couch. It would only be a moment and then he would come out and fetch her.

Sprinting up the steps and into his house, he could hear the televised EBS loop playing the same warning that had been running the past two days. He was beginning to doubt the validity of the idea of relocating to one of those FEMA centers. After all, shouldn't there at least be some sort of update after almost forty-eight hours?

Once Ashley was laid on the couch, Mike looked out the living room window. He could see Nettie still sprawled on the front porch where she'd fainted. He could also see that the street remained empty of any sort of movement. That confirmed, at least in his mind, that they were the last living souls on the street; either that, or the ones remaining were so callous that they could ignore the horrific screams of a child.

A flush of shame washed over him for the briefest instant as he recalled sitting huddled in the bedroom with his wife and daughter just last night when they heard a very similar scream from close by.

"Somebody's in trouble, Mike," Nettie had whispered.

"Probably too late to do anything about it now," he'd said, half-managing to believe his own words. He'd had no idea if they were a lie or the truth, but since it hadn't been one of his family members, he hadn't seen it as his problem.

With no signs of activity outside, he decided to rush into the bathroom on the main floor and grab the box they'd just packed full of first-aid supplies. Nettie was fine for the moment; his top priority was to stop Ashley's bleeding.

He worked feverishly, glancing out the window repeatedly as he did his best to at least staunch the flow of blood. As soon as he was satisfied that he could leave Ashley's side, he hustled outside and scooped up Nettie. She let out a soft moan and whimper that almost caused him to drop her.

As soon as he got her inside, he laid her out on the loveseat. Ashley had stopped making any sounds except for a rapid panting and Mike rushed back to her side.

Her eyes had shut allowing him a strange flash of relief at not having to see her tracer-filled gaze staring up blankly at the ceiling. Already, the dressings that he'd put in place were soaking through. Seeing the blood trickling down the cushions of the sofa triggered a hiss of frustration that morphed into a wail of despair.

The hospitals had been declared unsafe days ago. There was no sort of public service, and even if there might be, the phones had not worked for a long time. In a moment of coldness, he'd once had the thought that, after enough people died, the phone lines would free up. That had not proved to be the case and he was certain the problem was likely more of a technological issue than it was one of the circuits being overloaded.

As he knelt beside his little girl, holding her hand, he felt her start to twitch. That lasted only a few seconds before it grew to a convulsive fit. Instinctively, he reached for her mouth. Something flashed in his brain about not letting her swallow her tongue. However, the very next thought was that she might bite his fingers off if he did so and he instead tried to hold her down by the shoulders as he whispered her name over and over.

At last, her thrashing ceased. His little girl's eyes flew open as she gasped once, went momentarily rigid…and then seemed to melt in his grasp.

In that instant, Mike Pinkham went completely numb. It was as if his body had been dipped in liquid nitrogen. He sat, dumbfounded and totally at a loss as to what he could or should do.

"Ashley?" a groggy voice said from over his shoulder, causing him to jump.

He turned to see Nettie standing just a few feet away. She was looking past him, her eyes probably not even registering his presence as they quickly shed their sleepy appearance, growing wider every second.

At last, her eyes shifted to him. "Mike? Is she going to be okay?"

He could tell by her expression that she already knew the truth, she simply did not want to accept it. She was looking at him and expecting him to say that Ashley would be fine. He could not bring himself to say the words and instead simply dropped his head, slid to the floor beside the couch, his chin coming to rest on his chest, his eyes closing out the world for a moment.

He knew there were things that had to be done, but his mind absolutely refused to put itself in order. He was at a loss, his grief so overwhelming that he lacked the ability to latch on to one single thought. He was still trying to focus when a shriek of pain snapped him back to his senses.

It was Nettie. While he'd been adrift in his misery, she'd moved over and sat beside their daughter and apparently put her arm around the lifeless body. Ashley had clamped her mouth down onto her mother's forearm and was tugging at it, worrying it like a dog with its favorite chew toy as she sought to tear away a chunk of meat.

At last, the flesh gave and Ashley came away with her prize. Blood from Nettie's wound left a crimson trail across Ashley's face, and as Nettie scrambled to get away, her left arm caught for a moment in their daughter's frizzy auburn hair, turning it an unnaturally dark shade of red.

Mike yanked Nettie away from their daughter. His goal had been merely to separate the pair in hopes of saving his wife from being savaged by Ashley; underestimating the combination of his strength, his wife's petite size, and the rush of adrenaline coursing through him, he ended up throwing Nettie into the wall

across the room where she hit hard and slumped to the floor unconscious.

A hair-raising mewl came from his little Ashley and he returned his focus to his daughter...or what she had become.
Between all the blood, the way her skin was already starting to
pale even more than normal—which was making her many
freckles look all that much more dark and pronounced—and her
milky eyes seeming to writhe with the black tracers, there was
nothing in this creature that resembled his baby girl. And
yet...he could not look at it and not see *her*.

"Come with me, Princess," Mike cooed as he backed away
from the tiny horror.

Unsteady step by unsteady step, it followed. Its steps were
awkward, and its head would cock to one side and then the other
in jerks and fits. When he felt the knob of the garage door at his
back, he reached behind himself and gripped it, turning it without allowing his eyes to drift from the Ashley-zombie.

He backed into the bay of the garage and then made a wide
circle, leading her away from the door. As he backed into the
tool bench, his eyes spied a coil of hemp rope. He knew in his
brain what his daughter had become, but he was not ready to do
what those people on television and the radio said needed to be
done. It was one thing to say such things, but when you were
faced with a loved one—especially your own child—it was another thing entirely.

"This is how it is getting so bad," he whispered, finally un-
derstanding what had puzzled him for several days.

As soon as he brought the coil of rough rope around and
where Ashley could see it, she changed. Up to that point, she had
followed, but made no hint at attacking. That was what was
making this even more difficult. Now she was like Missus Bentley as she came at him with teeth gnashing and hands reaching,
swiping at the empty air between them.

He walked backwards in a circle around his car as he fash-
ioned a loop at the end of the rope. As he did, the war between
his head and his heart continued to rage. With the loop ready, he
stopped retreating and allowed Ashley to advance. He timed his

lunge and knocked her back against his black Ford Mustang GT. It was almost too easy to keep her subdued while he lashed her wrists together and, not knowing what else to do, he yanked open the car door, picked Ashley up, and dumped her inside.

He stepped back and saw her writhing on the seat as she tried to right herself. Unable to watch any longer, in addition to needing to get back to Nettie and check on her condition, Mike exited the garage with a sick feeling churning in his stomach. It had nothing to do with the stench that was still in his nostrils that wafted from his daughter—the same stink he'd encountered with Missus Bentley.

He entered the living room and felt his heart leap into his throat. He'd left the living room door wide open this entire time. It was already a certainty that the undead were drawn by noise, and his house had been a steady source these past several minutes. He rushed over and shut it, then returned to Nettie.

Kneeling beside her, he brushed her red hair from her eyes. Looking her up and down, she had the one nasty bite on her arm, but her chest was still rising and falling with her slow, deliberate breathing. Scooping her into his arms, he carried her up the stairs to their bedroom. As soon as he reached the second floor, his eyes could not help but rest on the open door to his little Ashley's room. Adorned with her beloved Disney princesses—her favorite was Ariel from *The Little Mermaid*—he carried Nettie to their room and laid her on the bed.

Rushing into the bathroom that sat at the top of the stairs, he grabbed the towels from the rack and knelt to rummage through the bottom drawer where he was pretty certain that a bottle of hydrogen peroxide was stashed. Hurrying back, he dumped generous amounts of the liquid on a hand towel and then went to work trying to clean the wound.

At first it was like trying to build a sandcastle as the tide came in. He would clean away the blood only to have more seep up like crimson crude. By the time he had a suitable bandage made from a pillow case he'd cut into strips, the room looked like a crime scene.

He got up, looked around and told himself that he would

clean up the mess later. He just needed to catch his breath for a minute and figure out what to do next. Obviously they would not be leaving for a FEMA center any time soon.

He had just slid down the wall and planted himself on the floor when Nettie stirred. It started as a whimper and became jumbled with her attempts to speak.

"Ash...no, baby...MIKE!" She'd screamed his name and then sat bolt upright.

Her eyes flew open and Mike Pinkham felt his stomach and heart tighten. The eyes staring back at him were laced with the darkness of Nettie's looming fate.

"Mike?" she cried.

"Right here," he said almost void of any emotion.

Rising to his feet with a grunt, he approached his wife and knelt beside the bed. He took Nettie's hands in his and made himself stare up into her eyes even though they were not really the ones he remembered from the night they shared that first kiss at her parents' doorstep.

Nettie Pinkham was not a stupid woman. She knew what was going on in the world around them, and despite her reluctance to accept it, she knew the fate of their daughter. And now, as Mike stared up at her, she knew her own as well.

"Please don't let me become one of them," she whispered, her hands coming free from his and caressing his cheek. She ignored his flinch.

For the next several minutes, there was a lot of crying, arguing...and denial. In the end, when Nettie pressed the small .22 caliber pistol that was kept in a lock box on the top shelf in their closet into his hand, Mike sobbed his agreement to honor her wishes.

The couple sat, foreheads pressed together until darkness began to devour the room with the arrival of the evening. Shortly after dark, Nettie began to slip in and out of consciousness. Mike continued to sit by her side and wait. When she shuddered twice and grew still, he stood, pressed the barrel of the gun to her forehead and pulled the trigger. The pop was almost entirely silenced, but he felt it slam into his bones like a hammer.

The Little Girl in the Garage

In his grief, he tossed the pistol away, not noticing as it ricocheted off the wall and slid under the bed. He could feel the desire to cry raging within him like a storm, but the tears refused to come.

There was nothing keeping him from escaping to a FEMA center now. But there was also no longer any reason to go. His will to continue had evaporated.

Like one of the walking dead shambling past his home, he scooped Nettie into his arms and carried her downstairs. He knew where she belonged, and this would be his final act.

When he reached the garage, he paused. He'd never noticed how dark the world seemed, nor how bright the moon's light could truly be.

He shifted Nettie's body in his arms and opened the door to the garage. The inky blackness was shoved into the corners by the silver square of moonlight burning with blue coldness in a near perfect rectangle on a section of concrete pad of the garage floor.

He took two steps and faltered. Ashley's face stared back at him from the driver's side window. There was enough shadow that she could just be his little girl for that moment. He finally felt the dam holding his tears shatter when her tiny bound hands slapped at the glass as if she was beckoning for him to let her out.

Mike had to fight for each step that brought him closer to the car. Eventually he found himself on the passenger's side. He took a deep breath, vowing to hold it as long as possible, before opening the door. He was reaching the point where he would have no choice but to take a breath when he realized that he'd been standing rooted to the spot. The zombie version of Ashley had made no move towards him the entire time. In fact, she almost appeared to be leaning away like she was the one afraid of him.

He knelt and placed Nettie in the passenger seat. As soon as he moved back, Ashley-zombie leaned forward, her hands seeming to try and pat her mother. He had no idea what was going on, but Mike knew two things for certain in that moment. He could not end Ashley as he had Nettie, and he would not leave her hands bound.

Reaching down to his belt, he drew his knife. As soon as he did, he caught a flash out of the corner of his eyes and looked up just in time to see the zombie side of his daughter re-surface. She was coming at him like she had before. He pushed her back easily enough and then reached in and pushed her against the door just long enough to cut the rope tied around her wrists.

Slamming the door shut, he waited for what felt like forever, but Ashley showed no sign of reverting to that version that had greeted his arrival just moments earlier. At last, he left the garage and trudged back up the stairs.

He walked into the bedroom, his senses dulled to the sights and smells that were the final moments of his Nettie's life. Opening the closet again, this time he pulled out the case that was stored behind the boxes of dress shoes and produced the shotgun that had been a gift from his late father.

Mike Pinkham exited the bedroom, absently shutting Nettie's bedroom door out of habit as he trudged to the bathroom. Shutting the door behind him, he dumped the box of shells onto the counter and plucked one from the little bunch of red cylinders. Climbing into the tub, he slid down the wall, opened his mouth to accept the barrel, and pulled the trigger.

MAY DECEMBER
Publications

**The growing voice in horror
and speculative fiction.**

Find us at www.maydecemberpublications.com

TW Brown is the author of the **Zomblog** series, his horror comedy romp, **That Ghoul Ava**, and, of course, the **DEAD** series. Safely tucked away in the beautiful Pacific Northwest, he moves away from his desk only at the urging of his Border Collie, Aoife. (Pronounced Eye-fa)

He plays a little guitar on the side...just for fun...and makes up any excuse to either go trail hiking or strolling along his favorite place...Cannon Beach. He answers all his emails sent to twbrown.maydecpub @gmail.com and tries to thank everybody personally when they take the time to leave a review of one of his works.

He can be found at www.authortwbrown.com

The best way to find everything he has out is to start at his Author Page:

You can follow him on twitter @maydecpub and on Facebook under Todd Brown, Author TW Brown, and also under May December Publications.

CPSIA information can be obtained
at www.ICGtesting.com
Printed in the USA
BVHW041144170419
545798BV00012B/85/P